A FORMER DETECTIVE
A DANGEROUS CON ARTIST

AN ELECTRIFYING GAME OF
CAT AND MOUSE

ONLY THE MOST CUNNING
WILL WIN

From the *New York Times* bestselling author of *The 6:20 Man* comes a new psychological thriller in which two women—one a former detective and the other a dangerous con artist—go head-to-head in an electrifying game of cat and mouse.

SIMPLY LIES

Mickey Gibson, single mother and former detective, leads a hectic life similar to that of many moms: juggling the demands of her two small children with the tasks of her job working remotely for ProEye, a global investigation company that hunts down wealthy tax and credit cheats.

When Mickey gets a call from a colleague named Arlene Robinson, she thinks nothing of Arlene's unusual request that she inventory the vacant home of an arms dealer who cheated ProEye's clients and fled. That is, until she arrives at the mansion to discover a dead body in a secret room—and that nothing is as it seems.

Not only does the arms dealer not exist, but the murder victim turns out to be Harry Langhorne, a man with mob ties who used to be in Witness Protection. What's more, no one named Arlene Robinson works at ProEye.

In the blink of an eye, Mickey has become a prime suspect in a murder investigation—and now her job is also on the line until she can prove that she was set up. Before long, Mickey is locked in a battle of wits with a brilliant woman with no name, a hidden past, and unknown motives—whose end game is as mysterious as it is deadly.

ACCLAIM FOR
DAVID BALDACCI'S THRILLERS

SIMPLY LIES

"Baldacci is at his best in this standalone thriller. [He] keeps the twists coming fast and furious in this tense page-turner, never losing credibility even as it takes bigger and bigger swings. Readers will fall in love with Mickey and hold their breath for her through to the very end."
— *Publishers Weekly* (Starred Review)

"Intriguing…Baldacci's readers will find plenty to enjoy here."
— *Booklist*

DREAM TOWN

"Baldacci paints a vivid picture of the not-so-distant era…The 1950s weren't the fabled good old days, but they're fodder for gritty crime stories of high ideals and lowlifes, of longing and disappointment, and all the trouble a PI can handle. Well-done crime fiction. Baldacci nails the noir."
— *Kirkus* (Starred Review)

"This was already my favorite of Baldacci's recurring series, and *Dream Town* only reinforces that, in large part because of Baldacci's brilliance in stitching his story across a tapestry of a bygone era of movie magic with a dark side. Nostalgia aside, this is storytelling of the highest order, rich in character and bursting with story."
— *Providence Journal*

"[A] welcome third outing for PI Aloysius Archer...Solid prose nicely evokes the traditional hard-boiled whodunit."
—*Publishers Weekly*

"In the Archer series, [Baldacci] proves to be a natural at handling the postwar setting. Baldacci's fans should be lining up for [it]."
—*Booklist*

"David Baldacci never fails to create an exciting story...the action is exhilarating. Fans of Baldacci will love this one from cover to cover."
—*Seattle Book Review*

"Baldacci keeps piling on the tension until the last chapters... Electrifying."
—*New York Journal of Books*

"Like his protagonist, Baldacci has a passion for details, especially those of the social variety. After a few pages you will feel as if you have time-traveled back to that era."
—*Florida Times-Union*

"If you like a whodunit with a complex plot and characters, you are going to love *Dream Town*. Baldacci's take on Hollywood in the fifties is quite refreshing and a great part of this mystery novel's charm."
—*TheMysterySite.com*

THE 6:20 MAN

"A complex, high-powered thriller that will keep the reader guessing...Readers will suspect nearly everyone in this fast-moving whodunit...This is a winner from a pro."
—*Kirkus* (Starred Review)

"Keeps readers guessing with an intriguing story...It seems like Baldacci might be planning more Travis Devine stories. Let's hope so."
—*Booklist*

"Corporate conspiracies, corruption, and murder—all come together in one of thriller fans' most anticipated books of the summer…Baldacci's experience in this genre truly shines as he builds complex layers of riveting twists and turns to keep you on the edge of your seat!" —*Reader's Digest*

MERCY

"*Mercy* is classic David Baldacci. It's full of heart and great thrills, with an intricate plot that only he can conceive."
—BookReporter.com

"Dips deeper into the dark world of noir, resonating at times as neo-gothic. This is Baldacci at his best, probing well beneath the surface of the story to create a thriller as richly drawn as it is wondrously realized." —BookTrib.com

"Baldacci at his best." —*Florida Times-Union*

"It's just too good…There's more than one case to be solved in this complex novel about very interesting women. One of Baldacci's best." —*Globe and Mail*

"With an interesting storyline, amazing characters, and packed with action, fans are sure to love *Mercy*." —*Seattle Book Review*

"Wildly entertaining." —*Winnipeg Free Press*

"Atlee Pine fans will want to get their hands on this one."
—TheMysterySite.com

A GAMBLING MAN

"David Baldacci is no stranger to hitting literary home runs, but his second book to feature World War II veteran turned avenging angel Aloysius Archer, *A Gambling Man*, is a flat-out grand slam…Few authors are able to frame period pieces for a contemporary sensibility, but Baldacci proves more than up to the task in fashioning a tale that's as close to perfect as a thriller can get." —*Providence Sunday Journal*

"Baldacci…definitely is onto something with Archer. He's a very interesting guy, in a rough-and-tumble way, and Baldacci renders Archer's postwar world with the kind of vivid detail that catches a reader's eye…Readers new to the series will definitely want to catch up on what they've missed."

—*Booklist*

"Fans of Baldacci should go all in for *A Gambling Man*. This spicy novel deals out a hand of brothels, gambling dens, drug operations, and government corruption—all a sure bet for a rollicking good time." —*New York Journal of Books*

"Baldacci establishes bona fides for this historical mystery with great delicacy, deftly navigating the cliché minefield and giving his readers a sense of the milieu without drowning them in minutiae. He delivers a cracking good suspense novel in the process." —*BookPage*

"With drugs, gambling, brothels, murders, and more, for historical crime fans, this one's got it all."

—CNN Underscored

"*A Gambling Man* is delicious crime noir with fascinating historical data thrown in to keep the story interesting…Archer is one of today's standout fictional characters, and you are missing out if you don't jump into this terrific series at the beginning." —BookReporter.com

"*A Gambling Man* moves at a steady clip, as Baldacci's plot pays homage to private eye novels by Raymond Chandler and Ross Macdonald. Archer is a well-drawn character, a man of

his times who tries to overcome his past and embrace new attitudes. Liberty is no damsel in distress but is a strong woman who knows how to protect herself and isn't fooled by any man, rising above clichés that may surround showgirls...A return to Archer and Liberty will be welcomed."
—*South Florida Sun-Sentinel*

"In Archer, Baldacci has plumbed postwar time and place. His story's personality is framed by Archer's snappy dialogue [and] infused with just the right amount of suspense to keep you glued to the narrative."
—*Jersey's Best*

"Good stuff from a master. Can't wait for another."
—*Florida Times-Union*

DAYLIGHT

"Baldacci is at his absolute best in the dazzling *Daylight*...a stunning success that sets our expectations high and somehow exceeds them."
—*Providence Journal*

"*Daylight* gives you everything you would expect from a David Baldacci novel and more. The title alone speaks to the promise of answers that have eluded Atlee in the first two installments...[Baldacci] is incapable of producing a less than superb read."
—BookReporter.com

WALK THE WIRE

"*Walk the Wire* solidifies Baldacci's status as this generation's premier storyteller...The perfect thriller."
—*Providence Journal*

"*Walk the Wire* may be the finest entry in David Baldacci's Memory Man series. The quality of his writing is at an all-time peak and, fortunately for his countless fans, he is showing no signs of slowing down any time soon." —BookReporter.com

"Intrepid...Although it's the sixth in a series, the book stands perfectly well on its own, providing many hours of enjoyable reading." —*Mystery Scene*

"Dire and complex...wildly entertaining."
—*Winnipeg Free Press*

A MINUTE TO MIDNIGHT

"Secrets and twists pop up seemingly on every page...an angst-riddled tale with a Southern Gothic tone. This is brilliant storytelling that will leave you reading long after the clock strikes 12." —*Providence Journal*

"A murder mystery that spooks and horrifies."
—Associated Press

"Baldacci has produced another remarkable novel with plot twists galore that let the pages practically turn themselves. His writing style allows readers to immediately enter the action and then forces them to strap in for another wild ride. He saves the biggest surprise for last in a moment that will provide an unexpected cliffhanger, which will have his audience eagerly awaiting the next entry." —BookReporter.com

"Baldacci does a fantastic job plotting things out and revealing just enough...to keep readers engaged and on the edge of their seats...A final surprise [will] leave fans begging for more...Few writers can hook readers faster and harder than David Baldacci." —*Real Book Spy*

"Baldacci shows off his mastery of the twist-and-turn-thriller, keeping us on edge throughout, right up to a surprise finale."
—*Florida Times-Union*

ONE GOOD DEED

"One of [Baldacci's] finest books. Great character, great story, great portrait of an era."
—Bill Clinton

"Insightful and entertaining, Baldacci has captured the time and events perfectly with authenticity, beauty, and flawless prose...Archer is a terrific antihero with plenty of longevity and originality, [and] the supporting cast is just as memorable. Gripping from beginning to end."
—*New York Journal of Books*

"David Baldacci is a master storyteller, and he invokes the classic feel of the postwar 1940s evident in the timeless literature and film of that time...[He] once again doesn't disappoint."
—Associated Press

"David Baldacci switches gears with magnificent results... Simmering suspense and splendid prose...Terrific-reading entertainment."
—*Providence Journal*

"Baldacci nails the setting—capturing everything from the way things looked back in 1949 to how people spoke, adding realism and authenticity to the story. The characters are developed nicely, especially Archer, who flashes real star power throughout...Fast paced and packed with plenty of suspense."
—*Real Book Spy*

"Mega-selling mystery writer David Baldacci's latest takes us back in time and introduces a new series protagonist that may become one of his most popular...A captivating page-turner."
—*Florida Times-Union*

"Baldacci has crafted an ingenious and addicting read in which each paragraph provides a new revelation. The time period and writing style immediately called to mind the works of the immortal James M. Cain...A terrific slice of crime noir."
— BookReporter.com

"An uproarious, tangled-web tale...David Baldacci knows how to pleasurably wind us up."
— *Washington Book Review*

REDEMPTION

"Baldacci turns up the suspense and surprises at a rapid pace without sacrificing character or story. With the personal stakes and the steep learning curve that Decker must overcome to find justice, the narrative carries a heavier emotional impact...Another great novel from a master storyteller."
— Associated Press

"Staying true to its title, *Redemption* is a riveting thriller, as relentlessly suspenseful as it is blisteringly original. Baldacci may be an old hand at this, but his grasp has never been stronger."
— *Providence Journal*

"No one will leave this story unchanged by the revelations and violent events that transpire one after another, making for a fine thriller that will please all of Baldacci's eager readers."
— BookReporter.com

"Little by little [Decker] thaws the case out, exposing a town full of secrets that have far-reaching, international ramifications. *Redemption*'s unusual plot will have you wanting to step back and say, 'Wait a minute.' But then you remember, this is David Baldacci, the master storyteller, and you keep turning the pages."
— *Florida Times-Union*

"The plot never slows enough to take a breath."
—*Winnipeg Free Press*

LONG ROAD TO MERCY

"A multi-layered protagonist; a plot as deep and twisty as the setting. In *Long Road to Mercy*, Baldacci is at the top of his game."
—Kathy Reichs, #1 *New York Times* bestselling author

"One of David Baldacci's best...FBI Agent Atlee Pine is unforgettable."
—James Patterson, #1 *New York Times* bestselling author

"David Baldacci's best yet. He keeps the pages flying and the plot twisting in this ingenious and riveting thriller. Best of all, he introduces a compelling new heroine in FBI Agent Atlee Pine. I can't wait to see what she does next. Baldacci delivers, every time!"
—Lisa Scottoline, *New York Times* bestselling author

"David Baldacci at his best, introducing an engrossing new heroine, FBI Agent Atlee Pine. Alternately chilling, poignant, and always heart-poundingly suspenseful."
—Scott Turow, #1 *New York Times* bestselling author

"David Baldacci is one of the all-time best thriller authors."
—Lisa Gardner, #1 *New York Times* bestselling author

"An epic thriller—fast moving, beautifully imagined, and vividly set in the Grand Canyon and its environs. From the opening chapter to the final twist, this novel will absolutely transfix you. A stunning debut to what promises to be a great series. Agent Pine is a character for the ages."
—Douglas Preston, #1 *New York Times* bestselling author

"David Baldacci is a name synonymous with excellence—a consummate storyteller who turns the conventional into unconventional. *Long Road to Mercy* strikes all the right chords: a perfect blend of action, secrets, and conspiracies—all combined with Baldacci's trademark sizzle."
—Steve Berry, *New York Times* bestselling author

"A fabulous new character from a master storyteller. Readers will love Atlee Pine. A mile-a-minute read that proves once again why David Baldacci has readers the world over flocking for more." —Jane Harper, *New York Times* bestselling author

"FBI Agent Atlee Pine is a heroine I'll never forget. I hope David Baldacci's hard at work on Agent Pine's next adventure, because I can't wait to dive into it."
—Tess Gerritsen, *New York Times* bestselling author

"What a blast-off for Baldacci's most memorable protagonist yet—Atlee Pine is a heroine for our times, a fighter for justice we'd all be glad to have on our side…A spectacular series debut. I can't wait to see what's next for her."
—Joseph Finder, *New York Times* bestselling author

"If you're wondering why David Baldacci is considered the best, look no further than *Long Road to Mercy*. In FBI Agent Atlee Pine, he has envisioned a new kind of heroine, forged in the fire of trauma and driven by a rare kind of strength. It should come as no shock that a thriller writer for the ages has created a character for the ages!"
—Gregg Hurwitz, *New York Times* bestselling author

"Baldacci excels as a storyteller…He knows how to craft a complex and compelling case for his stellar heroes to solve. Baldacci is at the top of his game here. The final reveal is both exciting and shocking. Readers will fall in love with Atlee, and hopefully Baldacci will bring her back soon."
—Associated Press

"Baldacci weaves an intricate tale full of action, adventure, and intrigue...Baldacci's latest page-turning thriller lives up to his readers' expectations and beyond." —*Killer Nashville*

"Baldacci at his finest." —*Dearborn Press & Guide*

THE FALLEN

"Baldacci is a wonderful storyteller, and he incorporates wonderful characters into baffling conspiracies. Mimicking the style of his Camel Club series of novels, he takes on small-town America, capturing both good and bad elements. He demonstrates why these small towns are worth saving. It's a theme he has explored before, but it still has potency and relevance." —Associated Press

"The pace picks up considerably with each passing chapter until the inevitable ending that most surely will deliver a resolution at about the same time you are catching your breath." —BookReporter.com

"Amos Decker shines again...David Baldacci at his very best." —*Real Book Spy*

"Amos Decker novels just keep getting better and better, and it's partly due to the careful in-depth characterization Baldacci gives his main character." —*New York Journal of Books*

END GAME

"Baldacci is a gifted storyteller." —Associated Press

"Fast-paced entertainment at its best." —*Florida Times-Union*

"Does *End Game* make for entertaining reading? You bet."
—*St. Louis Post-Dispatch*

"In true David Baldacci form, *End Game* starts with a bang and continues at a relentless pace to the very last page. Each chapter ends with a gritty cliffhanger. Putting the book down is simply not possible. This series is action-filled and highly satisfying." —BookReporter.com

"Hitting on all cylinders from beginning to end, David Baldacci brings back his best character with a bang."
—*Real Book Spy*

THE FIX

"A compelling puzzler...Baldacci is a truly gifted storyteller, and this novel is a perfect 'fix' for the thriller aficionado."
—Associated Press

"Crackling with tension...Reads at a breakneck pace... Bestselling author David Baldacci delivers a thrill ride, as always. Big time. Pick up *The Fix*, and you won't put it down until you reach the end. Guaranteed." —BookReporter.com

"Cleverly perverse, full of surprises, and touched throughout by the curious sense of congeniality." —*Toronto Star*

"[Baldacci] continues to show why he is a master of mystery."
Florida Times-Union

NO MAN'S LAND

"This thriller, featuring U.S. Army criminal investigator John Puller, has a very plausible theme with a compelling and action-packed plot...A riveting and heart-wrenching story…an edge-of-your-seat thriller. Readers will be hooked from page one." — *Military Press*

"David Baldacci is one of America's favorite mystery writers, and he has earned that adulation fair and square. He is constantly turning out one readable and enjoyable adventure after another. *No Man's Land* is his fourth John Puller story, and it is a good one. It is fast reading from the start as the pages grab the readers' interest and off they go." — *Huffington Post*

"[A novel of] dramatic depth and intensity…an unforgettable read…Action-packed and thought-provoking."
— Associated Press

"Bestseller Baldacci makes the implausible plausible in his riveting fourth thriller featuring U.S. Army criminal investigator John Puller…Baldacci maintains tension throughout and imbues his characters with enough humanity to make readers care what happens to them." — *Publishers Weekly*

"This fast-paced ride will leave you guessing until the last page." — *Virginia Living*

THE LAST MILE

"Entertaining and enlightening…a rich novel that has much to offer…In the best Baldacci tradition, the action is fast and furious. But *The Last Mile* is more than a good action thriller. It sheds light on racism, a father-son relationship, and capital punishment. Both Mars and Decker are substantive, solid characters…Utterly absorbing." — Associated Press

"[Amos Decker is] one of the most unique protagonists seen in thriller fiction…David Baldacci has always been a top-notch thriller writer…[His] fertile imagination and intricate plotting abilities make each of his books a treat for thriller readers. *The Last Mile* is no exception." — BookReporter.com

"A compelling mystery with emotional resonance. Just when the story line heads to what seems an obvious conclusion, Baldacci veers off course with a surprising twist. The end result is another exciting read from a thriller master."

— *Library Journal* (Starred Review)

"Baldacci excels at developing interesting, three-dimensional protagonists...Baldacci fans will not be disappointed, and *The Last Mile* gives good reason to look forward to the next Amos Decker thriller." — *New York Journal of Books*

ALSO BY DAVID BALDACCI

STANDALONES
Absolute Power
Total Control
The Winner
The Simple Truth
Saving Faith
Wish You Well
Last Man Standing
The Christmas Train
True Blue
One Summer
The 6:20 Man
Simply Lies
The Edge
A Calamity of Souls

ALOYSIUS ARCHER SERIES
One Good Deed
A Gambling Man
Dream Town

MEMORY MAN SERIES
Memory Man
The Last Mile
The Fix
The Fallen
Redemption
Walk the Wire
Long Shadows

ATLEE PINE SERIES
Long Road to Mercy
A Minute to Midnight
Daylight
Mercy

THE CAMEL CLUB SERIES
The Camel Club
The Collectors
Stone Cold
Divine Justice
Hell's Corner

JOHN PULLER SERIES
Zero Day
The Forgotten
The Escape
No Man's Land

KING & MAXWELL SERIES
Split Second
Hour Game
Simple Genius
First Family
The Sixth Man
King and Maxwell

THE SHAW SERIES
The Whole Truth
Deliver Us from Evil

WILL ROBIE SERIES
The Innocent
The Hit
The Target
The Guilty
End Game

SHORT STORIES
Waiting for Santa
No Time Left
Bullseye
The Mighty Johns (A Digital Novella)

DAVID BALDACCI

SIMPLY LIES

GRAND
CENTRAL

New York Boston

Copyright © 2023 by Columbus Rose, Ltd.

Excerpt from *A Calamity of Souls* copyright © 2024 by Columbus Rose, Ltd.

Cover design by Tal Goretsky. Cover copyright © 2024 by Hachette Book Group, Inc.

Grand Central Publishing
Hachette Book Group
1290 Avenue of the Americas, New York, NY 10104
grandcentralpublishing.com
twitter.com/grandcentralpub

Originally published in hardcover and ebook by Grand Central Publishing in April 2023

First U.S. Trade Paperback Edition: March 2024

Grand Central Publishing is a division of Hachette Book Group, Inc. The Grand Central Publishing name and logo is a trademark of Hachette Book Group, Inc.

The publisher is not responsible for websites (or their content) that are not owned by the publisher.

The Hachette Speakers Bureau provides a wide range of authors for speaking events. To find out more, go to www.hachettespeakersbureau.com or call (866) 376-6591.

ISBNs: 9781538750612 (U.S. trade edition), 978-1-5387-5059-9 (ebook)

Printed in the United States of America

LSC-C

Printing 1, 2023

*To Michelle, for providing the inspiration
for this story—and for a whole lot more*

SIMPLY LIES

CHAPTER

I

MICKEY GIBSON WIPED THE SPIT-UP off Darby's face, and then gave her two-year-old daughter a plastic squeaky ball, hoping that would hold her attention for a bit. The girl sat stoically in her playpen, eyeing the toy like it was neither foe nor friend. Gibson had learned in one of the many child development books she had read that two-year-olds should be able to play and entertain themselves for up to thirty minutes.

Whoever wrote that was on drugs, or else my kids have no future as adults.

She was hoping for simply a five-minute respite, just to finish her phone call.

Gibson hefted her three-year-old son, Tommy, who had been doing his best to use his mom as a jungle gym, and placed him on her thrust-out right hip. It was only eleven in the morning and she was already exhausted.

She said into her headset, "Okay, Zeb, I'm back. Like I said before, the paper trail is pretty clear. There's at least two hundred mill in six different bank accounts, three in Chad, one in Bermuda, and two in Zurich. Larkin must know we're closing in, so he's probably going to try to move that money ASAP, and I may not be able to track it again."

Gibson listened for a few moments as she deftly dodged Tommy's attempts to grab her hair and knock off her headset. Darby threw the ball out of the playpen and hit her mother in the back before starting to wail, then tried to climb to freedom over the playpen rails.

Gibson noted this and went into action. While still holding Tommy, she grabbed the ball off the floor, tossed it up in the air, and deftly caught it behind her back—one of the skills she had developed from her basketball days.

Darby stopped climbing, grinned, and started clapping. "Mommy, Mommy. G-good."

Tommy was also mesmerized by this enough to stop attacking his mother's hair. "Do it again," he ordered.

Gibson kept repeating this act while she said, "Right, Zeb, I understand. But the fact is I got lucky on some key clicks and ran down a couple tricky leads that paid off, but there's no guarantee that will happen again. The lawyers need to get injunctions filed and put concrete lids on those accounts before he can wire that money out to God knows where. I checked and we can get the assets frozen because all those countries are subject to the usual global banking laws, so Larkin can't grease their skids without severe consequences to their memberships in the international financial community."

Gibson paused for a moment and tossed the ball again so she could remove Tommy's index finger from her right eye. Nimbly catching the ball, she said, "Larkin's probably already regretting not burying those funds deeper, offshoring them in the Cook Islands or laundering them beyond our reach." As she continued to try to control her gyrating son, she added, "I've also already provided the evidentiary trail to the creditors' lead bankruptcy lawyers and they're following up, too. The wire rooms are closed in Zurich and Chad, but they're still running in Bermuda. So you need to hit this hard and you need to hit it fast."

As though he were waiting for Gibson to finish speaking, Tommy threw up all over his mother.

Gibson watched the vomit spiral down the front of her only clean outfit at the moment, with chunks of it landing on her bare feet. As a final touch, the slop soaked into the rug, to join all the previous stains there.

Darby started laughing and pointing. "G-good. T-Tommy."

Gibson looked at her son, whose expression told her all she needed to know. She ran for it and reached the toilet just in time to hold him over the bowl while simultaneously hitting a button on her headset to place the call on mute. Tommy managed somehow to miss the toilet completely and instead puked on the toilet paper holder *and* her pair of slippers. Gibson had left them there earlier after attempting to use the bathroom. Then she'd heard a crash somewhere and found Tommy sitting on the kitchen floor, covered with most of the wet dirt from a potted plant. She'd stripped the boy and thrown his clothes directly into the washing machine. Gibson had wanted to toss him in, too, only she didn't relish a visit from Child Services. But she'd forgotten the slippers. And her urge to pee.

Until now.

She set Tommy down and threw the soiled footwear into the trash can. She washed her face, trying not to look at the gunk that was sliding off her and down into the sink because it was making *her* want to vomit. She dried off, then she sat on the toilet, holding Tommy, and finished her long overdue urination.

After that, she unmuted the phone. During this whole time Zeb had been chattering away, oblivious to all her domestic drama.

"So, as I was saying, great work. Now go paint the town red tonight, Mick, on the company card, of course. Have a blast. You've earned it."

"Yeah, Zeb, I'll get all dolled up. Champagne and caviar and a long, slinky dress."

"Have fun. We all need downtime."

"Yeah, we do, don't we?"

"Hey, and next time, let's do a Zoom call. I like to see my people's faces."

Not this people's face, thought Gibson. *Not now. Not for maybe the next ten years.*

"Right, sounds good."

She clicked off, flushed the toilet, and looked at her son.

He rubbed his stomach and said solemnly, "Better, Mommy."

"I bet."

CHAPTER

2

LATER, WITH THE KIDS DOWN for brief naps, Gibson grabbed a quick shower, unlocked the door of her home office, and hurried inside. She had a cup of peppermint tea in one hand and an oatmeal almond cookie in the other. Her dirty clothes had been replaced with green gym shorts and a T-shirt and ankle socks. Until she did the next load of laundry this was mostly it for clean garments. The slinky dress would definitely have to wait since she didn't have one, or the time to "paint the town red," whatever the hell that meant. And with the tea and cookie, she was holding the mommy version of champagne and caviar.

At least this mommy.

The baby monitor was on the shelf. All she could hear right now was gentle breathing, and a series of small snores that she knew came from Tommy. She let out her own long breath and wondered if their usual one-hour nap timeline would hold today. The one predictable component of motherhood, she had found, was that no two days were ever alike.

Then she glanced at herself in the drab reflection of her twin computer screens.

Gibson was five seven if she stood absolutely erect, which she had never once managed to do since having kids. She figured her right hip was stuck out about four inches further than her left, and she had no idea if it would ever return to its original alignment. She didn't want to even think what her spine looked like. But if it reflected her chronic back pain, it was a real anatomical horror show. She still carried stubborn pounds of baby weight in her hips, buttocks, and belly, and they might be permanent for all she knew. Her dark hair was cut short because who had time to deal with long tresses? Her face was puffy, her skin blotchy—her OB-GYN had blamed postpartum hormone releases—which was something they hadn't covered all that thoroughly in the pregnancy books she'd read. The slender, dynamic athlete she had once been in high school and college was no longer readily apparent.

As a tough, feisty, ball-hawking, elbows-throwing point guard with a wickedly accurate midrange jump shot, impressive passing skills, and great court awareness, she could run all day. Later, first as a crime scene tech and then a street cop and after that a detective, she had won the 10K competition for the entire department six years in a row, besting both the men and the women. The guys had been initially faster than she, but their endurance had petered out around the 5K mark. She had tried not to smile too broadly as she blew past them at that point.

Now the stairs were a bitch.

She'd gone to Temple University in Philly and been coached by the legendary Dawn Staley. Gibson had also been a theater major, and had been cast as the lead in a number of student productions at Temple. People thought she might make it to Broadway one day.

After college she had actually contemplated dabbling in a career on the stage, but quickly found out that half-ass wouldn't cut it, because she would be competing against legions of immensely talented and driven people who were dead certain that Broadway was their destiny.

Gibson had been a computer nerd growing up as well as a serious gamer. She had taken college courses to enhance those skills because with that she knew she would almost always be employable. She had once also had visions of trying out for pro basketball, but quickly realized that she had neither the necessary athleticism nor the true game to play in the WNBA.

She had instead opted to follow in her father's footsteps and joined the police force. He had been thrilled, her mother not so much. She had worked her way up to being a criminal investigator, and then found who she thought had been the love of her life.

His name was Peter Gibson, and he was tall and handsome and gregarious and funny. And, she had come to find out too late, he was also the world's biggest prick. He'd told her that he wanted a large family, but as soon as one baby was out of the oven he had been a changed man, chafing at not being able to go out with his friends, or having his weekends "ruined" by the daddy do list. When she was pregnant with Darby, he had cleaned out their bank accounts and run out on her with his secretary, leaving Gibson with an infant and another baby on the way, and a mortgage and bills that could not be paid on her salary alone.

She had searched for him, but Gibson had vanished so thoroughly that she wondered if he had had some professional help in doing so. She had lost the house and had to leave her job with the force, and then she moved to Williamsburg, Virginia, where her retired parents lived. She had lucked out by joining ProEye, a global private investigation agency that did most of its sleuthing online. It paid well and allowed her to use her computer skills, and work from home pretty much full-time. And she had her mom and dad as a support group and free childcare.

Gibson was getting back on her feet, but the single-parent thing was a challenge, even with her mother and father nearby. They both had some health issues and were more apt to be twiddling their thumbs in a doctor's waiting room than be available to assist her. But Gibson was making it work because she didn't have a choice, and she loved her kids. Even when they were puking on her.

She now used her computer skills working for ProEye. The company specialized in hunting down the assets of rich delinquents who continued to live notoriously in the lap of luxury while blowing raspberries at both courts and creditors as they hid behind a wall of snarky lawyers, scheming accountants, and PR mudslingers. And there were so many of these monied deadbeats that ProEye and thus Gibson were flooded with work.

Some rich people obviously did not like to pay their debts, as though they were somehow exempt from the obligation. While positions like a car mechanic, grocery store cashier, or warehouse worker were routinely audited by the IRS for a few thousand bucks as low-hanging fruit, the zillionaires scared off the revenue man with their prodigious legal and accounting muscle.

She'd attended one deposition where a billionaire defendant had argued that his businesses created thousands of jobs and *those* people paid taxes, that he had very little actual income since most of his billion-dollar fortune was in stocks—which he got loans against to pay for his extravagant lifestyle, effectively bypassing the tax man—and that he gave to charity. When the counsel for the government had pointed out that that was not a defense to paying no tax at all on his actual taxable income, the billionaire hadn't told him to fuck off. He'd just said, "Wait until *we* officially *make* it the law. It won't be long now." And *then* he'd told the lawyer to fuck off.

Gibson took a sip of tea and a bite of her cookie, put on her headset, and started clicking computer keys. What she did now could never compare to the adrenaline rush of working cases on the street. But life was full of trade-offs. And this was one she had made. For the good of her family, something every mother would understand.

She might eventually find someone else to spend her life with, but right now that did not seem likely at all. Why? Because what Peter Gibson had robbed her most of, and it was a lengthy list, was trust. Trust in men and, even worse, trust in herself.

Gibson prepared to get to work chasing down a rogue business-man who had $2 billion in assets somewhere, but unfortunately also had $4 billion in debt. Just another world-class punk fraudster in a sea of them. Twenty years ago there were fewer than five hundred billionaires in the world. Now there were nearly three thousand. That was an enormous amount of wealth creation. For a very select few.

Everybody else, not so much, she mused.

But then her phone rang.

And everything in Mickey Gibson's suburban, single-mom life was about to get blown straight to hell.

Ms. GIBSON, THIS IS ARLENE ROBINSON from ProEye, I work with Zeb Brown. I know you were on the phone with him earlier."

"That's right. Is there a problem getting the funds locked down?"

"No, that's all going very well. They're acting on Bermuda, and they'll get Zurich and Chad done as soon as they open. You did great work as always."

"Thanks. I don't believe we've spoken before," said Gibson as she bit into her cookie and took another sip of her tea.

"We haven't. I've been with ProEye for eighteen months, but I was just transferred to Mr. Brown's division three weeks ago. He's always spoken highly of you." Then she chuckled.

"What?" said Gibson.

"He also informed me that he told you to paint the town red tonight or something to that effect, on the company dime, of course."

"Yeah, he did," said an amused Gibson.

"I looked you up before I called. You're a single mom with two little kids, right?"

Now Gibson understood the chuckle.

"That's right. And just as I was telling Zeb to lock down those accounts my son threw up on me."

"Well, I've got three under the age of five at home, so I can definitely relate. And I knew you weren't going to be painting anything red unless it's a room in your house."

Gibson laughed. "Spoken like a true mom. Where are you operating from?"

"Albany. I was told it was ProEye's headquarters about ten years ago, before they really took off and went global."

"That's right. I've been with them for about two years. It's a good firm."

"And it lets people work remotely, which is very nice."

"Yes it is. So, what can I do for you, Ms. Robinson?"

"Please, make it Arlene. Here's the thing, and it's a little different but I was told to call and run it past you."

"Okay," said Gibson expectantly.

"There's an old mansion near Smithfield, Virginia, on the James River, that went into foreclosure. That's why they thought of you, because you're in the area."

"Thought of me for what?"

"They want you to go there and take an inventory of the home's contents. The file says that there's a house key under a statue of a cat near the front entrance, if you can believe that."

"This *is* a little unusual. I usually do my sleuthing on the internet."

"I know. That's most of what ProEye does, as you know. But this is what I was told. And they'd like you to go out today if possible. You can talk to Zeb if you want, but I know he's in a meeting now. And they really wanted to get you out there fast. It sounded to me like there might be a nice field bonus in there for you, too."

Gibson was thinking that doing a little field work would be a welcome change from staring at a computer screen for the next few hours. And bonuses were always nice. She would have to call her parents and hope they could come over. She had their calendar and she brought it up on her screen. *Okay, they have no doctor appointments today. That's a miracle.*

"I think I can make that work. What can you tell me about the property and ProEye's interest?"

"I've got the info up on my screen. The mansion was built in the 1920s by a man named Mason Rutherford. He was a robber baron who made his money in railroad, timber, and mining. He owned a mansion in Colorado, a five-story town house in New York, and this place in Virginia. It's on land where a British Lord built his home; it was later burned down during the Revolutionary War." She added in a joking manner, "So there might be a ghost or two around."

"Just what I always wanted to be—a ghost hunter."

"Rutherford died in 1940 and his wife, Laura, who was much younger than he was, lived there until 1998. She was a hundred when she passed away. And the place had fallen into disrepair. Must have cost a fortune to keep up."

"And the current owner?" asked Gibson, who was wondering what she was going to wear on this field trip.

"Ah, that's the notorious Rutger Novak. He bought the place about seven years ago and spent an enormous amount of money undertaking an extensive renovation."

"Rutger Novak? I definitely know that name."

"Right. He and ProEye have a history, and not a good one. Forgive me if I'm telling you things you already know, but Novak is German. He was a big international businessman thirty years back, though always on the shady side. Arms dealer, Middle East strongman backer. He worked both sides on pretty much every deal. He had some setbacks over the years, and it looked like he would go quietly into the night with the bucks he had left. But he apparently made some bad decisions that sucked him dry and then he started to borrow heavily, and it turned out the assets pledged as collateral were mostly phony. ProEye chased him years ago on behalf of a whole coterie of clients, and they ended up with egg on their faces and not a dollar to show for their efforts."

Gibson said, "That part I know very well. It was before my time, but the firm has never forgotten it. It's part of the company lore. They even tell it to you during orientation as a warning sign against complacency and not going the extra mile."

"Well, time apparently caught up to Novak. Everything has now gone belly-up in the last couple of months."

"Is he around or did he hit the road like last time?"

"Vanished, or so the file says. He owes so much his creditors are trying to grab everything they can. This mansion is one of them. That's why they want you to go there. The firm wants to make amends for what happened last time."

"You said near Smithfield? Can you be more specific?"

She heard some key clicks. "It's between a place called Mogarts Beach and Rushmere on something known as Burwell Bay." Robinson gave her the street address.

"Okay, that gives me some context. The short route includes a ferry, so that would take me about an hour or so and that's if I hit the boat schedule dead-on. The long route will have me drive south through Newport News, cross the James River Bridge, head to Smithfield, and then it's about eight miles above that, like making a horseshoe. All told that's about an hour, too, depending on traffic, so that's the way I'll go."

"See? It pays to have someone who knows the local geography."

"I'm surprised no one has been there before now."

"Well, we didn't know about the property until an hour ago, which is why Zeb didn't mention it to you earlier. The title was in the name of a shell company. We just punched through that wall. Our clients have documented liens on all of the man's assets and have filed blanket legal papers allowing access to all his properties. We're hoping Novak left so fast he couldn't clean the place out, because our intel is that he loved the finest things in life and that place might be full of them. Paintings, furniture, sculptures—hell, the creditors will take Oriental rugs, silverware, the contents of a wine cellar or a library, whatever. Regardless, they'll be lucky to get a nickel on the dollar."

"Yes they will. Okay, I'll head out as fast as I can."

"And the kids?" asked Robinson.

"My next call will be to my parents. They're local."

"Thank God for local parents. Mine live on the West Coast. And I think that's by design."

4

THE BLACK PANTSUIT WAS SNUG around the hips and tight around the waist with her stomach pooch drooping over it, although the white blouse hung well on her frame. But Gibson was pissed because while the blouse was hers, she'd had to borrow the pantsuit from Dorothy Rogers, her *mother*.

You did birth two kids. You don't snap right back from that. Well, it has been two years since Darby was born, so you're well past snapping-back stage.

Now she regretted the oatmeal almond cookie.

And she had seen the look her mother had given her when she'd come down the stairs in her clothes. No words, just that look— no, that *smirk*. But then her mother did remark, "I just bought that outfit at TJ Maxx. But then I have been working out a lot more *and* watching my diet. It's very important as one gets older, although none of us is getting any younger, right, honey? But for now just button the jacket and no one will notice how tight it is on you. Baby belly can be a real bitch. Took me thirty years to get rid of mine. Many women never do."

That was about as subtle as her mother ever got. Maybe any mother ever got with her daughter.

Gibson steered her mommy van south down Interstate 64 East, and then worked her way through surface roads to US 17 that sling-shotted her across the burly James River. Next, she turned north, passing through what had once been the hog-slaughtering capital of the world at Smithfield. Her nav system showed it was another seven miles to the remnants of Rutger Novak's shattered empire. The whole journey would be less than fifty miles, but that was a long way in the tightly constricted parameters of this part of coastal Virginia. It was filled with military footprints, underwater tunnels, bridges, the ocean with wide sandy beaches, and the delicate lines of inland waterways that either crept along the earth like capillaries under the skin or gushed across it like fat arteries.

Gibson had thought about calling Zeb Brown back, but she knew he would be preoccupied with the case she had discussed with him this morning. And she was excited about getting out of the house.

She followed the directions until she turned down a long narrow road that was bracketed on both sides by mature trees that were just starting to bud out in early spring. Gibson reached down and touched the holster riding on her belt. In it was a Beretta eight-shot Nano, which was comparable in size and weight to the Glock 26 she had carried on the police force, and chambered the same ordnance. Its slightly smaller footprint fit her hand well. And the nine-millimeter Luger bullet that blew out of its barrel would stop pretty much whatever it hit.

She had not let her mother see her unlock the combo safe located at the top of her bedroom closet or put the gun in her belt clip. Her mom had never wanted her daughter to be a cop. One in the family was enough, she had often said. However, Gibson had wanted to follow in her father's footsteps. As the oldest child, with two brothers coming in behind her, she had held her uniformed father in awe. But, initially, bowing to the will of her mother, Gibson had joined the force as a forensics tech. That had mollified her mom, since Gibson would show up at the crime scene only *after* all the danger had passed.

When she secretly took and passed the written and physical exams to enter the police academy, her mother had thrown a fit. It wasn't until her father, Rick Rogers, stepped in that she was allowed to pursue her dream. Her old man was proud of her, Gibson knew, though he rarely showed it. Public displays of affection were not in the DNA of the Rogers family. Gibson could count on one hand the number of times her mother had hugged or kissed her. And she could count those times on *one* finger with her father—that was the day of her graduation from the police academy.

He hadn't done it at her wedding, for reasons he had made clear to his daughter prior to Gibson's walking down the aisle.

She turned off the road she was on and started down another. The property was just up ahead on the right.

And maybe I'll find some British ghosts living in the old mansion.

She slowed as she saw the stone monuments on either side of a driveway. The plaque on one of the monuments read: STORMFIELD.

Arlene Robinson hadn't told her the name of the place, not that it mattered.

There was a wrought iron gate but it hung open. Farther down and partially concealed by some overgrown bushes stood a mailbox. She drove up the cobblestone lane and swung around a bend in the road. Revealed was a sprawling old manor house that looked as though it hadn't changed a jot since it had been built. Rutger Novak's renovation must have all been on the interior.

She could only describe the architecture as an unruly blend of baronial, feudal, and gothic with a bit of Versailles thrown in for no apparent reason. It sat in front of her, stained and discolored after a long residence next to the unforgiving elements of an estuary reeking of equal parts saltwater and freshwater.

She parked in front and got out. The only sound was the breeze and the occasional bird opening its beak in anticipation of the dawning springtime. The tree canopies were still relatively bare, and the gloomy sky did not provide much light in the afternoon.

She figured when it turned dark it would be difficult to see anything. And then she decided to hurry because it had just occurred to her that the place might not have electricity.

She snagged a flashlight from her van, because, as large as the house was, it would be dark in some places, regardless of the light outside.

Gibson made her way up to the front doors, which were each twelve feet tall and constructed of solid oak. She found the cat statue and the key underneath. As she set the statue back in place, it seemed to her that the feline was warning her to flee from here before it was too late.

When she unlocked the door and stepped inside, the musty air abruptly hit her. That was strange, she thought, because the place, supposedly, had been recently inhabited. Yet maybe it always smelled like this.

She suddenly looked around for an alarm pad. A bit panicked, Gibson listened for the sound of beeping prompting the inputting of a code before it was too late. She saw the alarm pad to the left of the doors, but its panel was dark.

That's also odd.

But it was also lucky for her, since she had not been given the alarm code.

Gibson took out her iPad from her bag and turned on the video feature. She had no idea of the floor plan here, but since the place was nearly as large as a small shopping mall, this was not going to be a single afternoon's worth of work. She started in the foyer, where there were two suits of armor standing about eight feet tall and still looking dwarfed by the immense space.

There was a large dining room fully, if incompatibly, outfitted with Baroque pieces and a Chippendale sideboard. Gibson had become something of an expert about such things while hunting the assets of the rich and shifty over the last couple years. On the walls were oil paintings mostly consisting of colonial scenery and waterfront landscapes. She didn't think they were originals, or if they were, she doubted they were worth much. There was a nineteenth-century-era bar set up in a massive, hinged globe on rollers, and some nice Oriental rugs. Those might bring in decent bucks.

She walked down hallways and into other rooms, taking video and dictating pertinent information to the extent she could find any from either the objects themselves or her own expertise. She could Google everything later. She passed by a broad window and looked out at the dying sun. The rear grounds gazed out upon the James River, which looked dark and slick as it slid slowly past Newport News, turned to the east, and emptied into the Chesapeake Bay between Hampton and Norfolk. Beyond that was the unnervingly long Chesapeake Bay Bridge-Tunnel. After that, was the Atlantic.

Gibson had been across the Bay Bridge-Tunnel a few times and had never cared for the experience. It was over seventeen miles long, with artificial islands built along the route, and the bridge seemed to disappear right into the middle of the bay where the road entered the tunnels. It was like the highway was executing a suicidal dive into the water, taking all traffic with it.

Along the shoreline she spotted an old boathouse with an attached dock. There was a covered cabin cruiser there that might fetch some dollars. She decided to check on it while it was still light outside. She had already confirmed that there was no electricity turned on, which probably accounted for the musty smell, what with no air circulation.

Gibson headed down a slippery stone path to the shoreline of the James River. The boat was a Formula cabin cruiser, the hull white with blue and red accents. She estimated it was about forty feet in length and seemed to be in good shape, though it still had its winter cover on, so her views were limited. She took video of it and then tried the door of the boathouse, but it was locked. She peered in the window but couldn't see much.

She trekked back to the house and entered the library. The

shelves were mostly empty, so it appeared Novak had either cleared it out or wasn't much of a reader.

Gibson walked over to one section of shelves to look at a large vase placed there when she felt something on her ankles.

She stopped and eyed the wall. It didn't precisely meet the adjacent section of wood. There was about an inch sticking out. She set her iPad down, curled her fingers around the wood, and pulled. The wall swung open on a pivot pin set in the floor, revealing a darkened space. She could now hear something whirring close by. And there was the same sensation of airflow she had felt on her ankles when the wall was mostly closed.

She punched her flashlight on and adjusted the beam so it was concentrated. Her other hand rested on the butt of her Beretta. Four steps in she saw the source of the sound and airflow. A battery powered fan had been set on the floor within feet of the opening. She kept going.

And then the smell hit her.

Damn, I recognize that.

The hallway curved and she curved with it. She shone her light on walls that were damp stone; they probably dated back to the original construction.

She directed the beam back and forth in front of her as she walked along.

And then Gibson stopped and kept the beam on one spot.

From out of the darkness, a slash of white and twin pops of color representing a toothy mouth and bulging eyes.

The man was sitting in a chair. He was tall and elderly, with thin, gray hair.

And he was also quite dead, which accounted for the stench.

And by the decomposing state of him, his life had been over for a while.

THE POLICE CRUISER SPUN TO a stop in front of the mansion where Gibson perched on the steps. She rose and walked over to the car as two uniformed deputies from the Isle of Wight sheriff's department stepped from it.

"You the lady who called this in?" said one.

Gibson nodded, showing them her ID. "I'll take you to where it is."

She led them inside and to the room where the body was. One of the deputies stopped her at the threshold into the secret room, and asked her to go back and wait outside. One of the officers accompanied her—on the long shot that she was the killer, Gibson knew. Within thirty minutes more officers arrived, this time from the Smithfield Police Department and a lieutenant investigator from Isle of Wight. Five minutes after that another man showed up. He introduced himself to Gibson as Wilson Sullivan, a senior CID agent with the Virginia State Police's Bureau of Criminal Investigation.

Sullivan was about six two, muscular and broad shouldered and around forty, with a square-jawed face and short hair that was as rumpled as his off-the-rack suit.

His eyes were pure cop's eyes, thought Gibson. Alert, suspicious, roving, and contemplative.

They all went in to see the body just about the time a forensics team showed up, offloaded their equipment, and shuffled inside to look for microscopic clues that criminals always left behind.

Sullivan came back out later and sat on the steps next to Gibson.

"Will I have to stay much longer?" she asked. "I've got two little kids to get back to. I've already given a detailed statement."

Sullivan lit up a cigarette and blew smoke away from her. "I really need to quit this, but the patch doesn't work. Neither does anything else. And the fact is, I like it."

"I know a lot of cops who smoke. Sort of comes with the territory for some."

He ran his gaze over her. "You look like you wore the uniform."

She gave him an amused expression. "How can you tell? From my extreme fitness?"

"You found a dead body in a creepy mansion. You're not hysterical or crying or otherwise upset. That means you're either the killer, or you're used to seeing dead bodies. Plus, I see it in your eyes, the way you handled yourself around all the law enforcement flying around here."

"Okay, I'm busted. Jersey City. Forensic tech for two years, uniform for six, detective for four."

"And a mom of two small kids. And your husband?"

"Divorced."

"So, can you tell me how you came to be here? I know it's in your statement, but I'd like to hear firsthand."

Gibson explained who she worked for and the call that she received.

"Can I see some ID that shows you work for ProEye? Which I've heard of, by the way."

Gibson pulled out both her driver's license and ProEye credentials.

Sullivan studied the twin cards before handing them back. "They good folks to work for?"

"They are for me. And it gives me flexibility. I mostly work behind a computer at home."

"But not this time," said Sullivan pointedly. He finished his smoke, pocketing the butt. "Don't want to contaminate the crime scene," he noted. "So, Rutger Novak?"

"Yes."

Sullivan got a look in his eyes that Gibson did not like. "I've heard of him, though not too much lately. Didn't know he was living around here."

"I didn't even know this place *was* here. I'm a relative new-comer to the area. I was told it was built by some robber baron named Mason Rutherford back in the 1920s. And that a British Lord's house used to be here before it was burned down during the Revolutionary War."

Sullivan gave her another look that Gibson liked even less than the first one.

"What?" she asked.

"I've only been in this area a couple years, too. Came up from North Carolina. But I learn pretty fast. And I've never heard of a British Lord having a home here. Never heard of this Mason Rutherford, either. And I checked on this Stormfield place before I headed out here. Rutger Novak never owned it."

Gibson looked perplexed. "I...I don't understand."

"Neither do I," retorted Sullivan, giving her a sharp look that Gibson had given many suspects in her time as a cop and detective.

Shit.

Sullivan took out his phone and scrolled through some screens. "Stormfield wasn't built in the 1920s. It was built in 1950 by a man named Richard Turner. He was the great-grandfather of the people who lived here before the current owner. He made his money in advertising up in New York, but he was from Tidewater and returned home to build this mansion. The Turner descendants owned it until about six years ago." He stopped and eyed her.

"I...I don't understand any of this. I was told that Laura Rutherford lived here until she was a hundred in 1998 and—"

Sullivan turned when a uniformed officer came out and called to him.

"Excuse me," said Sullivan, standing up and joining the man for a minute. They had a whispered conversation that included several glances at Gibson, who was growing more uncomfortable by the minute. She looked at her watch and was expecting a call from her mother at any moment demanding to know where the hell she was.

After the officer went back into the house, Sullivan rejoined Gibson on the steps, his features grim but otherwise unreadable.

"Problem?" said Gibson.

Sullivan took out his cigarette lighter and clicked the top back and forth like his personal fidget toy.

"We called ProEye about you. They just got back to us."

"And they confirmed that I worked for them."

"Yes they did."

"I sense a *but* coming."

"But they never asked you to come out here to do an inventory on this place. They never called you at all about Stormfield. They have no idea what it is or where it is."

Gibson caught a breath and gaped. "Who did your people talk to?"

"Fellow named Zeb Brown. He said he was your immediate supervisor."

"He is."

"So care to explain the discrepancy? Because one of you seems to be lying. And I'd like to know which one it is."

"I told you. I got a call from Arlene Robinson from the Albany office—"

"There is no Arlene Robinson in the Albany office. There is no Arlene Robinson that works at ProEye, period. So let me ask you again, what are you doing here?"

Gibson looked at the old, ugly building as a number of scenarios played out through her mind.

"I got a call from someone identifying herself as Arlene Robinson a couple of hours or so after I spoke with Zeb about an unrelated case. The woman said she worked with him."

"And you just accepted that at face value?" He held up his phone. "It took me all of five minutes to look up the history of this place."

"Look, she knew that Zeb and I had spoken earlier and she even had numerous details of our conversation. She pretty much quoted a line that Zeb said to me this morning. So I just assumed that she worked there because how else would she know all that? And she also knew I had kids. She said that since I was local, which meant she knew I lived around here, they wanted me to come over and do an inventory of this place. She said the owner, Rutger Novak, had run out on some big debts and the creditors wanted to salvage what they could. And that's basically what ProEye does, so I had no reason to doubt the authenticity of the call or the nature of the assignment."

"As I already said, Rutger Novak does *not* own Stormfield."

"I didn't know that. Then who does?"

"The man you found in the secret room, Daniel Pottinger."

"Then you've identified him?"

"Preliminarily. He had a wallet with a driver's license. Photo matched the deceased. We'll confirm that, of course."

"Who is he?"

"Rich, obviously. I've never met him. He came here and bought Stormfield from the Turners. That's all I know."

"How did Pottinger die?"

Sullivan shook his head. "Can't get into that. We're going to need your phone records to confirm you got a call. Maybe we could trace it, *if* it actually happened."

"I *am* telling you the truth. Why else would I be here? Why would I have called the police when I found the dead body?"

"I don't know, Ms. Gibson. There are reasons on both sides why you would."

"What do you mean, 'both sides'?"

"Those that favor you being innocent. And those that favor you being involved in the murder of Daniel Pottinger."

"So he *was* murdered? I could see no wound," said Gibson.

"Your driver's license says you live in Williamsburg?"

"Yes, with my two young kids, as I mentioned before. And my mother is watching them and will be expecting me back. This was a spur-of-the-moment thing and I had to call her in to be the baby-sitter. I thought I was going to be spending the day chasing down assets on the internet, not finding a murdered man in a gloomy old mansion."

"Well, it would have been much better for you if you had stuck to being a digital detective. It's a lot more dangerous out here."

"What happens now?" asked Gibson.

"I'll follow you back to your house. And then we can talk some more and I can check on some things that, hopefully, will exclude you from the suspect list."

"Do you *really* believe I had something to do with this murder?"

"You were a detective once. How would you answer that?" asked Sullivan.

Gibson sighed. "Everyone's a suspect until it's proved conclusively that they're not."

"Good that you still remember that." He took her firmly by the arm. "Let's go."

6

On the drive back Gibson kept looking in the rearview mirror at Sullivan in his sedan. She was trying to gauge whether the man seriously considered her a suspect in the murder or not. His look was focused yet distant, as though he had a great many scenarios flitting through his head. He reminded Gibson of herself on a case, consuming all the facts of a crime scene, but then taking the time and distance to weave them into plausible theories that might, or might not, turn out to be supported by the facts.

When they arrived at her house, Gibson introduced Sullivan to her mother, but didn't elaborate on why he was here.

"It's work-related, Mom. Can you hang around a bit to watch the kids? I have some things to go over with Detective Sullivan. Thanks."

Dorothy Rogers eyed her daughter and then glanced at the tall and attractive Sullivan and smiled. "Well, I'll just leave you two *alone* then."

Gibson had to work extra hard to keep the groan inside her from coming out.

He doesn't want to date me, Mom, he wants to figure out if I'm a murderer.

She took Sullivan into her office and slipped out her iPhone. "*This* is my business phone." She scrolled down the screen. "Here's the number she called me from. It didn't have a name because it wasn't in my contacts, or a location tag, but I usually answer because my job pretty much requires that."

Sullivan punched in the number on his phone and held it to his ear. It rang and rang but no one answered. "Probably a burner or something like it. Or voice-over-untraceable-IP bullshit. We'll try to track it, but don't hold your breath." He looked around at her office setup and the two monster screens. "So this is where the investigatory magic happens?"

"If you want to call digital drudgery that, yes it is." Gibson sat down, took off her shoes, and rubbed her feet. "Sorry, not used to wearing even low-heel pumps anymore."

Sullivan sat down across from her. "Anything else you can remember from the call?"

Gibson knew he could have asked her all this back at Stormfield, but he obviously wanted to see if her suburban mom story checked out or not.

"I'm naturally skeptical like any good ex-cop, but she played every beat perfectly. She threw in the conversation with Zeb first, which took away any doubt I might have had."

"Which means either your boss is in on this—"

"—or she does work there, used a fake name and phone and overheard the conversation, *or* she tapped Zeb's phone or mine and got the necessary intel that way."

Sullivan nodded appreciatively. "You're not showing any rust at all from your detective days."

"Really? I think I need a full lube job after what happened. She reeled me in hook, line, and *sinker*. Like you, I would normally have checked out the place online, but she provided a history for it that sounded plausible, and they wanted this done really fast, or at least she said that. And she never told me the name of the place. That was probably so I wouldn't check it out and determine everything she said was bullshit. And, on top of all that, she used the name Rutger Novak."

"Why is that significant?" asked Sullivan curiously.

"Long before I joined ProEye they had a battle royale with Novak. He ended up winning because he disappeared and ProEye couldn't find a single asset to grab for their clients. It was a big black eye for the firm, so every employee that they hire, during the orientation, gets a snootful of info on Novak, as if to say, you better work hard and cover every angle, or the big fish slips away. She must have known that about the firm and mentioned his name to me so I would have no doubts she worked there."

"Mickey Gibson. It says that on your license. But isn't it short for Michelle?"

"No, my given name isn't Michelle. It's Mickey."

"Okay? Is there a story behind that?"

Gibson sighed resignedly. "To say my late grandfather was a diehard Yankees fan would be a gross understatement. He bled the navy blue pinstripes. Family lore has it that he threatened to strangle my father unless he named his first grandchild, regardless of gender, after *Mickey* Mantle. So voilà, here I am."

"Well, it *is* different."

"Very kind of you to say so. Growing up with that name I would have used a different word to describe it."

"Made you tougher, I take it."

"Made me something."

"Which then leads us to the question of why *you*? Out of the entire universe of people she could have made that call to?"

"I thought about that all the way on the drive back. I didn't come up with much other than I work for ProEye and live close to Stormfield. She obviously wanted me to go there and find that body. Today. The wall had been opened a bit and there was a fan just inside the space to create airflow and noise, and a vase had been placed on the shelf there to draw my attention. Chances were very good I would stumble upon it."

"Any possibility you could know the woman under another name?"

"I didn't recognize the voice, but she could have altered that.

I don't know all that many people around here, other than some other moms and dads in my neighborhood."

"So you think the crime scene was arranged?"

"There's no power on in that house; fan was battery operated. Wall left partially open, dead body, fan on. Yeah, it was staged and then the call came to me."

Sullivan said, "And the techs estimated the fan had a decent charge left."

"So whoever turned it on was there probably today. Maybe this 'Arlene Robinson' even called me from there. She knew where I lived and she knew how long it would take me to get to Stormfield, because I basically told her it would be about an hour after I left my house."

"So the question becomes: Did she kill him?"

"How long has he been dead?"

"It wasn't today. I can tell you that."

"I could see that for myself. Why would anyone want to kill Pottinger? Did he have any enemies?"

"Early for all that. We're checking out various possibilities."

"I was told the place was abandoned. But if Pottinger was still living there, where's all the hired help? He couldn't have taken care of that place all by his lonesome. But it was empty when I got there, and the power was off. And the place didn't really look lived in. There was stuff that I inventoried, but it just had the feel of being abandoned."

"Checking into all of that."

"So am I off the suspect list?"

"Not quite, but you're getting there." He rose. "We'll be in touch."

"Look, if you need another pair of eyes on this?"

"Not the way the Virginia State Police work, sorry."

Gibson took a symbolic step back. "Of course."

He eyed the computers. "I guess it was a big change. Going from the streets to this."

"It was. But being a parent is an even bigger change in your life, maybe the biggest."

He left Gibson there staring at the screens around which her work life now flowed.

What the hell have I just stepped in?

CHAPTER

7

Gibson put the phone down after having talked to Zeb Brown. He confirmed everything that Sullivan had told her. There was no Arlene Robinson. There was no assignment from ProEye.

Brown hadn't been at all sympathetic with Gibson. On the contrary, he'd clearly been pissed that she hadn't confirmed the assignment with him and saved the company and her a lot of trouble and egg on their faces.

"We *do* have a reputation to uphold," he had told her in a scolding tone. "So if there is a next time, just call me, okay? Then maybe we can avoid being part of a freaking police investigation. And maybe you should bag going out tonight to celebrate the Larkin matter and get your head on straight." He'd clicked off before she could reply.

She slowly set the phone down. *Okay, he thinks I'm either an idiot or I'm involved in a crime, and I'm not sure which is worse, because I cannot lose this job.*

Later, she fed her kids, played with them, bathed them, and put them to bed. She still had on her mother's pantsuit. The waist actually felt a bit looser, and she realized she hadn't had anything to eat other than the almond oatmeal cookie.

She went down to the kitchen, and pan-cooked her special and amazing Kraft Mac & Cheese and ate it standing up with a glass of cheap merlot to kill the taste.

Gibson looked out the window and saw nothing but darkness in the chilly springtime evening.

Darkness out there, darkness in here.

Darkness between my ears.

And then her phone buzzed. Her business phone. She looked at the screen. It was a text.

Can you talk? AR

She almost dropped her wine and then looked quickly around to see if she was being watched somehow.

She texted back: Okay. And waited.

The phone buzzed. She answered. The same woman's voice came on the line.

"Can I explain?" she said.

"What a great idea," snapped Gibson. "Maybe your real name might be the best place to start."

"They found the body, correct?"

"*I* found the body. Daniel Pottinger. Murdered. How'd you kill him?"

"I need you to go to your front door."

"Why?" said Gibson in a tense voice. She automatically looked up, to where her kids were sleeping.

The woman said, "You'll find a phone there in a box. I'll call it in thirty seconds." She clicked off.

Gibson rushed to the gun safe, unlocked it, slid out her Beretta, and slapped in a mag.

She hurried to the front door and looked out one of the side lights. She lived in a working-class, cookie-cutter neighborhood of 1,500-square-foot homes with carports or one-car garages, built mostly in the eighties. There were lights on in some of the houses, and cars were parked up and down the street. She saw no one out and about. A dog barked from somewhere, making her jump. She slowly opened the door and saw the small box on the porch. Gibson gently opened it just as the phone inside started to ring. She stepped back into her home and locked the door.

And then Mickey Gibson decided to lose her shit.

"What is this load of crap?" she yelled into the phone. "I don't appreciate getting sucked into whatever stupid game it is you're playing."

"It's *not* a game, but I'd feel the same if I were in your shoes."

"Easy to say since you're not *in* my shoes. You almost cost me my job and you still might."

"I'm sorry, but please let me explain."

Gibson bit back her anger and turned to cop mode, which meant, above all, listening. And this might be the only way to eventually get to the truth. Plus, she was curious as hell as to what was really going on. Not that she expected this woman to tell her anything except lies. But Gibson was really good at tracking stuff down. She just needed a lead, one tiny morsel.

"Okay, go ahead," she said in a calmer voice.

"I didn't kill him and I don't know who did. All I know is that I found his body and didn't know what else to do."

Incensed once more, Gibson barked, "How about calling the fucking police, that one ever occur to you?"

"I couldn't call them."

"You just had to hit 911 with your index finger, you didn't have to give your name or just use a fake one, like you did with me."

"I didn't want to do it that way. I had my reasons. Good ones."

"Then why involve me in your mess?"

"Because I had heard of you."

"Heard of me from where?" demanded Gibson.

"When you were a cop."

"That was back in Jersey. So you tracked me to Williamsburg?"

"I felt like I could trust you. I hope I still can?"

"Well, I don't trust *you*, seeing that the police now think I'm a suspect for a murder I knew nothing about until today." She drew a long, calming breath. This aggressive posture was going to get her nowhere. "Did you know Pottinger?"

"Yes."

"How?" Gibson said.

"He was very well-known in Miami. I was surprised that he moved to such an isolated place in Virginia."

So was she from Miami? "Why were you there?"

"He asked me to come to see him."

"Why?" asked Gibson.

"I can't get into that."

"You're going to have to get into *everything* if you really want me to trust you."

"He was someone I knew from way back. He said he was in trouble. I went to Stormfield to help. The door was unlocked. I went in. The wall in the library was open. That's how I found him."

"Was there anyone around when you got there?" asked Gibson.

"No, which surprised me. The place is huge. He must have had servants or some kind of help. But if they had been there they would have found the body."

"How did he die?" asked Gibson.

"Didn't the police tell you?"

"No, they don't tell people like me things like that."

"I don't know how he died."

"You're lying," retorted Gibson.

"I'm not. I saw no obvious wounds."

Okay, she might be telling the truth because I didn't see any, either. "Are you sure you didn't see anyone while you were there? Or hear anything?"

"No. The place was empty. Except for him."

"Did you put the fan in there and then leave the wall partially open and place the vase on the shelf?"

"Yes, I wanted you to find the body."

"Exactly who are you? And how did you know all that stuff you mentioned on the phone? You tapped my lines? Or ProEye's?"

"I did what I had to do to convince you to help me," she replied evasively.

"What exactly do you want me to do?"

"I thought that was obvious. Find out who killed Dan."

"Why?" asked Gibson.

"I told you. He was my friend."

"From Miami?"

"Yes."

"How exactly did you know him? Business? You don't sound all that old. He was at least seventy, if not older. It was hard to tell with him dissolving right in front of me."

"We were friends who did business together. My age was never an issue."

"What sort of business?" asked Gibson.

"I feel like I'm being interrogated," she countered.

"Good, because you are."

"Maybe I made a mistake with you."

Gibson said, "You made a mistake the minute you put me in this situation. And trust runs both ways. I need to feel some from you."

"I told you what I could."

"I need more than that."

"Has motherhood robbed you of your detective skills?" asked the woman.

"I don't like that you know so much about me. And if you so much as come near me or my kids—"

"I wouldn't do that."

"You dropped this phone off on my porch," retorted Gibson.

"No, I didn't. I had someone do that for me."

"Same thing. You've encroached on my territory, lady."

The line went dead.

Gibson went to a drawer in the kitchen and took out a small toolbox. She spent five minutes taking the phone apart to see if it contained a listening or tracking device. It held neither. She put it back together again and checked her front door camera using her phone app.

At nine thirteen a hooded figure had come around one side of her house, placed the box on the front porch, and hurried off. She calculated the person's height at five eight and weight at maybe 120, but that was iffy because of the bulky hoodie. Could have been a tall woman, or a small man.

She sat down at her kitchen table and stared at the reassembled phone before looking down at the butcher block table she'd bought from Wayfair with a signing bonus from ProEye.

Her life as a divorced woman with two young children had, up until today, been predictable and...safe. Her old job as a cop had been none of those things. For her kids' sake she'd wanted to leave that old life, and she had. Then her new life had become...tedious. Now today had come along to deliver her kicking and screaming right back to her old life.

She rose and made sure every window and door was secure and then Gibson set the alarm system. She locked her gun away, grabbed the baseball bat that she'd used on the girls' softball team in high school, and slept on the floor between her two kids. But she didn't really sleep, because every sound in the house made her open her eyes and check for would-be murderers.

This is getting downright creepy. Should I tell Wilson Sullivan about this?

But if the police took over, she would be cut out of the investigation completely. And Sullivan might not believe her, even if she showed him the phone and the camera footage. If someone was going to threaten her family, she wanted to be in the loop and have an opportunity to do something about it. For all those reasons, Gibson decided to keep quiet for now.

She awoke with a start the next morning when she felt something on her face. She gripped the bat and was about to—

Tommy was stroking her cheek. "I hungry, Mommy."

She blinked up at him, and looked around to see Darby staring at her from behind the side rail of her bed.

"Me too, Mommy," Darby said. "Hu-un-gry." She rubbed her belly.

Gibson eyed her watch. It was six thirty. She rose off the floor and took a moment to hold both her kids as tightly as she could.

If anything happened to them…

Tommy put his small hands squarely on his mother's quivering cheeks and held her gaze. "Okay, Mommy?"

"Sure, honey, Mommy's okay. Everything's awesome."

She changed Darby's diaper, helped Tommy do his business with the toilet, cleaned them both up, and got them dressed. They filed downstairs, where she made them cereal and buttered toast, and poured out glasses of milk.

She watched them eat every bite, while she rubbed at her tired eyes and yawned and sucked down a cup of coffee like it was a shot of tequila. She had a babysitter come three days a week during the day to give her a break and allow her to work uninterrupted. Thankfully, this was one of those days.

The kids really liked Carol Silva. She was in her late twenties, tall and lean with thick dark hair and a toothy, perpetual smile, and she brought games and puzzles and other fun things for the kids to do. She was not really in Gibson's budget, but the woman was worth every penny.

And when she arrived and took charge at eight o'clock, Gibson ran upstairs, showered in two minutes, and hit her computer. No delinquent billionaires today. Today was all about the dead Dan Pottinger.

And the anonymous woman on the phone.

CHAPTER

8

DANIEL POTTINGER HAD BEEN A recluse in life, and there was little information about the man online. There were a couple of local news stories about his donating money to a youth center, and Pottinger had also given funds to a retirement home for war vets. But there were no pictures of the man. He had no social media presence and, seemingly, no history. The only reference to his wealth was that he had been in retail investing, whatever the hell that actually meant.

Gibson did a search on Pottinger in Miami to see if he had any businesses registered there or had done any sort of commerce in the city or state. If the woman had been telling the truth there should have been some evidence of that, but Gibson found none in the usual places.

So maybe their business was in unusual places. Or maybe…

The absence of any real information about the man made Gibson's cop antennae tingle. So maybe she had to get off the computer and do some forensic fieldwork. And an opportunity occurred to her.

She opened a drawer of her desk and removed a leather kit. Inside were items Gibson had bought with her own money when she had worked at the Jersey City Police Department.

She kissed her kids, told Silva she would be back in approximately three hours, and drove off in her van. The ride went faster this time, since she knew where she was going. Once she drew close to Stormfield she slowed the van. They might still be working the crime scene, she knew, but her idea could work nonetheless.

She pulled off onto a side road, got out with her leather case, crossed the road, and walked about a hundred feet on the shoulder before turning down the lane where Stormfield was located. She slowed her pace, looking everywhere for cop activity, but saw none. She reached the gate and saw that there was no cop car there. They must have established their perimeter closer to the mansion, perhaps around the bend. It wasn't like the locals here had the unlimited manpower that larger cities had.

And thank God for that.

Just to make sure, she snuck through the trees until she could see the house. There was one police cruiser out front with an officer in the driver's seat. She couldn't see him clearly from this vantage point, but he appeared to be reading something on his phone. The forensics team must have finished up and gone on their merry way with Pottinger's body, and hopefully with some promising clues.

She couldn't see any other cars. If Pottinger had hired help, they wouldn't be allowed in the house right now, but she imagined they would have already been questioned by Sullivan or would be shortly.

She got back to the mailbox, which fortunately was set about ten feet off the road and screened from there by some large bushes. She made one more searching look up and down the road and then toward the mansion. All was clear.

She opened her leather kit and took out the fingerprinting equipment—a vial of latent powder, a fiberglass brush, black plastic lifting tape, and backing cards. Luckily, it hadn't rained or else she might have had to use a reactive spray to bring out the latent prints. The same would hold for curved or irregular surfaces. But the mailbox's sides and lid were mostly flat and the metal nonporous, so it was ideal for what she wanted to do.

She applied the titanium dioxide powder to her brush, spun off the excess, and, holding her light at oblique angles to highlight the surface and check for ridge detail, followed the whorls, loops, arches, and circles wherever they took her.

It was fortunate that she had started out her police career as a crime tech. Forensic evidence ruled the day in the world of criminal convictions. And the lack thereof almost guaranteed that guilty people often walked free, lifting their collective middle finger at the scales of justice.

She spread the powder to all areas of the mailbox, around the handle, the flag, the sides, anywhere someone might have touched the surface. She knew she would probably get the prints of the mailman as well, but she could work around that.

She identified ten sets of viable prints. Her next step was to use her lifting tape to grab them. She established an anchor point and set the tape down over the first print, smoothing away the air bubbles. She repeated this for all the other prints, including a nice palm print on the side of the box where someone had placed their hand, perhaps to provide a leverage point for pulling an oversized package from the box. She constantly looked around for anyone coming. She knew she was taking a risk, and would be in serious trouble if the cops showed up, or the officer on perimeter duty decided to go get some coffee. But right now she didn't care, and she would hear the car coming and could duck down and hope whoever it was didn't notice the print powder on the mailbox.

Gibson placed each print onto her acetate cards. She finished and wiped off the print powder with a spray bottle of water and a rag from her kit. She wasn't destroying evidence, she told herself. The cops would have lots of prints inside the house and they could always take them right off the dead man. Gibson was certain they already had, though they had preliminarily identified him as Daniel Pottinger. But that was not conclusive, Gibson knew. And that was the reason she was here. Because Pottinger's background, or lack thereof, just screamed that he was trying to hide his real identity for some reason.

She walked back to her van and drove off. Gibson suddenly noticed that her heart was racing and her cheeks were flushed. All in a good way. This was perhaps her most exciting moment since she was a patrol officer running down a suspected rapist and tackling him in an alleyway behind a Walmart back in the Garden State. And when he'd tried to attack her, a knee to his groin and a palm strike to his nose had been immensely gratifying.

She returned to her house, took pictures of each card with her camera phone, and then called a friend of hers who still worked for the New Jersey State Police. She asked the woman to run the prints for her through her databases and, if necessary, also through the NGI system, which had replaced the FBI's IAFIS fingerprint database and featured enhanced capabilities including palm prints, irises, and even facial ID.

"What's this for, Mick?" her friend asked.

"It's personal, Kate, but I really need to find out the ID of someone."

"Where'd you get the prints?"

"Off a mailbox."

"Is that legal?"

"Absolutely, public space," said Gibson, though she really had no idea if it was.

"I'll see what I can do," replied Kate. "How are the kids?"

"Adorable, especially when they're not vomiting on me."

That got a laugh out of old Kate, who was the mother of four. And hopefully extra incentive to run the prints for her.

Then the phone that had been left on her porch buzzed.

9

Aʀᴇ ʏᴏᴜ ʀᴇᴀᴅʏ ᴛᴏ ᴛᴀʟᴋ calmly now?" the woman said.

"I was talking calmly last time and you hung up on me," replied Gibson a little testily. "But I *am* ready to talk, and listen to what you have to say."

"Good. Do the police know the cause of death yet?"

"Again, they have no reason to share that with me. In fact, I asked and they refused."

"Can you ask again?"

"Why?"

"It could be critical. It could be instructive, like a *clue*. Cops like clues, right?"

"Okay, I'll see what I can do."

"Have you told the local police about me?'"

"No. I'm keeping it to myself for now."

"Good, because it might unduly complicate things if you do let them know."

"They're complicated enough. You mentioned Miami and business. Can you tell me anything else? I need something to go on if I'm going to make any progress. You want me to help you, so you need to help me. I hope you can see that."

"You're very manipulative," she replied.

Gibson wanted to scream out, *I'm manipulative?* Instead she said, "Just the cop in me. But I do need some information, otherwise I'm stuck in neutral."

"What do you want to know?"

"First, is Daniel Pottinger the man's real name?"

"Why do you ask?"

"Because there is really nothing on the guy online. Just stuff that could be fabricated."

"Not everyone bares their soul online."

"Preaching to the choir on that one, but my question is still hanging out there."

"Dan was secretive," she said cautiously. "He didn't like people knowing his business."

"So maybe he had a fake identity then?"

"I knew him only as Dan Pottinger. If he had a different identity it was before my time."

"Okay, were you in Miami with him?"

"For a while."

"How long ago?"

"Years."

"How long did you two work together?" asked Gibson.

"Not long enough. He taught me a lot."

"When did you learn he had moved to Virginia and bought Stormfield?"

"Recently. As I said, he communicated with me and told me to visit him there. I wish I had gotten to him before whoever killed him did."

Well, that's quite the self-serving statement. "Before then, how long had it been since you had heard from him?"

"Why does that matter?" the woman asked.

"I'm just trying to establish some basic facts and timelines here."

"What you need to establish is *how* he died."

"But for the police to share with me, I need something of value to barter with them."

"I hadn't thought of that."

"That's okay. Together, we can get there," replied Gibson encouragingly.

"Our interests are probably not perfectly aligned."

"That never stopped people from working together before. And *you* reached out to me. Can you at least give me a hint as to what business you two were involved in?"

The line went dead again.

On impulse Gibson threw the phone across the room. But then she rushed over, picked it up, and hit the redial button. It rang and rang. Finally she clicked off.

That evening, after Silva had left, Gibson got to be a mom again. She made dinner for the kids and they played in the living room for about an hour. This usually involved Gibson's giving the kids rides on her back, which wasn't great for her spine, and then reading to them or letting them toss a ball back and forth. She tried to teach Tommy how to dribble a basketball, but his coordination just wasn't there yet. Tommy also had a toy computer that he liked to peck on while his sister kept pestering him for a turn.

Tommy cracked silly jokes and said things that made Darby howl with laughter, and that, in turn, made Gibson laugh, too. This was the best part of being a mom. Just spending time with her kids. No agenda, no to-do list, no vomit hurling, or tears spilling, just…fun.

Then will come the teenage years when I'll have to stop being a friend and really become a parent and lay down the law.

Gibson thought of the stupid shit she had done as a teen, which had driven her parents crazy with worry, and caused her dad's hair to gray prematurely, or so the family lore went. She looked at her own kids. *Slow down, don't grow up so fast. I don't want white hair in my thirties.*

She put them to bed after reading them another story about a kindly farm animal that helped her friends get out of trouble.

I could use a friend like that, thought Gibson as she closed the book and put it on the shelf.

She was about to leave after turning off the light, but then Gibson lingered by the door, the moonlight from the window illuminating the sleeping forms of her kids. It was a perfect vision of peace and security in an imperfect and often violent world.

The dead Daniel Pottinger in his secret little room.

The mysterious lying lady on the phone.

Gibson's entanglement in something she couldn't understand.

She felt like a little girl again, alone, and afraid of unseen dangers lurking for her. As a single woman and a cop she had felt equipped to take on anything. As a mother of two little kids with her athletic and cop days behind her, she felt small and unsure and vulnerable.

She walked downstairs and called her father.

Rick Rogers answered on the second ring and said in his naturally gruff voice, "I was wondering when you were going to call, Mick."

"Why?"

"Your mother told me some police detective was at your house that you had business with. And before that you had her come and babysit on the spur of the moment. What's going on?"

Gibson told him about the call from Arlene Robinson, the journey to Stormfield, finding the body of Pottinger, meeting with Detective Wilson Sullivan, and then the revelation that she had been duped by the very same Arlene Robinson.

"And now she's calling me on this phone that she or someone else left on my front porch."

"You really need to let this guy Sullivan know about those calls, honey."

"If I sic Sullivan on her I might lose the only shot I have at solving this sucker."

"First of all, it's not *your* job to solve this *sucker*. You're not a cop anymore. And, second, you've got two little kids who depend on you. So let the people with the badges and guns handle this and you go back to your nerdy computer stuff."

The way he said this last part made Gibson's face flush. Her father had been the most vocal critic of her ex-husband. He had lectured his daughter over and over that the man was a scumbag and she should never, ever consider marrying him.

And I didn't listen to him. I sided with the guy who ended up breaking my heart.

She knew this had hurt her father deeply, because they had always been close. She didn't know if it was because she was his first child, or because their personalities were similar—everyone had called her a chip off the old block. Growing up, she had confided in her dad far more than in her mother, telling him things that were intimate and sometimes embarrassing. And her father had taken it all in stride and never betrayed her confidences. As a cop he had no doubt seen far worse, and he understood how imperfect the world and those inhabiting it were. And to his credit, after being proved right about her ex-husband, her father had never once said, *I told you so.* Though his criticisms had been delivered in more subtle ways.

But in speaking with him now, she wondered if he held it against her for quitting the police force and becoming, basically, a computer geek looking for bounty.

"I know that makes the most sense," she began. "And I hope you know I would never do anything to put my kids in danger."

"Then you're going to follow my advice?"

"I'm not going to actively investigate this case, but I want to let it play out for a bit, see where it goes."

"You may not like where it goes. This person sounds manipulative and slick. I worked with the fraud division for a couple of years. It made me disgusted with my fellow human beings. The ones who committed the fraud *and* the ones who, despite all the clear evidence to the contrary, refused to accept that they were being duped."

Like me and my ex, thought Gibson, who also wondered if this was another subtle dig from her father. "I know, Dad. And if it starts to go sideways, I'll go to the cops. I promise."

"Just to be clear, my advice is for you to go to the cops *now*."

"Okay, okay. Hey, I got some prints that I think are Pottinger's."

"Why?"

"Because I don't think that's his real name. I'd like to know who he really is."

"How are you getting them run through the system? The outfit you work for?"

"No. Just somebody I know from the old days."

"I thought you said you weren't going to actively investigate this case?"

"Running prints is not exactly *active*."

"Yeah, sure it isn't."

They said their goodbyes and Gibson slowly put down the phone.

He's right, Mick. You need to drop this thing, right now.

But they knew where she lived. They were on her front porch.

Do I have a choice to drop it?

And then the other phone rang.

10

The room was dark, as she preferred it. Light was revealing, obviously, and it also showed too much that might be true.

She used the computer audio, channeling the burner phone through it.

She never held a phone to her ear. She liked separation, a buffer. Nothing truly close to her.

She stared at the computer screen, where there were a half-dozen videos showing various places she needed to keep an eye on, including Gibson's home.

On the screen were Post-its with helpful, encouraging notes like: *You can do this. Sweat the small details and the big plan becomes a fait accompli.* And the one she liked best of all: *No one will ever know you.*

She readied herself.

"I apologize for hanging up on you," she said in the same measured tone and voice she had employed with Gibson from day one. That was critical.

Gibson said, "It is frustrating, especially when I'm trying to reach common ground with you."

She had checked the record of Gibson's phone calls from a reliable tracking source she often used. Ten minutes before, Gibson had called her parents' number. Probably spoken with her father, the former cop, for advice in dealing with the shitstorm she was in.

There is no more privacy. Except for people like me, who pay attention. "I can understand that, Mick."

"Don't call me that. That's reserved for friends. And we're not there yet."

Agree with her to build that common ground and a degree of reasonableness.

"I understand, Mickey, or do you prefer Ms. Gibson?"

"Mickey is fine. And your name?"

"Just call me Arlene."

"So sticking with the fake name then?"

Use her own words against her.

"As you said, we're not there yet, *Mickey*."

"So, the business you and Pottinger were involved in?"

"The business *he* was involved in was not legal. The business he and I were engaged in was perfectly aboveboard."

"Then why the fear of the police?"

"I didn't say I was afraid of the police, did I?"

"I think you did."

She frowned and wrote in her spiral notebook: *CHECK THAT.*

"If I did, then I misspoke. There are others involved here, and anyone in their right minds should be afraid of them."

"Let's focus on Pottinger and his business for now."

She looked over at the adjustable mirror next to her computer. She slipped off her dark wig and put on a blond one.

"Okay, that sounds like a plan."

"Good," said Gibson.

She worked with the strands, letting some dangle in front of her eyes, giving her a mysterious look. She picked up a tube of lipstick and applied a bright cherry red color to her lips. It was the subtle things that changed you the most. And color was near the top of that list. Along with how you carried yourself, your voice, the eyes, the walk. It was a long list, really, and she was coming up with new items for it all the time.

Total transformation. Why be one person your whole life when you can be…anybody?

"What do you want to know?" she asked as she brushed out her new look, and applied some highlighter to her cheekbones and jawline. She hit her face with a small light and checked her reflection in the mirror.

"Principally the nature of the illegality of what he did."

She glanced at a Post-it note. *Start slow and build. Tap on, tap off. Make them want it.*

"It was more than one thing. And it's complicated after that. Very complicated."

She looked at another note. *Employ self-deprecation and vulnerability to encourage sympathy and subsequent bonding.*

"In fact, I can't say that I completely understand it. If you want the truth, I feel way over my head with this. And I can't get the vision of Dan's dead body out of my mind. I haven't slept well since."

Gibson said, "It *was* disturbing, and I've had some experience with that."

"I've had none, until now."

She looked at another note. *Drop deity reference for gravity and sincerity.*

"And I hope to *God* I never do again."

"I'm sure."

Thanks God, whatever you are.

She took off the wig and put on an auburn one. That worked better with the highlights but clashed with the lipstick. She removed the cherry red and applied a subtler shade. Her own mother would never recognize her. But then again, she never had anyway. Not deep down.

"Getting back to Pottinger's business," prompted Gibson.

"Some of it was the usual. Drugs, prostitution, sex trafficking, pornography. That's where the money is. Men and their penises make the dark world go round."

"You said *some of it*; so there's more?"

She read down the list from her notebook.

"Theft of historical artifacts from the Middle East. Trafficking in elephant tusks from Africa. Importing endangered shark fins from Japan." She paused. "You want more?"

"Sure, why not," said Gibson offhandedly.

Right, wow, I wonder what's coming next from you?

"Okay, he was also involved in the illicit transfer of biomedical weapons out of Crimea and money laundering for terrorists based in the Sudan."

Gibson growled, "Why don't you throw in nuclear weapons, the plague, and fake Gucci purses for good measure?"

Just as expected.

"So you don't believe me?"

"One guy in all those lines of criminal activity?"

"How do you think he afforded Stormfield? And he's probably got a dozen places just like it. And you ask me to tell you what I know and then you don't believe me. This will get us nowhere."

"How do you know all this?" Gibson asked.

"When I go into business with someone I try to find out as much as I can."

"If you found that out about Pottinger, why did he let you live?"

"Easy. Because he didn't know I found out. I don't leave tracks. I did it all electronically. Just like you do with your work, Mickey."

She listened to the other woman's breathing. Even, but slightly elevated. *She's thinking of the right response, knowing there probably isn't one.*

She used a new eyeliner and studied the effect. *Yes, much better. I can mess with anybody with this look.*

"You still there?" she prompted.

Gibson said, "And knowing what you did about him, you still decided to do business with him? What does that say about you?"

Okay, that was also totally expected and this was not a long call so far. Her respect for Gibson slipped a notch. *But then again, I am better than you, and I'm going to prove it.* "That I compartmentalize well. As we all do. As *you* do."

"I don't deal with criminals."

"Even when you worked undercover back in Jersey City? You shacked up with some real scum there, did some questionable, borderline illegal things."

"I won't ask how you know about that, though I'd like to. That was part of my job and the object was to catch the bad guys, not make money."

Cocked and loaded. Fire away. "And you just assume that my goals are different?"

"Are they?"

"Maybe I just want to catch bad people, like you used to do as a cop."

"Are you saying you're a cop?"

"Do you have to be a cop to catch bad people?"

"A snitch then? Or a plant working with the cops?"

She looked at her notebook, running down a few possibilities. *Play shrink for a bit to shake things up.* "And how does that make you feel?"

"What the hell does that mean?" Gibson snapped.

"Does that make you feel more comfortable working with me? That we're on the same side?"

"I don't know that."

"Not yet. But we could get there, right?"

"It all depends. Who are you working with?"

"Did you ever reveal that to a stranger while you were under-cover?" She put a checkmark in one box next to a line of goals in her notebook. *Okay, she's tacitly accepted that I am what I say I am.*

"I think this situation might be a little different, don't you?"

She looked at the computer clock and smiled. *Terrific segue because I have another appointment.* "On the contrary, I think we've accomplished a lot with this call. It gives us something to build on next time."

"You really haven't told me anything!"

"Of course I have, Mickey. Let me recount for you. Pottinger was a criminal on a global scale. I managed to find out about this. There are people out there who want to kill me. The same ones who probably killed Pottinger. I know you were skeptical of the breadth of his heinous actions, but I can assure you that what I gave you is not an exhaustive list by any means. Now you have some things to check out."

"It would help a lot if I had his real name."

Praise her. "I'm sure with all your talents and experience you can discover that. I didn't involve you in this because you're second-rate, Mickey."

"I actually *have* taken some steps."

"Excellent. And who knows, before much more time passes, you'll let me call you Mick."

And next time don't make it so easy. People grow from challenges and I'm no exception.

She clicked off and finished her makeup. She rose and took off her robe. She was naked underneath. She wrapped a pushup bra around her bosom, slid on a thong, wriggled into a tight black dress, and completed the outfit with dark stockings and four-inch heels.

She checked her image in a full-length mirror.

It was good, no, better than good. She was not beautiful. She was even better. *I can sell the line with average looks and a tall, thin, small-chested frame because I exude confidence, refuse to back down, and can read a room better than anyone. And really, what else does one need to do to make it in this life? Hell, with just the right eyeliner I can rule the world.*

She walked over to her desk and looked at the open spiral note-book. She closed it, revealing the cover on which she had placed a label that read MICKEY GIBSON AND THE PLAN. It sat next to a half-dozen other notebooks with their own little neatly organized esoteric worlds lying therein.

She wasn't full-on OCD. Yet. But it was probably only a matter of time.

But then, with my history, what else could I expect? You build walls to keep the boogeyman away as long as you can.

She grabbed a large tote bag with things already packed neatly in it, and a wrap, and walked out the door.

To go to work.

II

THE CAB DROPPED HER OFF at the corner of a major thoroughfare in Washington, DC's Georgetown neighborhood, which gleamed bright and full of possibilities.

"Clarisse," exclaimed the woman. The lady approaching her was towering and busty and hippy and dressed for success of a certain kind, with men of a certain kind.

Clarisse turned and smiled with her muted, burgundy-tinged lips.

Hit the play button and enjoy yourself. "Angie, how long have you been waiting?"

"Ages, meaning ten minutes. Girl, we have work to do."

"Yes we do."

They started down M Street. There were money and powerful people in abundance here, which was the only reason the two women were trolling the area.

They entered the lobby of the hotel, looking guest-worthy but with just enough glam to cause sedate heads to turn. DC was not New York or even close to LA. Somber and conservative were still the accepted fashion marks of the day here. But something different and alluring could be appreciated, and every bit of clothing worn by the two women had been carefully calibrated to elicit heightened attention but *not* scrutiny.

Angie hit the elevator button and they rode the car to the fourth floor.

"Room 412," said Angie, her booming voice gone; she was all business and focus now.

"The Washington senator," Clarisse whispered back.

"All five feet six of him. And another four inches of you know what, poor, pitiful thing. But that's okay, in his mind he's LeBron James with a Louisville slugger in his pants."

That was as playful as Angie got on these things. Still, Clarisse frowned.

Influencer mode. "Time for games later, Angie. Tight is tight. You're a pro. You know this."

"Yes I do, girl."

Angie keyed the door to Room 410 and let Clarisse inside. Clarisse took Angie's purse, and a few moments later she heard Angie unlocking the door to 412.

Clarisse opened up her small laptop and ran it off the hotspot of her ultra-secure "fortress" phone, as she liked to call it. No ludicrously unsecure Wi-Fi for this mission. She connected a wireless camera to her computer, fired up a program, and said into the computer, "Copy, Angie?"

"Copy loud and clear."

With the line of communication established, Angie would now take her mic, which was sunk so far in her ear that it was invisible but not untraceable, and place it in a small lead container that she had carried on her person. That container would be inserted in the showerhead pipe in the bathroom. She would wait for the electronic sweep to be completed and then, unless she did it before the senator arrived, nature would call before the show would begin. In this intimate situation, no man would deny a woman that. The earbud would be reinserted and the connection resumed.

The placement of the tiny camera would have to wait for the sweep. The senator's detail placed too much faith in this electronic vetting. If it had been Clarisse, she would have rented out the rooms on either side and placed trusted people there. Apparently the senator was too cheap or too stupid to do that.

She readied herself as she heard the *troop-troop* of the dutiful and dullard personal security detail. These guys made middle-class wages and had no incentive to go the last mile. The criminal syndicates did it so much better. You messed up there, you were fish food. You screwed up here, and you just slouched off to work for the government.

She heard murmurs next door.

The sweep took five minutes while she could envision Angie waiting patiently on the bed, her eyes not making contact with any of the men, as instructed. And they were always men. Put a girl on the detail and then people like Clarisse started to sweat. Men were clueless about everything having to do with women. That was the one principle that drove her entire business plan.

The detail left but with a man posted outside. They always did it that way. One lucky guy was picked to listen to the fun.

When Angie opened her connecting door a crack, Clarisse was there, having done the same with her door. Clarisse secured the tiny camera to the edge of Angie's door with a Velcro sticker, its silhouette invisible against the dark wood of the door.

"Okay, going to mic up now while the getting's good," whispered Angie. Both women eased their doors shut and secured them.

Clarisse returned to her computer and watched as Angie disappeared into the bathroom, coming out a minute later with the mic in her ear. Her glam reverberated to all four corners of the room in the little white nighty that she had worn under her dress.

The knock on the door came a few moments later. Angie opened it and in strode Senator Wright, who was, despite the name, all wrong in too many ways to count. He was four inches shorter than Angie in bare feet, flabby, bald, and the second wealthiest politician on Capitol Hill, all inherited. Back in the fifties, his grandfather had invented a new type of windshield wiper motor, invested the royalties well, and allowed his descendants to be lazy, rich, and obnoxious about it.

And the senator's wife, a petulant Princeton grad with her own trust fund, just didn't get him, or so he told women like Angie. And neither, apparently, did his three kids.

He smiled, wrapped his arms around her, his hands dipping down and sliding up the nighty.

"I like them really voluptuous," he said, giving her the same campaign trail smile he had probably practiced in front of a mirror for months on end. "And you damn sure fill that bill."

Clarisse could not speak without fear of the senator overhearing through the mic. But she and Angie had devised another method to communicate.

Clarisse tapped her mic twice, telling Angie to deliver the line they had practiced.

Angie said breathlessly, "I will be your best friend tonight."

"Oh, I can see that, babe."

One tap.

"But this will be our little secret, okay?" said Angie.

"What do you mean?"

Three taps.

"I'm married."

He smiled. "Perfect. He's a lucky guy."

"And tonight, I'm a lucky girl."

That was it for the chitchat. The rest was a mud wrestle on the bed that was energetic if not epic. Clarisse had seen better and worse.

The gasps, the moans, the squeaks of the embattled box springs. The nervous chuckle of the lone security guy outside.

You won't be laughing tomorrow. Tomorrow you'll be unemployed.

Clarisse now put things on autopilot. Angie knew how to string the guy along. She somehow could tell right when the cork was going to pop and she pulled it back, let the guy calm, allowing a bit more time to film, because the more footage they had, the more the men tended to pay.

Clarisse pulled another notebook out of her bag and began

jotting thoughts down on another project, the sounds of sex next door becoming white noise to her.

Later, when the couple was done, the senator washed up and was gone, leaving an exhausted (he thought) and sleeping (he hoped) and absolutely sexually fulfilled (he was sure) Angie on the bed, naked, along with a stack of cash on the nightstand.

Oh, this night is going to cost you so much more than that, thought Clarisse.

Ten seconds after the door closed Clarisse checked her security peephole and tapped the all-clear signal on the mic. She watched on the screen as Angie rose, washed up, got dressed, and then methodically wiped down everything in the room she might have touched. Prints she could do something about, DNA not so much, but DNA was probably not going to come into play, particularly after the maids cleaned the room. And Angie was on no database anywhere, so DNA could go screw itself.

Clarisse had worn gloves, because her prints *were* on file.

Angie then knocked on the connecting door and was let in to 410.

Clarisse had already put all the equipment away, and now she took the ear mic back from Angie.

Angie worked away on some fasteners and a scalp adhesive patch, and finally pulled her long hair free, revealing a bald head. She put the fake tresses in her purse.

She said in a resigned tone, "How come the richest, cheating assholes are the shortest and the fattest with the smallest dicks?"

"Somehow, in the universe, it all makes perfect sense."

"I'd much prefer tall, rich, handsome, with a six-pack."

"Try the NBA, Angie. They've got plenty of free cash flow."

"Oh, I've worked that garden, baby."

"I thought so."

"And you don't have to blackmail those suckers. They just give you a Ferrari for a blowjob."

"Right."

Before parting Angie said, "When?"

"Very soon."

"You know how much?"

"To start, half a mill. You managed him well. I've got twenty-five minutes of film. The good, the better, and the really better."

Angie blew her a kiss. "See you next time, bay-bee."

Her coat was reversible. She went from black to white, which looked stunning.

She left, her cavalier stride now transformed to a normal gait.

Clarisse watched the door for a moment. She had six Angies, but Angie only had one Clarisse.

She took her auburn wig off as well, and put on a short blond one she had in her bag. She teased the hair in the mirror, reapplied her makeup, and changed the colors of her eyeliner and lipstick. She slipped out a different outfit from her oversized bag and went from slinky dress to a women's tailored suit and black, square glasses. The sky-high heels got replaced with flat and professional. With slumped, rounded shoulders she shrunk from high-priced hooker to mousy CPA. The hotel had CCTV everywhere and if the senator later had it pulled, he would be very confused as to the women coming out of this room. And tomorrow she and Angie would look nothing like either of the two women the film would reveal coming and going.

She hailed a cab outside and rode it back to within three blocks of where she was staying. You never took anyone all the way home.

Clarisse walked in, got on the phone, and confirmed her reservation on NetJets. She slept well, rose early, walked the requisite three blocks, picked up her Uber and rode it to Dulles with big sunglasses covering her face. Clarisse was wheels up to Greenville, South Carolina, at eight a.m. sharp.

Time to visit Mommy.

12

I HEAR THE WHISPERS. THE dutiful daughter from somewhere else who comes here on private wings, because Greenville is growing but still small; and someone works at the Greenville-Spartanburg Airport who knows somebody who knows somebody. And the tattle commences like two cans on a string line.

Is Mrs. Leland's daughter a movie star under another name? A socialite with a Wall Street husband? A TikTok influencer earning major bucks? Or maybe even a high-dollar whore?

I might be all of those things. And more.

She sat in the chair and watched the woman lying in the bed.

The assisted living facility was top-notch, or so she had been told. At six grand a month it had better be.

Indeed, she thought, for that price they better wipe the woman's ass and give her a daily mani-pedi and feed her with a silver spoon. None of that happened, of course. She had a roof, enough food, aides to dispense her stack of pills—little pearl-like trinkets of sustained geriatric life—afternoon Scrabble, a library with actual books, an ice cream shop with an aged soda jerk, though no one here could manage to digest lactose except the staff, a four-hundred-square-foot room, and the bed. There was a memory center for when you went fully gaga. She knew this because they had given her a tour when it seemed Mommy had reached a tipping point. That was an extra two grand a month because the gagas could get unruly, and really did need to be wiped.

There was a pool table, which was hard to navigate with a walker or rollator or shaky limbs, an outdoor courtyard with picnic tables and cushioned chairs, and an outdoor fireplace where one could sit and stare off at nothing much. She knew this was true; she had done it herself when Mommy got to be a little too much.

There was a cute and cuddly therapy dog that slept all day. There were myriad clubs organized by residents, which only a handful utilized, namely the ones who organized them. Mostly people here sat and waited for visitors who never came.

But I come, once a month.

A timer on her watch went off. She reached into the half fridge and pulled out an Ensure, placed a straw into it, woke her mother, got her to sit up, and helped her drink down the liquid. Her mother was diabetic and had COPD from the cigs, and swollen feet from the same. She was also obese from a life of crappy, fat-laden food, had a tricky liver and failing kidneys, and wore a chemo wig from her last dance with the cancer in her breasts. She was seventy-one and looked a hundred and seventy-one. The tragic irony was her mother had once been a beautiful woman. Many men wanted her. Only one had gotten her. And that man had not been a good one, but so many of them weren't.

She would probably go straight from here to hospice and bypass gaga land.

Her mother's given name was Agnes. Of course it was, she thought. Her parents had given their daughter nothing, not even a decent name.

Instead they had bestowed one upon her that sounded like someone trying to hock up phlegm. Thanks, Me-maw and Paw-paw.

Her mother opened her one good and cataract-less eye and said in the hollowed-out, gravelly voice of a Camel smoke queen, "You look too thin. Don't they feed you?"

"Does *who* feed me?"

"Your man!"

Post-it note to self: Never ask Mommy another question again. But you know you will because you can't help it.

"I feel like shit," said Agnes, not waiting for an answer and probably already having forgotten the question.

"You actually look better than last time."

"Can I come and live with you?"

"We tried that, remember? You tried to stab me with a cheese knife. Putting you here was actually a pretty fair compromise in lieu of my having you arrested."

"I forget things," said Agnes.

"That's okay. I don't. Especially cheese knives to the jugular."

"You look rich. Are you rich? Is my little girl rich?"

"I do just fine. That's why you can afford to live here. Because of your little girl."

Her mother would never remember this, because her brain was full of rot, too. But it made her feel good to say it.

"I never thought you'd make anything of yourself," Agnes said with a yawn.

"You always said I was full of surprises."

"Did I?"

"No, I'm lying."

"How's your father?"

"Dead to us. Over twenty years. We covered this before." She pantomimed the shotgun to the mouth, pulled the invisible trigger and jerked her head back, although her mother wasn't even looking.

That was okay because the pantomime had been bullshit.

"I forget things," said her mother, promptly forgetting it but then surprising her daughter by saying, "Did he treat you nice? Did he love you?"

Clarisse's fingernail rubbed the arm of the chair she was sitting in. She rubbed it so hard, part of it broke off and fell to the floor. She looked down at the fuchsia-colored piece of herself resting on the cheap, stained carpet and said, "How have your bowel movements been lately? Firmer?"

Her mother sucked down the last of the Ensure and handed the empty to her daughter, who promptly disposed of it.

"Why do you keep coming here?" asked Agnes, licking her cracked lips, caused by oxygen deprivation, caused by the COPD, caused by the Camels. "You hate me and I know it."

"I'm your daughter. And I *am* paying for this place. So I like to make sure you're getting *my* money's worth."

"Do I have other children?"

"Not that you ever mentioned," she lied.

"What is your name again?"

"Lucretia."

The older woman sniggered. "That is one funny-ass name."

"Says Agnes."

The lips curled back. "I don't like you much, you little bitch."

"Yes, you made that quite clear over the years. Not so much the words, but the actions."

Or, more accurately, inactions.

"You must love me, too, though. To pay for this shit, to come here and give me the chocolate milk and ask about my *bowel* movements."

"It's called Ensure. And I will bury you nice, or do you prefer cremation?"

"Just burn me to ash and be done. I'm almost there now."

"And sprinkled where?"

"Who gives a shit?"

"I will see you next time."

But her mother had fallen asleep. That often happened when your body could barely breathe. As she looked down at the wrecked woman, she had to fight back the urge to put a pillow over her face and be done with her and that part of her life.

You're right, I do hate you. And you earned that. But it also wasn't all your fault, either. Part of me feels sorry for you. But only part. But you have nothing and I now have a lot, so here we are.

Sometimes life didn't just suck, it made no sense at all.

Because people often make no sense.

Later, as the plane shed altitude on its way to land, she looked at her Mickey Gibson phone—that, like her notebook, was actually labeled that.

Gibson had tried to call her three times.

You could have been so much more, Mickey Gibson. And you just threw it all away. You had every opportunity, and now look at you. And me? I had nothing. And now look at me. Right on the same playing field as you. Because this is a competition even if you don't know it yet.

But all the phone call attempts were interesting. She might have found out Pottinger's true identity now. Other things being equal, that had to be it. Fingerprints from Stormfield was the most likely angle. If she had passed that test, things were about to get interesting.

Mickey Gibson would have her full and undivided attention for the allotted twenty-five minutes, because she had a schedule to keep.

She looked out the rounded window of the Gulfstream as the tarmac flew at her. A few moments later the jolt of landing brought her back to terra firma in more ways than one.

She deplaned, and the waiting car service dropped her four blocks from the place she was using as a temporary residence. She walked the rest of the way.

Later that evening it took ten minutes to type out the message to Senator Wright and append a little attachment that would forever change the man's life, and not for the better. Yet it would do wonders for her bank account. This was her version of ransomware, only she would never accept cryptocurrency in payment. It fluctuated too much in value from day to day, which was the last thing you wanted currency to do. A wire to bounce-around bank accounts in Zurich and Istanbul would suffice.

With the senator about to receive a gut punch via the "very" personal online account he had provided Angie so she could write dirty to him over the digital ether and hopefully sext him a time or two, she opened her MICKEY GIBSON notebook, lined up her Post-it notes, stared at the video sectors on her screen, and tapped the speed dial.

Mickey Gibson, Round Three.

She was fully prepared and scripted, but actually hoping that Gibson had a few surprises for her.

Truthfully, after Mommy time, she needed the diversion.

13

GIBSON WAS IN HER HOME office. Tommy was playing in the corner, and Darby was sound asleep on her blanket in a miniature wooden rocking chair Gibson's father had made for his granddaughter.

The phone buzzed. It was her police friend, Kate, from Jersey City.

"Only three sets of prints were in the system," she said. "One matches a fellow named Paul Gerald. He works for the post office."

"The mailman, then," said Gibson.

"Right, that's what I figured, too. The second set was a Mary Tatum, she's also a postal worker."

"And the third?"

"Harry Langhorne."

"Not another postal person?"

"No."

"So where'd you get the print match, then?"

"I always check local databases first before I hit the national pipeline. The two mail carriers were on the fed databases. I had no idea if Langhorne was from or had any connection to New Jersey. But apparently he had his prints taken when he was doing some volunteer work at a school. That particular school district required a background check. So I didn't even have to tap the FBI database to nail him."

"So where in Jersey?"

"Trenton."

Near my old stomping ground.

"Could he be your guy?"

"Maybe. Thanks, I owe you, Kate."

Gibson clicked off and tapped a finger against her desk. She glanced over at a still-passed-out Darby, and then at Tommy, who was getting all droopy-eyed because he had been running a million miles an hour since six a.m. and was about to fade into a nap.

Me too. If only.

Her phone buzzed again. It was her ProEye boss, Zeb Brown.

She watched as Tommy lay on the floor with his dinosaur pillow tucked under his head and his thumb in his mouth. *And now we have nap launch, thank you God.*

She spoke quietly into her headset. "Hey, Zeb, what's up?"

"I'm sorry if I was a little stern with you earlier."

"I did think about calling you before I went out there, but then stuff happened. But it was my fault, buck stops with me."

"The detective on the case, Sullivan I think his name was, contacted me. He said the person was super slick and would probably have talked him right out of his badge."

"He did?"

"Yes, so I'm sorry for flying off the handle."

"Apology accepted."

"Do they know anything more about who killed that man?" he asked.

"Not that they're saying, but I'm not involved in the investigation, either."

She crossed her fingers on that one. *White lies are good for the soul.*

"Right, right. Well, I wanted to let you know that we nailed Larkin's assets. All two hundred million. The clients are very happy."

"That's great."

"Look, you might want to take some time off before jumping back in on your other assignments."

Gibson's eyes narrowed along with her thoughts. "Time off?"

"With pay, of course. And I've recommended a performance bonus for you in connection with the Larkin matter."

"That's great. Thank you so much. But as far as the time off, I'm fine, Zeb, I can keep—"

"Jesus, Mickey, you *did* find a dead body. And you do have someone out there who made direct contact with you and who was obviously listening in on our phone conversations. I have to be honest, it freaked lots of people out here. We're doing a full, internal security audit."

"I saw lots of dead bodies in my old career. And why would time off help with the rest of what you just said?"

"I just think you need to decompress and—"

A terrible thought bolted through her head and she voiced it without really thinking. "Zeb, will I have a job to come back to?"

But he had already clicked off.

Coward.

Gibson looked at her kids. *Damn.*

She used her thumbs and index fingers to squeeze her eyeballs tight. To make the image of her and her kids kicked to the curb go away. But they could live with her parents for a bit.

No, you did nothing wrong and you haven't lost your damn job. Yet.

She had a sudden thought and called her father.

"What's up, Mick?"

"Got a lead on something. Harry Langhorne? Name sound familiar?"

"Hell, if that ain't a blast from the past."

"So you recognize it?"

"Oh, yeah. Harry Langhorne was the bookkeeper for the Giordano crime family back in Trenton."

"Giordano? Doesn't ring a bell."

"Way back. I was just a beat cop myself in Jersey City when it happened, and you were just a little kid. It was all over the news."

"What did they do?"

"The usual. Drugs, hookers, blackmail. And they had the local garbage-haul business, a string of storefront laundering operations, and their street enforcers cracked the heads of any merchant who didn't pay them protection money. All local politicians were in their pocket. They robbed and kidnapped and assaulted and killed, right up until the Feds came down on them like Thor's hammer. They took out some of the New York mob at the same time. It was a big deal back then, let me tell you. Lots of heads rolled and it wasn't just the Giordanos."

"And Langhorne was the bookkeeper? He doesn't sound Italian. He sounds Presbyterian."

"If memory serves me, his mother was…let me think, Ida Giordano, yeah, that was her name. She was a cousin or sister of the top guy, Leo Giordano. Funny, I remember that and I have no memory of what I had for breakfast. Anyway, she married Langhorne Sr. I'm not sure if he knew what he was getting into, but their son Harry apparently did. When he grew up, he got his CPA license, went to work for the mob, and kept all the books, knew where all the bodies were buried. I guess he was a whiz with numbers."

"What happened?"

"Big-time trial, witnesses murdered, evidence tainted, cops paid off, political pressure brought to bear, but, still, all the sons of bitches were convicted."

"And Harry Langhorne?"

"He didn't even testify. Wasn't even charged. But I think he gave them lots of dirt and named the names and opened the cooked books. Then he just vanished. I mean, like gone, gone. You know, like your dick of a husband."

"Thanks for the reminder, Dad, I'd almost forgotten. So what about all the money generated by the Giordano family?"

"Funny thing, you never heard much about that. I bet we were talking big bucks. They had a ton of real estate and other hard assets that the Feds confiscated, but there must have been mounds of cash lying around. It's not like they accepted barter or IOUs. And I never heard about that being recovered, and I think I would have. Why are you asking about Langhorne?"

"Because I think he was the guy who I found dead in the creepy mansion."

"Bullshit, seriously?"

"Seriously."

"I'm sure he did a preemptive plea. If so, he was smart. Government comes after the mob, the first thing they do is deep-six the accountants with cement shoes."

"Spoken like a true Jersey cop with lots of experience in that realm."

"Hey, I know what I know, you know?"

She could almost see her old man grinning.

"So what are you going to do?" he asked.

"Keep digging."

Her father's tone instantly turned serious and warning. "You do not want to get mixed up in anything like that, Mick. I know it was a long time ago, but there are still Giordanos out there. They couldn't get them all. And little mobsters grow up to be big mobsters. And if they did just off this guy, some of them are alive and killing, so you don't want to be on their radar."

"I don't want to be involved with any of this. The thing is, I may not have a choice. But if there is an exit ramp, I promise to take it."

"Shit. You got your gun?"

"Of course."

"Should I come and sleep over at your house?"

"For what, the next forty years?"

"This is not good, Mick. I can feel the ulcer forming in my gut right this minute."

"I promise to be really careful. And thanks for the history lesson."

"I'm not telling your mother."

"Smart man."

She clicked off, drew a deep breath, and let out a silent scream that made a muscle in her face lock up. She put her head down on her desk and took several long breaths.

"Mommy, you okay?"

Gibson looked over to see Tommy staring anxiously at her from the floor with his dinosaur pillow. She gave him a reassuring smile.

"Mommy is just fine."

Around six thirty, she fed her kids dinner. Then they had some play and reading time. Later she put them to bed.

When she got back to her home office after cleaning the kitchen and taking a quick shower, the phone rang.

That phone.

CHAPTER

14

"WHERE THE HELL HAVE YOU been?" said Gibson, clearly irked at the lapse of time. "I've been calling and calling you."

"I do have another life, Mickey."

"What are you going by today? Still fake Arlene?"

"Clarisse will do."

"Is that your real name?"

"What do you think?"

"Okay, *Clarisse*."

"Have you made progress?"

"I'm not taking orders from you and I'm not working for you. Actually, I don't want to be involved in this at all."

"I'm sorry if I implied that you were working for me. But I thought we were working *together*."

Gibson decided to cut to the chase. "Harry Langhorne?"

"Yes, Mickey, that is excellent."

"You could have saved me the trouble and just told me his real name."

"But you feel far better having discovered it yourself, right? And even if I had told you, you would have had to verify it, correct?"

Gibson grimaced, because she knew the woman was right. "The cops will have that information by now, too."

"Oh, I'm sure. What will you do with it?"

"He was a mob bookkeeper who turned state's evidence back in New Jersey. Did you know that?"

"That all sounds quite intimidating."

"You didn't answer my question."

"I have since learned of his relationships with other unsavory types."

Now if that wasn't a bullshit word salad answer, I don't know what is. "If they were the ones to take him out, then they have long memories. And they all would be old guys by now."

"Or it could be their descendants. *They* would be younger men. And *women*."

Gibson drew in a breath. Was that last reference important?

"Could be. I wonder how they found him."

"I have no idea. But if the motivation is strong enough, people can accomplish anything."

"You sound like you know that very well."

"I've lived life, just like you have. Are you scared?"

"Should I be?" asked Gibson.

"*I* am. But I think I'm several degrees removed from where you are. They might know you've been out to the mansion. They'll know you discovered the body and alerted the police."

"*You* actually discovered the body."

"Yes, but no one knows that."

"I do."

"And who are you going to tell?" Clarisse asked.

"I've recorded our calls. I can share them with the police."

"Do you really want to do that?"

"I may not have a choice," noted Gibson.

"Well, that would be unfortunate."

"Is that a threat?" demanded Gibson.

"No, Mickey, it's just me thinking out loud. What did your father say?"

"How do you know I talked to my father?"

"I just assumed you had. He was a cop in Jersey right around the time that Langhorne turned on the mob."

"So you know all that?"

"I told you I had educated myself. So what did he say?"

"He gave me some useful info and told me to keep the hell away from all of this."

"Okay. So what will you do now?"

"I'm not sure I'm going to do anything. The police are handling this. And it could be dangerous."

"You were a cop. *Danger* was part of the *job*. I hope you haven't forgotten that."

Gibson thought she could detect a bit of resentment in Clarisse's tone and wondered where that might be coming from.

"I didn't have two little kids back then."

"But you want to be part of that investigation, surely?"

"Why?" said Gibson.

"Because sitting behind a computer looking for assets to seize has gotten boring and you miss your old life."

"Nice guess."

"I never guess. And I don't deduce, either. I gather evidence, develop theories, and draw conclusions, like Sherlock Holmes. I hate that Conan Doyle got deduction and induction mixed up, don't you?"

"Never really thought about it." Gibson rubbed her temples. She could feel one helluva migraine coming on.

"And you were a good cop and detective, right?"

"I'd like to think so."

"But then you switched careers. Threw all that away."

"I didn't *throw* anything away," Gibson snapped. "I had *kids*. And I'm a single mom! Not that I have to justify anything to you about my life decisions."

"Okay, fine. How is ProEye treating you? I hear they're good to work for."

"Things are fine," said Gibson in a calmer tone. *Do not let her wind you up, because that is clearly what she wants.*

"Really?" she said incredulously.

The way she said it, Gibson was sure she knew all about her call with Zeb Brown.

One or both of our phone lines have been breached.

"Yes, really."

"So you are backing off this?"

"What exactly do you want me to do?" asked Gibson.

"Can I be frank?"

"Oh, go right ahead," replied Gibson, girding herself for what she felt was coming.

"Aside from any personal connection I have in this matter, I thought it would give you something interesting to do. I can't imagine how bored you've become. The detective in you must be champing at the bit over this sort of case. You solve this and you could start your own investigation firm."

"How many times do I have to say this? I have little kids. I'm not going to be some sort of modern-day gumshoe trying to build an empire from scratch."

"One can buy excellent day care if one has enough money. That goes for children *and* parents. And when your kids are old enough to go to pre-K, which is right around the corner, what then? How will you spend your days?"

Sleeping, thought Gibson, but she said, "My days are plenty full, thank you very much. And why pick me in the first place? I know what you said before, but I didn't believe it."

"There simply aren't that many female detectives. It's still very much a male-dominated space. I just thought you would do a great job. And I like working with women more than men. But if you're not interested, so be it. Have a nice life, *Mommy*."

Before Gibson could respond, the line went silent.

She slowly put down the phone.

Shit. What a manipulative piece of crap. And yet, she still got to me. She really did.

But the woman had said something important without it seeming important at all.

And maybe Gibson had her first real clue.

But you can't go there, Mick. You just told that woman three times that you have little kids. And you promised your dad. And if something happened to them because of your decision to pursue this?

She sat back and closed her eyes.

God help me.

CHAPTER

15

THE NEXT MORNING GIBSON PULLED the card out she had been given and punched in the number. She had made up her mind. She didn't believe she could just walk away from this case, regardless of the peril it might bring her and her kids, for the simple reason that Clarisse knew she was involved. And there was no telling what that woman was actually up to or what she really wanted. She could have killed Langhorne for all Gibson knew. And the woman might have a beef with Gibson somehow, which had led her to seek out Gibson in the first place.

She knows where I live. She knows about my kids. She knows everything about me, apparently. She is probably dangerous as hell. So if I have to be stuck in this nightmare, I need some reinforcements. Some official *reinforcements.*

The voice answered two beats later. "Sullivan."

"It's Mickey Gibson."

"Ms. Gibson, what can I do for you?"

"Please, just make it Mickey. I wanted to thank you for calling my boss and putting in a good word for me."

"Well, it was an unusual situation, and I'm not sure how I would have handled it."

Sullivan knew nothing of the conversations she'd had with the woman who had initially called herself Arlene Robinson. Or Gibson's trip back to Stormfield to get the prints off the mailbox. Or her now knowing Pottinger's true identity.

And while part of her wanted to tell Sullivan some or all of this, her gut was not inclined to do so. And she almost always listened to her gut. Here, it was pretty easy because Sullivan could charge her with obstruction of, and interfering with, a police investigation. And she did not care to find out what the view was like from the other side of the bars.

"So how's the case going?"

"It's going," he said carefully.

"It occurred to me that Pottinger might not be the man's real name," she began.

"Really, why is that, I wonder?"

"I Googled him. And really found nothing. Like he didn't exist until recently. Now, he might be a recluse, but a rich guy like that? There has to be some online footprint. Even Wikipedia. But there was nothing."

"We shouldn't be having this conversation."

"I totally understand."

"I'm going to hang up now."

"If I were still a cop I'd probably do the same thing."

"Probably?"

"My father was a beat cop his whole career. But he did some investigating, too. It's not like they have detectives for every little thing. Anyway, he always taught me that you use whatever resources and assets you have at hand to solve a case."

"He did, did he?"

"He did."

"And you consider yourself such an asset and/or resource?" said Sullivan.

"I do, actually. And I'd be happy to work with you. And if whatever I'm involved in goes sideways or I need some backup, you guys would be there."

Please, please, please.

"If things go sideways call 911."

"Look, I see no reason why we can't share resources. We might solve this thing faster."

"I have plenty of resources at my disposal."

"And if you ever need more, I'm here," she said.

"Right, thanks."

He clicked off and she put the phone down. Her heart was beating fast and she wasn't quite sure why.

Yes you are. You tried to guilt-shame a cop into having your back. Your father would shit a brick. Especially considering that you're technically still a suspect in Pottinger's murder. But it was worth a shot to possibly get some coverage for yourself and the kids. Now what do you do? Sit here as an open target waiting for the ax to fall? Or do something? Anything.

That, she knew, was a choice in theory only.

Even though she had already done a search she went online and put in the name Daniel Pottinger once more. But now her search was taking her to the dark web, as it often did with her work for ProEye; some debtors she chased were also criminals. And even the legit ones often used shady devices to hide their money. *You sleep with scum, if only digitally, to find other scum.*

She dialed up some sites she had used before, trying to dig up dirt on Daniel Pottinger the tusk-trafficking, drug-dealing, biomedical-horse-trading, Sudan-terrorist-money-laundering douchebag.

Nothing.

Okay, that'll take some more time and will have to wait. Let's try some low-hanging fruit.

She Googled Harry Langhorne. A great many articles from decades ago came up on her screen. She read through them, but they didn't tell her much more than her father already had. She did gaze at a grainy photo of Langhorne from the late 1980s. He had a thin face, high cheekbones, long, wavy hair, and glasses that made his eyes frog-like. She was pretty certain it was the same man she had found at Stormfield, even with all the intervening years and the fact that Langhorne's face had been decomposing for a while.

She didn't like his look in the picture. She had liked it even less in death.

She finally found an article that talked about Langhorne's family. Langhorne had married Geraldine Mercer when he was in his thirties. A few years later they had a son named Douglas Langhorne, and a year later a daughter, Francine. She found pictures of all of them. Geraldine was a lovely woman who looked like the unhappiest person in the world. Douglas was around eight in the photo. He seemed big for his age, a hulking towhead, and not overly bright looking. Gibson scolded herself for being so judgmental. Sometimes Tommy didn't look so smart, either. And at age three the child would be expected to wipe himself better than he apparently could.

But I digress.

Francine looked intense and guarded even as a little girl. In her wide eyes Gibson thought she could see depths of complex thoughts competing for attention. Way too much going on for someone that young.

She wrote this information down and then searched for more on the family.

She found nothing really of significance. Back then there were no armies of people adding info to the internet every millisecond of every day, even though they were now playing a spirited game of catch-up on that score. You would be hard-pressed to name a topic that you couldn't find something out about online. There was a YouTube video about every conceivable thing a human had ever done or would ever attempt to do.

She had repaired the internal guts of her outdoor water faucets by watching one DIY video put up by a very helpful fellow in Illinois.

Yeah, what a thrill that had been. But it saved me paying a plumber like three hundred bucks.

But there also weren't any other in-depth newspaper articles on the family, and what had happened to them. It was like they had simply vanished.

They might have changed their names. In fact, it was probable. The Feds might have put them all into WITSEC, or Witness Protection. If so, she would probably never find them.

But then how did Langhorne end up dead at Stormfield under the name Daniel Pottinger? Had he abandoned his family? Were they all dead?

There was no way for her to answer that. At least not right now. She refocused on Clarisse.

Until I find out her real name. And I will find it, if it's the last thing I ever do.

She was under no illusions that Clarisse's business with the man was aboveboard. Innocent people didn't play the kind of elaborate mind games she did. And they went to the police when finding a dead body unless they had guilty secrets of their own to keep hidden.

On the phone Clarisse had said that some of the mobster descendants could be men or *women*. That was the clue Gibson thought she had unwittingly let slip.

Is she referring to herself? Is she somehow connected to Langhorne and the Jersey mob from way back? She sounded way too young for that, but maybe she's a child of one of them? Grandchild, even?

Gibson really believed nothing Clarisse had told her. But there was usually an element of truth mixed in with a lie, at least for the really excellent liars like Clarisse undoubtedly was.

And there had been something else the woman had said. But Gibson couldn't think of it right now.

A clue? As Clarisse had earlier said, somewhat comically. Yes, it might be a clue.

If I can think of it.

CHAPTER

16

LATER THAT DAY, GIBSON FED the kids lunch, then sat there watching them and continually wiping their mouths, and the table, and the floor when Tommy, and then copycat Darby, got particularly adventurous with their meals.

Afterward she put them in the van and drove them to a nearby park, where they walked around and threw pennies into a fountain, and played tag and then hide-and-seek, though neither of her children were all that good with following the rules.

But then neither am I.

As she sat and laughed and applauded their spirited antics, she wondered about what her father had said. If something happened to her, where would her kids go? Her parents couldn't take care of them, not full-time. And she would never allow her ex to go anywhere near her kids, even if the jerk could be found. And one of her younger brothers had his hands full with his own family. Her other sibling was single and had never managed to get his crap together; he couldn't take care of himself, much less two toddlers. She had tried to dial up some cover from Sullivan, but he had turned her down flat.

So I'm it. And no matter how much I want to follow this through, should I? Can I risk it? Can I risk them?

She giggled as Darby ran in circles so fast she fell down dizzy and laughing, while Tommy sprinted around growling like a bear, or a reasonable facsimile thereof.

She had brought the phone with her. She looked at it.

You can walk away right now. Never call this number again. And never answer it when and if she does call. But if she's a psycho, which certainly might be the case? If that sends her over the edge? Do you have a shot at controlling this by keeping on it?

She stared at the phone for nearly a minute as this mental back-and-forth ping-ponged inside her head. Finally, she hit the number and waited. It rang so long she was just about to click off.

"You surprise me," said Clarisse.

"Don't you keep the Batphone right next to you at all times?"

"I wanted to see how tenacious and patient you were. Those twin attributes can tell pretty much everything you need to know about someone."

"Have you found someone else to get the glory?" she asked Clarisse.

"Not just yet."

"Do you know where Langhorne's widow and children are?" Gibson asked.

"No."

"I was thinking they were in WITSEC," noted Gibson.

"Maybe."

"Do you think they know he was here? And that he's dead?"

"I have no way of knowing."

"You still going by Clarisse today, or do you have another name?"

"Clarisse it will stay. It'll avoid unnecessary confusion."

"Have you always been this weird?" said Gibson, perhaps more frankly than she intended.

"No, I'm much better. Years of therapy has worked wonders."

Maybe another clue. And what was the other one, dammit?

"Okay, *Clarisse*, what if we were to continue on this case together?"

"It would be my preference. You were my first choice, after all."

"Why do you need to know who killed Langhorne?"

"Because they will be coming after me next, I'm sure of that."

"Because of who Harry Langhorne was, or because of your business with his alter ego, Pottinger?"

"Does it matter?"

"Of course it matters, because depending on the answer, the investigation will take me in very different directions. But according to you, your business with Pottinger was entirely legitimate. So how would his criminal partners even know about you?"

"Dan never compartmentalized very well. At least when I knew him. He would slip. He did so to me, so I'm sure he did so to others *about* me."

"And what were some of the slips that he made to you?" asked Gibson.

"I've discussed some of them. That's what made me suspicious of him and his past. I did some digging and found more."

"You said he contacted you and wanted you to meet him at Stormfield. Why?"

"He didn't say."

Tommy fell down and hit his knee and started to cry. Gibson went over to him and, cradling the phone against her ear, checked the spot and soothed his tears.

"Sounds like someone's not happy," commented Clarisse.

"He's fine, just a skinned knee." She took some sanitizer, ointment, and a Band-Aid out of her fanny pack and proceeded to doctor her son's injury.

"You ever regret having kids?"

Gibson tensed. "Why do you ask?"

"Because I want to know."

"I take it you never had kids?"

"Never found the time."

"If you wait around for the perfect time or situation, you'll be waiting forever. And no, I don't regret having them. They're the best thing I ever did. But I guess all mothers say that."

"Not all mothers," said Clarisse.

Yet another clue? thought Gibson. She said, "Come on, why do you think he wanted to meet? You must have an inkling."

Clarisse replied, "Well, considering he was murdered before I got there, I would imagine he wanted to see me because he was fearful for his life."

Finished, Gibson slid Tommy's pants leg down and tousled his hair. "And what could you do about that?"

"Not sure. But then again, maybe he didn't have many friends left."

"Were you surprised to hear from him?"

"No, because people are unpredictable."

Gibson thought, *That may be the only completely true thing she's said to me.*

Clarisse said, "So what are you going to do?"

"I'm not sure. In fact, I'm not sure I'm going to do anything."

"I thought you were in."

Gibson looked down at Tommy and then glanced at her daughter, who was making grass angels. Her father's warning came back to her.

"I've got other priorities, more important things in my life. So you might have to find another patsy after all."

"Well, that is very unfortunate. But you're a smart girl, so you surely realize you're already knee-deep into this."

"That's your opinion."

"And there's something else," said Clarisse.

"What?"

"I sense we are running out of time."

"Running out of time for what?" asked Gibson sharply.

"Until the next person dies, of course."

The line, appropriately, went dead.

17

WHY THE HELL SHOULD I tell you anything else?" barked Rick Rogers in a clearly annoyed tone on the phone with his daughter the following morning. "Since you clearly didn't take my advice."

Gibson said, "Look, don't get pissed at me, but I have to work this thing a little longer. And I'm not saying I won't go to the cops. In fact, I tried to, but it didn't work out."

"What happened?"

"It doesn't matter. I went in for cover and got none."

"What are you angling for here, Mick? I've told you all I know about Langhorne."

"But you might know someone from the old days who knows more," countered Gibson.

He let out a long sigh and she waited, patiently. Experience had taught Gibson that her father almost always reached the right conclusion when it came to him, meaning the conclusion she wanted. She just had to give him time, space, and the understanding that it was ultimately his decision and not hers.

"I actually might know a guy. He was a detective in Newark, but he worked on the case because it crossed all sorts of jurisdictional lines. He and I talked shop about it over the years."

"Is he retired?"

"Oh, yeah, he was older than me. Let me make some calls and I'll get back to you."

"Thanks, Dad, I really appreciate this."

"Yeah, yeah. I shouldn't be doing this, you know."

"You're just trying to help out your little girl."

"Right, my little girl who has Daddy wrapped right around her little finger."

"You need to stop listening to Mom."

"*You* try that. And I wish you luck. You'll need it."

He clicked off and she headed to her office.

The kids were with Silva. With the situation the way it was, she had arranged with the woman to come over every day for the next week, and luckily Silva's schedule allowed for that.

As soon as she got to her office her phone buzzed. It was Wilson Sullivan.

"You busy?" he asked.

"I'm never too busy to help you, Detective Sullivan," she replied brightly.

"You know, you're very good at that."

"At what?" she said innocently.

"Exactly. Anyway, we have some developments. Can you meet me at Stormfield? Or do you have kid stuff to do?"

"I have a babysitter today. I can be there in about an hour and a half. What developments?"

"I'll fill you in when you get here."

Gibson thought, *Did I just get my official cover?*

She quickly changed into jeans, a white blouse, and a dark jacket, checked in with Silva, hugged her kids, and drove off in the van. When she arrived at Stormfield, Sullivan was standing out front. Nearby, a trooper was sitting in a marked car.

She walked up to Sullivan, and he said, "Let's go inside."

As they entered the home, she suddenly had a weird feeling that this might be a setup.

Did someone see me dusting the mailbox for prints and rat me out? Am I about to be arrested for obstruction of justice, tampering with evidence, or for just being stupid?

He led her to where the body had been discovered.

"What I'm about to tell you goes no further, okay?" he said.

She made a show of locking her lips and throwing away the key.

He pointed to the chair where Pottinger had been found. The fan had been taken away and everything was coated in fingerprint powder.

"First of all, like you intimated before, Daniel Pottinger was not his real name."

She managed, she hoped, to look suitably surprised. "But you said people around here knew him."

"He hadn't owned the place for all that long, and he wasn't here full-time. In fact, he was almost never here. So local people never got to know him."

"So who is he really, then?"

"Fellow named Harry Langhorne." He studied her in the dim illumination provided by a pair of battery-powered police work lights set on tripods. "Ring a bell?"

She pretended to think on this. "Not really. Should I know the name?"

"I only asked because he was from your neck of the woods, but a totally different generation."

"He was from Jersey City?"

"No, sorry. In the south we just tend to lump all of New Jersey into one place. He was from Trenton."

"What do you know about him?"

"He was an accountant for the mob decades ago. Apparently he turned state's evidence on them, and brought down some mafia families."

"So you think they finally caught up to him? All this time later?"

"I don't know. I don't have much experience with the mob."

She smiled. "And since I'm from Jersey, I do? Is that why I'm here?"

"I didn't mean to imply that. But I suspected he was mob related even before we had identified him."

"Why?" asked Gibson.

In answer Sullivan held up his hand, palm facing her. "He had a burn mark here on his right hand."

"How'd he get it?" she asked.

"As an initiation the mob would prick the person's finger, smear the blood on a picture of a saint, and set the picture on fire, and the initiate would have to hold the burning picture while repeating the oath of loyalty to the mob."

"Holy shit."

"Yeah. And if you break the oath, you burn like the saint did. I didn't know that beforehand. I had to research it after I was shown the mark."

Gibson decided to take control of this opportunity. "Look, I've got contacts back in Jersey. I'll talk to them and maybe they can put us in touch with somebody who knows something."

" 'Us'?" said Sullivan.

"Look, you called me. I'm just trying to help. But if I'm going to call in some markers to help you, I feel an obligation to at least be in the loop on this sucker. I do have a reputation to maintain."

He studied her for an uncomfortably long time. For some reason her gaze dipped to his ring finger, and she saw that it was naked of gold, silver, or platinum.

"Well?" she finally said.

"Deal."

"Do we shake on it? I don't want to do the burning-picture thing," said Gibson.

They did so and she said, "So how did he die?"

"Why do I think I just got suckered?"

"My request is pretty reasonable if I'm going to help you on this."

"He was poisoned," said Sullivan.

"If it was poison, how do you know he was murdered? It could have been suicide."

Sullivan touched his wrist and pointed to his ankles. "He was restrained."

"I didn't see any evidence of that."

"You wouldn't. The restraints were removed after he was dead. The marks were under his clothing."

"So they watched him die?" said Gibson.

"Could be. Which might dovetail with this being a revenge killing."

"Okay, I'll call you as soon as I know something from my sources."

"Thanks."

"You could have told me all this on the phone," Gibson noted.

"I also wanted to show you something."

"Where?"

"Follow me."

18

DO AS I SAY, NOT AS I DO.

Gibson was reading this off the wall at the end of the secret room. It had been written in foot-high letters using a broad-tipped red marker.

She turned to look at Sullivan, who was shining his flashlight on it.

"What do you take it to mean?" she asked.

"I have no idea. I mean, I know what it's supposed to mean in a general sense. 'Don't follow my example or actions, only my words.'"

"Yeah, it's a way for people to do what they want and then hold others to a higher standard."

"You sound like you speak from experience."

"Every woman I know can speak from experience on that one."

Sullivan coughed into his hand. "Right, I get that. Especially in police work."

"In *any* work, where there are lots of guys around. When did you find it?"

"Just recently. The team spent most of its time with the body and crime scene, but they finally made their way down here and found this."

"And you think it ties the killer to Langhorne somehow? Presuming they were the ones to write it."

"My people examined it and told me it hasn't been here any longer than the body."

"Okay," Gibson said. She was wondering whether the killer had written it, or Clarisse, her new phone friend. Or whether they were one and the same, because she had no reason, right now, to believe otherwise. "If it does tie into Langhorne somehow, we might be able to track it down. But the nexus is pretty vague."

"But not to whoever wrote it," Sullivan pointed out.

"No, to them it's crystal clear. Can I see the flashlight?"

He handed it over and Gibson shone the light over each letter, going slowly and studying the marks thoroughly. They were done in block lettering, which made it harder, but since there were three words repeated, it also made it easier.

"I think it was written by two different people," she concluded, handing him back the flashlight.

He stepped forward and shone the light over the letters. "Really? I'm no handwriting expert, but those who are usually examine cursive writing, not block letters."

"True, but handwriting is handwriting. Take the three words *I*, *do*, and *as*. They obviously appear in the first *and* second half of the message. Take a look at how the *d* is formed in both, and look at how the *a* and *s* are done. Different arcs and upward and downward strokes, varied stopping points. The flourish on the first *d* is not seen in the second *d*. The first *s* is smooth, the second one choppy, as though the person wasn't quite sure how to do it. Even the *I*'s are different. The height is dissimilar and the top caps are not close. The penmanship is totally different."

"How do you know so much about handwriting analysis?"

"Like I said, I started out as a forensics tech. And with my job now I review thousands of documents online and compare signatures and other handwriting all the time. But I would suggest you get your experts out here to do their own exam. My opinion wouldn't count for squat in court."

"But it does with me."

She gave him a look. "So does that mean I'm off the suspect list?"

"I think we can safely say that."

Gibson scrutinized the space where Langhorne's body had been as they passed by it.

Had Clarisse killed the man? If so, why involve her? Because she was afraid? She didn't sound afraid. Because she wanted something? Yes, that was the far more likely answer.

Langhorne had probably stolen a ton of money from the mob. Gibson wasn't really speculating on that. For how else could he have bought this place? Did that represent all of the money he'd taken? If not, where was the rest? But if Clarisse had done the deed, had she also written the phrase on the wall? And taken the pains to make it seem like two people had done it? She seemed like just the sort of person who would sweat those kinds of details. But what would have been the point of that deception? Or maybe she *was* working with another person.

Out in the daylight, Sullivan turned to her. "Thanks for coming out and thanks for the 'expert' analysis back there."

"You're welcome. And thanks for taking me off the suspect list. I'll make those calls and get back to you."

She paused and that made Sullivan hike his eyebrows and say, "Yes?"

"So how did a mob accountant end up here under an assumed name?"

"We're looking into it."

"Did he have a family?"

"Yes, wife and two kids."

Part of Gibson felt badly for doing this dog-and-pony show with Sullivan, asking him questions she already knew the answers to. But the other part of her, the professional part, knew it was necessary.

"Any idea where they are now?"

"None," he said.

"You would think a mob accountant, after turning on his employer, would be put into Witness Protection."

"I was thinking the same thing. In fact, I have a meeting with a representative of the US Marshals Service in Norfolk this afternoon. Want to tag along?"

Gibson was surprised by this offer and her expression showed it. "I would love to tag along."

"We have time to grab something to eat, if you want."

"In for a dime, Detective Sullivan."

"Just make it Will, Mickey."

"I'll follow you over."

They got into their vehicles and drove off. As they passed the mailbox, Gibson shuddered with her guilty knowledge of having dusted the metal and come away with Langhorne's true identity right under the nose of her new bestie, *Will* Sullivan.

19

Clarisse studied the numbers on the screen.

Five hundred thousand dollars, not a penny more or less, had just landed at its final destination after taking an untraceable digital whirlybird tour of financial accounts and money havens around the world.

She shaved off 30 percent and catapulted that amount into Angie's pocketbook.

The message that came back from the big bad little senator was full of quite colorful language and threats and other things, none of which he had a chance to actually do, since he would never find either of them.

And in one week's time she would send another demand to the senator, this time for an even million dollars with a pledge that such would be the last request for compensation. And it would be. She was always fair on that. And Angie would get another three hundred grand. A girl could have fun pretty much anyplace with that level of funding, tax-free as it was.

She glanced at her reflection in the little vanity mirror set next to her twin computers.

She was a blonde once more. She didn't know why she liked that particular color so much. It seemed to her to represent light and transparency when she was anything but. But maybe that was the explanation for her affinity for light hair. Her physical appearance, on its face, was itself deceiving.

She opened her MICKEY GIBSON notebook and read over some notes she had jotted down.

Their last conversation had been intriguing. Gibson had wanted to back out and the reason was clear.

She was fearful that something would happen to her and leave her kids in the lurch. Or that working with her could place them in danger.

She could understand that. From a *normal* person. Yet children got screwed over every day by their parents and lots of other people. And no one apparently gave a damn unless they were rich or famous or powerful, or all three. That was just her little old opinion, but what did she know.

I only know myself. But I know myself really, really well.

She had deployed the standard "the next murder is coming" warning to entice Gibson to keep going, but she also believed it to be true. She had an idea who had killed Langhorne, perhaps more than an idea. And if she was right, she could use the help. Her job was to remain in the background moving her chess pieces around. And Gibson was her queen on the front lines, or at least she hoped the woman had the potential to become such a powerful tool.

I've already filled up multiple notebooks on her. I hope it's going to be worth it.

Her fingers skimmed over the computer keys as she sent NSA-level encrypted messages, searched for information on people and things she needed to understand better, and, finally, focused on a picture she had brought up on the screen.

"Wilson Sullivan, of the Virginia State Police," she read off.

He was good-looking in a rugged way that appealed to some women but not her. Steady career in law enforcement. He was not spectacular; he was above average. He might be a Goldilocks "just right" as an unwitting if useful tool for her, working through Gibson, of course.

As a matter of principle, she absolutely refused to work directly with the police. They were not dependable, she had found. And they lied. A lot.

Google Maps showed her that Sullivan lived in a two-story town house with a deck on the back, in a Norfolk suburb that looked like a thousand other such neighborhoods. A million other such homes, a billion other such people.

That could have been me if something called "my life" had not intervened. But then, existence itself is a trade-off.

The cops would now know that Pottinger was Langhorne. From secretive, reclusive rich guy to secretive, on-the-run former mob accountant. But that was not all Harry Langhorne was and had been. He had been a lot more than that, as well she knew.

Men like Harry made women stutter and shudder. And every woman would know exactly what she meant by that.

So would she wait for Gibson to engage, or would she insert herself back into the conversation? To drive this mission forward with speed and urgency? People needed to be pushed. Otherwise, the human tendency was to slow everything down. People hated change. And they hated to make decisions. Her job was to turn those tendencies on their proverbial head.

The surveillance device she had placed on Gibson's property showed that the babysitter was there, the kids were engaged with her, and Gibson had driven off in her van an hour before. If she had to guess, it was back to Stormfield because her phone log showed a previous call from Wilson Sullivan.

They would discuss the revelation of Daniel Pottinger's being Harry Langhorne. Perhaps Sullivan would want to use the Jersey girl's knowledge of Garden State mobsters. If they teamed up, wonderful. But then it would all be about the timing at the end.

Because this would have a definite denouement. And it had to terminate on her terms and to her benefit, and Clarisse would sacrifice anything or anyone to make sure that would be the case. She had worked too hard, filled up too many notebooks, played too many different people to be denied that.

And after this is over? Do I retire to that lovely villa in Aix-en-Provence that I saw in the magazine? Or the hilltop estate in Tuscany that was in that foodie show with the adorable Stanley Tucci? Or the other lovely residence on Costa del Sol that I actually went to? I could see Africa from my villa, although it was really just Morocco. Do I give my fantasy up to be a poor little rich girl in splendid retirement?

Probably not, but so cool to have the choice. Right?

She winked at herself in the vanity mirror and shook her fake, fabulous blond locks.

She hit the speed dial on her super-duper, compartmentalized Mickey Gibson burner phone.

"Hello?" said Gibson.

"*Action,*" cried out Clarisse, at least in her mind.

CHAPTER

20

I'T'S YOUR FAVORITE PHONE PAL." She looked at her notes, which read: *Keep tone fresh, appealing, and casual. To start. And play off her energy, if she has any.*

"I'm busy right now," replied Gibson as she steered her van.

"Out and about on our case, or home web-sleuthing the next pesky billionaire who refuses to pay his bills?"

"You have a funny way of putting things."

"Is it incorrect in any way?"

"Not at all. It's spot-on, actually. That's why it's funny."

She's getting more comfortable, Clarisse wrote in meticulous penmanship in her notebook. *Work that for a bit before dropping the hammer.* "I thought our last conversation ended badly, so I wanted to reach out."

"Ended badly? You mentioned the next murder and then hung up on me."

She flipped back two pages in her notebook: *Spin this positive before it flips negative. Stakes are high. Impress that. Do not end conversation. That will be on her.* "I also mentioned that you were out there, the public face as it were. Knee-deep in it. That makes you vulnerable."

"Meaning *you* made *me* vulnerable."

"There was no getting around that, Mickey. It was always going to come to that. The only question was the timing."

"So what exactly do I get out of all this?"

"I thought I made that clear before. You solve this, you are a girl who calls her own shots. Unless you want to work for ProEye until you drop dead from boredom. And if so, we can do a full stop here because half-ass won't cut it. I think you can already see that, can't you?"

"But I also do not want to die prematurely."

"You want to see your kids grow up. We talked about that before."

"But you still want me to see this through, and maybe *not* see my kids grow up."

Clarisse brought up pictures of Tommy and Darby on her screen. They were absolute cuties, innocent, still forming in every way. They were clueless about how much shit life had in store for them. And that was if they had a normal life, whatever the hell that was.

"I don't like going over old ground. Did you find out how the man died?"

"Poison. And he was restrained."

"So they watched him die?"

"Apparently, yes."

"Okay, now can we talk tactics and strategy?"

"I thought that was up to me."

"I can help you get there, faster."

"And what do *you* get out of this?"

Page one of the Mickey Gibson notebook.

"I might get to live a little longer, Mickey. I might get to see *my* kids grow up."

"You said you didn't have children."

"But I still could." *Pour on guilt, because why not?* "Anything wrong with that?"

"Nothing at all," replied Gibson. "Just be prepared not to sleep or eat a decent meal for about eleven years. And I hope you enjoy the comingled smell of Cheerios and banana puke. It's quite unforgettable."

Clarisse turned to page twenty-four. "Tactics and strategy? Shall we?"

"Okay."

"The man I knew as Daniel Pottinger, businessman with his fingers in lots of pies, both legal and illegal, has now been revealed as Harry Langhorne, an accountant for the New Jersey mob of yesteryear. I know you know this," she said because she could sense Gibson was about to interject. "But it doesn't hurt to lay out everything precisely and in order. Now, whoever killed him did so for specific reasons. And I don't think it was related to his mob activity."

"Why not?"

"The mobsters who went to prison for the crimes Langhorne provided information on are either still in prison or dead. Without exception."

"Not all of them went to prison."

"The ones who did not go to prison are also dead, either from old age, ill health, via police shoot-outs, or at the hands of their fellow gangsters. As an interesting factoid, did you know the life expectancy of a mobster on the East Coast from 1950 to 1990 was forty-nine years?"

"Where the hell did you get that statistic?"

"I put together a database and ran the numbers myself. It was forty-six years on the West Coast and in Nevada during that same time period. Now that Lake Mead is drying up they're finding lots of mob murder victims from long ago."

"If not the mob, then who?"

"It could be the business he did later on."

"The ones *you* were involved in?"

"I was all legit, as I told you before. But *he* wasn't. Which is what put me in the crosshairs. Which I also told you before." She glanced at her notebook. "Don't you write this stuff down?"

"I *do* write it down. But that doesn't mean I believe it unless I can corroborate it by other means that to me are unimpeachable."

"Are there really any unimpeachable sources anymore? I'm not being facetious, I really want to know."

"I suppose you want me to think *you* are an unimpeachable source?"

"That was a nice touch, Mickey. I could *almost* feel the tip of your foil against my chest. Look, all I can do is provide information to you. You, in turn, have to evaluate its veracity and arrive at your own conclusions."

"Now you sound like lawyers I ran into in the courtroom when I was a cop."

"Maybe I am a lawyer. Or was. Or would like to be. But getting back on topic, I can provide you a list of known associates of Daniel Pottinger. You can run them down."

"Are these his legal or illegal associates?"

"These people are dangerous, Mickey. Extremely so. And one of them is in your area. You might want to start with that person. But tread cautiously."

"If you have names, why don't you take them to the cops?"

"I could tell you exactly why, but it would take too long. Now, do you want me to text you the list, or not?"

"Knock yourself out."

"I hope you realize that I was not bullshitting you about them being dangerous."

"Why, are you worried about me? You don't even know me."

In some ways I know you better than you know yourself. "I worry about you for one reason."

"What? My kids?" she added skeptically.

"No. I don't have time to train someone new for this job. You'll have the names in sixty seconds. Bueno suerte."

CHAPTER

21

Y OU OKAY?" ASKED SULLIVAN.

They were sitting in a café on the outskirts of downtown Norfolk. Gibson was staring into her iced tea like it was a drowning pool and all who she cared about were trapped in it with her.

"What? No, I'm fine. Just thinking some things through."

What she was thinking through was the short list of names she had gotten from Clarisse.

Daniel Pottinger had not been messing around if the names of his business associates were actually on the up-and-up. She had heard of three of the four names. Pretty much everyone in law enforcement had. One was from Mexico. One from Russia. One from China. That was the one she hadn't heard of, and couldn't pronounce his name.

The last name was all American, and he was the one living in the area. And he scared the crap out of her. All these guys were way out of her league.

Yeah, I used to be a cop but now I drive a Chrysler minivan. My daughter spit all of her scrambled eggs back onto her plate this morning just because she found out she could and thought it was the funniest thing ever. I am not Gal Gadot as Wonder Woman. Not in real life. Not in the movies. Not even in my dreams unless I'm drunk. These guys eat Feds for breakfast. They throw prosecutors off buildings in a dozen countries. I would be roadkill to them, plain and simple. No challenge, no sweat at all.

The American was Nathan Trask. A real piece of work with the shadiest of connections, and neither the Feds nor the states, nor anyone else in the world, could lay a glove on him. To the ignorant public he was a legit businessman, if they even knew who he was, which they probably didn't. To the cop world he was a criminal heavyweight that they were itching to indict, but just could never seem to get there. Evidence disappeared; police and prosecutors were compromised or bribed. Witnesses missed their time on the stand because they were no longer living. And unless you could prove Trask was behind it, the judge just ended up screaming at the prosecutors for not being able to keep their witnesses breathing, while Trask's high-priced lawyers tried hard not to laugh their asses off.

"How are your kids doing?"

"Fine. Just being kids. They're at an age that wallops the crap out of you physically and it's also the time that as a parent you would never want to miss. Their mess-ups now are easy to clean up. Not so when they're teenagers and then young adults."

Sullivan looked at her strangely. "You have teenage children, too? Must've started young."

"No, I was speaking about the misery *I* put my parents through at those ages. Getting back to the case, you didn't mention the poison that was used to kill Langhorne."

"Botulinum toxin, type A. Apparently it's considered the deadliest poison in the world, or close to it. Prevents your muscles from working. Heart stops beating, you can't breathe, everything shuts down. Just a tiny dose can do it. A far tinier dose and you can get rid of those annoying frown lines on your forehead for a bit. Just don't get the amount wrong or the only place you *won't* be frowning is in your coffin."

"Yeah, sounds tempting."

"There was something else that came up on the post."

"What was that?" she asked.

"Langhorne had terminal brain cancer. The man had maybe a few months to live."

"Shouldn't he have been in a hospital or hospice, then?"

"You would think. But he apparently went to his house, laid off his entire staff, and settled down to die."

"He must have been in a lot of pain."

"The medical examiner also found a ton of morphine in his system. He was apparently self-regulating for his pain."

"I think you might be off about one thing."

He cocked his head at her. "What do you mean?"

"It was like he went to Stormfield, fired the staff, and waited, not to die, but for someone to come and *kill* him."

"That's an extraordinary theory."

"It's an extraordinary case, at least so far." She glanced down at his hand. "I don't see a wedding band, but I know lots of cops who don't wear them on the job."

Okay, where did that come from, Mick?

Sullivan rubbed that spot on his finger. "I was engaged, once. Didn't work out."

"I wish I hadn't pulled the trigger on my walk down the aisle."

He grinned and turned his head a bit. She noted the scar that poked above his shirt collar.

"Work souvenir?" she said, pointing at it.

He flinched and then nodded. "I was a little sloppy on an arrest when I was in uniform. Didn't search the perp carefully enough. He pulled a knife. Another half inch to the right, I'm not sitting here with you."

She shook her head. "However much they pay cops, it's not enough. So, tell me about the US marshal we're going to be meeting."

"Earl Beckett. Been doing his job for well over twenty-five years."

"So was Pottinger/Langhorne in WITSEC?"

"I don't think Earl would bother meeting if he wasn't."

"But what is he allowed to tell us?"

"Considering Langhorne's been murdered, I hope a lot."

"Pretty much no one who stayed in WITSEC and followed the rules has ever ended up being murdered by the people they were being protected against," Gibson noted.

"So either Langhorne is the rare exception or—"

"—or he voluntarily left WITSEC and got himself killed. Which seems far more likely, since I don't see WITSEC springing for a place like Stormfield."

"Hopefully he can tell us what happened to Langhorne's family."

"I'm not sure *hope* is going to cut it," noted Gibson.

"But even cops can hold out for it," said Sullivan, grinning and tapping her hand. That was a first in their relationship, thought Gibson, who immediately caught herself.

What relationship? She recalibrated. "Maybe whatever Daniel Pottinger has been up to lately got him killed. It may have nothing to do with what he did decades ago as Harry Langhorne."

Sullivan slipped a French fry into his mouth and munched on it. "Come on, what are the odds?"

Yeah, but I have a list of global psychopaths Pottinger was doing business with and you don't.

"Apart from the little you told me about *Pottinger*, I know nothing about what he's been doing all this time, or when Langhorne changed his name."

Sullivan shrugged. "I don't know all that much, either. Like I told you, Pottinger came here around six years ago and bought the property from the Turners."

"Have you been in contact with the Turners? Did they know why he was coming to the area?"

"I *have* talked to them. They say they never met him. It was all handled by his representatives. Lawyers, real estate agents, financial people."

"All that money and he was living alone in that mausoleum at the end."

"People make choices."

"Was that secret room always there?"

"I asked John Turner that when I talked to him. He said his great-grandfather had put that in. They used to play hide-and-seek, and that was a popular destination. Until people caught on, that is."

"So do you think the Stormfield acquisition was just a money-laundering bit?"

"Why do you ask that?"

"You mind?" She eyed his fries.

"What? No, go ahead. I should have ordered the fruit salad as my side, but I have a weakness for things that aren't good for me."

I think I have you beat in that department, buddy, thought Gibson, thinking of her choice in husbands.

She snagged a couple of fries, bit into one, and almost purred. "I've been trying to cut this stuff out and lose some of the baby weight, but it's harder than I thought it would be. As my mother loves to point out."

"Well, as someone who will never have to go through that, all I'm going to say is hat's off to you whatever you do or don't do."

She smiled. "I'm beginning to like your style, Will." She inwardly groaned at such a stupid line. "So getting back to the money laundering. What did Stormfield sell for?"

"The property records say five mill."

That drew a whistle from Gibson. "Langhorne was a mob accountant. It's not like those folks are millionaires. So why do I think that when Langhorne disappeared he didn't do so empty-handed?"

"Stealing from the mob is pretty much suicidal."

"So is turning state's evidence against them. Langhorne had already crossed that Rubicon. So why not go for the brass ring in the process?"

"So you think the money-laundering angle is legit?" he asked.

"Look, I spend all my time now looking for assets just like that. 'Dirty money' means it goes through multiple washing machines and comes out smelling like it was filled with nothing except healthy doses of Febreze. If he was smart enough to hoodwink the mob and take their money, I think he was smart enough to keep moving it around in an elaborate shell game. And it's not like the Feds would have known about him stealing any money. If they had they would have confiscated it. At least in an ideal world. But maybe the world wasn't ideal back then."

"Hell, and you think it is now?" retorted Sullivan with a chuckle, but it was clear he was intrigued by her theory. "But your point is valid. So the guy had the mansion and probably other assets."

"And if he managed to invest it all somehow, over the years, I would imagine those assets have grown exponentially."

"I do know that he paid cash for Stormfield. And they would have checked that the funds came from legit sources."

"After thirty-plus years, you can make anything look legit," replied Gibson. "Even mob money."

"You know, your experience in ferreting out assets might come in handy for our investigation."

"Now, I like how that sounds."

"How *what* sounds?"

"*Our* investigation." She checked her watch. "And it's time to go add to it."

22

Earl Beckett looked like a US marshal, thought Gibson. Tall, lean, ramrod straight. Weathered good looks, wavy salt-and-pepper hair. A grim smile coupled with flinty eyes and a crushing handshake. Gibson thought that in another era, the man could have walked on to an old movie set and been an instant star, especially if he'd had on a ten-gallon hat and was sporting twin pearl-handled Colt .45s.

After Sullivan had introduced her, Beckett led them to his office in the federal building in Norfolk and sat down across from them. He had a manila folder in front of him.

"Had to get this sucker overnighted. It was in the record morgue, in yonder parts." He smiled. " 'Yonder parts' are what folks expect to hear from a US marshal, or maybe I'm just getting old."

"Works for me," said Sullivan.

Beckett opened the folder and got down to business. "Harry E. Langhorne. A name right out of the past."

"Yeah, and he's in *our* morgue," said Sullivan.

"So you told me over the phone."

"Then he *was* in WITSEC?" asked Sullivan.

Beckett slid a finger over his top lip. "You *confirmed* the dead guy is Langhorne?"

"Yes. We checked and rechecked. And the FBI sent us a notification as well."

"Right. All WITSECs are on their database. And if any law

enforcement agency sends a print ID request that ends up being a WITSEC, the Bureau gets pinged. They usually let us know, too. They may have, but I'm not necessarily in the loop on that."

Gibson inwardly cringed. *Thank God my cop friend Kate didn't have to access a Fed database but got Langhorne's print off a local one.*

Beckett said, "Okay, yeah, he was under our protection starting around the time of the mob trials."

"With his family?" asked Gibson.

"That's right. His wife, Geraldine, and the two kids." Beckett took a few moments to read over the file. "They were initially relocated to Eugene, Oregon, about as far away as you can get from New Jersey. Then to Butte, Montana, and finally to Albuquerque, New Mexico, where they spent a number of years."

"Why so many moves?" asked Gibson.

"Not unusual at all. Might have been they suspected someone had found out where they were. Or there was a problem of some kind with the current location. We always err on the side of caution."

"What's the process for a WITSEC family?" asked Gibson.

"We determine how many members will be entering the program, adults, children. Then they're all given a psych evaluation."

"Why a psych eval?" asked Gibson.

"The transition is not an easy one," noted Beckett. "So we need to know what mental state they're all in. You don't enter WITSEC because your life is a bed of roses, quite the opposite. The program will support them for six months financially. After that, they need to get a job. Now, we do cater to certain requests if feasible."

"Like what?" she asked.

"Well, I can tell you that we've paid for breast implants, face-lifts, and boxing lessons, but that's atypical."

"O-kay," said Gibson slowly.

"The jobs these folks get are usually not going to be high paying. They have no work or credit history. Early on the Marshals

Service reached out to the business community and got commitments from over a thousand national businesses to provide jobs to WITSEC members. In the past, we've also placed protectees in certain government jobs."

"Doesn't that jeopardize their safety?" asked Sullivan.

"We have protocols to prevent that, but I can't get into them with you. Langhorne was working at a local car dealership in Albuquerque until about twenty years ago."

"As a salesman?" asked Sullivan.

"No, as a vehicle detailer. Guy liked the details, apparently."

"A long fall from mob accountant to cleaning cars," remarked Gibson.

"What happened?" asked Sullivan.

"Langhorne vanished."

Gibson and Sullivan exchanged glances. She said, "Vanished? Alone, or with his family?"

"Alone. After all those years, maybe he didn't appreciate the lifestyle or the working-class life that came with it. Or the family he had."

"Damn," said Gibson.

"I always thought the guy was odd."

"Wait, you knew him?" exclaimed Gibson.

Beckett nodded. "That's why I agreed to meet. See, I was in Albuquerque at the tail end of Langhorne's time there. Did several years with him and his family and some other families out there in WITSEC. Don't tell anybody, but we sometimes clump them together in the same neighborhoods to conserve manpower. None of the families knew the others were in WITSEC, of course." He eyed Gibson. "Will told me you were a cop for a while and now work for ProEye. Said I could trust you."

"You can. What names did they go by back then?"

"They're no longer in WITSEC, so I guess it won't hurt to tell you." He glanced at the file again. "Harry and Geraldine Parker. The kids went by Fran and Doug."

"But those are their actual first names," Gibson pointed out.

"Way we do it at WITSEC. Theory is people will not be able to get the memory of their true given name out of their brain. Someone calls out Harry and Harry turns. But if the first names are the same, so what? Last names are different, of course."

"Do you change their appearances?" asked Gibson. "Especially if their faces had been in the media?"

"On a case-by-case basis, we do what we need to do to keep them safe," said Beckett. "And that's really all I can say."

"So he just left his family?" said Sullivan. "You're sure nothing happened to him?"

"We're sure. I think he'd been prepping it for quite a while. This was in hindsight, of course. And he might have had a stash of money to help him on his way."

"What makes you say that?" asked Sullivan.

"Rumors. Scuttlebutt."

"Maybe in addition to ratting out the mob he might've raided their piggybank, too," said Gibson.

Beckett shrugged. "The man had helped take down a bunch of really bad guys. You're not gonna jump the dude's bones over money at that point. And if they made him out to be dishonest that way, maybe it would have hurt the prosecution. You give a good defense attorney an opening, well, look out."

"Right," said Gibson. "Well, the man he became, Daniel Pottinger, paid five million dollars in cash for an old estate near Smithfield."

"Damn" was all Beckett said to that.

"You said he vanished. How so?" asked Sullivan.

"Went to his job one day and never came home. We checked everything, talked to everybody. He went out for lunch, the folks at the dealership said, and then called in that he was feeling ill, so they didn't expect him back. That was the last they saw or heard of him. We checked the buses, trains, airports, car rentals. Nothing."

"So maybe he had help?" noted Gibson.

"I have no doubt of that. But he worked it so he had a good head start. His wife didn't contact us until the following morning."

"Why so long?" asked Gibson.

"She said that Langhorne had phoned and told her he was working late and not to wait up for him. He said he'd probably sleep on the couch downstairs, so as not to wake her. She went downstairs around eight the next morning and there was no sign of him. But she thought he'd just gone to work early. She didn't call us until the dealership phoned her asking where the hell he was. All told, he had a long runway to make his getaway. And, look, it's not like what he did was illegal. Being in WITSEC is a choice. We looked for him mainly because we were worried someone had snatched him. But as more information came out, it seemed clear that he planned it."

"And his family? What happened to them? You said they were no longer in WITSEC."

"Geraldine walked out of her house about a month after her husband vanished. No one's seen her since."

Gibson said, "And the kids?"

"Doug was nearly eighteen by then, a senior in high school. Francine was about a year younger. Not little kids anymore. It was a helluva mess. Technically, they couldn't opt out of WITSEC until they were eighteen. And we, of course, couldn't inform their extended family about the situation so they could help or make decisions for them. And traditional foster care was out, so we just kept watch over them. Doug hung around until Francine hit her eighteenth birthday, and then they both opted out and moved on. Haven't seen or heard from them since."

"What a miserable existence for them," said Gibson.

"We did the best we could," Beckett said defensively.

"Not saying you didn't. I'm just talking generally. They had nothing approaching a normal childhood. Then their father abandons them, and then their mother does, too."

"Right, yeah," said Beckett. "I did feel sorry for them. But even if they leave, we ask them to stay in touch. We try to help them regardless of their official status. But they never did contact us." He looked between them. "What else do you need to know?"

"A lot more than we do right now," said Gibson glumly.

CHAPTER

23

Darby was in the stroller and Tommy was walking next to his mother. It was a brisk morning and the sun was ascending into a cloudless sky. Tommy would occasionally hold his mom's hand or walk right next to the stroller and talk to Darby, who talked right back to him in childish staccato.

Gibson was half watching them and half watching everything else around them. She had plenty of reasons to be paranoid.

Clarisse on the phone, the list of global criminals, and a dead mob numbers guy with maybe more mobsters involved had put her very near the edge. She was a few mental beats from chucking it all, selling her house, and taking the kids as far away as possible.

But could I ever get far away enough? And what about Mom and Dad?

She felt trapped because she was. She had called Zeb Brown a few times to see how long her "vacation" was to last. And whether she would have employment when she came back from said vacation. He had not returned her calls. But her latest paycheck had cleared the bank and there was a nice bonus added on for her work on the Larkin matter.

Yeah, I singlehandedly find two hundred million bucks and they tack on five grand for my bonus. I wonder how much Zeb got? But I'll take it.

Every car that passed by and that she did not recognize received extra scrutiny. She had slipped her baseball bat into the mesh bottom under the stroller.

She had the burner phone with her; part of her was hoping it would ring and another part was hoping it would remain forever silent.

Tommy chased a squirrel while Darby begged to get out of the stroller and do the same. Gibson obliged, and she watched her kids pointing and doing inch-high jumps off the ground as the squirrel peered curiously down at them from ten feet up a tree.

Tommy looked at Gibson and said, "Mommy, skirl!"

"Yep. But it's *squirrel. Squa-earl.* Fast, huh?"

"Vewie fast," agreed her son.

"Me take home, Mommy?" pleaded Darby. "Pease, pease, pease."

"It's not a pet, sweetie. It needs to be free."

"Pet, pet, pet," chanted Darby, and Gibson silently berated herself for walking so freely into that one.

Five minutes of intense drama later, they were heading back home, Darby in tears and Tommy saying "Skirl" over and over.

She handed the kids off to Silva, who had just arrived when they got back.

Gibson ran to her office and fired up her computer.

Nathan Trask.

She hit the send key on her search, and a data dump ran down her screen. The man was wrapped up in numerous lawsuits, all civil litigation, at least currently. His business deals were immense, and his background was shady as hell. His Wikipedia page begged for more information on the man; the fourteen current pages on him apparently didn't cut it.

The photos she saw were of a man who looked carefree, intelligent, and maybe even kind.

But they had said that about Ted Bundy, too.

She dug deeper. He had homes all over the world, but his principal residence, at present, was in Virginia Beach. A thirty-thousand-square-foot behemoth he'd built right on the ocean with its own helipad. His superyacht was kept at a nearby deepwater marina. His Dassault Falcon tri-engine jet was hangared at a corporate jet park.

He presumably had security out the wazoo. She had about as much chance of getting in to see the man as she did the president.

And even if I managed it, what would I say? "Excuse me, Mr. Gazillionaire, did you kill Daniel Pottinger by any chance, or pay to have someone do it?" Yeah, if I want to be dumped in a grave no one will ever find.

She slumped in front of her computer, a weapon she had used in her time at ProEye to slay mighty beasts. But this situation was different, far different.

What the hell does Clarisse expect me to do with this list, anyway?

She looked up the other men. They all were rich and looked arrogant and cruel and were probably criminal in myriad ways. But from the sources she could find that seemed legit, none of them were anywhere near here when Pottinger had bought it. Sure, they could have hired someone to do it, but she didn't think so. Pottinger had died from poisoning. That was not what hitmen did. They shot you, usually. Anyone could poison someone and watch while they croaked. It took something altogether different to pull the trigger on someone and see their head explode right in front of you.

But why would a guy like Trask go to Stormfield and inject Pottinger with this botulism stuff? Did he stiff the man on poached elephant tusks or stolen biomedical crap?

Not that I really believed any of that from Clarisse. She's a liar, plain and simple. But there were elements of truth in what she said.

Normally, one could tell if someone was lying by the number of words they used in response to questioning. People telling the truth used far more words, because they were unafraid of being trapped in a lie. Those lying used far fewer words. They consolidated them as a cautionary measure because they were wary of being jammed into an inconsistency. They were making it all up, and that always allowed for a mistake to creep in if they hadn't practiced enough. Truth tellers could be inconsistent as well because no one could remember everything. But a pro could tell the difference.

I *can tell the difference.*

She tried to find some more information on Langhorne's family, but there just wasn't anything there. That actually made sense after what Marshal Beckett had told them. Doug and Francine Langhorne had vanished when they were old enough to voluntarily leave WITSEC. They had no doubt changed their names once more. That was a dead end.

She joined some dark web chat rooms using an untraceable online ID that she employed for her ProEye work. She had to be subtle about this because the last thing she wanted to do was warn anyone that someone was digging into their pasts. She dropped innocuous-sounding queries in some comment threads and then exited. She had an auto-ping that would alert her if anything interesting came out of these searches.

So now she had Clarisse on one end, Nathan Trask on the other, and a dead ex-WITSEC mob bean counter in the middle.

She grabbed her keys, snuck past the kids, who were enthusiastically telling Silva all about *skirls* as potential pets, and drove away in her minivan. She had plugged the address into her navigation. It took her about an hour to get to Virginia Beach.

Holy shit.

Trask's compound made Stormfield look small. But it was as unlike that place as it was possible to be. It was all glass and metal and concrete. It looked more like some funky-ass factory of the future than a home.

There was a big gate that looked like the one at the White House. There were men in suits by the gate. As she watched, one of them climbed into a golf cart trimmed in what looked to be some sort of gold leaf and raced off toward the house. A few moments later a chopper came into view, tracking over the ocean below. As she continued to look up it came to a hover over the rear of the mansion and slowly lowered like a descending elevator car, until it passed from her sight line.

The king had apparently arrived back at his castle.

She drove off, and later stopped for a cup of coffee. As she was sitting in her van, snuggled in her coat and drinking her Starbucks, a gentle, chilly rain began to fall. The next moment the phone rang. She looked down at it, not really wanting to answer it, but still.

Damn.

24

THE GOOD FOLKS IN GREENVILLE, South Carolina, had called late last night. Her mother had taken a turn for the worse. Clarisse wasn't unduly concerned, since the woman took a turn for the worse at regular intervals.

"I'll be there as soon as I can," she had said. "Tell her to hang on until I arrive." She clicked off the line.

That had stopped the woman on the other end of the call in her tracks, she felt sure. Clarisse could imagine the silent gasp, the brow wrinkled in outrage at a daughter's callousness.

Oh honey, if you only knew. And it's complicated. You can care about someone and still hate them at the same time. At least I can.

With that last thought she picked up her Mickey Gibson phone and made the call. Clarisse had just downloaded an app on her computer that would analyze a person's speech pattern and spew out findings on a variety of emotional measures including anxiety and fear, which Clarisse knew all too well.

"Hello," said Gibson.

Clarisse eyed the screen to see if this simple greeting had caused any alarms to go off.

Nothing yet.

"You got the list. Have you checked it twice?"

"If you're trying to be funny."

"I thought it would work well for a mom with two little kids."

"Christmas is a long way off," noted Gibson.

Not for me, not if things go according to plan. "So what have you learned?" Clarisse asked.

"Nothing that I'm sure you couldn't have learned already. But I did go by Trask's house. It's a fortress. I'm not sure what you expect I can do about it."

"I wasn't suggesting a frontal assault, if that's what you're implying. You're a stealth girl, remember?" added Clarisse.

"I've been online. There's a ton of stuff on the guy, but so what?"

"Have you checked his assets?" said Clarisse.

"Why, is he a deadbeat and I need to find something to grab before he can hide it?"

"His net worth puts him at number eighty-nine on the *Forbes* list."

"He's not on the *Forbes* list. I *did* check that," said Gibson.

"That's only because they don't put suspected criminals on there, since their wealth can't be verified using traditional measures. That's why you won't see Putin on there, but for some odd reason, they *do* list a number of his oligarchs. I simply estimated his net worth and placed him within the *Forbes* list rankings."

"Again, so what? That doesn't help us find out if he had Pottinger killed. And Trask is only fifty. He's really too young to have been much of a player in Langhorne's mob days."

"What did you learn about Trask's past?" Clarisse asked.

"He was born in Chicago. He seemed to have a normal upbringing. Hell, his father was Sam Trask, an FBI special agent of some note. But then again maybe that's a variation of the 'preacher's kids gone wild' theme. Anyway, he got into some scrapes with the law, managed to dodge any jail time, and after that he headed to South America. Probably cartel business. Then he came back home flush with cash, and he built on that footprint to get where he is now. He owns a lot of businesses and properties."

"Laundering fronts?" said Clarisse.

"Probably. He doesn't tweet or post or say anything publicly.

He just makes money and lives in a grand style. But there were a lot of gaps in the story. My thinking is those gaps represent the man's true history, but people are afraid to post it, because they'll get sued or, more likely, killed."

"I'm impressed, Mickey. You've covered a lot of ground and your analysis is perfectly acceptable."

She studied the screen and finally had a hit. The analysis of Gibson's speech pattern showed stress and doubt and conflict.

Amazing that your words can show all that.

She wrote in her notebook: *Speak far less.*

"Okay, but I don't see where it gets us."

"Remember that I only threw out that list as *possibly* being connected to Langhorne's death. You're right that Trask is too young to have really been part of the mob back then. But there are other alternatives that need to be explored."

"If he did kill or have Langhorne killed, it seems far more likely it was connected to whatever Langhorne did as Daniel Pottinger rather than stretching back to the mob days. Maybe he screwed Trask over some deal and the guy decided to punish him for it."

Okay, let the big one drop and see what it does to little old Mickey Gibson. "How is that reconciled with the phrase 'Do as I say, not as I do'?"

She listened to the woman's breathing, and waited for the words to come and be analyzed.

"If you knew about that, why not tell me?"

She looked at the stress meter. *Oh, yes, straight-up pissed-off angry at me on that one.* "I assumed you knew if you were in the room. And obviously you did."

"Yeah, but only recently."

"You *were* in the room with the body," she repeated.

"I didn't search the whole thing. I found the body, got out of there, and called the cops. They wouldn't let me back in there—it was a crime scene."

Still angry but mellowing. "But now you do know, so someone told you, or showed you."

"Does it matter?"

"I suppose only to you."

"What does that mean?" exclaimed Gibson.

"I don't know. What does it mean to you?"

"I'm not playing the patient to your shrink, okay?"

Clarisse said, "My take is that either Trask did it or paid someone to do it because *Pottinger* screwed him over fairly recently, as you suggested. The writing on the wall might be mumbo-jumbo, or it might have some meaning between Trask and Pottinger. Or Trask is not involved, and someone else killed Pottinger for recent dealings."

"Or," Gibson said, "this *does* date back to Langhorne's screwing the mob over."

Oh, Mickey, you missed an obvious one, babe, but that's for me to know and you hopefully never to find out.

Gibson continued, "If the latter, then I can start digging into the mob from back then." She paused. "Langhorne might have escaped with a shitload of mob money. The mob, at least the one today, may have discovered that, and wanted it back."

Oh, how right you are, at least partially. "The question becomes, did they find it?"

"Is that what you want, too? The mob treasure?"

She analyzed the screen and saw that Gibson had been remarkably calm when uttering these lines. Clarisse automatically wrote some thoughts in her notebook. *Her anxiety goes down when she believes she's right about something.*

"I could lie and say it never crossed my mind, but what would be the point? Besides, don't girls multitask really well?"

"I'm glad you can see it that way," muttered Gibson.

"Are you? It brings me no particular joy."

Her other phone silently buzzed. She looked at the screen. It was Greenville. *What now?*

Frowning, she said, "I'll have to get back to you."

Only in her hurry, her finger didn't hit the right button.

She answered the call. "Yes? I already said I would be there as soon as I could."

The woman's voice on the speakerphone was trembling. "Ms. Frazier, I'm afraid—"

"Afraid? Don't tell me she died already."

"No, ma'am. But it seems that…that…"

"Oh for God's sake. It seems *what*?"

"It seems that she's gone missing," the woman said.

It was only then that the other line disengaged, as Gibson clicked off her phone.

25

THE HARD BED, THE HARD chair, an empty bottle of Ensure on the nightstand, the cheerless room cluttered but now without its occupant. Her mother had come here with basically nothing and had now left with the same.

Clarisse sat in the chair and gazed around.

The management had groveled at her feet for an hour, begging for mercy, pleading for her not to sue their asses off. The police had been called and looked around and asked some questions. They came back to meet with Clarisse when she arrived. They told her that her mother might have simply wandered off. They had started a search. No foul play was suspected, they told her. Just an old woman wandering off. She would turn up soon. The weather was nice, not too hot, not too cold. She couldn't have gone far. They'd find her soon enough. They left, their boredom barely concealed.

Clarisse slipped one glove off and then the other. She had gotten off the jet dressed to the nines. She wanted them to know who was in their presence. She wanted them to quake.

Though I'm really a nobody, I can act like SOMEBODY better than any other person on the planet.

The manager poked her head in the doorway. "If there's anything you need, anything at all, Ms. Frazier?"

"My *mother* would be nice. See what you can do about that, why don't you?"

The head disappeared like it had been jerked away, and the door closed.

Her mother had not gotten up and walked away, although it would have been easy to do so in this place. Except for the memory unit, the facility had not been built to prevent old people from fleeing. It had apparently never occurred to the dolts here that their charges ever could or would.

But her mother didn't have the lungs to walk down the hall, much less out the door. She had told the police this but they clearly didn't believe her. She hadn't pushed it because the last thing she wanted was to start answering a bunch of questions about her and her mother's past.

One cop had asked her, "Do you or your mother have any enemies, ma'am?" She knew the way he asked it, he was being tongue-in-cheek.

Oh, you have no clue, asshole. She truly hated men in uniform.

It was clear that someone had taken her mother. The puzzle was how they had found her in the first place.

She walked to the office, opened the door, and said, "Any CCTV? I saw what looked like cameras."

A few minutes later, on the camera feed, she saw her mother come around the corner of the building, and the woman was not alone. She was in a wheelchair being pushed by someone in jeans and a bulky hoodie.

She was wheeled out of the building while the front desk was apparently unoccupied. The exterior cameras next picked her up being loaded into a van, then the hoodie driving them off. Only the first three letters of the license plate could be seen.

She looked at the manager, who was standing behind her, riveted by this spectacle.

"And no one saw this?" Clarisse said. "Do you have no one who actually watches this stuff? And no one thought to show the police this while they were here? They didn't ask if there was footage? Is this a joke or what?"

"I...I don't know what to say. We're a little short on personnel. And we never really saw the need for security. We thought the cameras were enough. And who would want to hurt any of our dear, sweet residents?"

"You do realize that I could end up owning this place, right? And if I do, I sure as hell won't be requiring *your* services."

The woman swayed on her feet. "We can get the police back in here and show them the footage."

Clarisse had already leapt ahead and thought this through. No police. She would handle this on her own. "I'll make a deal with you. Say nothing to the cops and I won't file a lawsuit against you and this place."

"But—"

"It wasn't really a request."

"Thank you so much."

"Now I need to transfer that video file to my computer, and then I want you to get out of my face. I don't want to see you ever again."

After the file was delivered, she returned to her mother's room, sat down in the chair, rubbed her temples, and shut her eyes.

Hoodie and white van stealing her mother away. Not good in so many ways.

My defenses have been pierced.

She was sure the van was already abandoned and the hoodie abductor was long gone with their hostage, for that was what her mother had become. They hadn't realized her mother was missing until her meds were due. That was five hours after she had been rolled out of the place. Wheels up on a private jet, she could be in another country now. Just being driven somewhere, she could already be in any number of states.

And what am I going to do about that? Because I'm not sure who it is, though I have my suspicions, strong ones. But the worst part is, I'm apparently no longer anonymous, when that's all I've ever wanted to be.

This was a race, a competition of sorts. That was why she had brought Gibson in. And it was the first time Clarisse thought that she might lose.

And now I have somewhere else to be.

It wasn't connected to this, but it was connected to something else important. The most important of all.

My survival. Because I've damn well earned the right to keep on living.

26

"Thank you for meeting me on a Sunday, Phillip," Clarisse said, though that was not the name she was using today. She and Phillip Crandall were in the lobby of a building in North Carolina. She had just let him in and was escorting him to the elevators. They got on using her security card.

Crandall looked wealthy and was. But he was also too arrogant for his own good. He'd always wanted to be a player, a big-deal investor when he had neither the brains nor the discipline to be one. Which made him perfect for her.

She was not blond for this encounter. Her hair was a demure but professional-looking brown. She had on tinted specs and blue contact lenses. Her dress was businesslike, with a measure of underwire-bra-aided cleavage. It had always amazed her how little it took to completely gain dominance over a man. Their dicks were their Achilles' heels. And Crandall was not only arrogant, he was also a pig.

She liked pigs. All they cared about was eating, rolling around in the mud, doing whatever they pleased, and feeling like the boss of all bosses.

And then they were killed and eaten by others.

"Well, I wanted to see your operation for myself. You know, kick the tires now that we're going to be partners."

"I think you'll be impressed with what you see."

"I already like what I see," he replied, giving her the eye.

They laughed at his wit.

He was dressed in a dark blue blazer and khaki slacks with an Untuckit shirt to look hipper and younger than his fiftysomething age. A pocket square completed the package. She could tell he was so impressed with himself. Just like he had looked when he'd climbed out of the Aston Martin two-door after he'd pulled up in front of the building.

"Wow, you don't see many Aston Martins around here," she said, smiling adoringly from the other side of the elevator car.

He smiled right back. "One thing you'll learn about me, I don't like to have the same toys as all the other guys."

She applauded him with her eyes. "I like your style."

He ran his gaze over her again, his intentions as clear as the elevator buttons. "And I like *yours*."

He was married, but unhappily, he had told her. Which meant, of course, that he wanted to screw her. She had let him think that was a real possibility because that's just what you did with a guy *you* were trying to screw, but in a completely different way.

He had told her over drinks that he read people really well and trusted his instincts. "That's how I made my fortune."

"Brilliant," she had said. She was actually referring to Crandall's father, Richard, who *had* made a fortune in real estate.

This Crandall had taken a $250 million inheritance, and over twenty years managed to lose $50 million of it by investing in stupid deals that never rose above the scam level.

If he'd just put his inheritance in the stock market back then he'd probably be a billionaire by now.

They got to the fifth floor and she led him down the hall to a double office door with a sign proclaiming it to be the home of LASER FOCUS, INC.

She opened the door with her key card and led him inside. The lobby was spacious; the firm's name, on a much larger sign, was behind the receptionist's desk.

"Nothing fancy but we're not into that. All our money goes

into product and people. And the branding push will come next. Of course no one is in today."

"I've been to your website. Very impressive."

"Thanks. It's a very different world than the one I had at IBM."

"Yes, IBM. A great company but maybe a little bit of a dinosaur now," he said.

"Wow. You are so up-to-date on everything," she said. "We're lucky to have you as an early investor."

"I keep my nose to the ground." His gaze drifted over her legs. "Look, maybe we can have dinner and drinks later."

"I can do it on Wednesday, if that works. I'm off on a business trip to Montreal early tomorrow. We're trying to go full bore in Canada right now."

"I'd like that. I know a place."

"I knew you would. In fact, we can celebrate your investment in Laser Focus. But I have to warn you, I'm not much of a drinker."

"Then I'll order a case of red for our table."

They both laughed.

"Now to business." She led him into a conference room where she had set up a slide deck on a laptop. "We've already been over pretty much all of this but I wanted you to see it again, in a more comprehensive way."

They sat down, inches apart.

He touched her arm. "I appreciate the *private* showing."

Stranger danger, stranger danger.

"And let's appreciate that this is strictly business, as I owe my partners a fiduciary duty." She touched his hand. "But there's always Wednesday."

"Here's to always Wednesday."

"And then we'll bring you in for a full meet and greet. The rest of the team are dying to get to know you."

"I really enjoyed meeting your partners, Joe and Bill. Rock solid, both of them."

"Yes, they are."

She went over the plans for Laser Focus, which she had written on her laptop, cobbling together bits and pieces from other such plans she had gained access to. It all had a professional appearance because she was really good at Excel and Photoshop and what she didn't know she could always find out. She actually thought the business concept wasn't bad, but she wasn't going to be the one to see if it would work or not. All she needed to do was get the $2 million wire transferred tomorrow.

"Love the name by the way—Laser Focus," said Crandall.

"I wish I could claim credit for it, but it was that before I came here. However, I wouldn't leave a VP slot at IBM for nothing. You remember our main concept of pop-ups, of course. But leveraging them in a totally unique way. We refer to it as a latitude-based, instant market supply coordination factored, gross throughput decision-making process." She glanced at him. "It's all algorithm-centric, of course. No human can operate at the speeds we need to balance out supply and demand and also definitive location-focused stratagems. Pop-ups must literally 'pop up' right when and where the customer needs them to."

He looked utterly bewildered by all of this but said bracingly, "Pop-ups, of course. Great idea. Always loved the concept."

"Now, as we discussed before, postpandemic a great many people have or will be starting their own businesses or can work remotely. However, the future dynamic of work has been fundamentally altered, and they don't want the office space and headaches that come with that. And many businesses have cut back on their office footprint and don't have the requisite flexibility anymore. And workers don't always want to sit at their kitchen table and do Zoom meetings while their kids are screaming in the background. That's where we come in. And while there are temporary office space companies galore, like WeWork, Impact Hub, and Regus, we thought why not make the temp workspace *also* 'temporary.' That way we, as landlords, don't have to bear the underlying brick-and-mortar property costs. And then we simply pass some but not all of those savings on to our clients. In essence, instead of their coming to us, we go to them."

"Love it!"

She smiled and touched his arm. "It's a hybrid system that I think will come to dominate the space in the very near term. Our physical structure has been engineered so that it can be put up and then disassembled in less than one hour, and that includes all equipment provided to the customer on a semi-customized basis. It's trucked off and either sent to a new site where there is an algorithm-based demand, or warehoused until it's needed again. But our goal is to have an eighty-five percent deployment at all times. Idle inventory does not make us money."

She clicked some keys and a new screen appeared. "As you can see, our projections, while conservative, are quite eye-popping. We're cash flow positive after only eleven months, and in two years' time, with costs under control and a firm book of business, we're forecasting net profit margins at over twenty-eight percent. That beats our benchmark by a good eight hundred basis points. We have painstakingly built solid relationships with all necessary vendors and space owners. I've had this business plan vetted by a dozen seasoned businesspeople whose opinion I really value, and they all deem it an unqualified home run."

She glanced at him to see if his eyes were glazing over. They were. *Bingo.*

"But I don't have to tell an experienced investor like yourself anything. You either see it as a good deal or not."

"And I do see it as a *terrific* deal."

"And your investment gets you fifteen percent of the company on a *post* money basis."

"An incredible opportunity at a very fair valuation."

"We plan to align with a SPAC or other appropriate vehicle within two years, and take it public for *at least* a three-hundred-

million-dollar valuation, making your ownership interest worth—"
She pretended to be calculating in her head.

He said, "Forty-five million. A nice return on investment."

She smiled. "No fair—you're quicker on the draw than I am."

"Hey, I'm not just a pretty face."

She saw him out, letting him kiss her on the cheek.

Wednesday, Wednesday. But by then I'll be a thousand miles away. Enjoy dinner and drinks and tears alone, or maybe try taking your wife out, you jerk.

27

Clarisse looked over at the electronic marquee in the lobby where the name Laser Focus did not appear. But Crandall had never even looked. She knew he wouldn't, especially with her gushing self in the lobby to distract him.

Life was a shell game. The winners could just hide the truth better than everybody else.

She walked upstairs and let herself back in using the duplicate key she'd had made. She had gotten the passcode to the firm's security system by working as an office cleaner in the building for a week. And the security card she'd been given as a cleaner granted her access to the building at all times.

She walked behind the receptionist's desk and curled her fingers around the sign there. The magnetized backing on the Styrofoam sign pulled free from the metal letters bolted into the wall.

Revealed was the name of the company that really called this place home.

Creative Engineering. A well-respected company with lots of projects worldwide.

She had come in earlier today and made sure nothing that said "Creative Engineering" was visible anywhere. She had led Crandall right to the conference room and then right out the front door. She felt like a stage director.

Enter and exit only when and where I say to.

It was a role she enjoyed.

She had learned that all the personnel from this office had been redeployed to Austin, Texas, for a special four-week project, which was why she had chosen this space for her "office."

She broke her sign into two pieces and stuffed it into a large trash bag, then slipped her laptop into her briefcase. She next wiped her prints from every surface she had touched. She closed the door behind her and took the sign off the wall next to the exterior door. Underneath was, once more, revealed the name Creative Engineering.

But not as creative as me, I'd wager.

She added the small sign to the trash bag and left the building, but first took a moment to glance out the glass front door just to make sure Crandall had not doubled back.

Of course he hadn't. Arrogance again. He was probably stopping off to get the pack of Trojans for their Wednesday dinner followed by a romp in a hotel room with her all drunk and helpless against his preening manliness.

She got into her rental car and drove off. She threw the trash bag away in a dumpster about two miles away.

By one o'clock the next day $2 million had been wired into the bank account of Laser Focus, which had been set up only two months earlier. Crandall's banking people would have made certain he was really authorizing the wire because they needed to cover their asses. But it was not their job to make sure Crandall was not being scammed. That was all on him.

Thirty minutes later the money had been wired out, and the account was closed.

In the next five hours, the money would be divided up and sent to four different accounts around the world on preauthorized transfer instructions, until it disappeared into a sea of digital funds, never to be seen by its original owner again. But to be utilized fully by her.

She was on a commercial flight an hour after that. She didn't like to fly private all the time. And she sometimes found marks in first class. That was where she had first met Crandall, on a red-eye to London, where she let him "innocently" caress her leg and arm on the night flight over the Atlantic. That was followed by a peck on the cheek, a hug that lingered a bit too long, all with the implicit understanding of much more to come if business could be done.

On the plane she had just been thinking about leaving IBM, she had told him. He had never checked, of course. Men like him never did. She had taken her time reeling him in on Laser Focus, a scam she had been working on for some time. She had put the website up and gotten the slide deck together and spent some of her money on dinners with just the two of them.

She had also introduced him to her two *partners*, Bill and Joe. She had used them in the past for things like this. They weren't cheap, but they adhered to the script like the pros they were, more than earning their compensation. During several meetings they had talked of financial projections and marketing plans and corporate org flowsheets and cost itemizations and hiring initiatives, and all sorts of business items ad nauseum. This had overwhelmed Crandall and caused him to finally stop asking questions and simply nod at their fancy-sounding gibberish lest he reveal that he actually knew very little about business.

It really was all in the psychology. If you knew what made your mark tick, you knew everything you needed to know. And playing to the mark's ego was usually golden.

When she had learned while sitting next to Crandall in first class that his wealth had been inherited, her interest had been piqued. Those who inherited wealth either let the professionals handle the business matters while they simply enjoyed the benefits of being born into the right family, or else they went the route that Crandall did, convincing themselves that they had somehow earned every dollar and had the business acumen to earn even more.

Well, Phillip Crandall would have to content himself with the many millions he still had left. And knowing his ego, he might not even report being ripped off, because that would make public the fact that he was an idiot. But this also might be a nice wake-up call for him. He hopefully would take the rest of his huge fortune and put it into a proper stocks-and-bonds portfolio and let people who actually knew what they were doing manage it for him. That way he could spend his days driving around in his ego machine and chasing younger women until his pecker gave out.

She was much richer today than yesterday, but really only focused on one thing.

Where in the hell is my mother? And who took her? And what am I going to do about it?

28

AND PARENTS.

The clue had finally come to Gibson as she made pancakes for her kids while they impatiently watched her.

Clarisse had said, *One can buy excellent day care if one has enough money. That goes for children* and *parents.*

And days later she had taken a call, presumably unaware that Gibson could still hear. It seemed like a woman had gone missing.

That was what the person on the other end of the line had said.

And the woman had called Clarisse "Ms. Frazier." Another alias. Gibson wondered how many she had.

Probably more than the number of shoes I own. She looked down at her ratty pair of Adidas sneakers. *Yeah, definitely more.*

No one would really say that about their parents, not when talking about day care. But they might if they *had* parents in assisted living or a nursing home. So did Clarisse have that in her life? Until her *mother* went missing?

She had an intriguing thought. Could Clarisse be Francine Langhorne? She sounded around Gibson's age, which would be in the ballpark with what she knew about Francine.

She buttered the pancakes, ladled syrup on them, and put them on plates with the scrambled eggs, and the turkey bacon already cut up into easily swallowed pieces. She then poured the milk into plastic cups with snap tops and built-in straws, making them spill proof.

Whoever invented these cups must *have had kids.*

Tommy asked for more syrup and said, "Me do it," when she brought it over. He made a mess of it, but she said nothing. She had long ago learned to pick her battles, and making a lake on your plate with syrup was not a hill she was willing to die on.

As Tommy and Darby ate, Gibson munched on a piece of bacon. She pulled out her laptop and looked at the material she had downloaded on the Langhorne family, studying the image of Francine Langhorne in particular. It looked like the kids were being rushed into a car by their mother, Geraldine. The hulking Doug Langhorne, his face dour and pinched, had turned to stare into the camera. She didn't like that look at all.

Gibson next turned to Francine. Her look was far more nuanced than her brother's. The girl's large eyes were sad, but there was an underlying determination that spoke of strength, of resiliency. Such a person could survive much, Gibson surmised, including a crooked dad, the murderous mob, and a stint in WITSEC. And, finally, abandonment by her parents.

Earl Beckett had said Doug had stayed with his sister until she was old enough to voluntarily leave WITSEC. Under the circumstances, they probably had only each other, and a circling-of-the-wagons mentality would be perfectly understandable.

My problem is, I don't know enough about the Langhornes, particularly the kids. But then it occurred to her. *Idiot, you have a source that can help you on that.*

When Silva arrived and took over, Gibson rushed to her office and made the call.

Earl Beckett was actually in Williamsburg for a meeting today and could meet her for coffee nearby in about an hour, he told her.

She ran upstairs, showered, and changed, and was at the coffee shop in the historic district of Williamsburg five minutes early. When Beckett came walking up, she greeted him, and they went inside and ordered their coffees.

Once they were settled at a table, Beckett said, "I thought I might hear from you."

"Why is that?"

"I looked you up after you and Sullivan came to see me. Even talked to some folks who knew you. 'Dog with a bone that won't let go' is how you were described."

"I guess I don't like unanswered questions."

"So what questions can *I* answer for you?"

"I'd like you to tell me about the Langhornes. The kids. The family dynamic. The relationship between husband and wife, but particularly about the kids."

"You think one of them tracked down their daddy and doled out their own justice?"

"It's certainly a possibility."

He nodded and sipped his coffee. "Family dynamics are a strange thing. You see similarities in some families, but every one of them is unique, too. Now, WITSEC families are not the norm. They are as far from the norm as it is possible to be, in fact, except if you're in a family of serial killers."

"You mean the stress and the upheaval?"

"Yes, and having to build a new life from scratch, but it can't be any kind of, well, special life, I guess is what I'm trying to say. You're not going to grow up to be a rock star or CEO or a pro athlete after being in WITSEC. At least I've never seen that happen. Your opportunities are definitely limited, and that's a damn shame, really."

Gibson fingered her coffee cup, thinking of her own children at the moment. "And for the kids it had nothing to do with them and everything to do with decisions their parents made. Well, in this case, Harry Langhorne mostly."

"Exactly. And let me tell you, that can build up to a volcano of resentment. I've seen that happen to quite a few WITSEC families."

"Is that what happened with the Langhornes?"

Beckett nodded. "When I got assigned there the kids were young teens. And Harry, to put it politely, was a Class A asshole. He rode both of them hard. Whatever they did, it wasn't good enough. Whatever bad happened, it was their fault. And he seemed to resent when either of them had any fun or tried to be normal." He eyed Gibson. "I mentioned the psych eval we do for all of the people coming into the program?"

"Yeah?"

"Well, the Langhornes read like a horror story. Harry was a psychopath with some creepy tendencies. Geraldine was a lush who never made a decision in her life, and had so many insecurities the shrinks stopped counting. And the kids?"

"What about them?"

"Let's just say they were not very well-adjusted. Remember, they'd been living the mob life since they'd been born, unwittingly or not. That is not healthy for anyone. And Harry? Well, let's just say his actions didn't help matters."

"Can you give me an example?"

"I sure can. I remember it well. Francine was a junior in high school, and she was the lead in her school's Christmas play. She was quite the actress, and she had been involved in local theater and performed in all the school productions. Hell, when I was off duty I went to some of them. She was good, I mean real good. A born actress, you could say. And, despite what I just said about nobody in WITSEC going on to do anything exceptional, she might have broken that rule if she'd had the chance."

"I majored in theater in college. It's intense as hell, but there's no rush like being up on that stage," said Gibson.

"I'm sure."

"Which play was it?"

"I don't know why, but I remember it all these years later. *Twelfth Night*. You know it?" asked Beckett.

"Yeah, we did a lot of Shakespeare in college, but not that one. So what happened?"

"The night came for her to do the play. They'd sold out the show. But before Francine left for the school the house alarm went off. Not the normal burglar alarm; this was the alarm tied directly to our office. Our protocol was strict. When that alarm went off, the family was taken to a safe house, no exceptions. And kept there until we determined there was no threat. Well, we followed our procedures, and because of that Francine missed the play."

"I'm sure she was devastated."

"She was even more devastated when she found out her father had intentionally set off the damn alarm, not because there was a threat, but because she had brought a stray cat home to feed it, and the thing had crapped on the floor. And he thought a good lesson would be to have her lose out on starring in the Christmas play."

"How did you find that out?"

"Hell, he told her, and us. He laughed. But I read him the riot act. I told him if he pulled something like that again, I would rip his hand off. Shortly after that, he vanished."

"So he presumably had already decided to disappear?"

"Oh yeah. No way he could have vanished so effectively without some planning."

"And the son?"

"Dougie was strong as a horse. Wanted to play sports and all, but his old man wouldn't let him. So he just stayed in the garage and lifted weights. At age eighteen he was six two and over two hundred pounds and none of it fat. Blond hair, nice-looking kid. He had all the girls swooning over him. But he didn't seem to care about that. He sort of closed off that part of his life. He wasn't a typical teen and he knew it. Why get close to someone if nothing was going to come out of it? At least that was my take. So he stayed in the garage and lifted weights."

"How about Geraldine? What was her role in the dynamic?"

"She did what her husband told her to do."

"Didn't stand up for the kids?"

"Not that I ever saw. The kids pretty much raised themselves.

I'm not saying Geraldine was a bad person. But her life basically fell apart after the family got moved into WITSEC. She didn't cope well. But she apparently liked the mob money that Harry was paid. They had a good lifestyle back in Jersey. But he was no millionaire, at least not back then. Strictly upper-middle-class."

"Did she work outside the house while in WITSEC?"

"Yep, like I said, that's a rule. Got to get a job. And it's not just about the money. We don't want people sitting at home moping. Only bad things come out of that. So she was a maid for a while at a motel chain, and she also worked at a bowling alley. Then at a Walmart. There were other jobs. All menial stuff. But after the mob business, it was like every bit of energy and ambition left her. I didn't get all that just from my time with them. Other marshals filled out the story for me."

"And the kids resented their mother's not taking their sides, not being there for them?"

He eyed her. "You got kids?"

"Yes, very little ones. And we were all kids once."

"Well, then you probably know the answer to that."

Gibson let out a long, subdued breath. *Yeah, I guess I do*, she thought. "How did the kids get along?"

"Francine could get Dougie to do whatever she wanted. She just had that way about her. Now, I might have given you the wrong impression before about Dougie staying in the garage and lifting weights. The boy was not stupid. He was a brooder, but intelligent. His grades weren't the best, but not because of ability. He just seemed bored. But he loved his sister. Would do whatever she told him to do. I think that's why he waited around for her before heading out."

"Well, a good actress can be very manipulative," said Gibson. The conjured image of Clarisse and the image of the young Francine Langhorne from the photo appeared in her mind's eye. She mentally blended one into the other and got a real mess in return.

"Yes, they can. And she was."

"Manipulative enough to have him kill their mother? I mean, you said she vanished, but do you really know that for sure?"

"We never found a body, and the kids disclaimed all knowledge of her disappearance."

"Would someone have seen anything if they did do her harm?"

"Another WITSEC family with kids, name of Enders, lived near them. The Langhornes would socialize with them. The fathers got along, I mean really well. It was like Harry had found a kindred spirit in Darren Enders. We talked to them, but they weren't home the night she vanished. Geraldine's kids reported her missing the next morning. Part of me thinks she went to join her husband. We never found a trace, but, like her husband, she had a good head start."

"One last thing."

"Sure."

"Can you find samples of Francine's and Dougie's handwriting?"

"Handwriting?" asked Beckett.

"Yeah."

"You have something you think they both wrote out?"

Do as I say, not as I do, she thought. "Not right now, but I might stumble on something in the future."

"You're talking a long time ago."

"I'm not expecting miracles. Just asking you to make some phone calls to see if something turns up."

"Okay, I'll see what I can do," replied Beckett.

"Thanks, and thanks for all the info."

"You really think his kids found Harry Langhorne and killed him?"

"It's certainly possible." *And I might be working with one of the killers*, thought Gibson.

CHAPTER

29

On the drive home, Gibson mulled over things.

If Clarisse was Francine, she could have found and killed her father at Stormfield. Whether her brother, Doug, was around and part of it, Gibson didn't know.

But then why involve me? If she did kill him, then she basically engaged me to find her.

Since that made no sense, Gibson had to conclude she had it all wrong, or was missing something vital that would make her initial speculation right.

Later, she turned into her driveway and sat there for a bit.

If the "and parents" comment made by Clarisse meant she had a parent in assisted living, then Geraldine Langhorne might be alive. Had Francine found her mother, and made her tell where her father was? Then she went and killed him? But that still didn't explain Gibson's involvement in all this. And had something just happened to Geraldine, if that's who it was? Based on the partial conversation Gibson had overheard, it was possible.

And if Clarisse is Francine, how did she even know that I exist?

Based on what Beckett had told her about the school play, Francine had been a thespian, too. She and Gibson were close in age. Had Francine gone to Temple while Gibson had been there? Had she used the name Francine Parker? Or had she used another name? And where was Doug? Had he followed his sister across the country? From what Beckett had told him about Doug

Langhorne, he didn't sound much like the college type, but one never knew.

But that's something I can check.

Gibson went inside to her office. She could hear the kids playing with Silva in the backyard. She picked up her iPad that she had used to take pictures of the items at Stormfield.

Gibson sat down and scrolled through picture after picture of the mansion's interior. The thing was, there wasn't millions of dollars' worth of assets there. She had gotten particulars on the Formula cabin cruiser. Brand-new, it would go for well over a million. But this model was four years old, so it would be worth far less. And if the millions were the ones Langhorne had already spent on purchasing Stormfield and the boat, he couldn't imagine how Clarisse intended to get her hands on those proceeds. She would have to prove that she was Harry Langhorne's daughter. And if she had killed her father, that would not exactly be smart. Plus, even if the place was sold and millions resulted from that sale, it could be argued by the government that the monies Langhorne had used to buy the place were stolen from a criminal organization. In that case she might not realize a penny. And while Harry Langhorne might well have been a Class A asshole, as Marshal Beckett had said, that didn't give anyone the right to murder him.

Yet how many times have you dreamed about killing your ex?

Her small attic had an access door in the middle of the upstairs hall. She pulled on the cord and a set of stairs dropped down. She clambered up and turned on the light. There was no room to stand, so she stepped across the loose plywood boards set over the ceiling joists until she reached the pile of cardboard boxes.

She opened one and pulled out her yearbooks from Temple. She went over all four of them. There was no Francine or Doug Parker, not that she had expected to find those names. Next she went through all the photos of the students. The problem was, the only pictures she had of Francine and Doug Langhorne were from when they were children.

As they were leaving the cafe, she had asked Beckett if he had any photos of them as teenagers, but he had told her no. As a routine, he said, they did not take pictures of their protectees, in case they fell into the wrong hands. That meant Gibson really had no idea what Francine or Doug looked like now.

She stopped at one page in her junior yearbook, which showed Mickey Rogers onstage in the role of Eliza Doolittle from *My Fair Lady*. She smiled and ran her fingers over the images. The cockney accent had been really hard for the Jersey girl to master, but she had worked her butt off to nail it. The camera angle showed the audience, and also some of the crew in the wings.

She heard her kids screaming and playing in the backyard. She took the yearbook with her, left the attic, and walked over to a window where she could see Tommy and Darby running in circles, using their arms as plane wings, while Silva clapped and danced around them.

She glanced down at her far younger self on the page as she beamed out at the audience.

I thought I was going to be the next great thing on Broadway, even though my pipes weren't the best and my acting chops, though decent, were not exactly Tony Award level. Now I'm approaching forty, divorced with two little kids, and I'm embroiled in something I can't even begin to understand.

But whoever said life was predictable?

She put the yearbook down and hurried outside to be with her kids.

30

CLARISSE HAD MANAGED TO TRACE the van that had been used to abduct her mother. It had been rented. The identity used to lease it had been stolen. She found that out on her own. The rental company could do nothing to help her. They apparently spent every dollar of their budget on ads demonstrating how amazing their customer service was, and none on their actual customer service. All she got were recorded voices sending her from one voice mail to another until the system just spit her out.

Clarisse looked at her computer screen.

The vehicle had been picked up in Asheville, North Carolina, driven to Greenville, South Carolina, used for a felony abduction of one Agnes Leland, and then abandoned somewhere in between. No leads, no clues, no nothing. The interesting thing now? How would communication to her occur?

True to her habit, she had started a new notebook. On its cover she had written RECOVERY OF MOMMY.

Short and to the point but with a lot of work ahead and not much to go on.

She hacked into what she needed to hack into and watched Hoodie rent the van in Asheville, which was only about an hour or so across the state line from Greenville. The world was all connected now. What that actually meant was that there was no more privacy, ever. She zoomed in on the figure, but the person's face was never pointed toward the camera.

Using an app, she calculated the height of the person at over six feet, but that included shoes. The clothes were bulky, so an educated guess on the weight and build was likely to be well off. The ID used to rent the car was in the name of Daryl Oxblood of The Plains, Virginia. The DMV records in Virginia showed there *was* a Daryl Oxblood of The Plains, Virginia. The credit card used was also in Oxblood's name.

She sat back and thought about this.

Do I go to The Plains, Virginia, or do I wait for them to contact me? Or maybe they already have.

And there would be only one way to do it.

She used a burner phone to call the facility in Greenville.

The manager said in a cowed voice, "You're not going to have me fired, are you? I really need this job."

"How good are the firewalls on your computer network?"

"I don't know anything about firewalls. But we have a guy. He's a cousin of someone who works here and he gave us a good deal to—"

She hung up on the woman and checked the email she had given the facility in case of emergency. She had provided a phone number, too, which they had called when her mother went missing. But she felt sure the first contact would not be by phone. If ever.

And there it was.

Sitting in her email's spam folder.

Hello and surprise. Took a while, but, like you, I don't give up easy. The old bitch is well and full of shit, as always. We'll need to talk about things. I'll let you know when. Get cranked and buckle up because we're taking this ride to a whole other level. It's going to be a wild one, hon.

Take it to another level, will you? Well, that can cut both ways. But how did they find Mommy, and then me?

She let the possible scenarios flow through her mind.

The background cover was solid. Agnes was gaga so she wasn't telling anybody anything. Greenville out of all places. So how?

The answer didn't please her but it was inevitable.

They didn't track Mommy to me, they tracked me *to Mommy.*

She went back over the last six months of her activity to see where the penetration might have come from. She consulted her notebooks and computer files and...

Frankfort, Kentucky. A scam run on a horse breeder who thought himself a demigod of sorts. It was only a $250,000 operation, plus a racehorse that she'd later sold for a tidy sum. There had been no glitches.

The dickless senator with Angie. Again, nothing there. She hadn't appeared on the scene until the very end.

Phillip Crandall. Now, that had been more involved. She had been invested in that one both digitally and in person. She flipped through her notebooks and then checked her schedule of appearances on the computer. She pulled up footage of the places where she had been seen on camera, but always in disguise. A disguise no one could see through, especially after all this time.

She flipped through screen after screen. The airport, the restaurants. The meeting places. Her conferring with her two conspirators, Bill and Joe. There was nothing that looked out of the ordinary. No one paying her the least bit of attention.

The building housing the fake Laser Focus.

It had nothing to do with Creative Engineering, the office space that she had used to dupe Phillip Crandall.

But Creative wasn't the only business in the building. There was a wholesale jeweler, Stewart and Sons. She had previously read the news article but thought nothing of it at the time. They'd been robbed. Two million in uncut gems taken from a vault that was guaranteed as being pick-proof. It had been opened without any force whatsoever, which had led police to think it was an inside job. People had been questioned and arrested and then released for lack of evidence or alibis. Insurance paid the claim. The authorities were befuddled.

She was not. Not now.

The cleaning crew, of which I was a member for a short time. There was another woman my race, my age, and the right size.

She thought back. No, she never let me get a look at her, and she wore a COVID mask the whole time. But the crew had cleaned the jeweler's shop. Clarisse had seen the impressive vault with its digital pad and laser trip wires and alarms all around. They had been strictly instructed not to go anywhere near it.

Two million in uncut gems, the easiest of all to fence. It would have netted her around half a million. Not bad for the time and effort.

How she had defeated the safe wasn't all that complicated. Clarisse was surprised the local police were puzzled. She envisioned the vault in her mind. The laser trip wires were the first obstacle.

Needed: a number of mirrored surfaces built on a collapsible frame that when set up would redirect the lasers over their surfaces so the loop was unbroken, but leaving a gap in the middle to be exploited, like a running back going through a hole in the line created by his blockers. When done, it would collapse flat, go into a bucket of water, and become invisible.

Next, a ten-digit alarm pad was formidable with all the possible combinations. But knock it down to four numbers and it was quite doable by an app you could download on your phone. How do you knock it down to four?

She pantomimed shooting the digital pad with a substance that would luminesce under the right light. The person opening or locking the safe would hit only the requisite keys, leaving their luminous prints behind. That was how you eliminated six out of the ten possibilities. And that turned ten billion different possible combinations into ten thousand. That could be defeated in seconds.

Then, a place to secret the gems? The pole on the mop. It's hollow. Open one end, slide them in, then drop in a long strip of precut Styrofoam so the gems would make no noise. She could have gone into that room and done it all in a couple of minutes.

And if she hadn't been focused on separating Phillip Crandall from his money, she might have.

But somehow, against all the odds, she recognized me. She followed me. She found out what she needed. She knew I had traveled to Greenville. I flew commercial there twice. She was on the plane. She followed me to the assisted living facility. She bribed the people who worked there. Or, more likely—to avoid interacting with anyone there and leaving behind witnesses—she probably snuck in by pretending she was visiting someone else, and then sat down and gotten out of Agnes, in her lucid moments, all that she needed.

And Agnes wouldn't tell me about it because she probably thought she was having one over on me. But then they took her and it's obvious why.

So now I know how it could have happened. And I think I know who did it. But there my advantages stop. So they have Mommy and I have no idea where they have her. But I have one thing to do: close up this shop and open another. The trail on me goes cold now.

And Clarisse set about to do just that.

Mickey Gibson would have to wait a bit.

31

GIBSON WATCHED HER CHILDREN EAT their dinners, or rather Tommy wolf his down and Darby pick at hers. It was annoying but she could understand it. Gibson had been the same way when she was a kid. Her brothers had eaten everything in sight while she had been indifferent to food and thin as a rail. She touched her hips and closed her eyes.

Those were the days.

Later, she put the kids to bed and went to her office. She stared at the Batphone for about ten minutes before hitting the send button.

"Now is not a good time," Clarisse said.

"Then why answer?"

"I thought it might be important. Is it?"

"I went by Nathan Trask's place."

"You told me that already."

"But we didn't finish our discussion. How in the hell do you expect me to ever get a face-to-face with the man? Stealth, as you suggested, isn't going to cut it, unless I can become invisible."

"I didn't think it was *my* job to do *your* job."

"I don't remember being hired by you to do a job!" Gibson snapped. "Or did my paycheck go astray?"

"You are in this knee-deep, no, make that ass-deep. If Trask *is* involved in Langhorne's death he knows all about you already."

"You sound flustered."

"Maybe I am. And maybe I don't need to be your self-starter, Mickey. I thought you could motivate yourself. You're a smart girl—act like it."

"Maybe *we* should meet. On a Zoom."

"Why?"

"I like to know who I'm dealing with."

"You already know who you're dealing with. Me."

"You're just a voice on the other end of the ether."

"A voice who has spent quite a bit of time holding your hand and leading you down the path you need to go down. I suggest, from now on, you take it from here."

The line went dead and Gibson slowly put the phone down.

She picked up the yearbook and went back over the pages. Her focus was now on some of the people in the audience. She went through them one by one. But that didn't make sense to her. Why would Francine Langhorne be in the audience in Philly watching a college performance starring Mickey Rogers?

But then her focus changed—to the stage wings.

The backstage crew. They were typically all students at Temple and also some folks who worked at the university. She had helped a number of the students, becoming a mentor and shoulder to cry on when auditions or their tests went badly.

She took pictures of all the images with her phone and then sent them to her email. She fired up her computer and brought the images up on the large screen and then zoomed in on the faces in the wings. There were a lot of them. Stage productions needed a great deal of manpower whether in college or on Broadway. She went through the pictures one by one. Nothing clicked.

But why would it? You have photos of Francine Langhorne as a child.

Wait, could our paths have crossed when I was a cop? She knew I had been on the force in Jersey City. Did I arrest her at some point? I met a lot of people back then. And she obviously knew I worked at ProEye. But I really haven't met anyone in person at ProEye. It's basically all done on the computer.

She sighed and sat back. This was getting her nowhere fast.

Okay, set this aside for now and work to your strengths.

And that meant trying to find Pottinger's assets by way of her cyber-sleuthing.

She obtained some of Pottinger's personal information from his purchase of Stormfield. She used this to start building a baseline of the man's financial activities.

And then, surprisingly, the Batphone rang. She answered it.

Clarisse said, "I apologize for being so abrupt before. I *did* have something else on my mind, but it was no excuse for rudeness."

"Okay," said Gibson grudgingly, taken aback by this abrupt turnaround.

"As for Trask, here is some advice. He has an army of aides and bodyguards and all the entourage of the king he thinks he is."

"Which was my point. So how can I—" began Gibson.

"Why do you think he built a place in Virginia Beach when he could live anywhere in the world?"

"Okay, why?"

"His father, Sam Trask, lives in Virginia Beach, too," said Clarisse.

"What! And you didn't tell me this before because why?"

"I like to see people find out things for themselves."

"Trask Senior obviously knows what his son really is," noted Gibson.

"He does. Apparently during his career at the Bureau, they built a formidable case against his son. His father, of course, would have been no part of it because of conflict rules, but I heard that he was actually the leading force behind the scenes. But the case fell apart when a group of women, who could have sent Trask to prison for sex trafficking, were burned up in a hotel fire in San Antonio."

"Trask's work?" asked Gibson.

"Obviously, but nothing could be proven. Sam Trask retired

from the Bureau at age fifty-seven, which is mandatory for special agents. After that he worked at Kroll International for over a decade. You know them?"

Gibson said, "Of course, one of the biggest and best known private security and investigation firms in the world. They're a competitor of ProEye."

"He did specialized work for them, using his breadth of knowledge and Rolodex acquired at the Bureau. His cases took him all over the world, and there was overlap with the sort of crimes his son was engaged in."

"So you mean the father was still trying to take down his son?"

"It's almost biblical, isn't it?" remarked Clarisse. "Sam Trask is now eighty years old, retired, widowed, and has lived for five years at The Feathers, an assisted living center in Virginia Beach. He has some health issues, but word is the man still has his mental faculties."

"And his son built that monstrosity after his father moved there?" said Gibson.

"Sort of like, 'Look at me, I have this awesome place and *you're* the one imprisoned at an assisted living facility.'"

"If I were Sam I'd up and move somewhere else. Make his son shell out the bucks to build another place."

Clarisse said, "I'm not sure Sam Trask would give him the satisfaction of knowing that his son is still getting in his father's head."

"Does Nathan ever visit him?"

"His father obviously wants nothing to do with him, so he has refrained from trying. So maybe there's your in."

"What do you mean?" asked Gibson.

"Sam Trask knows more about his son than maybe anyone alive."

"If that's so, why hasn't the son taken out the father?"

"He would be the prime suspect if that happened, and that would turn the FBI's attention to him again. His father can't really hurt him now, so why make that sort of trouble for himself?"

"So you want me to go and talk to the father?" asked Gibson.

"Do you have a better idea? Apparently not, because you called me initially complaining you had no shot at nailing Nathan Trask."

"Whoa, *nailing* him?"

"Okay, getting information about him," amended Clarisse.

"But the Langhorne murder was very recent. Sam Trask has been out of the game for years. What would he know about his son's activities since then?"

"I said he *retired*. I didn't say he was out of the game. And what will it hurt to go and ask the man?"

"But won't Trask have him watched, especially if his father knows so much?" noted Gibson.

"Nothing that Sam Trask knows has been enough to touch the son. And if he *is* being watched, then you need to use ingenuity to get around that."

"You make it sound so easy," retorted Gibson.

"I didn't involve you in this because it was easy. I brought you in because you're good."

"I'm a former cop. I can't flit around conning people and doing illegal things."

"Really? Then how did you find out that Daniel Pottinger was really Harry Langhorne? I would imagine you did some *conning* and *flitting* and *illegal* shit to score that info."

Okay, I walked right into that one. "What do you think Sam Trask can tell me?"

"Isn't that the whole point of asking? Okay, I'm done hand-holding. Oh, and one more thing."

"Yeah?" said Gibson.

"A much younger Sam Trask was on the FBI task force that took down the mob bosses Harry Langhorne was working with. But I'm sure you already knew that, right?"

And with that Parthian shot, the line went dead again. And Gibson didn't think Clarisse would be calling back a second time.

And maybe she's right. I am half-assing this because I keep oscillating between whether I really want to be involved or not.

She went online and looked up The Feathers. It was quite an upscale place, about a dozen rungs above any place Gibson would be able to afford when her time came to *retire*.

The resident list wasn't available, of course; she looked over the facility schematic. It had a memory wing for dementia patients, a library, a game room, a hair salon, an outdoor courtyard in the very center, fireplaces, a dining room, and other community spaces.

She was surprised when her Batphone dinged. Not a call but definitely a communication.

She opened the email and saw a picture of a distinguished-looking, elderly man. Written under it was: "Sam Trask. Good hunting."

She studied the picture, and then thought how best to do this.

And when she had struck on a plan, Gibson had to admit that a bit of the excitement lost from her earlier professional life was starting to seep back into her. And it wasn't just her time as a cop, but also her stint as a college thespian.

She checked on the kids, and woke Tommy from a devilish nightmare and held him until he fell back asleep. She had had night terrors as a child and understood quite clearly how bad they could be.

Gibson went to her room, set her alarm, and pulled the covers over herself, thinking of what she had once been and perhaps what she still could be.

32

With the kids bathed and fed and Silva in charge, Gibson set out for The Feathers the following morning. She had on an outfit that she had last worn about two years ago. She had delivered Darby about three weeks before, and had still been carrying some of her pregnancy weight. She refused to borrow any more clothes from her mother.

She drove past The Feathers twice, each time looking for anyone surveilling the place. She didn't believe that Nathan Trask was keeping his father under eyeballs 24/7, but the man had enough resources to justify Gibson's going through the pains of checking.

Nothing looked amiss to her, so she drove into the parking lot, and went inside with a little gift bag and small bouquet of flowers she had purchased as part of her cover. There was a sign-in sheet, so she signed in, in an undecipherable scribble. She took her temperature with the device sitting next to the sign-in ledger, and saw that it was normal. A woman at the front desk, on the telephone, nodded at Gibson, who smiled back and held up the gift bag and flowers. The woman mouthed the words *Very nice*.

Another lady in blue scrubs walked by pushing a basket of soiled laundry. She nodded at Gibson and moved on.

Gibson turned left and walked down the corridor, passing the library and community spaces. The nurses' station on this hall was unoccupied. Retirement places had a hard time keeping workers because of low pay, she knew, and less than ideal circumstances.

Working with the elderly, who were often in pain, depressed, and sometimes not in their right minds, would challenge anyone. Plus, even the upscale facilities operated on a shoestring, and to make a profit they had to keep the employee head count down as much as possible.

None of that was good as far as patient care went, but it was quite good for Gibson's efforts today.

Each resident room had a name plate on it. She passed by twelve rooms without finding Trask's.

She eyed a resident slowly making his way down the hall on a rollator. She asked him if he knew what room Sam Trask was in. He just looked back at her blankly, gummed his lips, and kept going.

She turned the corner and ran into another employee.

"Can I help you?" she asked, the woman's features an intriguing mix of friendliness and suspicion.

"I was looking for Mrs. Edison's room?" Gibson glibly asked, using the name she had seen on one of the rooms she had passed. She didn't want to ask for Trask's room in case the son had plants here. "She's an old friend of my mother's." She held up the gift bag and flowers. "I thought this might brighten up her day."

"I'm sure it will. Kate loves flowers. But you passed it. It's back around the corner. Third door on the right."

Gibson smiled. "Thank you. I guess I really do have to get those eyeglasses."

The woman chuckled and went through a door marked EM-PLOYEES ONLY.

Gibson kept going and turned the corner. She met an elderly woman pushing herself along in a wheelchair and whistling a tune that Gibson did not recognize.

The woman stopped and looked at Gibson. "Are you lost?" she said.

"I think I might be. It's my first visit here to see my great-uncle."

"His name?"

"Sam Trask."

"Room 223, upstairs."

"Thank you so much."

Gibson found the stairs, headed up, and ten seconds later was knocking on Trask's door. She noted the sign next to the door that warned of oxygen being used inside.

"Come," said an authoritative voice.

She opened the door and, breathing heavily—not from the stairs, but from apprehension—walked in.

Maybe I can get some of that oxygen.

33

THE FIRST THING GIBSON NOTED about the front room was how neat it was. There was no sign of clutter, just minimal furnishings. Two chairs, one coffee table, one towering shelf bulging with books with wide-ranging titles, a small kitchen area with a sink and cabinets and an under-the-counter fridge. The pictures on the wall looked like they might have been bought at the same print shop: birds, landscapes, a mountain. There were no personal photos, no knickknacks. On the carpet she saw the recent vacuum lines. The counter had a microwave and a few neatly arranged cards wishing happy holidays, and she spied one birthday greeting. Across from the kitchen was the bathroom.

There was an oxygen concentrator machine plugged into a wall outlet, and she saw the tubing snake down the floor and into the rear room. There was no doorway leading into the back room, just a short hall.

"Who is it?" called out the same voice.

"Mr. Trask?" Gibson said as she set the gift bag and flowers down on the counter and walked to the rear of the space. "I wanted to have a chat if that's okay?"

She took a moment to look around. There was a large flat-screen TV on the wall playing CNN. There was a bed, and a nightstand with several books stacked on it. A recliner was angled next to it. A bookcase standing against one wall was full of tomes with serious titles, mostly dealing with geopolitics. A small window overlooked a courtyard below.

Sam Trask was seated at a desk with a laptop in front of him. A rollator stood at the ready next to him. What Gibson *wasn't* seeing in the small apartment intrigued her.

Trask wheeled around in his chair and looked at her. The oxygen tubing was connected to a cannula, which was inserted in his nostrils.

She figured he would be at least six two standing; he was trim and fit looking, despite the need for oxygen. His hair was thin and snow white, his features were chiseled and rugged, his eyes were flint chips, and he had a pugnacious chin. All told, the man seemed to be looking for a confrontation.

"Who are you? And what do you want to *chat* about?"

"My name is not that important. But why I'm here *is* important."

"Explain."

She could see how he would have done well at the FBI. He was confident but curious. Direct, but there was a subtlety to it.

"Have you ever heard of a man named Harry Langhorne?"

"Mob accountant. He turned state's evidence and helped to take down several New York and New Jersey crime families, including the Giordanos. He and his family were put into WITSEC. I lost track of him after that."

"You worked on the task force that brought the mob down."

"I was only one of many."

Humility too, thought Gibson. How was Nathan Trask spawned from this?

"What exactly does all that have to do with you?" He looked her over as he took several deep breaths, sucking in extra manufactured oxygen from the tank down the hall. "You would have just been a child at the time."

"Harry Langhorne had a home in the area under the name Daniel Pottinger. He was found murdered a few days ago at that home."

Trask took all of this in. Watching him, Gibson could imagine his doing the same mental calculations back at the Bureau as he was briefed by a junior staffer.

"What area exactly?"

This surprised her but she answered him. "An estate called Stormfield, a bit north of Smithfield, right on the James River."

"How was he murdered?"

"Botulinum, type A."

"Nasty stuff. It's not a painless death."

"I'm sure. But he was already terminal with brain cancer."

"And so Harry Langhorne finally met his end?"

"Had you met him?"

"I had. Not a nice person, but what would you expect? Out to save his own skin, like the rest of the scum."

"And his family?"

"What of them?"

"Did you meet them?"

"Yes, briefly. Geraldine, the wife; Francine and Douglas, the children."

"You have a good memory." She eyed the cannula.

"My mind is fine but I smoked too much," he said in answer to this look. "It was my one weakness, but it's a big one now come home to roost. That and the beginnings of Parkinson's." He held out his hand and she saw it quivering slightly.

"I'm sorry."

"At my age it's not unexpected. At some point my mind will go, and that will be that."

"I hope I can handle all that as well as you can when my time comes."

"I hope you can, too. You remember how you were, and it's…not easy."

"I'm sure."

"You're not police or you would have flashed your badge. What's your interest?"

She took out her ProEye credentials.

He inspected them and nodded. "Good firm. You were a worthy competitor to my old shop, Kroll."

"Thanks. It was rumored that Langhorne got away with a great deal of the mob's money. He paid cash for the estate to the tune of five million. But word is there was more, a lot more. And if he invested it over the last thirty years or so, the sums would be far larger."

"And you're trying to claw these assets back for clients of ProEye? Who exactly would that be?"

"Confidentiality bars me from telling you. I'm sure you can understand."

There was a twinkle in his eye now that she didn't particularly get.

"Oh, I know confidentiality rules better than most. You can't be working on behalf of the descendants of mobsters. ProEye is a legit outfit, so they wouldn't have accepted a client seeking to get back ill-gotten gains. So I wonder who the client is?"

"Without giving away too much, perhaps those from whom the mob money was originally taken?"

"That would be a lot of people and entities."

"Yes it would."

"And what do you want with me?"

She began the spiel she had practiced on the drive over. "We found out about some of Daniel Pottinger's business associates. They would be prime suspects in his murder. The fact is Harry Langhorne kept right on being a criminal in the persona of Daniel Pottinger. He was operating on a large scale; his list of known criminal endeavors stretches the globe and goes deep into some of the vilest stuff on earth. And he partnered with some people who had the wherewithal to play in that sandbox."

Gibson stopped talking and just looked at him. Her heart went out to the man when his broad shoulders slumped and his handsome face collapsed and his breathing accelerated slightly.

"I guess that explains why you're here, then," he said without much behind it.

"And please believe me that I would not bother you with this if I had any other viable leads."

He looked her over once more. "Not to sound sexist or misogynistic, though my generation is guilty of that generally, you don't strike me as the type to be hunting down the likes of my *son*."

Gibson thought of her mommy van outside with the two kiddy car seats inside. "Maybe that's my superpower," she said. "Everyone underestimates me to the point that I'm ignored when I shouldn't be."

He now looked at her with fresh respect. "I can see that. We had some female agents during my tenure that fit that description precisely. Other agents would tell them to get coffee. The next week they'd trump the same guys on a big bust. They just worked harder."

"There you go."

"But even so, you never said what you want from me."

"Whatever you have on your son and his possible dealings with Harry Langhorne aka Daniel Pottinger."

"I've been out of the game a long time."

She glanced at his computer screen. "When I came in you were on a site that I use to track stolen assets. On the dark web."

She eyed the open journal next to the computer. "And it doesn't look to be just for fun."

He glanced down at his journal. "It keeps my mind active."

"Other people do Sudoku and Wordle to keep their brains sharp. You hunt criminals."

"Don't get carried away. I just mess around to keep busy. People here play bridge endlessly. I hate card games."

She looked around. "You also have no ego wall. Diplomas, commendations, awards, photos of you shaking hands with presidents. Nothing to show what you used to do. And I know you have all of those things to show off because I researched you before coming here. You have every award the FBI gives out, plus a slew of other ones from the federal government in general, and five other countries with which you worked on complex multijurisdictional investigations. France and the UK made you an honorary member of the DGSE and MI6, respectively. You're on the Wall of Fame at Interpol. Four presidents called you to the White House to take a picture for a job well done. But you choose not to display any of that. Now, that doesn't strike me as a man in retirement looking to the past. It smacks of a person still very much engaged and looking ahead, despite some age-related infirmities."

He sat back, drumming his fingers on the arm of his chair. "How much time do you have?"

"All the time *you* need, Mr. Trask."

CHAPTER

34

THE SIGHT OUT OF THE United Airlines jet window was a beautiful, soothing landscape with clusters of homes, some quite large in scope and ambition, but most were small, dulled jewels in a less luxurious chain. And then there were the farms situated along the legendary rolling Virginia hills. There seemed a peace and serenity to all of it.

Clarisse imagined real estate companies would use a drone to film it all and then put these images in their brochures to sell a dream that was only just a dream.

She turned away because the sight—and not the turbulence they were encountering—was making her sick to her stomach.

Dulles International Airport loomed in front of them and the jet touched down and finally slowed. She retrieved her suitcase from baggage claim, confident in her new identity pack: driver's license, passport, and credit cards; she even had Global Entry based on an interview that had never happened, but a computer only spit out what was put into it. All professionally done and paid for. Easy if you knew where to get such things.

She rented a car, a neat little white convertible, and headed out. She had researched The Plains. It was rural and equal parts poor and chic. But not too many inhabitants. She would be noticed. She did not want to be noticed, at least not right now. But she had no choice.

There was money in the surrounding countryside, some of

which she had seen from the air. She had read that Jacqueline Mars, of the Mars candy company, lived in The Plains. She was worth about $40 billion, she had heard, all from making people fat, diabetic, and dead prematurely.

But the town itself was strictly working-class. In May well over fifty thousand people came out to attend the Gold Cup steeplechase here. She imagined the local businesses prospered greatly during that time. Some of the outside dollars would stick here for a bit, like slick leaves on cracked pavement.

She drove slowly past the small pile of clapboard and shingles that Daryl Oxblood called home. It was a cracker box with a failing foundation, an adjacent lean-to where a dirty tan Ford F-150 sat, and a picket fence that was no longer white and no longer all standing up. Except for the truck, the place looked deserted. There was no smoke coming from the brick chimney, though the day was cold and windy. No lights on that she could see. The fenced-in paddock was empty.

As she gazed around she noted there were four homes on this short dead-end street, one next to Oxblood's and two across the narrow, disintegrating macadam. Smoke was curling up from the chimney top of one of them while the other sat silent and dark. The home next to Oxblood's had a Range Rover from the 1980s parked out front and a muddy ATV parked next to a tree. A horse whinnied from behind the structure. A crow flapped its wings and lifted off from the branches of a sprawling southern magnolia set in the front yard and taking up far too much space.

Clarisse parked her car and got out. She was dressed casually in jeans and low boots and a fleece-lined jacket. Her bag was slung over her shoulder. Inside the bag was a cylinder of potent pepper spray that she'd had in her checked bag. She never went anywhere without it. Because you just never knew who you might run into who would require an eyeful of it.

From her bag she pulled out an iPad. An element of cover but also a useful tool if need be. She slipped on fur-lined leather gloves. She stood next to her car and checked out the four houses: Oxblood's and the other three.

She headed up to Oxblood's place, approaching from the rear. She knocked but there was no answer. She peered in one of the windows and saw a dingy interior with furnishings that looked like carryovers from several generations back. She knocked on the front door and got the same result. There was a decrepit John Deere tractor parked right behind the house. It looked like it hadn't been touched in years.

She headed to the house next door. There was permanence there, she concluded, not a trap.

I hope.

35

THE WOMAN WHO ANSWERED HER knock was in her late sixties and looked like she had spent most of her life outdoors doing things that required a lot of physical labor and determination. Her frame was blocky and strong. She had on faded jeans encasing thick legs, dirty muck boots, and a light blue cotton sweater with several holes in it. A pair of leather work gloves stuck out of her front jeans pocket. Her white hair was pulled back in a tight knot. Her face was lined and absent of any artificial coloring.

"Yes?" the woman said, her voice as husky as she appeared.

Clarisse held up her iPad. "Hello, I'm here taking surveys of certain people for my company. My information tells me that Daryl Oxblood lives in the house next door. We were supposed to meet today, right now in fact, but I knocked and no one answered."

"What company?"

"Online marketing."

"I doubt Daryl owns a computer. It's not really his thing."

Without missing a beat Clarisse said, "That's why I was sent out, to meet with people like that. They have no online presence and that's in line with the audience we want to survey." She glanced over the woman's shoulder and saw the desktop unit on a farm table in the small kitchen visible from where she was standing. "I take it you don't suffer from that affliction."

The woman said, "I suffer from *an* affliction. It's called having to spend too much damn time on my computer. Whatever happened to a phone call or meeting someone for real?"

"I sympathize. I've been trying to get my own screen time down from a ridiculously high level. But Mr. Oxblood doesn't indulge, which is why we so wanted to talk to him."

The woman now looked over *her* shoulder at Oxblood's place. "His truck is there, which means he should be, too. It's the only vehicle he has."

"And he lives alone?" She glanced at her iPad screen, which was blank. "At least that's what our records show."

"That's right. His ma died, oh, four years ago. Daryl's never been much of an outside guy, if you know what I mean. He would have never left the house if his mother hadn't made him go out and get a job. Just sit in his room and do God knows what."

"What exactly does he do?"

"He's actually good with anything mechanical. And there's a lot of stuff around here, farm equipment mostly, that constantly needs fixing."

"I saw the John Deere tractor in his backyard. It looks like it needs a lot of work."

The woman smiled. "I guess it's 'do as I say, not as I do' with old Daryl. He makes all our stuff run good and doesn't lift a finger for his own."

Clarisse had frozen for a moment on the woman's first words. The same tagline in the secret room where Harry Langhorne had died.

"If he's an introvert he might not want to open the door to a stranger."

"You said you had an appointment with him?" the woman asked.

"Yes, but he doesn't know what I look like. I called out and said who I was and why I was here, but no one responded."

"Now that *is* strange."

"Maybe if you…"

The woman stepped out, and Clarisse followed her over to

Oxblood's. The woman knocked hard on the door. "Daryl, it's Barbara. You okay? There's a lady here you have an appointment with. Daryl!"

No sound came from within. Barbara looked at her. "Okay, now I'm getting a little worried."

"What should we do?"

"I think we're justified in going in and seeing if he's okay."

"Maybe we should call the police."

"Hell, the county sheriff's department's the law around here and they got a lot of ground to cover. So by the time they showed up we could have taken Daryl to the hospital, if he's fallen and hurt himself."

"Okay, but how do we get in?"

Barbara scooted back to her house and came back waving a key. "He has one for my place if something happens to me, too. Way it is out here."

"I'm sure."

Barbara unlocked the door, and they walked into a house that was filled with junk and clutter.

"He really let the place go after his ma died. He makes decent money, but Daryl has never been much of a housekeeper. Hell, neither am I."

"I'm sure," Clarisse said, her gaze roaming around the small space. "Maybe upstairs?"

There were ten steps up, and on the fifth one Clarisse reached into her bag and gripped the pepper spray. On the ninth step her hearing was as concentrated as was possible.

When they reached the second floor Barbara turned right.

"He's usually up here reading comic books and such. His ma used to complain."

"And his father?"

"Never knew him. He died before they moved here."

"How long have the Oxbloods lived here?"

"Nearly twenty years. I'm born and bred."

Barbara knocked on the door and got no answer. "Daryl, if you're in there, say something or we're coming in." She looked back at Clarisse and shrugged. "He's overweight and has diabetes and he's not good about taking his insulin. He's not that old, around forty, but maybe a heart attack?"

"One way to find out."

Barbara gripped the doorknob as Clarisse got ready to deploy her pepper spray. She didn't expect to find her adversary inside, but stranger things had happened to her.

The door opened and Barbara stepped through.

"Oh my God," she cried out.

Clarisse pushed past her and looked at the bed.

The dried, congealed blood was everywhere, and the assailant long gone.

She made a sweep of the room and then stepped closer to the corpse on the bed, avoiding the spots of blood on the wooden planks.

"Is this Daryl?" she asked.

Barbara hung back by the door. "Y-yes. All that blood. What the hell happened? Did he have some sort of accident?"

She looked at the cut that ran from one earlobe to the other.

"I think you should call the sheriff's department."

"And tell them what?"

"That a man has been murdered."

"Murdered! Here?"

Clarisse turned back to look at Barbara. "Go do it now," she said in a strained voice.

Barbara turned and clattered back down the stairs. She could hear the older woman bouncing off the walls in her haste.

She bent down and scrutinized the dead man's face and then recoiled in horror.

No way. It cannot be. Please.

She stepped back and glanced at the man's arm. She edged the sleeve up to the elbow and then slowly turned the arm toward her so she could see the inside of the forearm.

She saw what she needed to see and pulled the sleeve down and put the arm back.

It was a tat of Superman's insignia.

Shit.

Unfortunately for Clarisse, she had chosen burgundy gloves to wear today. And thus she didn't notice the small bit of congealed blood that had leached onto one of her fingertips.

Clarisse stepped away and looked at the shelves lining one wall. They were filled with comic books. She rushed over and then stopped and stared at the one on top of a large pile. It was, she knew, a copy of a special edition Superman comic. But was it *that* one? She opened the cover and looked on the first page.

The initials *BD* and *RE* housed inside a drawn-in heart.

She thrust the comic back, her panic rising. Now she had something else to look for, and she needed to do it quickly.

She rushed across to the opposite room she had noticed when they had reached the second floor. Clarisse pushed the door open using her gloved hand. It was a small room that was obviously used for storage. Boxes and old bed frames and the clutter and castoffs of seemingly several lifetimes were piled in here.

Her sweeping gaze stopped at the far wall. And there it was. She lifted her iPad and took a picture of what was written on the wall in black Magic Marker.

DO AS I SAY, NOT AS I DO.

She didn't want this found. She pulled a pen out of her bag and had started to mark through the words when she heard Barbara on the stairs. She quickly put her pen away as Barbara appeared in the doorway.

"They're on their way." She looked at the message on the wall. "Oh my God, what does that mean?"

"I don't know. The police will have to figure it out. And I have to be going."

"What! Aren't you going to wait for the cops?"

"Look, I came out here because it was part of my job. I don't know anyone here. I certainly didn't know Daryl Oxblood. You'll be able to tell the police a lot more than I ever could. And while I don't want to sound heartless, I have twenty more people to survey before the day is out, and they live all over."

Barbara glanced at the message and shrugged. "Well, all right, I guess. But I'm not staying in the house alone."

"You can wait for them outside."

They walked down the steps and out into the yard.

"Oh, what's your name, in case the police ask?" said Barbara.

"Julia Frazier. Good luck. And I'm very sorry about what happened to your friend."

"Well, we were more neighbors than friends. His mother was my friend, though. I bet it's drugs. That opioid stuff. Maybe he owed money or something and they came and did that to him when he couldn't pay. Bastards."

"You're probably right."

Barbara went back over to her house while Clarisse hustled to her car. She reached the main road and turned left. A few seconds later she saw two sheriff's cruisers in her rearview mirror. Sirens blaring and lights swirling, they turned down the road where there was a dead man waiting and disappeared from sight.

A few moments later, so did Clarisse.

CHAPTER

36

Clarisse sat in the airline's first-class lounge at Dulles. She had had a return ticket to her previous location but had opted to take a flight to New York instead. She had changed her appearance in the bathroom stall. Clarisse was a redhead now and her clothes were far more businesslike. Her delicately applied makeup had softened her previous harder edges. The lipstick was muted, the eyeliner the same. She could be going to close a big deal or coming back from doing so. And in a way she was.

Do as I say, not as I do. She had seen that phrase twice now. They had anticipated her drilling down to the theft of Daryl Oxblood's identity to rent the car and get the credit card. But the truth was they did not have to kill him. They didn't have to do anything to him. The fact that they had brutally murdered a man for no reason at all had changed the equation of all of this for her.

But there was a reason. I know who Daryl Oxblood was. And they know who Oxblood was. He was the BD in the heart drawn in the Superman comic book, a comic book that he had proudly shown me over twenty years ago.

They had found him, used his identity to rent the car, and killed him in the process, apparently just for the hell of it.

She sat back in her comfortable chair, not feeling comfortable at all. She sipped on flavored seltzer water and munched on a sesame seed cracker topped with Gruyère cheese.

She gazed around the room where well-to-do people lounged while waiting for their flights.

So many marks, so little time.

But that would have to wait. And truth be known, her heart was no longer in it. At least not right now.

They had killed before, she knew that: Daniel Pottinger aka Harry Langhorne. They had used a nasty poison and watched him croak. But there had been a good reason for killing him, at least to her mind. But Daryl Oxblood, not so much.

Which means things have changed and so have they.

She boarded the flight to New York and an hour later looked down upon the delicate spires of the city right before they landed at LaGuardia. She deplaned and took a cab to her hotel. She had made her reservation online from the airline lounge at Dulles. During the drive she scoured her phone for news of the very recent murder in rural Virginia, but found nothing yet. It might take a while out there, she assumed.

She got to her hotel, a chic boutique in SoHo that charged more than it should, but she liked it because no one looked you in the eye, except for the front desk people and they only did so once. It was an organization that understood privacy and boundaries, and right now she was feeling exposed and thus welcomed both.

She took a hot shower, then lay wrapped in a luxurious towel on her immensely comfortable four-poster bed staring at the ceiling, which was done in a quiet gray silk damask. In the very center was a three-bulbed chandelier that looked so modern that it, counter-intuitively, seemed rooted in a distant past.

Three bulbs, three players in this little drama, if I don't count Mickey Gibson, but I probably should. She's more than a pawn. She's at a rook or knight level now, and maturing fast. Hopefully. Because when I beat her I want to beat her at the woman's absolute best.

She dressed in jeans and a T-shirt, ordered room service, and sat down to eat thirty minutes later. She had indulged with some steak and potatoes and a glass of cabernet, when she usually didn't eat meat or many carbs and she kept her alcoholic intake to a minimum, mostly because of the example of Mommy. And she had never put a cigarette in her mouth or *voluntarily* done drugs for the very same reason. Mommy was a poster child for the consequences of shitty life choices.

After her meal was done she slid out her computer, set her notebook next to that, pulled out her burner phone, and placed it on the other side of the computer. Then Clarisse drew a long breath while complicated thoughts flooded her mind.

Focus! This is no way to play for real and for keeps. We're not kids, not now.

She flushed her brain, took a sip of the red wine, and hit the number.

"I assume the kids are in bed," she said when the other person answered.

Gibson said, "They are. For now."

"What do you have to report?"

"I spoke with Sam Trask."

"Did you now? Congratulations."

"You can keep the snark to yourself, Clarisse. I'm not in the mood."

"What did he tell you?"

"Basically that his son *is* capable of all the things I told him were going on with Pottinger/Langhorne."

"Let's just call him Harry for simplicity and consistency," interjected Clarisse.

"All right," said Gibson. "Nathan Trask is involved in all sorts of illegal things, but the cops can't prove them. He's had people killed, including maybe Harry, but again there's no proof of that. And why would he write 'Do as I say, not as I do' on the wall of the room where he was found?"

"Did you ask Trask about that?"

"Did you want me to?"

"I wanted you to go with your gut. So what did your gut tell you to do?"

"My gut told me not to ask him because I don't think Nathan Trask was involved in Harry's death."

"Based solely on your gut?"

"Not solely, no."

"What then?"

"I did some research on Trask. Even though they couldn't make anything stick he was clearly old-school when it came to snuffing out people he wanted snuffed out. Two shots to the head. But Langhorne was killed by poisoning, Botulinum type A, which takes a while and is incredibly painful. Things could happen in the interim, all of them bad, for Trask."

"Maybe he wanted him to feel the pain. Two head shots wouldn't do that."

"Maybe. But Harry was already terminal with brain cancer, for which he was on morphine."

"Really?" said a stunned Clarisse.

"Yes. The post on his body revealed that. And the writing on the wall? It was done by two people, so how does that make sense in the context of Nathan Trask? There's no way he personally offed Harry. He would never have been near the place. So why would he have his execution team write that?"

"How do you know two people wrote the message?"

"Among other things, I used to analyze handwriting for a living when I was a forensics tech. And I do it today working for ProEye."

"Did you tell the cops that?"

"So what if I did?"

"So you're ruling Trask out, just like that?"

"I think Trask was busywork for me for some reason," said Gibson.

"Meaning I gave you an assignment that I knew was pointless?"

"I don't know—did you?"

She's gaining confidence, which is good and bad.

Clarisse said, "I don't really see the *point* of that, do you? How did you leave it with Sam Trask?"

"He gave me a secure email to communicate with him. He said he wouldn't be surprised if his son had paid off people at The Feathers to keep watch over him."

"What does Sam hope to achieve?"

"He's still working, as you alluded to. I don't mean for a company. I mean, he's working the case against his son by himself. He showed me some of the research and leads he'd run down, all from his little retirement room. He even hired a cab to drive him by his son's fortress in Virginia Beach. He wanted to see it for himself. As added incentive to nail this guy."

"Did he ask you to help him?"

"Let's just say we talked about mutually beneficial action we could take."

"Did you tell him about me?"

"No. But I did tell him about the situation. He remembered Harry. Has no idea what happened to him or his family after WITSEC. He was intrigued about a possible connection between Harry and his son. He's a formidable guy, even with an oxygen tank. We agreed to keep each other informed."

"You took a big risk going to see him. His son probably knows all about you by now."

"You basically told me I had to go see him."

"Do you really do everything you're told, Mickey?" she said condescendingly.

Shit, why did you say that?

All Clarisse heard now was…nothing.

Do not lose your control. You own this. Now really own it by doing what any decent human being would do. So pretend you are a decent person for once in your life.

"I'm sorry, Mickey. This is on me. I had a preconceived notion that Trask was involved. The other guys on that list, you're right, they were white noise. Why I did that, I don't know. Sometimes I'm too clever for my own good. Now, Trask was the only player who could do all the dances with Harry *and* also have a motive to take him out. But I agree with you—if the writing on the wall was done by two people, it does not make sense that Trask was involved. And the poison instead of the bullets? Same thing. Okay? So again, I'm sorry if I was pulling your chain a bit. I really do want to get through this intact, and want the same for you."

You're rambling, and rambling is always weak, so shut up.

She caught herself breathing fast. Clarisse put herself on mute as she waited for Gibson to answer.

Come on, come on, come on…Just say something so I can spin it.

Only Mickey Gibson didn't answer. She ended the call.

37

GIBSON POCKETED HER PHONE AND walked out of her home office. She headed to her kids' room, where she opened the door and peered in.

Dead asleep. Both of them.

No, don't use that phrase, ever. Not with them.

She used her phone to take a picture of the pair that she would no doubt look at when she was an elderly woman and wanted to relive the good old days.

Gibson went downstairs and made herself a cup of tea. She drank it while staring out the picture window at her scraggly front yard. She'd planned to redo the flower beds and fill up some pots with colorful plants for the porch.

Yeah. Until she *came into my life. Do I do everything someone tells me to do? You don't know a fucking thing about me, even though you think you know everything.*

The picture window seemed a nice viewpoint to run the frames of her life—past, present, and whatever future was hanging out there for her, bleak or shiny.

And my kids' future, because they are the biggest factor in all of this.

And then she saw the darkness out there that seemed more than just what it was supposed to be. There was a solid shape to it. She ducked out of sight and then came back over to the window and peered out. Just across the street, behind a parked car. There was someone there. Someone staring at her house.

She looked down when her phone buzzed. Her father had just texted her with a name and phone number.

Art Collin is going to call you right now. Answer it. Dad

She looked back up and gasped. Whoever had been there was now gone. She rushed to the door and opened it, leapt out onto the porch, and gazed up and down the street. Breathing heavily, she shut and locked the door.

That was not my imagination. Someone was there.

A few seconds later her phone buzzed again. She saw on the screen that it was the phone number her father had just texted her.

"Hello, Mr. Collin?"

"Just make it Art," said a loud, gruff voice. "Knew your old man from way back. Says you're interested in Harry Langhorne. When Rick Rogers needs a favor I step up. He's a good guy. So here I am."

Well, Art doesn't waste any time.

As if in answer to her thoughts he said, "I gotta make this snappy. I live in Florida. Got plans. Cards, cocktails, and then me and my lady friend are going out to have a little fun."

Gibson checked her watch and saw that it was nearly nine o'clock. And he had cards, cocktails, *and* a lady friend still to come? He obviously stayed up way past her bedtime. This blew her whole image of Florida retirees eating the blue plate special for dinner at five p.m. and going beddy-bye at eight.

"Okay, I'll try to make it *snappy*. How did you know about Langhorne?"

"I was a detective in Newark. I worked the case. Slimeballs all around. Langhorne maybe the slimiest of all. But he walked; the others got iron bars and strip searches till kingdom come."

"Did you know Langhorne?"

"I was actually the one who turned him to our side."

Gibson tensed. "You did? How?"

"With my natural grace and charm, can't you tell? Seriously, my old man was a bean counter, too. I knew how those guys ticked, so I started watching Harry, taking pictures, recording phone calls, the works. Oh, I had warrants for everything. I'm not getting tripped up over that penny-ante shit. It wasn't easy, but we finally got the goods on him. Then we had him tied up in a neat little basket and he would be going up the river for a long time. And he probably wouldn't make it back down if he wouldn't agree to come over to our side. They eat dorks like Harry for breakfast, lunch, and dinner inside prison. So I met up with him one fine morning, showed him my hand, and gave him a choice. And he decided to save his own ass. What a shock."

"But he was never arrested, or charged. And he didn't testify at the trials."

"That was part of the deal. He pointed us to where all the goods were, got us the docs, signed, sealed, and delivered. He was one detail-oriented prick. He even had this substitution cipher or code or whatever you want to call it for the accounting books he kept. Without him we never could have figured out what was really going on. Based on that we got a bunch of the low-hanging fruit dead to rights and they all turned on the higher-ups, just like those scared little shits always do. It was their testimony, along with all the docs, that put the nails in the coffins. And three of those suckers ended up dead for their troubles, but it was Harry who put it all in motion. He didn't want to appear in court and say one word under oath because there would have been twenty hits out on the guy before he got down off the stand."

"But regardless of that the mob had to figure out that he had crossed them. Otherwise, he would have been indicted, too. Or called as a witness."

"Oh, they did. That was why all the man wanted to do was disappear."

"With his family, you mean."

Collin chortled. "If Harry Langhorne could have figured out a way he would have left his wife and two kiddies high and dry. But he couldn't, so he didn't. Heard they went into WITSEC."

"Harry Langhorne was found murdered recently at an old estate in Virginia. He was using the alias Daniel Pottinger."

"So your father told me. Well, it's not like he didn't deserve it. What goes around comes around. And shit stinks forever, especially shit like him. Sure, he was the bean counter, but he knew what was going on. Where all the bodies were buried, and I mean literally. He was like Robert Duvall playing the consigliere in *The Godfather*, only Duvall's character had some principles. Harry Langhorne had zip. Now, that don't sit well with me. But you got to take your shots where you can, and Harry was my one shot at taking the kingpins down. So you let scum go to get bigger and more dangerous scum."

"Any theories on who might have killed him?"

"The guys he helped put away are either dead or still in prison with long gray beards."

"Their children?" suggested Gibson.

"Could be. But my experience is that the stuff you see in the mob movies about family loyalty is mostly horseshit. The young bulls probably were thrilled to see their fathers go down. Now they were the capos and they all had their own problems rebuilding the family empires. I don't see them going out on a limb avenging anybody. Too much trouble and risk."

"Now, that's very interesting and it does make sense. So the question becomes, who did benefit from Harry going down all these years later?" asked Gibson.

"Was Geraldine with him when he got deep-sixed?"

"No. Harry walked away from WITSEC about two decades ago. His wife disappeared shortly thereafter, but we don't know if they hooked up later by plan, or whether she disappeared on her own, or—"

"—or whether someone popped her," Collin interjected. "Which

I think is more likely. I always had the distinct feeling Harry hated his wife. And she didn't make it easy to love her. I had limited interaction with Geraldine, but back then she was always drunk and/or doped up."

"I understand that Langhorne might have made off with a mountain of mob money."

"That was definitely a rumor."

"You didn't run that down?" asked Gibson.

"Wasn't my job. My job was to nail and then turn Harry to get the big boys, which I did."

"The place where he was killed? He paid five mill in cash for it."

Collin whistled. "So the rumor just went to fact. He *did* take the cash."

"I'm thinking there's a lot more than five mill lying around after all this time."

"Any idea where it could be?"

"No, but I think people are looking for it," replied Gibson. *Like Clarisse.*

"And what happened to the kids?" Collin asked.

"As soon as Francine hit eighteen they both voluntarily left WITSEC."

"They were only little kids when I knew them, but they were an odd pair even then."

"One of the WITSEC marshals told me that Doug was totally hamstrung by his father, never allowed to play any sports, and he sat in the garage lifting weights and brooding."

"And the girl?" said Collin.

"Had her own run-ins with her father. Maybe even more bitter and lasting. The marshal said that Doug basically took orders from his sister."

"Okay, that makes sense."

"What do you mean it makes sense?" said Gibson.

"As I mentioned, even back then they were an odd pair. I didn't get to really know them all that well. They were kids and my business was with Harry. Now, I'm no shrink, but my opinion is that whole household was royally screwed up. Harry was the king and taskmaster, and he relished that role. Geraldine drank and popped pills, and when it came to Harry she had a spine like jelly. The kids were silent and staring and maybe thinking shit I don't even want to contemplate. You ever see that flick *Children of the Corn*? It's based on a Stephen King story."

"No."

"Hell, it probably came out before you were born. Anyway, it was this perverted religious cult of kids from the cornfields who murdered all the adults to ensure a good harvest. Bloody and sadistic as hell, at least by the standards back then. But the kids in that movie? The ringleaders Malachai and Isaac? Well, let's just say Francine and Dougie would've fit right in. Hell, she'd be ruling the roost, handing out death sentences, and Dougie would be her enforcer. And I got that impression when they were little kids!"

"So a formidable pair, then?" said Gibson.

"Let's just say that I wouldn't want to run into them now in a well-lighted shopping center with a million people around. And, shit, I worked undercover for five years in the human garbage dumps of *Trenton*. I was with the Newark police force, you understand, but they recruited me for an undercover post in Trenton because I wasn't known in the area as a cop. Now, some people are just born evil and some people are made evil by a shitty life. I've seen both types. And my opinion is Francine and Dougie aren't one or the other, they're both."

"So maybe Geraldine didn't vanish voluntarily."

"Maybe not. And you think the kids finally caught up with the old man?" said Collin.

"I'm thinking that's likelier than not."

"One more thing."

"Yeah?" said Gibson.

"I know I just laid out my thoughts on the kids, you know, born evil?"

"Right."

"But there was something else. And I might walk back the born-evil spiel I just gave you. I could never prove anything, but I got the definite cop gut feeling."

"About what?" said Gibson.

"Harry Langhorne was one sick son of a bitch. He was the furthest thing from a mild-mannered accountant as you could get."

"What are you trying to say?"

"Despite her sullen nature Francine was a real cute girl."

"Can you just spit it out, Art?"

"I saw how Harry was around the girl. Let's just say he acted in ways toward Francine that no father should ever act around his daughter."

"Wait, are you saying he sexually abused her?"

"I have no proof, but if you want a veteran cop's take, yeah, that's what I'm saying."

"Jesus."

"Some maggots like them that age. And no telling what sort of shit he did to his son. So maybe they weren't born evil. Maybe Harry made them that way."

Gibson's thoughts went to her own kids. *If anyone ever so much as—*

"So is your job to track them down?" asked Collin.

Gibson refocused. "It might come to that."

"Well, let me give you a piece of advice."

"Okay."

"Shoot first and don't ask questions later. Now I got to go, my lady friend is giving me the evil eye. Good luck."

"Yeah, thanks, Art. I really appreciate the info," she said as her heart settled into her feet.

She clicked off, drank her tea, and looked out the picture window again.

People watching the place.

Francine and Doug Langhorne, apparently sociopaths on another level.

But Francine and Doug perhaps abused by their father in horrific ways. That would shatter any level of trust a person could have. It could make you into something less than human.

Am I already in the well-lighted shopping mall with twin monsters?

Gibson saw one terrifying scenario after another march across the breadth of that picture window. She finally looked up to the room where her kids were sleeping peacefully, oblivious to all the danger their mother might have exposed them to.

She closed her eyes as the panic rose in her.

What the hell have I done?

38

AFTER A MOSTLY SLEEPLESS NIGHT, Gibson woke early, got the kids up and fed, and then called her dad. She had decided that she could either assume the fetal position and wait for bad things to happen to her and her family, or she could use her skills and her brains and her work ethic to get ahead of the tidal wave she felt coming at her. And Silva had called the night before. She had taken ill and would not be coming over.

"Yeah, Dad, if you and Mom could watch the kids for a few hours, that would be great."

"Sure we can, honey, but where are you going?"

"Just to run some errands."

"You haven't gotten any better at lying to me since you were fifteen and said someone snuck that gin into your water bottle and those joints into your backpack."

"Okay, okay, I'm just running down a few leads."

"Harry Langhorne leads?"

"What else."

"My buddy Art any help?"

"Oh, yeah, he was. Thanks for setting that up."

"He's apparently doing okay."

"Sounds like he's doing *very* okay. Hey, Dad, what do you know about a guy named Nathan Trask?"

He didn't answer for such a long time she thought the connection had ended.

"Please, God, don't tell me you're getting mixed up with *that* guy."

"No, I'm not. I swear. But what can you tell me about him?"

"He's scum. Richer than God, and twice as evil as the Devil. And smarter than Einstein because not even the Feds have ever managed to lay an indictment on him. He's got this fortress down in Virginia Beach."

"Oh really? Didn't know that," she lied, hopefully better this time.

"How does he figure in things?"

"I was told that Langhorne might have had dealings with him, but I think that was just bullshit."

"Well, don't you go poking around that guy, Mick. You will not be coming back."

"Amazing how a scum like that gets to walk around free while some poor sap cracks the skull of his friend in a drunken argument and gets twenty years in prison."

"This is America. Poor and stupid go to prison while money walks. We'll be over around eleven thirty if that works. Your mother's getting her hair de-grayed at nine."

"'De-grayed'? I hope to God you've never used that term in front of her."

She could imagine her father's shit-eating grin over the phone connection.

"I'm still alive and kicking, ain't I?"

* * *

When her parents arrived, Gibson's father went for Darby, swooping her around in the air and making silly noises, while her mother automatically brushed Tommy's hair out of his eyes and straightened his shirt and wiped off his dirty chin with a Kleenex and sanitizer.

Mars versus Venus, thought Gibson.

Her father finally set Darby down and looked at his daughter, while she stared resolutely back at him.

Rick Rogers was built like a tank, and as a cop he had the rep of being firm but fair. He knew what living paycheck to paycheck was like, and what that sort of stress made people do.

"You got scum everywhere, but you don't know anybody till you've walked in their shoes. And a hungry belly or a sick kid or losing the roof over your head, or being the wrong color and having to live your life with that unfairly hanging over your head every damn day, can make bad things happen to good people, Mick. It doesn't mean the law won't be enforced. It just means they're human beings who you know very little about. You ever lose that bit of truth, go do something else for a living."

And she had never lost that sense of truth. If anything it had been more forcefully thrust upon her, since, at ProEye, she spent most of her time chasing folks with far too much money who not only didn't want to pay their fair share, they didn't want to pay anything because they thought they were above it all.

"Well?" he said to his daughter. His wife was now smoothing down Tommy's cowlicks as the boy gamely fought back.

"Well what?"

"You *know* what. You want to go somewhere and talk about this?"

"No. But when I get back we can talk, if you want."

"How about I go with you wherever it is you're going?"

She looked at his waistband that was hidden by his jacket and arched her eyebrows.

"I'm not packing," he said in a low voice, casting an anxious glance at his wife. She was now trying to corral Tommy, who was clearly done with her attempts to clean up his appearance.

"Then what good are you?" she replied.

"You really are a piece of work," her father said, but he tacked on a grin.

"I'll be back in a few hours."

"Call if you need help, okay?" he said, no longer grinning.

"You're first on my speed dial, Dad, always have been, always will be."

His smile came back with extra force.

She snagged her keys, hugged her kids, and drove off in her mommy van.

CHAPTER

39

STORMFIELD LOOKED AS DREARY AND intimidating as ever.

Gibson pulled to a stop and got out. No police presence at all. A storm was coming in off the bay. The temperature was already starting to drop, and she tugged her jacket closer around her.

Unlike her father, she *was* packing, the Beretta riding snugly in her belt clip holster.

She bypassed the house for now and headed to the dock. She didn't know if the cops had searched down here but she assumed they hadn't.

She walked out onto the dock and ventured to the stern of the boat. She climbed on the rear teak deck pad and managed to duck under the cover and slide in on her belly through the walkway into the boat. It was dark enough under the cover and the cloudy skies that she had to pull a flashlight out and sweep it around in order to see. It smelled musty and her nostrils crinkled. She sat on her haunches next to the telescopic poles holding up the heavy winter cover and looked around. She didn't know what she was looking for, but that was usually the case when she started on a search.

There were lots of compartments on the boat in which to secrete things, some obvious, others not. She had looked at the plans for dozens of yachts that debtors had tried to hide from their creditors. New names, new flag registrations, new paint colors, but you couldn't really change the superstructure of the thing. That was like a fingerprint.

She made a careful search from bow to stern. The luxurious interior had pretty much every bell and whistle Formula offered. Gibson didn't care about that. She focused on the fact that she had found exactly one thing of interest.

It was a note inked on the bottom of a fender in the forward storage hatch.

Look harder. It's worth it.

Okay, that was something. She thought more about Harry Langhorne. The guy, by all accounts, was an asshole, a bully, spiteful, vindictive, manipulative, and cruel and maybe a pedophile on top. And he was also terminally ill with brain cancer. She could imagine him seeing this as a game, his last chance to screw with the world.

Gibson crawled back out to find that it was now raining. She hustled through the storm to the front door of the house to find it locked, and the key no longer under the cat statue. She pulled out her pick kit and defeated this obstacle quickly. As she went inside a crack of thunder made her jump.

She took out her iPad and went through all the photos and video she had taken before. Paintings, sculptures, some furniture, and rugs. She had logged all that inventory and gone online to get prices for them. She figured it was nowhere near enough to constitute the man's stolen mob treasure.

She might have thought that he had sunk all his money into Stormfield. After all, five million bucks would have been big money back in the nineties. But she didn't think that was it. The note confirmed this.

Look harder. It's worth it.

So if his killers were Francine and Doug, had their father told them anything? If the treasure was in some bank account or safe-deposit box, or other financial hiding place, Gibson might have a shot at tracking it down. It was what she did for a living, after all.

But Langhorne's note showed that he was well aware that people were looking for something he had. And he was egging them on, daring them to find it. Seeing if they were smarter than he was.

Am I smarter than he was?

She drifted through room after room, looking for anything that might be a clue or lead to a clue. She needed to know more about Langhorne and even more about his time as Daniel Pottinger. The first she could possibly get from Earl Beckett. The latter she might have to get from Clarisse.

If I ever call her back, and right now I'm not sure I want to.

She didn't like being shit on, not that anyone did. But she liked it even less from a person who was clearly enjoying pulling Gibson's strings.

And what is the woman's beef with me, anyway? It's not just standard manipulation technique. Something else is going on. Something personal.

She heard the noise a second later and her hand flew to her gun. She aimed the Beretta in front of her and walked toward the sound. She wanted to meet the intruder on her terms.

Gibson rounded the corner and slipped down the dark hall. The sounds were coming closer and her finger edged to the trigger.

"Shit," she exclaimed.

Virginia State Police detective Wilson Sullivan was staring at her.

"You don't seem surprised to see me here," said Gibson, putting her gun away.

He frowned and said tersely, "I'm not. I saw your van outside."

"Of course."

"But I want an answer as to what you're doing here. And I want it right now." He took a step closer. "Because the fact is, you shouldn't be here. I could arrest you for being here."

"It looked to me like you guys released the crime scene. And I thought we were working together. I was just trying to find a lead of some kind."

He studied her for an uncomfortably long moment. "And did you find a lead?"

She told him about the message she'd discovered on the boat.

"So there *is* some treasure out there that he's playing games with?"

"Sounds like it. Or he could be bullshitting everyone and there's no treasure at all."

"Which do you think it is?"

"You know as much about Harry Langhorne as I do," she said. "He's obviously a complicated guy. So I'm not sure which way to go on that question."

He nodded and looked around. "Find anything else besides the note?"

"Not yet. Still raining hard out there?" she asked, noting his wet coat and hair.

"Bucketing."

"We might want to stay inside then and go over the place."

"Treasure in plain sight, maybe?"

"Maybe. But it all depends on how you define 'plain sight.'"

"I thought you went all over with your iPad."

"I couldn't hit every room. That would have taken days. Have your people searched the whole place?"

"Yes, but they weren't looking for treasure."

"Any leads on the murder?"

He shook his head. "I have a feeling this one is going to take a while. Who's watching the kids? Your mother again?"

"Both parents."

"Shall we go room by room?" he asked.

She smiled and said, "Yes." Inside, though, she was frowning.

Ninety minutes later the rain had finally subsided and so had their search. Without result.

"If there's a treasure in here, I'm not seeing it," said Sullivan.

"What about a safe-deposit box? Bank and other financial accounts? The normal hiding places?"

"We're trying to access some of that. But we've had a hard time tracking anything down."

"He didn't bank with some local entity?"

"Not that we can find. And there were no financial records at the house, at least that we could uncover. He may have them somewhere else, but we can't even find a checkbook or a list of bills. He could be renting a storage facility somewhere, but we have no idea where it might be. But these days, you can hide stuff anywhere."

"Tell me about it," replied Gibson dryly. "But no one has come forward? Law or accounting firm? Financial advisors who worked with him?"

Sullivan shook his head. "They might have worked with him under another name and have no idea the guy's even dead."

"His murder's been in the news," she countered. "It mentioned he was killed at Stormfield. You would think his financial people would know he owned it."

"We got some names from the Turners' Realtor. Big surprise, we can't find a single one of them. It's like they ran for it."

Gibson looked around the dank interior of Stormfield. "Well, the note I found clearly shows he knew someone would be looking for something. Either he hid it somewhere, or he didn't and it's just a whole lot of nothing."

"Maybe you can work your magic and crack it. If you do, let me know."

She frowned again but wasn't facing him when she did so. "I can give it a shot. Hey, you know anything about Nathan Trask?"

Sullivan looked taken aback. "Trask? What does he have to do with anything?"

"Maybe nothing. But he's a big mover and shaker in the criminal world, though I need to watch my words or else he'll sue me for slander and probably win."

"You think he was working with Langhorne aka Pottinger?"

"He might have been."

Sullivan said, "I was told about him when I moved up from

Carolina. He has a bunch of politicians in his pocket who cover for him."

"What a world we live in."

"Isn't it though," said Sullivan, who was also now frowning as the rain picked up again.

CHAPTER

40

Clarisse had not called Gibson back, figuring it would be the height of weakness on her part to do so. She would let Gibson contact her, if she ever did.

Yet she has to, doesn't she? She can't leave it like this.

She refocused and went over the current state of affairs.

Harry Langhorne had been murdered. But he was already dying of brain cancer, which was stunning news to Clarisse. Her mother had been kidnapped. They had killed Daryl Oxblood and in doing so had also slaughtered BD.

So have they already killed Mommy?

But they wouldn't, not yet. And if they were using her as leverage, they would have to make contact again.

She would rather head them off and make contact with them. There was no real advantage in that, other than she wanted to show strength in the face of her antagonist's grab for dominance. Only the person facing her now was not so easily fooled. And Clarisse would not mention BD. She didn't want them to know that she had figured that piece out.

She pulled up the email she had received.

Hello and surprise. Took a while, but, like you, I don't give up easy. The old bitch is well and full of shit, as always. We'll need to talk about things. I'll let you know when. Get cranked and buckle up because we're taking this ride to a whole other level. It's going to be a wild one, hon.

She opened another notebook. On it Clarisse had affixed a label that read OLD SCORES TO SETTLE.

She had already written a great deal in it. Memories that might prove useful, factoids to float around in her mind. Strategies and tactics. She read through it, added a few things, and sat down to compose her reply.

Hello, right back at you. Clever girl on the jewel heist. You make a wonderful maid by the way, in a cheap sort of way. Servitude must be in your DNA. Mommy means less to me than you think so FYI leverage limited. And really, poor Daryl Oxblood whoever the hell he is? When you steal a schlep's ID you don't have to kill him on top of it. I would have thought you had more class. So the issue becomes: where do we go from here? We want the same thing, I take it. Payment in lieu of services is how I see it. Maybe you see more. I have people working on it and progress is being made. Your plan, as I see it, is to let me find it and you ransom Mommy for your share, since you didn't find it on your trip to Stormfield when you took care of HL. If I'm wrong, let me know. I have other things to do with my time. Cheers, hon.

Her finger hovered over the send key as she read and reread the missive looking for anything that shouldn't be in there. And for something that should be and wasn't.

Next moment, her finger plunged and off it went.

She wondered how long it would take for a reply. Her response might also go to spam, but they would be checking that, no doubt. She had to watch herself for sure. Langhorne's murder had been as she had expected. But the murder of Oxblood had been out-of-control bloody.

Maybe Oxblood was a message to me. If they're willing to do that to BD, what will they do to me?

She now pondered Mickey Gibson. The woman had been to Stormfield. Her geolocator on her phone had told Clarisse that. What had she discovered, if anything?

The problem was what the problem was always going to be, she knew.

If Gibson beats me to it, I need to get the treasure from her. And I will, regardless of what it will take. Or what it will cost. I will survive this, even if Mickey Gibson won't.

The thought of Gibson's possibly dying made her freeze up for a moment, which, in turn, made her furious.

Never forget, it's just you and you alone. Nobody else gives a shit and neither should you.

And now you better bring your A game, girl. Because where you're going right now? Anything less and you are dead.

41

CLARISSE HAD LIED TO GIBSON. Of course she had. It was what she did.

You simply lie to everyone about everything.

But she actually hadn't lied about Nathan Trask. The man was in the wheelhouse of everything important to her at the moment.

She had made calls. Surprisingly, her request had met with success. A meeting had been arranged. She was now out on the street, observing the man's Virginia Beach fortress.

For this meeting, she was using a different name, of course. But still, it was not without risk. Trask was smart, ruthless, not a man to be toyed with. And not a man easily scammed. And she was here to do exactly that.

She walked up to the gate where two men were stationed. They were in sharp suits, with sharp eyes and bulges under their jackets where the ubiquitous guns were kept. On the rooftop she spotted two more men in black jumpsuits. Both held long-range rifles. A third guard was manning a set of expensive optics while performing a near constant 360-degree surveillance of the area, from beach to street.

After she told them who she was and why she was here, one of the gate guards asked to see her ID. The other one patted her down and then wanded her, taking his time and missing nothing. She appreciated the professionalism. He didn't even try to cop a feel.

Clarisse had dressed carefully for the meeting. Black jacket and matching skirt. A quick blond dye job, reading glasses, muted lipstick and makeup, low heels. No bag. No phone, no wallet. They would have confiscated them anyway.

She was driven up to the main house by another man in a golf cart outfitted with gold trim. She viewed the multibuilding complex. It was mostly hidden from the street by the wall and massive landscape plantings, boulders, and other architectural features. She watched as an AgustaWestland chopper lifted off from the rear grounds, banked right, and drifted out over the ocean.

"I hope that's not Mr. Trask leaving," she said to the man next to her.

He didn't even bother to answer.

She was dropped off at the front door and it was opened by a woman dressed as a butler, right down to the starched collar and bow tie. She was about fifty, trim, and without a hair out of place; she looked pleased with her lot in life.

"This way, Ms. Peters," she said, her voice low, her gaze pointed at her well-polished shoes.

So she can have plausible deniability with the cops if I end up as a corpse somewhere, Clarisse thought.

She was led down a long plushly decorated hall, from which rooms of considerable size and luxury branched off like ribs from a spine. They came to a set of tall double doors. The butler knocked, was told to enter, and held the door open for her.

Clarisse stepped through and listened to the other woman's footsteps marching away.

The room was small and minimally furnished.

There were only two upholstered chairs with long, straight backs.

A man was sitting in one of them. He lifted a hand and pointed her to the other one.

She came forward and sat down, adjusting her glasses and taking him in.

Nathan Trask was smaller than she would have expected, since he loomed so large in life in all other ways. In her bare feet, they were about the same height, she calculated. He was fifty-one, she knew, from her research. His build was stocky but strong. His suit was tailored, but he wore it with indifference. The ring on his finger was probably worth more than the first payment she'd gotten from Senator Wright. Yet it was the only item of excess on him. His shoes were ordinary, his tie and shirt the same.

He looked back at her with unblinking eyes the color of asphalt.

Okay, that was a bit unnerving, she had to admit.

He lifted a hand. "Drink?" he asked in a raspy voice that might speak to a cold coming or going.

"No, thank you."

He nodded and let his hand fall to his lap. He never took his eyes off her. She had been told by some in the know that this would be the case. It was as though he was imprinting every bit of her onto his memory. Never a good thing with a sociopath.

And don't I know that?

"You asked to meet?" he prompted her. "You said you had some information that might be useful to me?"

She nodded. "I do."

"Normally, I would have ignored the request, and you wouldn't be sitting there. I had you checked out, of course, Ms. Peters. But it's all bullshit. *Of course.* Made up. But your background cover is good. My people couldn't punch through it and they usually can. So kudos to you. And that intrigued me enough to allow you in the door. Otherwise, it never would have happened. And I like new things, keeps me young. So impress me. Or not."

"Why let me in if you can't confirm who I am? I could be a threat."

"There are six guns pointed at you right now from inconspicuous holes in the walls. You can't see them, nor can I. But they're still there. You'll never feel a thing. At least they tell me that. I have no personal experience, you understand. But maybe you don't believe me."

On cue, she heard, one after the other, six gun slides being racked.

"Impressive," she said demurely.

"Flashy, actually, and I'm more into substance." He cleared his throat. "So, the information?"

"Daniel Pottinger?"

"Yes?"

"He's dead," said Clarisse.

"I'm aware of that."

"You did business with him."

"Did I?" asked Trask.

She sat back and allowed herself to get comfortable, fall fully into the role she was playing. You had to believe your own bullshit. But it wasn't all bullshit. The important stuff was true. "For purposes of this discussion, let's assume you did. Of course I have no way of holding you to that."

He inclined his head a notch in a show of agreeing to these terms, for now.

"He was murdered with arguably the world's deadliest poison. But he was already dying from brain cancer."

"And how do you know this? Are you working with the police?"

"If I were working with the police, I would have to identify myself to you as such. And I don't think you would have agreed to meet me."

"Undercover?"

She shook her head. "I don't have the stomach for it. And the pay is far too low to support my lifestyle." Clarisse thought she saw the trace of a smile play across his lips.

Had he been thinking about his FBI father just now?

"I found out from someone who *is* working with the police."

"And why would they tell you?"

"I can be very persuasive."

"I'm listening."

"A mysterious message was also left near the body. And a note was hidden in Pottinger's boat that might be meaningful to you."

She had not told Gibson that she had previously found the note on the boat fender. But she didn't know that Gibson had also found it, although Clarisse expected her to at some point.

"And what did the note say?"

"Basically, to try harder if you wanted to find the real treasure."

"So this is a treasure hunt then?" said Trask.

"Apparently so."

The black eyes drilled into her with a calmness that was disconcerting. "But *whose* treasure?"

Curious question. Let me throw something else out as bait and see if the pole bends.

"Pottinger was not his real name. He stole a lot of mob money from decades ago. And he did deals as Pottinger that made him even more money in various ways."

She stopped talking and studied him with her green contact lens eyes. She wondered if they were as intimidating as his dark ones. Somehow, she doubted it. Which was good.

Underestimate me at your peril.

"He *did* make a lot of money. Off certain people who would like it back."

"Can you tell me how?"

"Why would I?" said Trask.

"I came here to see if I could help bring this thing to a conclusion. A mutually beneficial conclusion."

"Why do I need you to do that?"

Okay, that was a bit predictable, she thought. *But then, don't underestimate him, either.*

"Maybe you don't. You have lots of resources. You might be close to finding the money already. If so, I'll just go. No harm done."

She started to rise until he lifted a hand, which seemed to have the power to force her to sit back down.

"He paid five million for Stormfield. Did you know he was living there?"

He gave another slight incline of the head.

"That money will be going to the government. The funds used to purchase the estate are mob connected, at least the government will see it that way. But if you knew he was nearby, why didn't you—"

"Why do you think I came here and built this place, Ms. Peters?"

"Enemies closer. Was it worth it for the geographical proximity?"

"Not just him."

She nodded slowly. "Your father is also nearby."

"As to Pottinger, he also *made* certain people a lot of money. He had talents for both making it and then hiding it from the government. It created in him a certain value, at least to some people."

"So he was a good partner to these 'people'?"

"Apparently so. Until he turned into a bad one."

"But again, if that happened and he was right here...?"

"Just because someone has a home doesn't mean they're in it. As a matter of fact, he was hardly ever there. I took pains to know that. And so we had really no opportunities to...chat about matters. But after his mob racket, I suppose he got in the habit of biting the hand that fed him."

"Well, he finally came back here. If only to die."

"Ideas on that?" asked Trask.

"Several. But we need to conclude some business first."

He spread his hands. "I'm listening."

"In the way of a finder's fee."

"How much?"

"Fifteen percent."

"Five."

"Twelve and a half?"

"Five."

"Ten?"

"Five. It's a big number. You won't know how to spend it all. Or maybe live long enough to."

"You had me right up until that point. It sort of dilutes the incentive."

"Then let me fire it back up. If you can pull this off, I have no reason to wish you ill will. Your ideas?"

"I have several." She sat forward. She did not mind getting lowballed on the finder's fee for one simple fact.

Clarisse never intended to collect it.

About a half hour later, Trask walked her out. At the front door he said, "Someone visited my father recently. A woman. Know anything about that?"

"I may. But I need to be sure. She could be friend or foe."

"I don't need friends and I don't like foes."

"Then it may not matter."

"It always matters. But just so we understand each other really well, you fall into the same category, business associate or not."

"I never expected anything less, or more."

"You're a strange one. I can't quite figure you out, and that's unusual. I've seen just about everything."

"Don't beat yourself up about it, Mr. Trask. I'm a little beyond 'just about everything.'"

CHAPTER

42

Clarisse walked for two miles. If they were going to follow her, she was going to make them work for it. She entered a store from the front and went out through the rear, after a pit stop in the ladies' room where she had previously left a bag underneath the bottom of the trash bag with some fresh clothes and other disguise elements, and her phone.

When she came out she was transformed, blond to brunette, skirt and jacket to torn jeans and a sweater, heels to flats, glasses, makeup and lipstick shorn from her face. She could pass for a fresh-faced teenager with AirPods in her ears and a vape in her hand.

She grabbed an Uber and took it to within two blocks of her hotel. She went to her room, sat at her desk, and opened her notebook.

Then her phone dinged as the email dropped in.

You haven't matured a bit, it seems. Same old snark. If no leverage on Mommy then I guess she becomes superfluous. What a word. Didn't expect me to conjure that one, did you, darling? A bullet to the head, or a ligature display? Poison down the pipe. It won't take much. Huff and puff and blow the old bitch down would do it actually. What shitty care you took of her. Way I see it, I found HL. That was the big part. Your part, finish the job. Then we divvy. And don't take your time. I'm tired of mops and little diamonds where the fence screws you over after you do all the planning and take all the risk. A faraway beach beckons. I want to get there. But I want to get there in unassailable style. Wow, another SAT word. But I see you've been keeping busy too. Poor Mr. Schmuck. How much did you take him for in the offices of Creative Engineering? Saw him giving your ass a rubdown. Hope you enjoyed it. You always were poor at relationships. Have you even had sex yet, whirly-girl? I mean, not against your will of course. Not sure you're capable, but I could be wrong. Let me know on Mommy. She eats a lot and she snores and her gas, well, it's a problem. Tick, tock, tick.

Cheers, hon.

Her bluff on Mommy had been called, it seems. So what to do, what to do? She consulted the appropriate notebook, even as her mind lingered on the "had she had sex" part. That had been a low blow, and she knew the bitch had meant every word of it.

I could say the exact same about you, babycakes. Isn't that what they called you? Young and just meant to be eaten up, with no other purpose in life?

But no reason to antagonize, not yet anyway. And she had not even mentioned her comments on Oxblood's murder. She would give it a bit. No need to rush a reply. *She* had obviously taken her time in answering.

Plus, I have other things to do.

She turned to another notebook and flipped through some pages, making notes and crossing out other ones.

What would I do without these? They allow me to make sense of my world. To put things in precise, logical steps to achieve a precise, logical outcome.

And they also prevent me from losing my damn mind.

Clarisse had told herself she was not going to do what she was just about to do. But things had changed. And when things changed, your plans must as well.

She looked at her computer screen and hit the key. A few seconds later Mickey Gibson answered.

"I wasn't sure you would pick up," said Clarisse.

"I almost didn't."

"Things weren't left well, I know. But I have information pertinent to you."

"Okay."

"Just like that? No rehashing of what went down before?"

"Do either of us have time to play it that way?" asked Gibson.

Okay, unload H-bomb and see what happens. "Nathan Trask knows you visited his father."

She thought she could hear Gibson's breathing accelerate, but only slightly. The woman really did have stainless steel balls, Clarisse had to give her that.

"How do you know that?"

"He told me personally."

"You mean you got in to see him? How?" asked Gibson.

"The only way I could. I had information that was relevant to him."

"Relevant information such as?"

"Treasure," replied Clarisse.

"You'll need to flesh that out."

"Harry Langhorne left a lot of mob money behind. We've gone over this."

"So why does Trask care about that? *Was* he involved with Langhorne in that laundry list of crimes you told me about before?"

"Maybe not all of them, but enough. He also told me he built his fortress in Virginia Beach because Langhorne—or Pottinger, to him—was nearby."

"And you believed that?" said Gibson.

"Doesn't matter. His father is nearby, too. That could be the real reason, or it could be both. The point is, he was connected to Pottinger at some point and in some way."

"So he doesn't know who Pottinger really was?"

"I didn't tell him, but I did reveal that he had taken a great deal of mob money from decades ago. Some of it he used to buy

Stormfield. But the rest? It has to be somewhere. And I think that Pottinger ripped off Trask as well, at least he strongly intimated that was the case. So the treasure might even be larger than we think."

Gibson said, "If Pottinger had ripped off Trask, how come Trask didn't take care of him? He was right next door and had been for years. The man should have been dead a long time ago."

"I asked him that."

"And his response?"

"Something to the tune of just because he owned the place didn't mean he actually lived there."

"Well, he was *killed* there. Did Trask do that?" asked Gibson.

"We covered this before, too. The poison, the strange message left. Not his MO. And do you think he'd confess the deed to me?"

"Did Trask have any idea how much money he got ripped off for? Or how?"

"I'm sure he does, to the penny. And again, he didn't exactly admit to being ripped off at all. But it was meaningful enough for him to agree to see me. And it's not just money with those guys. It's reputation. If they can get taken, it's a sign of weakness. In that business, you don't want the other sharks to see your blood in the water."

"Trust me, I know that," said Gibson.

"Did you find any clues to a treasure at Stormfield?" she asked.

"I found a note, in the man's boat. It basically acknowledged that he was aware people would be looking for something, and suggested they try harder."

Okay, her giving that up without a fight does surprise me. "Do the police know about this note?"

"They do," replied Gibson.

"And?"

"And I don't think their priority is finding money. It's finding a killer."

"Perhaps to find the killer, you have to locate the treasure," noted Clarisse.

"I can't tell them how to do their job."

"But you can suggest things," said Clarisse.

"Maybe. But if the police find the killer *and* the treasure, where does that leave you?" asked Gibson.

"It will make me stop looking over my shoulder."

"Bullshit, you want the money. I doubt you're worried about your personal security."

I wasn't until Mommy went missing. "We can agree to disagree on that. So what will you do next?"

"I've got some leads. I'll run them down."

"Will you be working with Wilson Sullivan on this?" asked Clarisse.

"I won't bother to ask how you know about all that, but yes, I will, at least on some of it. And what will *you* be doing?"

"Don't worry, my plate is full."

"Did Nathan Trask know *who* I was?" Gibson wanted to know.

"Not that he said, just that you visited. But he could easily find out your identity."

"He must keep eyes on his father."

"Of course," said Clarisse.

"So you did walk me right into a trap."

"Look, Mickey, I want you to survive this." *Actually, I don't care,* thought Clarisse. *You had your shot, Mickey Rogers Gibson. You had everything, and you pissed it all away.*

Gibson barked, "*You* don't care about me, which is why you let me put a bull's-eye on *my* back with Trask."

"In case you forgot, *I* went to visit the man directly. He knows about me, too. I didn't use my real name, but with his resources, he could find me as well."

"I don't know for sure that you *did* visit him."

"He has a female butler. Two guards at the front gate who wanded me. They took me up to the main house in a golf cart trimmed in gold. The place is enormous but not furnished over-the-top. He met me in a small room with a couple of chairs. He's around five eight, fit build, early fifties, and has the darkest pair of eyes I've ever seen. I can hold my own with most people in pretty much any situation, but I have to confess, he intimidated me by saying almost nothing."

"I'll be in touch," said Gibson. The line disconnected.

Clarisse looked down at her MICKEY GIBSON notebook. But she had nothing right now she wanted to write in it.

She stared at the muted reflection in her computer screen. There might be two or three people in that reflection, she thought. Depending on the day and the need. And whatever else was swirling around inside her head.

She wanted to punish Gibson for not living up to her potential. Why Clarisse should care about that was complicated. But, essentially, it came down to the haves and the have-nots. Gibson had had it all. Clarisse had had nothing. When you have it all, it was your duty to capitalize on it. Otherwise, you were disrespecting everyone. Including people like Clarisse.

Nothing like a little pressure, Mick, she conceded, if only to herself. Some days she wondered why she was so obsessed with the woman. But she had an obsessive personality; every shrink she'd ever been to, and they had been legion, had diagnosed that about her. She could have saved them the time and herself the money because she had already self-diagnosed. It hadn't been hard.

In her more rational moments she had seen that Gibson owed her life's choices to no one other than herself. And she couldn't have foreseen marrying a louse and having two kids to raise on her own. And she was making the best of it that she could.

But another side of Clarisse refused to yield any ground on the subject.

I am giving her the chance to do something extraordinary. All she has to do is succeed and then survive. And maybe a part of me, deep down, actually wants her to.

CHAPTER

43

Gibson let out a long breath. It seemed like every call with the woman made her blood pressure rise and her nerves fray.

And with Nathan Trask now aware of her she had good reason to be anxious.

Yet the visit with his father had been illuminating, so there was that. Plus, he was a nice old guy and Gibson was glad to have met him. He reminded her of her dad. And he might be of use on this case. A lot of use, in fact.

She wasn't entirely convinced that Clarisse had actually been to see Trask, despite the details, which included the golf cart Gibson had seen on her reconnoiter of the place. But for some reason, she thought the woman was probably telling the truth.

She must have some chutzpah to go into the lion's den with that guy. Or a death wish.

She sat back and mulled over things.

Langhorne was dead, murdered. A treasure might or might not be out there to be found. Clarisse might or might not be Francine Langhorne. She had no idea where Doug Langhorne might be, if he was still alive. Nathan Trask might be involved with all this somehow. And she was informally helping Wilson Sullivan in his investigation but not getting very far with it. And there was something about Sullivan that was bothering her.

She felt fairly sure that if Clarisse was Francine, she just wanted the treasure. But had she killed her father attempting to locate it? But what didn't make sense, as she had thought before, was why involve her? Why not just keep looking for it, with no one the wiser? And why leave the weird message on the wall? She could maybe understand the choice of poison. Francine might have told her father, *Tell me where the money is and I'll give you the antidote*, that sort of thing, though she wasn't sure there even was one for botulinum. But a man who had swindled the mob, then brought them down and lived to tell about it, did not seem gullible enough to buy that sort of line. And he was dying anyway. What did it matter to him?

I've got to find out who Clarisse really is. If she's not Francine, then what's her interest in all this? Without knowing that I'm spinning in circles.

The kids were down for short naps, so she went on her computer and read the news stories so far about the murder of Daniel Pottinger. Withheld from them was the message on the wall written presumably by two people—which might mean Francine and her brother were working together. The police had also not released the fact of Pottinger's real identity. That was definitely an item to hold back, though she was sure they had told other law enforcement agencies. She knew her father and Art Collin would know to keep that on the QT.

Gibson didn't necessarily believe that some old mob guy or their son or daughter had found Langhorne and taken him out. But stranger things had happened. If so, looking into Langhorne's history was a no-brainer from an investigative point of view. Indeed, it would have been gross negligence not to.

DO AS I SAY, NOT AS I DO.

She had looked it up. It apparently had originated in the Book of Matthew. Jesus was speaking to the multitudes and his disciples, and he told them that the scribes and the Pharisees sit in Moses' seat. After that it got a bit muddled, but the message was, apparently, watch them but don't follow what they actually do, because what they say and what they do are two different, and probably diametrically opposed, things.

She had heard that growing up from her father. He'd been a rabble rouser as a kid, always getting in trouble. But don't you do that, Mick, he would tell her over and over. There was something logical and instinctive about an adult wanting their kids to avoid their parents' past mistakes, but it still seemed disingenuous. Yeah, Dad, you weren't mature enough to avoid all that crap but you expect me to just because you say so? Easier said than done. And you probably had the same lecture from your parents, so there.

She stared at the words on the screen again. They were important to the killer or killers.

But were they something every cop looked for in trying to solve a crime? *Were they an MO?*

In her job at ProEye she had access to databases that most people did not, since ProEye sometimes worked hand-in-glove with law enforcement. She decided to use that access right now.

She entered the database and filled in her request:

Do as I say, not as I do. Has that phrase turned up in any homicide over the last two months?

If nothing came back she could always modify the request.

She didn't have to modify it though. Not the least little bit.

A police bulletin from the Fauquier County Sheriff's Office showed up on her computer screen. A murder of one Daryl Oxblood, resident of The Plains, Virginia. It was about fifty miles west of DC and had fewer than three hundred inhabitants.

He'd been found nearly decapitated. And on a wall of his home had been written the words, DO AS I SAY, NOT AS I DO.

She sent Sullivan the link to the bulletin, with the email labeled URGENT.

She drummed her fingers on her desk and read through the rest of the bulletin while she awaited his reply.

Two minutes later her phone rang. It was Sullivan.

"Shit," he said.

"Yeah, I know. But is it or isn't it?"

"One way to find out. We go to The Plains, Virginia."

"'We'?"

"You found it. Can you come with me, today?"

"Let me check with my parents." *Great, Mick, you sound like a preteen who wants to go to the movies with a boy.*

"I'll wait to hear from you."

44

I'M GOING WITH A POLICE DETECTIVE, Dad, I'll be fine."

Gibson's parents had come over to watch the kids. Gibson had packed an overnight bag, and was saying goodbye to her father on the front porch of her house.

"I think you're getting in this sucker so deep, you'll never get back out."

"One way of looking at it."

"Is he picking you up?"

"Yep, in fact that's him now," said Gibson as Sullivan's trim dark sedan pulled onto her street and turned into the driveway.

"You be careful, cop escort or not. I'm too old to be raising little kids. My knees and back are shot."

She hugged him, surprising her father, and said, "I'll call with my status."

"You got your Beretta?"

"Of course."

She got into the car with Sullivan, who flicked a hand in greeting at Gibson's father. Rogers merely nodded back, his hands stuffed in his pants pockets as he stared down the police detective.

"Still looks like a cop," noted Sullivan. "Intimidating."

"My dad will look like a cop until he takes his last breath."

They headed north and rode Interstate 64 to 95. At Fredericksburg they branched northwest onto Route 17. A little under three hours after starting their trip they were rolling into the little hamlet of The Plains.

"Don't think they see many murders here," noted Sullivan as they cruised along.

"I would hope not. Did you make a call?"

"Yeah. Someone from the Sheriff's Office will meet us at Oxblood's place."

"What do we know about him?"

"Not much. He was around forty. Lived with his mother until she died. Then he kept living in her house. Did equipment repair work locally. Kept to himself."

"They from The Plains?"

"Don't know, but I'm going to ask."

When they pulled into Oxblood's drive they didn't see a sheriff's car. But a woman did come out from the house next to Oxblood's. She was dressed in jeans and a flannel shirt. She looked weathered and tough.

They got out and introduced themselves and told her why they were there. She eyed Sullivan's police credentials and nodded.

"I'm Barbara Cole. As you can see, I live next door."

"You knew Daryl?"

"Yes, and his mother, when she was alive."

Sullivan took out his notebook. "And her name was?"

"Cindy Oxblood."

"How long has she been dead?" asked Gibson.

"Oh, four years now. Time flies."

"How'd she die?" asked Gibson.

"Car accident, on the road coming in here. Don't know how it happened. Critter might have run in front of her. She went off the road and the truck flipped. She wasn't wearing a seat belt, unfortunately. Not sure she would have survived anyway. Cab was crushed from the impact."

"Do you know where they moved from?" asked Gibson while Sullivan wrote all of this down.

Cole screwed up her features. "I think I recall her saying the west coast. Oregon, yeah, Oregon."

"She ever mention her husband? Any other kids?"

"No, and I'm not one to pry. I don't like talking about my ex, either. Just makes me feel stupid all over again."

Gibson smiled at the woman's frankness. "I feel your pain," she said, drawing a glance from Sullivan.

"And you found Daryl?" asked Sullivan.

"Me and the other gal."

"What other gal?" said Gibson sharply.

"She was here taking a survey and had an appointment with Daryl. She knocked on his door but he didn't answer. She came to my house and we went over there together. That's when we found Daryl." She shivered. "Still have nightmares about it. Been keeping my door locked and my gun under my pillow ever since."

"I'm sure. Can you describe the woman?"

Cole did so and Sullivan wrote it all down while Gibson listened intently.

"There was no mention of the woman in the police report," said Sullivan.

"Yeah, she had other appointments to get to and didn't want to get involved. She lit out of here before the cops showed up. So I didn't see any need to mention her."

"Can you tell us anything else about her? What she said. The car she was driving."

"Think the car was a rental. Looked like one that you get at the airport. She was thin and tall and pretty and real put together, if you know what I mean. Nice clothes, carried herself real well."

"Did Daryl seem like the type who would make that sort of an appointment?" asked Sullivan.

"He would if they paid him, or gave him free stuff."

"What was she taking a survey on?" asked Gibson.

"She said with people who didn't have an online presence, or some such. The company she worked for was sort of researching those types, I guess to figure out how to sell them stuff another way. I think every day about chucking the whole internet and going back to the way it was, but I never seem to get there."

"Did she act suspicious at all? Nervous?"

"No, nothing like that. She just seemed like she was out here doing her job. Look, she didn't have nothing to do with what happened to Daryl. She knocked on *my* door. I had to get my spare key to Daryl's house to let us in. When we found him, we were both shocked, let me tell you. I came close to throwing up and she didn't look much better."

"And then she left?"

"She needed to get going. And she couldn't tell the police anything I didn't."

Gibson looked at Sullivan, who shrugged.

He looked at the door to Oxblood's place. There was no police tape there.

"Local cops finished up in there?" he asked.

"Yeah, they were here yesterday taking stuff away, and then they took off a lock they had on the door."

"Can you let us in while we wait for the sheriff?"

"Sure thing."

She opened the door with her spare key and led them inside. She showed them around Oxblood's room, where his body had been found.

Cole shivered as she looked around. "There was so much blood. It was horrible."

"Did he have any enemies that you knew of?" asked Gibson.

"Hell, nobody around here has enemies like that. Daryl kept to himself. No troubles."

"Drugs?"

"No, not that I know of. He never seemed like that, anyway. I thought it might be something to do with opioids, even mentioned it to that gal. But when I thought about it later, I just didn't think that was possible."

"What was his mother like?"

"Sort of like Daryl. Cindy kept to herself. I probably knew her best, being right next door. But she didn't go to church, or join any of the local organizations."

"Did she work?"

"No. Cindy didn't really go anywhere. When they first moved here she mentioned something about a settlement her husband had gotten from an accident."

"But her husband didn't come here with them?"

"No, she said he had died."

"Why move here all the way from Oregon?" asked Gibson.

"She said she had lived in Virginia once and really liked it."

"How was Daryl when he was younger?" asked Sullivan.

"He drank some, drove his car too fast, got into some minor scrapes here and there with some buddies. But then he sort of pulled back into a shell, I guess you'd say. Didn't go out. Sat home with his ma. Got a job at the vehicle repair place in town. Was a good mechanic. He worked on some of my stuff. Fixed it right up."

They heard a car pulling into the driveway and Sullivan glanced out the window. "It's the sheriff. I'll go out to meet him and then bring him in."

When he ducked out Gibson turned to Cole. "Where was the writing on the wall found?"

"In here."

She led Gibson to the other room and they stood looking at the words.

"Did the other woman come in here, too?"

"Oh, yes. In fact, she was in here before I was. I found her here after I called the police."

She had the presence of mind to look around after finding a dead body, thought Gibson.

Gibson's gaze roamed over the words until she came to where Clarisse had tried to obscure the writing.

"What happened there?" she said, pointing.

"I don't know. Guess the folks who wrote it did that."

"Did the woman give you her name? I think Detective Sullivan forgot to ask."

"Yes, she did. I asked for that in case the police would want to know even though I ended up not mentioning her. It was, let me think, yes, Julia, Julia Frazier. That's what she said."

Frazier. The same name used by the lady on the phone talking to Clarisse.

"It seems that she's gone missing." That's what was said.

Clarisse's mother, perhaps?

CHAPTER

45

THE DEPUTY SHERIFF WAS NAMED Billy Dawson. He was tall with broad shoulders, and around forty-five.

Dawson said, "Fauquier County is pretty big, but very rural and safe. Now, you have some areas that aren't as safe as others, but most of what we see here are property crimes." He looked at the blood on the walls of Oxblood's bedroom. "Not this."

"I'm sure," said Sullivan. "What can you tell us about Oxblood?"

"So you had a murder down in your neck of the woods that had similar elements?"

"The writing on the wall principally, yes."

Dawson led them into that room. "Heard the phrase a million times. But you don't see it written on the walls of homicide scenes. So you think it's the same killer?"

"Trying to piece that together. So, Oxblood?"

"I knew Daryl. He worked on my truck and a couple of my ATVs, and some of my brother's stuff, too. He kept to himself. His mother was the same. Just nice, quiet people."

"Did you know anything about them before they came here?"

"No."

"How long had he been dead?" asked Gibson.

"A few days, the ME said."

Gibson looked at Cole. "You didn't get suspicious when he didn't leave the house?"

"I was gone for nearly a week. Visiting family over in West Virginia. And like Billy said, Daryl kept to himself."

"Didn't where he worked report him missing?" asked Gibson.

Dawson said, "I talked to them. They said Daryl had taken a few days off."

"Any family pictures in the house that would show his father?" asked Gibson.

Dawson said, "Funny thing, no family photos. In fact, no photos at all."

"You find his phone?" asked Sullivan.

"No. We pulled the phone records, though. He didn't make many calls and the folks he texted or emailed all dealt with normal stuff. There were no incoming calls."

Gibson looked at the shelves of comic books. "Your guys go through all those?"

"We looked through some. I guess adults collect stuff like that, baseball cards, you name it. Maybe sell it on eBay."

"Only he wasn't online," pointed out Gibson. "There are no electronics in the house that I saw."

"Yeah, that's right," said Dawson. "So what do you think is going on?"

Sullivan shrugged. "What we're trying to find out."

"Mind if we look around?" asked Gibson.

"Knock yourselves out. I'm not too proud to ask for help. I can email you the file we have, Detective Sullivan."

"Sounds good, thanks."

Dawson and Barbara Cole left.

Sullivan eyed Gibson. "Thoughts?"

She didn't want to share what was on her mind right now, but Sullivan looked determined.

"I don't think we know enough to draw any preliminary, much less definite, conclusions. Why don't I search the upstairs and you check the rest of the house? If something pops we each call the other."

"Okay. Do you really think this is a coincidence—the two phrases on the wall, I mean?"

"There must be a connection. We just have to find it." What she didn't say was that the handwriting on Oxblood's wall was quite different from the handwriting back at Stormfield. But Sullivan might have already noted that.

Now that Gibson had committed herself to solving this case, as the only way to protect herself and her kids, she wanted to do it as rapidly as possible. Thus, she was itching for Sullivan to leave, because she had seen something that she wanted to check out.

As soon as he left she made a beeline for the comics.

They were all neatly laid in their respective piles. All except for one.

On top of one pile a comic book was sticking out, like a sore thumb, she thought. She didn't know if the cops had done it, or someone else. Like Ms. Frazier?

She put on latex gloves and picked it up. She opened it and stopped.

Was that blood on the inside of the cover? She looked closer; it seemed like blood. Had Oxblood's killer taken the time to pick up this particular comic book?

Then she noted the initials in the heart shape next to the drop of blood. *BD and RE?*

She had brought an evidence pouch with her and slipped the comic book into it, then folded it over and put it into her bag. Gibson was sure that someone, either the killer or killers, or Clarisse/Julia *Frazier*, had picked up this comic book out of all the others and opened it to that page. And seen the initials inside that heart. And what had that meant to them or her?

And what does it mean to me?

CHAPTER

46

THEY STAYED OVERNIGHT AT AN inn near The Plains. They had dinner in the small, quaint restaurant. Sullivan said, "So we didn't really find much back there, did we?"

Gibson thought of the plastic evidence pouch in her room containing the comic book with the dried blood on it. She had brought her kit and checked it, but found no prints on the blood mark. The person had probably worn gloves.

She knew removing potential evidence from a crime scene was a crime in itself. But she had thought long and hard about this and had arrived at one difficult conclusion.

I can't just walk away from this or bury my head in the sand, because I'm exposed. I've been exposed ever since I stepped foot into Stormfield and found Harry Langhorne dead. And Clarisse is probably a psycho and she knows where I live. And after I visited his father, Nathan Trask can easily find out who I am. Or, hell, Clarisse might decide to rat me out to the man, if she already hasn't. The only way to protect myself and my family is to get to the truth as fast as possible. And the only way I can do that is to become a detective again and hope I'm still good enough to solve this mess.

She said, "Maybe it's staring us in the face?"

Sullivan dipped a chunk of bread in the olive oil and bit into it. "Meaning?"

"No family photos? No online presence? Came from Oregon all the way here? Father dead? Mother had some money, and didn't work? They kept to themselves?"

"Wait a minute, are you thinking, what, WITSEC?" asked Sullivan.

"Aren't you?"

"Maybe I am. I'll have his prints run through the national databases and see what pops."

"I'm surprised the local cops hadn't already done that."

"I guess, to them, he's Daryl Oxblood, end of story."

"I guess," replied Gibson.

"So do we have a whole bunch of ex-WITSECs on the run causing mayhem or getting killed?"

"At least maybe the children of Harry Langhorne," she replied.

"Well, Oxblood wasn't Francine, obviously. And he does not fit the description for Doug Langhorne, who Beckett said was around six two. I saw the file on Oxblood. He was only five eight. No disguise can subtract six inches."

"Right," agreed Gibson.

"What do you think of this gal Julia Frazier?"

"Wrong place, wrong time probably. Didn't figure walking into a murder and didn't want to hang around to get more involved in it," answered Gibson. *Liar, liar, pants on fire.*

"I suppose you're right."

They finished their dinners and left the restaurant to get some fresh air on the broad front porch.

"Nice of you to let me in on the investigation. I know it's not the norm."

"I *am* getting some heat for it," admitted Sullivan.

"Don't cause yourself career trouble, Will. You can cut me loose any time."

"I thought you wanted to be in the loop."

"Oh, I'll still be working it, with or without you," she said, grinning.

He smiled, albeit reservedly. "For now, we'll just let things play out."

"Sounds good."

"I'm going for a quick smoke out back."

"And I'm going to bed. Good night."

"Good night."

They parted company and she took the stairs up to her room. She checked her watch and called her dad. She could tell by the background noise that he was watching basketball.

"How are the kids?"

"Sound asleep. Ate all their dinner. Never made any trouble. Just little bundles of joy. I don't want to hear you complaining ever again about how hard it is, Mick."

"Meaning Mom took care of them and you were somewhere else the whole time?"

"Well, I had some errands to run, yeah."

"Right."

"Jesus, he hit that three from the parking lot," he said, obviously watching the TV. "Damn kids these days. NBA's recruiting out of pre-K. Jump a mile in the air and dunk like it's nothing."

"It's not all about dunking," said Gibson. "I couldn't dunk."

"That's because you're too short. And you're a girl."

"Girls *can* dunk, Dad."

"Hell, I know. I just didn't want you to think I was getting soft. How'd it go today?"

She told him about what she had found and what she had done, and she thought her father was going to come through the phone and punch her.

"You did what?" he exclaimed. "You took evidence? Do you know that's a felony? Of course you do. What the hell are you thinking, Mick?"

"I'm playing it safe, Dad. For now, anyway. I need to know where things stand."

"I'll tell you where they stand. You don't do what you just did.

Now either go give it to the cop, or put it back where you got it and let them figure it out."

"Are those my only two choices?"

"Do you need a third? Because I told you before. I am not raising your kids while you're in prison for the next eight to ten years."

"You going to rat on me?"

"I know you pushed the envelope back in Jersey City, Mick, but this is not a game."

"Let me tell you my motives and then we can talk."

"I don't think you're going to change my mind."

She told him about going to see Nathan Trask's father. "And Trask knows someone visited his father. And he can find out it's me, if he really wants to."

This did not mollify her father in the least. It only made him more irate. "Son of a bitch! Do you have a death wish? I told you not to go anywhere near that guy."

"That guy is apparently part of this case. If I'm going to solve it, I have to go where I need to go."

"Let the police solve it and go back to your computers."

"Says the guy who hated the fact that I quit the force."

"I understood why you did it," her father corrected.

"But you still hated it."

"Yeah, I did. Because what's-his-fucking-name cratered your finances and your career. You expect me to be happy about that? And you were a damn good cop."

"*I'm* not happy about it, either. And I'm not walking away from this."

"Why the hell is this case so important to you? It got dumped in your lap. And you're taking a risk, I told you that. Think of the kids."

"I *am* thinking of the kids. And you. And Mom. I've crossed the Rubicon, so I'm involved in this thing whether I want to be or not. I can either wait for something bad to happen to me, or the kids or you or Mom, or I can work this thing like I worked my other cases."

"Is that really the only reason?" asked her father.

He could read her so easily sometimes, mainly because the two were so much alike. "Someone used me, okay? I don't like that. When that happens, I don't run away with my tail between my legs. You taught me to punch the bully in the face, Dad. I can't change who I am."

She heard him let out a long sigh. It was the same thing he had done after every argument he had lost with her, which was damn near all of them.

"So what are you going to do with what you found out?"

"I'm betting Julia Frazier is Francine Langhorne. I need to find her."

"How will you do that?"

"By digging. Isn't that what cop work is?"

"Just be careful. Some folks really need you to stick around."

"I know, the kids—"

Her father interrupted. "I was talking about *me*."

The silence hung heavy for a few seconds before he added, "I gotta get back to my basketball game. You take care, honey." He clicked off.

Gibson stared at the phone and realized for the first time just how worried her father really was about her.

CHAPTER

47

CLARISSE SAT IN FRONT OF her computer screens writing something down in a new notebook. It was labeled WAR ON THE PAST.

Things were happening quite rapidly now.

Her surveillance camera had shown that Wilson Sullivan had picked up Gibson and they had driven off together. She had an overnight bag, so wherever they were going it was some distance away.

Where would you go with the cop on an overnight, Mick? Where would you need official muscle to get to what you want to get to?

Something occurred to her.

She went online and did a search. There were a number of results, but the very first one would do.

The front-page story in the *Fauquier Times*: "Murder in The Plains. Daryl Oxblood Slain. No Suspects." And there it was. On the wall in a room of the house the phrase, DO AS I SAY, NOT AS I DO.

The Fauquier County Sheriff's Office had not been as tight-lipped as their colleagues to the south, who had kept that piece of information zealously guarded. They had actually let someone take a picture and run with it.

So Gibson did the search I just did, found this item, and she and Sullivan went there to see about possible connections.

They would have talked to the neighbor, seen the crime scene, talked to the cops. A search on Daryl Oxblood would have turned up nothing after twenty years back.

She will know what that means. They'll run his prints.

Clarisse thought back to what she had done and not done while there.

I tried to erase the phrase but I was stopped. Gibson will surely see that. I wore gloves, so no prints...the comic book! Did I put it back exactly...

She closed her eyes and let that recent memory flow back into her hippocampus where she analyzed it thoroughly, although the result was not to her liking.

No, I didn't. I should have taken it with me. Stupid.

"BD and RE." Gibson will know about that now.

Something else occurred to Clarisse. She ran and got the gloves she had worn that day. On one fingertip the fabric was soiled. With blood.

BD's blood. Not mine. With the gloves I left no prints or DNA behind, but it still was a blunder. You are truly getting sloppy, girl.

Clarisse took several deep calming breaths as she composed a reply to the last email.

Okay, let's cut out the high school snarky babble. We're older and hopefully wiser now. Yes, I want Mommy back, so put up with her for a bit longer. Once I find what I'm looking for, we can arrange the trade. It will be complex but what isn't, right?

She paused, wondering whether to go there or not. *Oh, what the hell.*

And FYI I know who Daryl was. It was unnecessary. Why do that to him? We had a history, all of us. Granted he was not the brightest bulb, but he got out. You could have let that sleeping dog lie, right? He had a life. He was doing okay. You snuffed him for no reason. I know we're all messed up. But let's try to get this done the right way. You want the nice, quiet life with bags of money? Well, so do I. We act appropriately, we get there. We don't, we all go down. Because there are others on the trail here and they have badges. So don't screw this up. We have one shot. And only one.

Clarisse's finger again hovered over the send key. This was serious shit. The person on the other end of this email trail was serious shit.

The key went down and the email went poof into the ethereal darkness. She wondered how long before the reply came, if there even was one. Clarisse's email had been logical, rational, made sense all around, for their own well-being, their own survival. But the thing was, the person she was facing could not be counted on to see it that way. The most dangerous enemy of all was the one who, consciously or not, didn't care about dying.

But in another way, it placed the person in danger of being anticipated by an adversary.

And that will probably be the only difference between my surviving this or not.

Because seeing Daryl Oxblood with his head nearly cut off changed everything for me.

Clarisse brought up some financial documents from a previous hack she had done. They belonged to Daniel Pottinger. They represented a dozen accounts from a similar number of financial institutions both foreign and domestic.

The problem was every single one of these accounts had been cleaned out and closed within the span of one week nearly seven months ago. Clarisse had only a guess on the total amount of money, but based on other things she had found and the cash price paid for Stormfield, she estimated it to be about half a billion dollars.

Now that qualified as a treasure under any definition. And she had always loved round numbers.

She figured Gibson would be able to snag these same documents at some point if she already hadn't. Whether she would drill deeper was the question. Clarisse was banking that she could. ProEye could get into places no one else could.

I may not have ProEye-level resources, but I'm cleverer than the great Mickey Gibson is or ever will be. She was the great one everyone loved. I was the one no one loved or even knew existed. But I will show her. And everyone else.

She hit a key, and all those empty accounts disappeared from the screen.

Still, if I get there first, all well and good.

If Gibson gets there first, still all well and good, possibly.

She changed her clothes and hair and makeup and personality and demeanor.

She stopped at her laminator and pulled out the item she had encased in heated and hardened plastic. She trimmed off the edges and punched a hole in it, then ran it through a lanyard and placed that around her neck. She walked out the door because she had an appointment to keep.

Somehow I am loving every minute of this.

Even though I'm scared to death.

CHAPTER

48

THE HOME WAS SIXTY YEARS old and on its last legs, and the yard undernourished and hence withered. The woman who lived here seemed to be all of these things rolled into one.

"Ms. Betty Gross?" Clarisse said.

"Yes?"

"I'm Sylvia Devereaux." She held up her laminated card. "With the Virginia Employment Commission."

"I don't understand."

Clarisse produced an iPad from her bag and said, "May I come in?"

"Am I in some sort of trouble?" asked Gross, clinging to the tattered screen door.

"Not at all. I'm here to *help* you, at least I hope. I understand that you were recently employed by a Mr. Daniel Pottinger at his home, Stormfield?"

"That's right. I was his housekeeper, but he let me go. He let everybody go."

"I know, that's why I'm here. To see if I can help. May I come in?" she asked again.

Gross stepped back. "I hope you can help me, too. I haven't found another housekeeper job yet. And the money is running low."

"I quite understand."

She was led into a small room off the kitchen. The place was decorated with what seemed to be spare parts from lots of different homes and decades. Clarisse assumed the woman had accumulated all this over the years and kept using it, since new items never came in to replace what was clearly worn out.

"Now exactly when did Mr. Pottinger let you go?"

"It was three weeks ago yesterday."

"And the reason given?"

"He didn't give no reason. Just told me and the others to get out."

"My goodness. How rude."

"That's what I thought. And he owed me wages, a week's worth. Never seen a dime and that big house he lived in, I know he had the money. Now he's dead. Doubt I'll be getting anything." She paused. "I filed for unemployment. Is that why you're here, Miss?"

"It's one of the reasons, yes," said Clarisse, keying some items in on her iPad. "How many staff did he have?"

"Four inside, three outside. All locals, hardworking. And he left them high and dry, too. Seems like the more money someone has, the less they care."

"Yes, it does, doesn't it. So he owed you a week's worth of wages. How much was that?"

"I got ten dollars an hour times forty-five hours for the week."

"So four hundred and fifty dollars then?"

"Yeah. Backbreaking work, it was. That place was huge. And he wanted the floors scrubbed and the marble to gleam."

"A difficult employer, then?"

"You could say that. You could say a lot more than that. The thing was the man was almost never there. He'd talk to me on the computer. Made me walk around with it, show him the state of the place. He'd read me the riot act if the least thing was out of place or something wasn't done to his liking, or if he didn't think we were working hard enough. It was a real bitch."

"And you mean to say he was almost never at Stormfield?"

"I could count the times he was there on one hand with fingers left over."

"Very interesting."

"And the few times he did show up he never gave me any notice. He was just there. Almost like the man was afraid to be in his own house."

Clarisse thought about Nathan Trask and knew the woman had unknowingly hit the nail right on the head with that one. "And how long did you work for him?"

"Nearly four years."

"Your annual income from that job would have been, around twenty-three thousand?"

"About that."

"Any paid vacation or health care?"

Gross smiled bitterly. "I asked for it, he never gave it. Said if I wanted a vacation why should he pay for it. And then he told me it was my fault if I got sick. Not his problem."

Clarisse looked around at the small space. "Could you live off that income?"

"Got one adult child and two grandbabies living with me, so the short answer is no. I work another job at night. Cleaning some buildings over in Smithfield. On the weekends I waitress at the local diner."

"You must be run off your feet."

"I'd rather be working, actually. The night job and the waitressing don't pay enough. I was hoping someone might buy that Stormfield place and hire me back, but I guess that will take a while."

"Yes, I think it will. Now, it seems that Mr. Pottinger failed to pay into the unemployment insurance fund."

Gross's face fell. "Does...does that mean I won't get no money? Like I said, I filed, but I ain't got nothing yet."

"Well, that's one reason I'm here, to help with that. Now, before he fired everyone, did Mr. Pottinger have any visitors?"

"Why does that matter?" Gross said, her expression suddenly wary.

Clarisse leaned forward and said in a confidential tone, "Just between you and me, it seems possible that Mr. Pottinger was engaged in something that might be criminal."

"Criminal!"

"Nothing has been proved yet, of course, but the state is looking into it. If you could assist us in our investigation, well, it certainly would help your chances of being compensated."

Gross smoothed down her wrinkled shirt and said, "I'll help you if I can, Miss, I swear. It's not like I owe Mr. Pottinger nothing. Man made my life miserable."

"I can understand that. So, any visitors?"

"He only had the one, Miss. We used to joke that the only friend he had was the devil."

"When was this visit?"

"About a week before he let us go. I remember it because he showed up out of the blue again. I walked in one morning and there he was, standing right in the foyer staring at me. I don't know how my heart didn't stop."

"Do you think he showed up because he knew he was going to have a visitor?"

"I thought that might be it, but he never said nothing until right before the person got there."

"And what can you tell me about the visitor?"

"It was a man. About your age."

"Can you describe him?"

"Tall man. Thin."

"Hair and eye color?"

"Why does that matter?"

"Well, we will want to find this man, of course."

"Oh, sure, yeah. Blond hair, thinning, and green eyes, least I think."

"How was he dressed?"

"Jeans and a sweater. He was very polite, but there was something about him, I don't know, gave me the creeps."

"Did you find out his name?"

"It was Mr. Marshal."

Clarisse sat back. *Marshal? Touché.* "Did you happen to hear what they discussed?"

"Oh, no. I took him to Mr. Pottinger's study and left them there. I went off and continued my work."

"Did you see him leave?"

"Stormfield has its own phone system, you know, so you can call room to room. Mr. Pottinger phoned me and told me to let Mr. Marshal out."

"Did either of them say anything as he was leaving?"

"Mr. Pottinger didn't. But when I opened the front door for Mr. Marshal he looked at me funny and what he said was even funnier. Not laugh funny, but strange funny."

"What was that?"

"He said, 'I hope you'll be able to find other work.'"

"Really? And what did you take that to mean?"

"Well, I thought Mr. Pottinger might be selling the place to this man and he'd bring in another staff. Never thought about him getting killed instead."

"Did you see the car he'd driven up in?"

"Oh, yes. It was parked out front. She was in the driver's seat."

Clarisse sat forward again, tensed. "'She'?"

"Yes, it was a woman. Couldn't get a good look at her, but I noticed the long hair. And she had on a necklace. It was all shiny in the sunlight. He got in and they drove off."

"And a week later you were given your notice?"

"Yes."

"Did Mr. Pottinger ever mention the visit to you?"

"No, never."

"Did you know about the secret room where he was found?"

"No, ma'am. When I read about that in the paper it nearly knocked me over. Me there all that time and never once noticed it."

"Was the place fully furnished? Books in the library, that sort of thing?"

She knew the answer to that, but she wanted to hear it from Gross. And things might have been taken.

"Well, it wasn't furnished like it ought to have been. Most rooms had nothing in 'em. Don't know why he bought that place. He was never there and when he was he only ever went into a few rooms, but he demanded that we clean everything. There were never any books in the library. I remember I asked him about that once when he showed up."

"What did he say?"

"He said he didn't like anything that was written down. That's pretty durn strange."

"Anything else you can think of?"

"No, I think that's all."

"Have the police been by to see you?"

Gross started and said, "Oh, that's right. I forgot."

"A Detective Sullivan?"

"I think that was his name, yes."

"Did he have a woman about my age with him? Around five seven, short, light brown hair, big blue eyes, by the name of Mickey Gibson?"

"No, he was alone."

"What did you tell him? What you told me?"

"Not everything, no, I mean, he didn't ask the same questions."

"Did you tell him about the visitor?"

"Yes, I did mention that."

"All right. I understand."

"So about my money? Can you put in a good word for me?"

"I can do better than that." Clarisse reached into her pocket and took out a certified check in the amount of five thousand dollars made out to Gross. It was drawn on an account that would be closed as soon as the check was cashed.

When Gross saw the amount she exclaimed, "My God, I don't understand."

"It's a new program at the VEC. Sort of like a whistleblower thing. But I do need you to sign this NDA," she added, drawing out a piece of paper from her bag. "It basically says you must not tell anyone about what we discussed, or even the fact of my visit. If you do, you have to pay the money back. That includes talking to the police if they come by again. But that doesn't matter, because I will inform them. But you can say nothing. Do you understand?"

With her eyes on the check Gross said, "Yes, ma'am, I'll mention it to no one. Cross my heart."

Gross signed the document and Clarisse took her leave. As she was getting into her car she thought, *After all this time they were right there at Stormfield. Both of them. What an exhilarating and terrifying thing to contemplate.*

49

THE NEXT DAY CLARISSE MADE the call.

"Long time, no hear," answered Gibson.

"Been busy. As I'm sure you have."

"I've been making some inquiries, as I said."

"And?"

"Heard of The Plains, Virginia?" Gibson asked.

"Tell me."

And Gibson did. Daryl Oxblood's being murdered. The phrase on the wall. But she didn't mention that someone had tried to rub it off. She didn't talk about Julia Frazier. She said nothing of a comic book with initials inside a heart.

"What do you take that to mean?" Clarisse asked.

"The murders are connected. Or else it's a copycat. But I don't see it that way."

"So who was Daryl Oxblood, really?"

"Cops are running his prints right now," replied Gibson.

Okay, then they'll know. The noose is tightening, and not in a good way for me.

"So that's why I was picked by you? So you can piggyback on ProEye resources?"

"It's a good reason, don't you think?" replied Clarisse.

"Francine and Douglas Langhorne?"

"What about them?" asked Clarisse.

"Know where they are?"

"I think we covered this already. I don't."

"When the fingerprint results on Oxblood come back, that will provide quite a few leads."

"Good." *Shit, I know it will.*

"Geraldine Langhorne?" asked Gibson.

"Again, no clue. Before my time. I dealt with Pottinger, not aka Langhorne."

"You like comic books?"

She felt an anxiety attack coming on. "Excuse me?"

"Comic books. Superman, Batman?" said Gibson.

"We don't have time to waste."

Gibson stared up at her computer screen where she had her own voice analysis program running. She used it when she was interviewing people on the phone in her search for assets. The indicators on the screen were often truer than the words spoken. And after she had preliminarily concluded that Julia Frazier and Clarisse were probably one and the same, she had decided to deploy the analyzer to help gauge whether this conclusion was right or not by asking Clarisse some unsettling questions.

And Clarisse's stress indicators had just spiked.

Clarisse, who was running a similar program on her computer, watched in dismay as she saw the arrow shoot north on *her* answer.

"Okay," said Gibson. "Just checking."

Clarisse looked at her Gibson notebook and decided to fire off her own salvo. "Are you worried that your father will do something stupid and endanger you and the kids?"

"What in the hell are you talking about?"

Now Clarisse watched the screen in satisfaction as Gibson's own stress level spiked.

"I know you told him about visiting Sam Trask because you're both former cops and have a tight bond. He obviously knows who Nathan Trask is. He's scared for you. What if he does something rash? I'm not doing this to pull your chain, Mickey. This is business with me. And I'm not claiming to have a big heart, but I don't want to see anyone get hurt. Especially little kids."

Gibson didn't say anything for a few moments and Clarisse had no intention of breaking the silence. Nathan Trask was a real threat to Gibson, to them both really. And she wanted the woman to understand that.

Plus, it might make her forget about the damn comic book.

"My father is not stupid," Gibson said finally. "He's not going to start a war with Nathan Trask."

"I just thought I'd mention it. Now, where do things stand with your and Sullivan's investigation?"

"Sullivan doesn't think the woman who was at Oxblood's home is important. Wrong place, wrong time."

"What woman?"

"The survey taker. She called herself Julia Frazier. Mean anything to you?"

"No. What sort of survey was she taking?"

Clarisse now kept watch on her stress level on the screen. She needed to keep it at an even level and she did so by taking silent, deep belly breaths and chewing the gum she had just popped into her mouth.

"Some BS. I think she was there for another reason. Sullivan didn't agree."

"What makes you think that she's important?"

"Call it my cop instinct."

"Sullivan's a cop, too," Clarisse pointed out.

"And we all have different instincts."

"I found out something, too."

"What?" asked Gibson.

"Langhorne had a visitor very close to the time he died. A man. Tall, thin, blond hair, green eyes."

"And how do you know this?"

"Proprietary source," replied Clarisse.

"Any idea who this visitor was?"

"That's for you to find out. Work your ProEye magic. And my source also told me that there was a woman waiting out in a car for the man."

"What did they want with Langhorne?" asked Gibson.

"My source didn't know. But when the visitor was leaving he told the person that she should look for another job. My source took that to mean that Langhorne was selling the place to the man. But it also could mean that the man knew Langhorne would not be alive much longer. Which turned out to be spot-on."

"So your proprietary source was a member of Langhorne's household staff?"

"I just can't keep anything from you, can I?" chided Clarisse.

"Okay, I'll share that with Sullivan."

"He already knows. He spoke to my source previously and they told him everything I just told you." She paused and added, "Didn't he share that with you?"

Clarisse watched the screen to see if Gibson's stress markers spiked. But she was disappointed because they remained level.

"Thanks for the info," said Gibson.

"You're welcome. Be careful out there."

Clarisse clicked off.

* * *

Gibson sat back in her chair. The stress levels told her that she had struck gold with the reference to the comic book. And Julia Frazier and Clarisse were almost certainly one and the same. Now that she had a fingerhold, she could perhaps track her down.

She was not unduly put out by Sullivan's withholding information from her, because she was doing the same to him. And he was official police and she was not. But it raised some interesting questions.

A tall man visiting Pottinger, and a woman in the car.

Doug and Francine Langhorne?

But if so, who the hell is Clarisse?

CHAPTER

50

IT WAS THE NEXT DAY and the kids were with Silva downstairs. Gibson had her cup of tea and oatmeal almond cookie. She hurried to her office, ceremoniously cracked her knuckles in front of her computer screens, and got to work.

While Zeb Brown had been the one to suggest that she take time off, she knew this hiatus would have to come to an end at some point, which lent urgency to her mission. And she could not step away from this case until it was solved.

She started hitting keys and typing in web addresses. There were myriad ways to hide money, and just as many ways to look for it. It was a game of cat and mouse played out every second of every day across the world. And it wasn't just about rich debtors trying to hide their fortunes from creditors, but also law enforcement trying to pierce the walls hiding money that dictators had stolen from their national treasuries, as well as secret organizations funneling dark money into a hot commodity that was now being termed "weaponized capital."

It was a way for the rich's assets to be deployed not in buying one more superyacht or luxurious private jet, but in silencing critics, buying off politicians and making sure they won their elections by hook or crook. And destroying legitimate business competition and making an already uneven playing field tilt even more unfairly in their favor.

Gibson used an asset locator search to build a list of everything ever recorded in Pottinger's name in a public records database. This also included any entity in which Pottinger had any connection whatsoever, whether as an officer, director, investor, or other affiliation. She should have done this before, but hindsight was 20/20.

Within an hour, and using ProEye software and access to internet platforms unavailable to the trolling public, she had compiled a list of forty-four companies, myriad investment platforms, alliances, and bank accounts. They were located all over the world. But they all had one thing in common: They had been closed down within the last six months or so and all assets transferred out.

She knew he had to pay bills from somewhere, including the salaries of the staff he had at the estate. She performed search after search and kept running into dead ends. These accounts had also been terminated and any funds in them were gone.

As she sipped her tea Gibson continued the arduous task of following the money. It was not as easy as depicted on TV, where the computer screen would show arrows bouncing off satellites and dipping into bank accounts until the current location was identified seconds later.

Yeah, right.

She next did a LexisNexis search of plaintiffs' and defendants' names to see if Pottinger had been involved in any lawsuits.

There were a dozen, all settled with no financial amounts disclosed. But it still provided her with some useful information, which she wrote down.

She did a search of Stormfield and found the real estate transaction she had noted before. Cash deal coming from an account that had since been closed. But it was drawn on Deutsche Bank. Okay, that was a red flag, Gibson thought. The German financial institution just couldn't seem to get out of its own way when it came to unscrupulous associations.

She tried to trace any funds left over from the purchase but lost the digital trail somewhere around the Caribbean. Gibson next checked his credit history but found nothing much there, not so odd if the man paid cash for everything. She went on LinkedIn and ran a search on both him and the companies that she had previously uncovered. Unfortunately, there was nothing helpful.

She went on another site to see if any liens had been filed against Pottinger, any of his companies, or any other property he and his entities might own. There were none. So the guy never tried to stiff anyone, good former mafia bean counter that he was.

She pulled out her iPad and went through the inventory of the house she had collected on her first visit there. There had been two suits of armor. She had gotten serial numbers off them both. She had next tracked them to an antiquities dealer in London.

She checked her watch; it would be evening now in England. She sent off an email to the business. Gibson posed as a motivated potential buyer. She knew from past experience this would get her a far quicker reply. She went through the rest of the inventory. Wherever she could run down where any piece had been purchased from, she emailed the source and left a message.

And then there was the Formula cabin cruiser. She learned that Pottinger had purchased it new from a dealer in Yorktown. However, when she checked the website, Gibson found that the company had gone out of business.

Undeterred by this, she decided to try a different tack.

It was the mundane if esoteric world of the registered agents. A corporation was legally required to have a registered agent physically in the state for service of process and other issues. There were really no exceptions to this rule. However, it wasn't an arduous requirement. You just needed a human being/company with a PO box or street address.

Gibson knew that around $40 trillion worth of dark and criminal money was floating around the world, entirely hidden from everyone, including governments. Over a trillion dollars of this money was sitting just in South Dakota, Wyoming, Delaware, and Nevada. She was pretty sure Nathan Trask would have huge amounts of his illicit fortune socked away in such schemes that were totally legal, even if they were funded with illicit money.

On one case she had tracked down a woman who was a registered agent in Wyoming. The records showed that the lady had a portfolio of roughly eight hundred companies for which she was the registered agent. The woman had no idea who was behind any of them. Gibson wasn't speculating about that. She had found a video deposition taken of the woman that had been posted to a database to which Gibson, with her ProEye credentials, had access. In the deposition the elderly lady had said, "It's none of my concern who's behind them. I just do what the law says I need to do and that's it. Lot better than living just off my Social Security. And thing is, I apparently live in a fraud-happy state. If the law says it's okay, then it's okay by me."

She charged $50 a year to be the agent and a onetime $150 fee for formation of the company. She made about forty thousand a year serving as a registered agent, which, along with her Social Security, allowed her to live quite comfortably in retirement.

"I've got all my kids and grandkids doing it, too," she had volunteered. "Best job in the world because you basically don't have to do nothing except maintain the records and file what's needed and you get paid like clockwork. And if they don't pay, I just cut 'em off. Wish I'd known about it when I was younger."

Gibson learned that the lawsuit in which the woman had been deposed had emanated from her unknowingly having been the agent for two billionaire Russian oligarchs, and a cartel boss from Venezuela. The latter, upon his arrest, had said he had never even heard of Wyoming until one of his associates had seen an ad that the woman had placed on LinkedIn looking for new clients.

When informed of her clients' infamous identities during the deposition, the elderly woman seemed to be proud that she was representing such wealthy, if criminal, people.

"Little old me. Who would'a thunk it?" she said.

Yeah, lady, who would'a thunk it.

Gibson seized on one filing in Colorado that Pottinger had done under a d/b/a, or "doing business as." He had left one thread of his real identity attached to it. That was probably the mistake of a county clerk or junior attorney somewhere along the paper trail. That happened a lot and was one of Gibson's prime methods for breaking through the elaborate shields the rich and/or criminal threw up to protect their assets.

She then followed that to what turned out to be four layers of corporate shields that she had to break through one after another. Until she finally struck—hopefully—gold. She clicked on a registered agent for a company that Pottinger had set up only a year back and then buried under the shell companies' myriad corporate identities. It was called DPE, clearly after the man's initials, with "Enterprises" probably representing the final letter in the acronym.

The registered agent for DPE was located in Sioux Falls, South Dakota. The man's name was Dexter Tremayne. His was an actual street address and not the more typical PO box. There was also an email address. She wrote out an email informing Mr. Tremayne that she needed to urgently speak with him about DPE.

She sent it off not expecting to hear anything back, at least not for a while.

But it was only seconds later when the email dropped into her inbox.

Can we talk?

He had left a phone number. She immediately called it.

The man confirmed he was Dexter Tremayne.

"I started doing this registered agent crap about two years ago," he said. "Used to be a truck driver. Unhealthiest job there is except maybe for coal mining. Anyway, I live on disability and Social Security and what I earn as an agent. My cousin got me onto it. I've only got fifteen hundred companies right now. He's got nearly thirty thousand. He has spreadsheets and state filing software and credit cards on file for autopay so he doesn't get stiffed. Runs smooth as silk. And he's printing money. That's my goal. To beat him. Got a lot of catching up to do."

"I understand. But why did you want to talk?" asked Gibson.

"I never met anyone from none of the companies I'm an agent for. Not a single one. I remember I got an email from a lawyer once, but he didn't say much. Have no idea who owns any of this shit. My cousin thinks he's got one of them Mexican cartel boys on his roster. Maybe I got me one, too," he added eagerly.

"Okay. But—"

"Wouldn't that be something? Me representing him, so to speak."

"Yeah, really something to tell the grandkids," noted Gibson, trying hard to keep the sarcasm out of her voice.

"Now let me get to the point. Like I said, I never met or heard from any of the owners, *until* this fellow Daniel Pottinger called me up one day. Out of the blue. Could'a knocked me over with a stick."

"How do you know it was him?"

"He said it was. And why else would he be calling me?"

Gibson could think of a few reasons but said, "What did he want?"

"He wanted to tell me something. And I'm going to tell you."

"Why tell me?" said an instantly suspicious Gibson.

"He's dead, right? I saw that on the news. Pottinger was killed in, was it West Virginia?"

"Close enough. But he's dead, yes. Someone killed him."

"Well, he said, if anyone contacted me after he was dead, I was to tell them what he told me to tell them."

Gibson sat up straighter and took up a pen. "And what was that, exactly?"

"He told me to tell the person, 'Now you see it, but then you don't.' Seemed kinda stupid to me, but there you go."

"Did he say anything else?"

"Yeah, as a matter of fact, he did."

"What?"

"He said, 'Then tell 'em to take away the eight.'"

"'Take away the eight'?"

"That's right. The eight. Those were his exact words. He had me write them down."

"What's the eight? And take it away from what?"

"I don't know what to tell you, ma'am. That's what he said."

"Anything else?"

"Yep, then he said for whoever to 'use the leftovers for Sesame Street.'"

"'The leftovers for Sesame Street'?"

"Those were his exact words. God's honest truth."

"Is that it?"

"Yep. Ain't that enough?" he added, with a chuckle.

Gibson thanked him and clicked off.

What in the hell?

51

GIBSON SAT THERE FOR A bit after ending the call. Langhorne seemed to really be having fun with all of this from-the-grave crap. The man's first cryptic message had been "Look harder. It's worth it." And now this.

She had a sudden thought. Had *he* written the phrase *Do as I say, not as I do* on the wall of the room where he'd died? Perhaps writing with one hand and then the other to make it look like two people had done it? No, that probably couldn't be. The same phrase had shown up at Oxblood's home, *after* Langhorne was dead.

Gibson looked at the words again that she had written in her notebook: *Now you see it, but then you don't.*

It felt off to her somehow. She looked it up online.

The common phrase actually was: "Now you see it, *now* you don't." Although she found other references that had it as "Now you see them, now you don't." But the origin seemed clear: It referred to a magician's trickery and sleight of hand. You wanted to hide something, so you did something interesting with one hand to get the audience's attention, while you secreted what you really wanted to hide with the other hand while people weren't looking. And then what did it mean to take away the eight? What eight, and from what was it supposed to be taken away? And then Sesame Street with the leftovers?

Trickery and deceit and hiding shit. Langhorne had definitely chosen the right phrase to use.

But then her spine stiffened. *This is what you do for a living. And you got to Tremayne and he told you what Langhorne wanted him to tell. That was more than you knew five minutes ago.*

Which is why Clarisse picked you in the first place.

What Gibson still didn't get was that if she got there first, Clarisse wouldn't see a penny. So why bring her on if Clarisse could just find the stuff on her own? There was another thing. Gibson wasn't sure she would share this information with Sullivan, either, because her cop radar was telling her there was something off about the man.

So what is your goal here, Mick?

She looked around the modest room in the modest home she lived in. Two kids, no husband. Her working life would be a nonstop grind until the kids were grown and off to college or wherever their lives were going to take them.

But what if you found the treasure? College funds taken care of. Helping her parents. Another house in a nicer neighborhood, not having to juggle a million things at the same time. Having a life. All of that could be accomplished with…

Gibson stared into the screen at her reflection, suddenly unsure of who she was seeing there.

You're getting into dangerous territory, lady. You were a cop, for God's sake. An honest one. And you don't *want that asshole's blood money.*

Her phone rang, jarring her out of these disturbing thoughts. It was Wilson Sullivan.

"Prints came back on Daryl Oxblood. FBI has already called."

"Let me guess. They got pinged on the database search because Oxblood was WITSEC?"

"Yep. In fact, his whole family was. His name was Bruce Hall. His father, Tony, was a midlevel enforcer for a mob boss in New

York City. Turned informant and got put in the program with his wife and son."

"So how did the mother and son end up in The Plains, Virginia?"

"Tony Hall had a heart attack and died. Bruce and his mother opted out of the program after that and literally disappeared. No word from them since."

"Where were they located when they were in the program?"

"That I don't know. FYI, I got a call from an FBI Special Agent Cary Pinker. He's coming in from DC to talk to me about the case."

"Any idea why?"

"Nope. But just so you know, I did tell him about you."

Gibson said, "Okay, what are the odds of my sitting in on the meeting with him?"

"Zero and nada."

"Just thought I'd give it a shot."

"Yeah, I would have, too."

"Can you let me know what he says?"

"Within professional boundaries, yes."

"Thanks."

She clicked off and looked down at her hands. He was holding back. And she was holding back. And Gibson wasn't sure where that would get either of them.

But you've been taking your own tack on this. And he knows nothing about Clarisse, or Langhorne's cryptic message left with his registered agent in South Dakota. So just keep pushing.

She picked up the phone and called Earl Beckett. She told him about Daryl Oxblood's being Bruce Hall.

"Jesus," he exclaimed. "So he's dead, too? We didn't get an alert from the FBI yet."

"And we think there's a connection between his death and Harry Langhorne's."

"What kind of connection?"

"You tell me. Where were the Halls located when they were in WITSEC?"

"I don't know that offhand."

"Can you find out?"

"I could. But I'm not sure I can tell you."

"Why not? They're not in WITSEC any longer *and* they're all dead."

"Doesn't matter."

"You told us about Langhorne."

"I told you when you were with Detective Sullivan. But on your own you're just a civilian. And as a rule the Marshals Service doesn't talk about WITSEC without serious justification."

"Two people's being murdered seems like justification enough for me. And all I want to know are two things: Was Bruce Hall his WITSEC name or his real name? And where were they located when they were in the program? That's it."

"I'll see what I can do," said Beckett.

"And were you able to find handwriting samples for Francine and Doug Langhorne?"

But Beckett had already hung up.

She sat back and fiddled with her pen. *Okay, he's clearly not getting back to me.*

So who had the motive to kill Bruce Hall? Clarisse?

But why, if she and Julia Frazier were one and the same, would she go back to the scene of the crime? She had tried to erase the phrase on the wall, for sure. And she had looked at the comic book that Gibson now had. She was probably regretting that she hadn't simply taken it.

But according to the neighbor Barbara Cole, Frazier had seemed shocked by the discovery of the body. And she had told Cole to call the police before hightailing it out of town.

If not her, then maybe Francine—if Clarisse wasn't her—and/or Doug Langhorne had killed Hall. They could have also killed their father. Although Clarisse hadn't said so, it might have been Doug visiting Langhorne shortly before he was killed, with Francine waiting for him in the car.

She thought it too improbable that former WITSEC members would just run into each other. But why kill Hall? Was he looking for the treasure, too? Did he know something, and Doug and Francine had tracked him down and silenced him after getting that information?

Or was there another reason?

—————

52

Two a.m. and sleep would not come for Gibson; she was exhausted, but her mind would not turn off. She figured she and about eighty million other stressed-out Americans were wandering around their houses right now trying to get their shit straight and then go back to bed, with limited success.

She had already checked on the kids. Sleep came easily for them. Then they woke and proceeded to race a million miles an hour until collapsing from sheer exhaustion.

I wish I still had the energy to do that. But then again, they have nothing to worry about. That's my department. I have everything to worry about.

She walked to her office and settled in front of her computers.

Gibson had been searching for some lead on Pottinger and been mostly disappointed. The only thing she had really scored was the clue that Dexter Tremayne had provided her. But it wasn't much, because she had no context with which to figure it out.

She loaded in her search and the screen started filling up with all things Harry Langhorne.

Born in the town of Yarden in upstate New York in a modest home in a working-class neighborhood, died near Smithfield, Virginia, in an empty mansion. His family had moved to New Jersey before he was five. He'd gone to public schools there and then attended college at Pace in New York City. He'd gotten his accounting degree, and then obtained his CPA license. Then he'd gone to work for the Giordanos. He had married Geraldine, and later they'd had Francine and Douglas.

She read another article about Ida Giordano's being Langhorne's mother and the sister of Leo Giordano, which her father had already told her. That had been the portal, the article had reported, to Langhorne's becoming a mob accountant.

And Langhorne's father, Joel Langhorne, had been one of Giordano's muscle, probably something also connected to his marriage to Ida. Hell, it was probably the reason he had gotten permission to marry Ida, Gibson thought. The mob was not known to encourage outsiders coming into the fold.

You marry one of us, you become one of us, Gibson reasoned.

Joel Langhorne had been killed in a shoot-out with police when Harry had still been in grade school. Gibson wondered if that had changed Harry, made him willing and eager to go over to the dark side. The Giordano family had also taken care of the Langhornes after Joel's death. That had probably endeared Harry to them as well.

Langhorne, by the accounts she could find, had been damn good at his job. The books he maintained evaded all attempts by legal authorities to get to the Giordano family, and others.

Now Gibson asked herself something she should have thought of before.

Why had Langhorne agreed to help the Feds take down the Giordano crime family, if they had taken care of him after his father's death? If they couldn't get the evidence because he was so good at being the mob's accountant, what had happened to make him turn on the hand that fed and protected him and his family?

Art Collin had told her that his undercover work had nailed Langhorne to the wall, forcing him to turn on the Giordanos to save his own ass. But was that really the case? Langhorne struck her as a guy three steps ahead of everyone else. And while Art Collin might have been good at his job, it all seemed too neat and clean. Then something occurred to her which might explain that.

What if Langhorne *wanted* to be caught and then "turned"? And why might he want that? The reason was obvious. Money. He had ripped off the Giordano family. Sooner or later they would knock on his door and kill him. But if he helped the government take them down? He would get federal protection and years to effectively hide what he had stolen. Then he would do what he eventually did: disappear and take that fortune with him, and safely live in the lap of luxury for the rest of his days.

This revelation was so startling that Gibson had to sit there for a few minutes and probe it from all sides to see if it held up. And it did. But she wanted to make sure that her theory *was* correct.

But to find the treasure, she needed to know even more about Langhorne.

Gibson searched article after article from back then, until one, buried deep in the pages of the Newark *Star-Ledger*, fully captured her attention.

She read it twice and then sat back.

Shit, really? Why had no one mentioned this to me before? Why hadn't Beckett—

And then the answer came to her. That was part of the deal. Langhorne brought the mob down, and his own dirty laundry—and this story was explicit about what that dirty laundry might be—would be forgiven. And that was probably the other reason he had turned on the Giordanos. Not just to get the money, but to keep from going to prison over...this.

I guess they did things differently back then. Or maybe they still do today, but nobody ever hears about it.

She searched for any other articles that spoke to this same subject matter, but found zip. That was curious in and of itself, she thought. Then the reason occurred to her. The Feds had put the lid on this. If it had been widely published, the mob's lawyers could possibly have used that in their client's defense.

She emailed the article to Art Collin.

Gibson wanted his take on what this reporter had alleged.

She also Googled the reporter who had written the article, Samantha Kember.

Well, Gibson wouldn't be speaking with Kember. She'd died of cancer fifteen years back.

Hopefully, Art Collin would have some information for her.

Gibson also left an email with Jan Roberts, a reporter now with the *Star-Ledger* whom she had come to know during her time as a detective back in Jersey City when Roberts worked for the local paper there.

She went back to her earlier searches on Langhorne's upbringing.

Joel Langhorne sounded like your typical street enforcer: brutal, sadistic, hard-drinking, and loyal only to the capos above him. His wife, Ida Giordano, seemed to have been totally all in with her mob family. She had nearly gone to prison when her son had turned rat. She doubted that had made the woman love him more. She had died twenty years ago in a state-run nursing home. Langhorne had had no brothers and sisters. He was it for the Langhorne line.

Except for Doug Langhorne.

She looked at what she knew about Langhorne's wife, Geraldine. She had been born in the south, but her family had moved to New York when she was in her early teens. She had met Langhorne there and they had married. Now her husband was dead, and no one knew where Geraldine was. Probably dead, too.

Gibson closed her eyes and slumped in her chair. She had waffled back and forth over this case from the start. *Do I work it? Do I run from it?* Now she was doubting herself again.

This shit is so complicated it'll take you the rest of your life to figure it out, and even that probably wouldn't be long enough. Here you are dreaming about impossible wealth dropping into your lap. Hello, it is not going to happen. So why don't you just leave this to the cops? And now the FBI? And then you can go back to being a computer nerd for ProEye. Nothing dangerous, just nice, steady work.

She ceremoniously turned off her computer and then hurried downstairs. Gibson had remembered she had forgotten to set the house alarm.

She walked over to the panel to do so.

And that was the last thing Gibson remembered.

CHAPTER

53

Gibson came to slowly, and then, with a jerk of her head, she was fully awake and looking wildly around, but seeing only darkness.

She blinked when a light hit her in the eyes. She tried to shield her face but her hands wouldn't move. They were bound to the chair she was sitting in. So were her legs.

Her heart thumping in her ears, she tugged against her bindings and said, "Who are you? Where am I? What are you doing?"

It sounded lame, like lines from a bad movie. But what else was she supposed to say?

The light dipped so it was no longer in her eyes.

"Ms. Gibson, I have some questions for you," said a voice from the dark. "Answer them and you go free. Don't answer them and things get complicated."

Now, that really does sound like a shitty movie script. But it's not, it's real.

"Look, I don't have to answer—"

"Your kids are in your house all alone right now. They probably wake up pretty early. You want to be there when they do, or not?"

This statement drained all the fight out of her. "What do you want to know?" she said.

"Sam Trask?"

"What about him?"

"Why did you go to meet him?"

Now she knew who had snatched her.

"And we know enough that if you try to lie, well, again, it gets complicated. I suppose your parents can take care of your children, though."

Okay, the man was not beating around the bush.

"I was given Nathan Trask's name to check out. And I thought I might start with his father."

Is Nathan Trask the voice or is it one of his cronies? Am I important enough to get the big fish in person?

"By whom were you given that name to check out?"

"Someone I've only met online. I don't know who they are."

"That's hard to believe."

"I know that, trust me. I wish I knew more."

"Why check Trask out?"

"Because he was connected to Daniel Pottinger, the person said."

"Daniel Pottinger aka Harry Langhorne?"

"Yes."

"And the point of this search?"

Gibson thought quickly. *Give him the truth because he probably already knows.*

"Langhorne was a mob accountant turned rat from decades ago. He might have stolen enormous amounts of cash from the mob. There are people trying to find that money. And I got roped into this. If I'd had a choice, I wouldn't be involved."

"Have you found the money?"

"No."

"We have done a deep dive on you, Ms. Gibson. Ex-cop, ex-detective, now a ProEye sleuth, and expert in tracking down large, hidden assets. I'd say whoever roped you in knew exactly what they were doing."

"I'm thinking the same thing."

"We might have a dog in this hunt. It might be that the money that is part of this search did not all come from Langhorne's mob bosses."

"Okay."

"So if you find it, those amounts should come our way. With a finder's fee to you, of course."

This got Gibson's attention. "How much of a fee?"

"Five percent is standard. Do we have a deal?"

"Do I have a choice?"

"People always have choices."

From behind Gibson a garrote was slipped around her neck and pulled uncomfortably tight.

A panicked Gibson gagged and coughed out, "Deal!"

"We have ways of checking to make sure you hold up your end of the bargain."

The garrote was pulled tight one more time before being removed.

"Now what?" said Gibson hoarsely.

"Now you get back to work. For your new partner. Oh, and if you tell anyone, we'll know that, too. So, you talk, then it won't just be you who suffers the consequences. Son, daughter, mother, father, and two younger brothers. The Rogers/Gibson family wiped out. And we might just hunt down your ex-husband and do him, too."

Well, Peter Gibson biting it wouldn't be so bad, thought Gibson in her anesthetic-garbled, garrote-choked mind.

"But just so you know, patience is not a virtue. So pursue this like you're looking at your last sixty seconds on earth. And trophies only go to winners. Losers go into the ground."

Before Gibson could respond a hand pressed something against her face, and once more it was lights out.

54

SHE AWOKE WITH A JOLT and saw the first shimmers of daylight coming in the window of the front room.

Gibson scrambled to her feet, raced up the stairs, and threw open the door to her kids' bedroom. They were there and still sleeping peacefully. Her chest heaving and her heart racing, Gibson felt like she might throw up. She closed the door and sat on the floor in the hall, trying to calm her nerves and her stomach.

She was not doing well with either.

She put her face in her hands and quietly wept, finally leaning back against the wall to steady herself. A minute later she took one long, calming breath and sat up straight, wiping the tears off her face. She rose, trekked to the bathroom, and took a quick shower. When she looked at herself in the mirror afterward, she saw a woman who'd had the wits scared clean out of her.

She looked at her watch. It was after six a.m. Her day was just about to start and all she wanted to do was crawl into bed.

Do I go to the cops? What good will that do? I have proof of nothing. Do I tell my dad? No, God no. He'd go off half cocked and get himself killed.

She made a pot of coffee and then she heard the kids stirring.

Gibson hurried upstairs and hugged them tightly. She got them dressed and downstairs for breakfast, hovering over them as they ate to such an extent that Tommy started giving her worried looks. He was quick to pick up on her moods, Gibson had found.

She attempted a smile as she slid another pancake onto his plate and let him pour the syrup, using both hands on the bottle.

"Good, Mommy?" said Tommy.

She didn't know if he was talking about his syrup pouring skills or her emotional state.

"Good, sweetie," she replied, tousling his thick sandy hair. "Really good."

She spent the morning with them, then let Silva take over.

Gibson rushed to her office and picked up the phone. She hit redial and it rang and rang.

Where are you, Clarisse? Where the hell are you?

She put the phone down and sat in her chair, staring at her twin dark screens.

She had emailed Zeb Brown about her job status. He'd assured her that she still had a position there. ProEye was very pleased with her work, and the assets she'd found on the Larkin matter were so colossal that her taking time off was not a big deal. Take as much time as you need, Brown had told her.

Gibson didn't know if that was true or bullshit, but at least she now had an email trail if it came to a lawsuit. Virginia was an at-will state, but still, she wasn't going down without a fight.

She fired up one of her computers and started going over what she had found on Harry Langhorne the previous night. She even used Google Maps to look at his boyhood home in Yarden, New York.

One ninety-nine Button Road was the address. It seemed that someone was living there now. An old car was in the driveway. There were early spring flowers in the beds around the house. The front porch had a rocking chair.

She noted the few other modest homes on the street. They all looked like people lived in them, too.

Gibson now turned once more to the disturbing article she had found on Langhorne. Then she looked more closely at the date. She saw that the story had come out *after* Langhorne and his family had disappeared into the world of WITSEC.

Some girls in Langhorne's neighborhood in Trenton had come forward and accused him of molestation, of enticing them to take their clothes off while he took their pictures, of sexually abusing them, of even having sex with them.

However, each time Langhorne had convinced the girls not to tell anyone. He had used gifts and glibness and then threats to keep them quiet, the girls had reported. Apparently, their willingness to come forward now had been enhanced by the disappearance of the Langhorne family.

Old Harry couldn't threaten or bribe them anymore.

What the hell had the US marshals done with those revelations? Nothing, apparently. The government had made a deal with the devil, it appeared. But couldn't they have prosecuted the man, regardless of his WITSEC status? She supposed it was a legal gray area, though morally, it shouldn't have been. Gibson also knew that many folks in WITSEC were criminals themselves. If the government started prosecuting them for previous crimes after they had been accepted into the program, it would effectively kill any incentive these folks would have to risk life and limb to come forward and rat out their fellow criminals higher up the food chain.

The next moment she heard a noise outside. She rushed over to the window overlooking the front of the house.

A sedan with federal plates had just pulled into her driveway.

And the man who got out of it screamed Federal law enforcement all the way down to his slightly scuffed black wingtips. He buttoned his jacket, which enhanced the hump where his gun lay in its shoulder holster. He seemed so tightly wound that she thought she could see some wires sticking out of him.

He looked around, clearly unimpressed with Gibson's humble domicile, and then the man headed to the front door. Gibson stepped back from the window.

Oh hell.

55

"FBI SPECIAL AGENT CARY PINKER," said the man after Gibson answered his knock. He took out his cred pack and held it in front of her for a couple of beats too long, at least to her mind.

Intimidation conflagration, she said to herself. She had experienced this as a cop and detective and it washed right off her back. But this guy was a Fed, and she was now a private citizen, so she clearly didn't have the luxury of underestimating him.

"Please come in."

She ushered Pinker into the front room and motioned to the couch, to the one area that wasn't stained from her kids' antics. Tommy and Darby were in the backyard with Silva, which was good. She didn't think she wanted them to be around for any of what Pinker would be saying, even if they couldn't understand it.

They sat down across from each other.

Pinker looked around. "I hear you're a single mom?"

"That's right. I work from home. The kids are in the backyard with their babysitter."

"And you used to be a cop, first forensic tech, then uniform, then detective, all in New Jersey."

"Yes, Jersey City."

"And your father was a beat cop?"

"That's right."

"And now you're currently employed by ProEye as an asset finder."

"That's pretty much my whole story." She smiled disarmingly.

He appeared to ignore this gesture. "And you find yourself in the middle of this mess with Harry Langhorne and another former WITSEC murder in The Plains, Virginia?"

"That's correct."

"I'm surprised that the Virginia State Police are allowing you to work with them on the investigation, but maybe they do things differently down here."

"It's informal. Detective Sullivan knew I had some skills that might help, but it's not like I've been given any special confidences. In fact, he told me he was going to meet with you, but that I was not allowed in the meeting. I'm surprised you came to see me. You haven't even met with him yet, have you?"

"Not yet. But let me explain that."

"All right," Gibson said pleasantly.

"I'm here to find out what you *haven't* told Detective Sullivan. What are the things you've done that have crossed the line? And I want to know what your motivation is to do all those things." He looked around. "Could it be money?"

He settled his gaze back on her.

Gibson took a moment to process all of this. Her earlier daydreaming of riches, and then agreeing, under duress, to find Trask's money for a 5 percent cut, came roaring back, increasing her sense of guilt.

"Are you accusing me of something?" she asked.

He just stared at her for a moment, like she had many a perp in an interrogation room. "I'm here to get to the truth, Ms. Gibson, nothing more, nothing less."

"That's exactly what I'm trying to do."

"You went out to that mansion and found Langhorne's body. You claim that a person called you and conned you into doing so. Why you out of all the people in the universe, I don't know. But for argument's sake, let's say that's true. Why are you still involved? If you were brought into this under some sort of scam or subterfuge, why have you not just walked away from the whole thing? You have children. You have a job. So what the hell are you still doing messing around with this case? Do my inquiries seem unreasonable?"

This burned Gibson's butt more than anything because his inquiries *weren't* unreasonable. She'd be asking the same questions if she were him.

And right at that moment she decided to tell him the truth. Or at least some of it.

"I *didn't* want to be involved in any of this. But the moment I went out and found that body, I was involved. I still tried to get out. Like you said, I've got little kids. I didn't want to do anything to put them in danger."

"Then why did you?" asked Pinker.

"Because I didn't have a choice, okay? There are...there are people who are aware of my involvement. My only way out of this is to solve it. And I was a cop for a long time. It's just my nature." She paused. "Any of that sound unreasonable to *you*?"

He sat back, clearly reassessing her in light of this swift and frank comeback. "What people?"

"Not going there, sorry," replied Gibson.

"Okay, I'll accept that. For now. Have you made any progress?"

"A little. Pottinger is Langhorne. Langhorne probably stole a fortune from the mob. Someone is looking for that money. And I think that's why they got me involved. At ProEye, that's what I do for a living. I look for assets, big ones, in the most unlikely of places."

"And does whoever got you involved in this think you will find this treasure, if it even exists, and then, what, turn it over to them?"

"Maybe," answered Gibson.

He looked at her skeptically. "Have they made threats against you or your family?"

"I think my safest bet is to find the treasure, if it does exist, and then turn it over to the authorities. That way, I'm off the hook, at least the way I see it."

"You didn't answer my question. Have you been threatened?"

"That's all I'm going to say on the matter," replied Gibson.

"Which is an answer in itself. So, do you have any firm leads?"

"Yes, and I've shared them with Detective Sullivan."

Except for all the ones I didn't tell him. Sorry about that one, Will.

"So what do you plan to do going forward?" asked Pinker.

"I'm planning to do some online searches into Langhorne's assets."

"I'm sure the police are doing that as well."

"And is the Bureau?" asked Gibson.

"I can't tell you that."

"Why is the Bureau involved, anyway?"

"I can't tell you that, either. But I'm sure you know that WITSEC is a *federal* program."

"They were no longer in WITSEC," countered Gibson.

"Doesn't matter. They're dead. Someone killed them. We have to figure that out. Next, they might start killing people who *are* still in the program."

"I see your point," said Gibson.

"So I'm less concerned about this 'treasure' than I am about finding the killer or killers."

"I'm sure you know all about the Langhornes?"

"Geraldine disappeared shortly after her husband, and may or may not be dead. Their children, Francine and Douglas, left the program when they came of age. No one knows where they are. You think they might have found their father and, what, exacted revenge for his walking out on them?"

Gibson said, "From what I've learned about Harry Langhorne, his kids were probably thrilled when he left. But I can't say they didn't kill him. Not for sure."

"I take it you've been talking to Earl Beckett with the US Marshals Service?"

"Sullivan and I met with him, yes. He actually was the handler for the Langhornes at their last stop."

"But you still think they might be good for his murder? Get back at the old man for being such a tyrant?" asked Pinker.

"People have killed for less."

"Yes, they have. And Daryl Oxblood?"

"I understand his real name was Bruce Hall," noted Gibson.

"You understand incorrectly. Bruce Hall was his WITSEC name. His actual name was Bruce *Dixon*."

Bruce Dixon? BD? The initials in the comic book. Gibson tried not to show her excitement. "Okay, thanks for that clarification."

She loved it when know-it-alls like Pinker just couldn't resist showing their superior knowledge. But she bet the man would later regret telling her that.

She said, "It seems the same person who killed Langhorne killed Oxblood. Same phrase on the wall. Can't be a coincidence, not that I believe in those, anyway."

"But why kill him?" asked Pinker.

"Beckett wouldn't tell me anything about him."

Pinker said, "The Dixons were neighbors of the Langhornes in New Mexico. Bruce and Francine were friends, *close* friends, by all accounts."

Thank you again. And that one really is important.

She wondered why he was telling her this, when Beckett hadn't even told her the Dixons knew the Langhornes.

Gibson noted, "Beckett said they sometimes consolidated WITSEC families for budget and manpower purposes. But they weren't supposed to tell anyone their real identities."

"And you think kids or adults always follow the rules?" asked Pinker.

"My kids don't and they're just toddlers. I can only imagine what teenagers can get up to. No, I take that back. I remember my teenage years, so the sky's the limit."

Pinker nodded, looking thoughtful. "It might have seemed cool for them. Like being in some elite club that only they knew about. So, Harry Langhorne is dead. And Francine Langhorne's WITSEC friend from decades ago is dead, too. What do you think is going on? Is it connected to the *treasure*?"

"If I knew, I'd tell you, Agent Pinker."

"Why don't I believe that?"

56

CLARISSE SAT IN FRONT OF her twin computer screens staring down at assorted burner phones and notebooks conspicuously labeled for each project she had going.

Gibson knows about Julia Frazier's being in The Plains, Virginia. She knows about the comic book and the initials. She saw the phrase on the wall.

She opened a notebook labeled, simply, THE PAST.

She turned to one page and stared down at the initials she had written there.

BD and RE.

She had once been sentimental, sometimes even caring. She could no longer be that way. Part of her was okay with that, and part of her, a constantly diminishing part, wasn't.

She rubbed her fingers across the letters *B* and *D*. He had been one of them. They had taken an oath, like the Mafia. You never turned on one of your own. Obviously, the years had dulled that solemn promise for some of them.

She looked at her Gibson burner phone. What was the woman doing right now? Tracking Julia Frazier's rental from Dulles to The Plains and back? Had Barbara Cole been able to give enough of a description of Frazier? She wasn't really worried about that. Clarisse knew exactly the outfit and wig and makeup she had worn at The Plains. She would never look anything like that again, having already excised the items from her inventory.

And Gibson couldn't know that Frazier and she were the same person.

The name, driver's license, and credit card she had used at the rental car company were first-rate, with several walls of defense separating her and her alter ego. The problem was that Gibson was a trained investigator with ProEye-level resources.

And going forward those same resources might be used against me.

She went online and performed an extreme electronic scrub down to obliterate any pathway for Gibson to connect the dots on Julia Frazier.

Finished with that, she left her place and drove nearly three hours to an apartment she had been renting for several months. Inside the apartment she put on another wig, teased it into a dull, lifeless bowl shape, and wiped all the makeup off her face. She then put on a pair of jeans and a sweatshirt and flat canvas shoes. She grabbed a small duffel bag and headed out. She drove the rental car to her destination and parked in the back lot of a building after swiping her ID, which hung on a lanyard, against the reader port at the gate. She got into the rear door of the building using the same ID card with the name April Nettles on it.

She had her bag opened and examined.

"You over COVID, Nettles?" said the uniformed guard at the security checkpoint. She was in her forties, and did not look happy to be where she was.

"Yeah, it was a bitch the third time around."

"You're lucky they kept your slot open."

"You want me to come here and infect everybody? And who else would want to do this crap? You guys outsourced all this. No benefits, shitty hours, lousy soul-sucking work, and crummy pay. I wonder how long the line is to sign up? Ha!"

"Hey, it's the American way. Screw the little people, and I include myself in that group."

Clarisse crossed the hall to a locker room, where there was a fresh set of work scrubs that she put on. She joined a team of nine young women as they pushed their cleaning trolleys down a hall and onto a large freight elevator.

They rode it up to the next floor, where the doors opened. One woman, holding a clipboard, stood there and said, "Bowers and Nettles, this floor. Start right, go left." She handed each of them a sheet with instructions and office layouts. "Just in case you forgot, which you probably have, Nettles."

Clarisse hadn't forgotten, and the forewoman knew it. Clarisse had paid her five hundred bucks to let her work this floor tonight. And because they didn't pay the supervisors any better than they did the underlings, the woman had not hesitated to take the bribe.

The forewoman got on the elevator and rode it up with the other cleaning crews, while Clarisse joined with Bowers in pushing her trolley down the hall.

Clarisse said, "You're new, right?"

"Second night," said Bowers, a petite woman with short dark hair.

"Okay, I'll go right, you go left. No reason to double up no matter what they say. We get done faster, maybe we can sneak a smoke break," she added, seeing a pack of Marlboros sticking out of Bowers's pocket.

"Sounds good to me."

Bowers went on her way and Clarisse did the same.

She had a system in place and fast-cleaned her section in half the time allotted. She actually liked to clean. It was a process with an intended result. That was pretty much her life. Clarisse left her trolley in an office and slipped down the hall.

She knew where every surveillance camera was located and carefully threaded that needle.

Clarisse took the second key card from its hiding place behind her first one in the lanyard pocket. This was why she had come back tonight. After doing this crummy job she finally had the key to where she needed to go. Her time off had been necessary, though, since she had had other things to take care of. But one of them had been getting a clone of this key, and it was not an easy one to duplicate.

She darted into the office and went directly over to the desk. She had already secured the password for this computer. She sat down, entered the system, and began her search. She continually shot glances at the door as she worked away.

She accessed the files she wanted, inserted a thumb drive, which had been hidden in her Zippo lighter, and copied what she needed.

She put the thumb drive back into her lighter and secured the lid.

She left the office and met up with Bowers. They took their smoke break outside, propping open a door that was supposed to remain locked. Everyone took their smoke break here, and the ground was littered with butts. The powers that be, not wanting to scare off the few people willing to do this job, had turned the alarm off on this door for that very reason.

While Bowers wasn't looking, Clarisse dropped her Zippo on the ground behind a bush. After her shift was done, she went through the security process, which, on the exit, included X-rays and rigorous searches of both persons and bags. She had not wanted to chance that they would find the thumb drive.

Clarisse left the building, circled back around to where they had taken their smoke break, and plucked her Zippo from behind the bush. She got into her rental car and drove back to her apartment.

She walked up to her place, unlocked the door, and went in.

The voice told her not to move.

So Clarisse didn't.

57

THE PLACE WAS DARK AND it stayed dark.

Clarisse slowly took the Zippo containing the thumb drive from her pocket. She put it inside her jeans and then slipped it into her underwear, and finally secreted it inside herself. It hurt, but it might not hurt as much as what was about to come.

"Who are you? What are you doing in here?"

She observed movement to her right, a shadow only slightly darker than the dark.

"Up close and personal time," said the voice. "And you know the who." The shadow did not move. It didn't have to. Clarisse indeed knew who it was.

"Mind telling me how you did it?"

The shadow moved closer. "Yes, I do mind. I don't want you to reverse engineer. You were always damn good at that, better than me."

"What do you want?" asked Clarisse.

"Obvious, right?"

"Not to me. I thought we had done the communication thing and knew where we stood."

"Really? I'm disappointed. You were always quick on the uptake. You live by your wits. You falling down on the job now?"

"We *had* an arrangement, did we not?" said Clarisse.

"Maybe you *thought* we had one."

"You going rogue?"

"I was born rogue. I thought we all were."

Clarisse shook her head. "No, not born, made. You know that."

"Maybe."

"BD?" she asked.

"What about him?"

"Why?" asked Clarisse.

"Why not?"

"You broke the rule on that one," said Clarisse.

"I make my own rules now. Have for years."

"Still, you didn't have to do it. You just needed his ID for the van to take my mother."

"There are things you never knew. Things I protected you from."

"He was sweet. He was kind. He didn't deserve that. He loved comic books!"

"He loved lots of 'things,' not just comic books."

"You're lying," snapped Clarisse.

"Just you saying it doesn't make it so, babycakes."

The person came into the feeble light filtering in from outside, but she still remained largely a shadow. Then she took one more step forward and could be seen fairly clearly.

The woman had changed. Greatly.

"You don't look good," said Clarisse.

"You, on the other hand, look amazing. Good enough to eat, *babycakes*, even with the dopey wig and plebian clothes. Plebian? Have I educated myself over the years or what?"

" 'Babycakes' was *your* nickname, not mine," retorted Clarisse.

"It would have been yours, but for me," she said quietly, moving still closer.

Clarisse looked for a weapon on her person, even as her hand slipped inside her pocket. "Something I was always grateful for," she said, her fingers closing around the cylinder of pepper spray in her pocket.

"Well, then start appreciating me again. We were all each other had for a long time. And from what I've seen that hasn't changed.

Tell me if I'm wrong. Are you married? Do you have kids? A significant other?" She smiled. "I know you've got nobody."

"I had Mommy. But you have her now."

"Mommy is just fine, never better. She's costing me a mint in Ensure, though, but it'll take more than that to keep her alive. She, like me, doesn't look so good."

"She's had a rough life."

"She just sat there and stared at that rough life consuming all of *us*. Same as my bitch of a mother."

"I told you what I was going to do," said Clarisse. "So I don't know why you're here. And I don't know how you found me here."

"You think you're the only one checking out the Feds? I was on the day cleaning shift for a month and scoping out the night shift when the time came. What a treasure trove of shit that was. And then I found you."

"I thought you'd picked up my trail on the cleaning crew at the Creative Engineering building in North Carolina."

"I did, but I picked you up back there, too. Wasn't hard."

"What was it? What gave me away?"

"Okay, I'll tell you. It was the swagger. Change the hair, face, clothes, body, but you can't change the way you walk. At least not to me."

"But, really, how could you be sure?"

"I'll tell you," she purred. "No one else on the cleaning crew went to pick up a Zippo from behind a bush off the smoking exit."

"Great minds," said Clarisse, her fingers gripping the pepper spray.

"So did you find what you were looking for?"

"Maybe. Does it matter to you?"

"It all matters to me, babycakes. Where's the stash you found?"

"In a safe place."

She grabbed Clarisse's crotch. "Down there, right? Same old hiding place. You need a new location, babycakes." She let go.

Clarisse drew a quick breath. *Deflect and counterattack.* "'Do as I say'? Why use that?"

"It was his mantra. Did you forget?"

"I can't forget any of *that*."

"There you go, then. Seemed fitting, after all."

"Where is Dougie?" asked Clarisse.

"No idea."

"You're lying. He was always loyal to you. Did anything you wanted."

"If you don't want to believe me, don't. By the way, you gonna pull that thing you're holding in your pocket and try and hurt me with it? Go on and try. It might be fun."

"I was certainly thinking about it."

"Well, think about this instead."

Clarisse felt the tip of the knife bite into her neck. She felt the drop of blood freed from her body. It meandered down her long neck like a skier on fluffy snow. "Is that the knife you used to kill Bruce?"

"No, you're special. This one is even sharper."

"You kill me, no treasure."

"Maybe I have enough money."

"Nobody has enough money."

She made one more small nick, her hand wielding the blade like a surgeon. "Tomorrow is promised to no one, but I'm promising it to you, *babycakes*."

And then she was gone.

Clarisse locked the door, hurried to the bathroom, and checked her wounds. They were precise cuts, as close together as snake fangs.

Or a vampire's mark.

And all done in the dark. Impressive.

She cleaned them, bandaged them.

And then threw up.

58

Gibson was staring at her computer screen the next day when the phone rang.

That phone.

"Hello?"

"Mickey?" said Clarisse.

"Are you all right? You sound…shaky."

"So do you."

Gibson hesitated and then just decided to tell her. "I had a visitor the other night." She went on to tell Clarisse about her being kidnapped and interrogated.

Clarisse said nothing for a few moments. "Nathan Trask? You're sure?"

"I don't know if he was there personally, but it was definitely him behind it. And don't tell me you're sorry because I won't believe it. He wants the money that Langhorne stole from him."

"He's more concerned with the loss of face than the money. I made a deal with him to recover it. I would get a piece of the action."

"What!"

"Oh come on, don't act all surprised. I'm not doing this for the fun of it."

Gibson said, "Well, I made the same deal with him. I had no choice if I wanted to walk out of there alive."

"Winner takes all."

"You make it sound like some sort of competition."

"Maybe it is."

"And why do *you* sound off?" asked Gibson.

"I had a visitor, too."

"Who, Trask's goons, too?" said Gibson.

"No. Not Trask."

"Who then? And what did they want?"

"They want the treasure, too, Mickey. And maybe more than that."

"Meaning what exactly?"

"Something that has to remain between me and them."

"If we're open with each other, it might improve our chances of survival."

"I'm actually regretting involving you," conceded Clarisse.

"Why exactly *did* you involve me? You could probably find the treasure without my help."

"It's complicated."

"Only if you make it so."

"I make everything complicated. It's how I'm wired."

"I've never heard you be this candid. That visit must have really shaken you."

"I don't like it when people can find me. Do you?" Clarisse snapped.

"I'm not in hiding."

"Well, I *am*."

With this stunning admission Gibson sensed vulnerability in the woman, for perhaps the first time. And she wasn't quite sure how to play it. She decided to attack. The kidnapping by Trask's people had lent a sense of urgency that was undeniable.

"Julia Frazier?"

"Who?" Clarisse said offhandedly.

A few seconds before, Gibson had connected the phone to her computer's dongle and fired up her voice analyzer. She now watched on the screen as the arrow stayed rock steady.

She wondered what her next questions would do to the woman.

"Why were you in The Plains that day? Are you RE? And did you care for Bruce Hall aka Bruce Dixon aka Daryl Oxblood? RE and BD? I read it in a comic book. Just asking. Was it shocking to find his body like that?"

Clarisse ended the call.

Gibson stared at her screen where the stress arrow had crashed right through the top bar like a bolt of lightning reversing to the heavens.

For some weird reason, it didn't make her feel any better.

59

Clarisse was on a train, for the first time in a long time. She had decided against another plane ride. She wanted to be tethered to the earth right now. She could not jump out at 35,000 feet, but she could leave a train with relative ease.

She had packed everything from her rental into two bags and Ubered to the train station. Just to be safe, she had gone into the women's room, changed her appearance in a stall, and exited the bathroom with one small duffel.

She boarded the train and headed north. She stared out the window into the deepening darkness. As the train picked up speed and the ride became gently swaying, she closed her eyes and tried to process what had happened.

There were two major events, neither one of them good for her. *She tracked me down. All my precautions, all my work, and she still managed to do it.*

She touched the wound on her neck.

Would she have cut it all the way?

Look what she did to Bruce.

She pressed her fingers against the coolness of the window.

Next up were Gibson's stunning revelations. *She knows I was Julia Frazier in The Plains. And she's figured out the connection to Bruce Dixon.*

I've got two of them breathing down my neck, literally.

Then her spine firmed.

Come on. You've got this. They haven't beaten you yet.

She took out her laptop and inserted the thumb drive in the dongle.

She brought up the files and quickly sorted through them.

The one she was looking at now was, in a nutshell, all the US Marshals Service had on the Langhorne family.

She knew most of it, but not all. She saw pictures of Harry Langhorne when he had been the mob accountant. Tall, somewhat nice-looking, but the arrogance in those eyes, the evil lurking inside what most would assume was a mild-mannered dollars-and-cents counter.

She went through the man's history, from cradle to, now, the grave. The file had dutifully been updated to include the death (murder, technically) of Harry Langhorne, aka Daniel Pottinger. But that hadn't ruined the marshal's perfect record, since Langhorne had left WITSEC long before he was killed.

She glanced away when the pictures of the Langhorne family came up: the mother, the son, the daughter. She knew enough about all of them.

The images were suddenly coming to her again. As they once did on a daily, sometimes hourly, basis. She had managed that anxiety for a long time. Years, in fact. She had done so through her concentration on grifting, and in her piles of notebooks compartmentalizing her very existence.

Clarisse looked around, but all the other passengers within her sight line were asleep.

You suffer in silence, you remember that. Seen but not heard. Used, but never a word uttered. Things done to you. Never a protest. But there had been crying; she couldn't help that.

They actually liked the tears. They longed for the tears to be shed. It made them happy. And even more sadistic.

She refocused on the computer screen and the information there.

The man had his treasure and she meant to have it now that he was dead. It would not make up for anything. She just wanted it because Clarisse knew the dead man would not want her to have it. That was enough motivation. More than enough.

Dig deeper.

She opened the Treasure notebook and started writing in a precise hand everything that she knew to that point. She figured if she looked at it all comprehensively, she might see something connect to something else.

The treasure must be at Stormfield, she concluded after about a half hour. The note was left on the boat. The place had many nooks and crannies to hide things within. And the grounds were immense.

Do I go there and start searching? How much time will I have? Who gets the property? What was in the man's last will and testament, if he even had one? Why am I just thinking of all this now?

Clarisse got off at the next stop.

60

Stormfield rose from the darkness, like a nightmare from the subconscious. Its facade was shrouded in the fog that had settled in during the night along with a steady rain.

Clarisse had driven her rental car to within a quarter mile of the place and then walked the rest of the way in the wet with only an umbrella to shield her. She didn't want to be doing this, but what was the alternative, really?

Her flashlight beam stabbed the dark, and she arced it around before moving to the front steps. The door was locked and the key was no longer under the cat statue—she had found that on her first visit here—but she had tools sufficient to defeat it. The door creaked as she opened it, causing the woman to grit her teeth.

Clarisse closed the door and shone the light in front of her.

She had been here once before, stumbling upon the man's body in that secret room. He hadn't summoned her, as she had told Gibson. She had never worked with Daniel Pottinger in Miami. But after years of searching she had discovered that Pottinger and Langhorne were one and the same. But he was already dead. She knew who had killed him. The message on the wall told her that.

DO AS I SAY, NOT AS I DO.

That had been Langhorne's mocking, sadistic mantra. He could do anything he wanted to anyone, but he demanded complete obedience from all those under his power.

She stood there and let this memory take ahold of her for a few moments.

Her goal in finding him had been twofold: first, to find the location of the treasure, a fact that he had let slip long ago; and second, to kill him for his past crimes against humanity.

Against me.

She started on the east side of the building and slowly made her way west.

Then she trekked upstairs to find the only bedroom that was furnished. This was where Langhorne had slept, presumably. She looked through the meager items for a possible additional clue, but came up empty.

She headed downstairs and worked her way from room to room, finally entering the last room on the lowest level, which appeared to be a wine cellar. There were wooden crates etched with the names of vineyards from France, Italy, and Spain. There were a few cracked bottles in the shelving along the walls. But if he was never here, why have a wine cellar? And the whole thing appeared to her to be...what was the word...*staged.*

She sat on one of the old crates and peered around. The smell of the nearby water was particularly strong, as though the river had somehow encroached on Stormfield's foundation.

Harry Langhorne was the king of mind games. He would turn your own brain against you. But he had also been cagey, intuitively a survivalist. And he had to be because the people who had wished him harm were very good at killing.

So where would a vindictive, cagey asshole hide his ill-gotten money? She looked at the floor under her feet. Was it just under here? Crates of gold bars? Trunks of dazzling jewels? Paper currency? But all that would take up a lot of space. And in this climate unprotected paper would quickly rot. How was she to get to it? Jackhammer up the floor and concrete foundation beneath it?

Dig deeper. That had been his admonishment from the grave.

Well, this was the lowest spot in all of Stormfield. If one were to dig deeper, it would be here. Yet that somehow seemed too ordinary, too anticlimactic. The man had had ample time to come up with a more inventive location for his plunder.

So would he anticipate that I would come down here? To this very spot? To dig, while he laughed, hopefully from hell? Or had his message been literal, only in another sense?

She rose as an idea occurred to her. He had left behind one message, perhaps he had left another.

Clarisse started searching through the crates, but then another thought struck her. It would make sense, after all. In a classic manner at least.

There were only five bottles down here. Four were empty and cracked; one was intact but empty of any wine. Well, that was intriguing in and of itself. Why have a corked bottle with nothing in it?

Or was there something inside?

She used a rusty wine opener lying on one of the crates to uncork the bottle.

Nothing.

"Shit," she muttered.

Was she just wrong about all of this? Was it just a wine cellar only with no wine?

But the one constant in Clarisse's life was attention to detail. Her hundreds of notebooks compiled over the years would attest to that. So she examined the cork closely in case something was embedded in it. She hit the glass with her light to see if there was any writing or clue on it.

And then her attention turned to the wine label. It was not entirely affixed to the glass. One edge was curled up. She slowly and carefully removed it. The folded-up slip of paper secreted behind it fell out.

A message outside *a bottle. How quaint, Harry.*

However, the message was anything but quaint.

This is the twenty-first century. Act like it, you idiot.

She stared at the paper for a few moments before slipping it into her pocket.

Twenty-first century?

Okay, that could mean a number of different things, some apparent, others not. She had just started pondering a few of the more obvious ones when she heard a noise from above.

As she listened, it was repeated.

It seemed she was not the only person at Stormfield tonight.

61

CLARISSE'S HAND CLOSED AROUND THE pepper spray as she quietly left the wine cellar and made her way slowly upward. She didn't want to be trapped in the bowels of the place with no way out.

She felt her breath quicken as she reached the main level and cautiously peered around. Clarisse didn't dare use her flashlight. She listened for additional sounds, but the quiet remained unbroken.

Did they hear me? Are they waiting for me to show myself?

Who could it be? she wondered. The ones who had come here and killed Langhorne? She shuddered at encountering *her* again. Was it the police? But why would they come in the middle of the night? Was it Nathan Trask's men, looking for the treasure, too? And if they found her here?

That would likely be the end of me.

She kept moving forward, growing ever closer to the front door.

What she would give to be back in her safe quarters surrounded by her notebooks with their comforting details.

She heard another noise; it sounded like one person. Then it all depended on who that one person was. She put the message she had found in the bottle into her mouth, chewed it up, and swallowed the gummy remains. If the person found her, they would not find what she had.

Next, the assertive steps she had heard up to now turned to stealth.

Maybe she had left wet footprints in the entrance hall. Or had they noticed her car parked along the road?

She screamed when the hand clenched her shoulder.

She looked up into the face of the tall, strongly built man.

"What are you doing here? Who are you?"

The pepper spray hit him right in the face, causing him to drop his flashlight, clutch his face, and stagger backward. He slammed into the wall.

"God damn it!" he cried out in pain.

She ran down the passage and hurtled through the open doorway, her gloved hand reaching in her pocket for her car keys. She passed the sedan parked in front and ran flat-out away from Stormfield, and reached her car. She drove pell-mell to the main road, turned left, and gunned the motor. When she got to a highway Clarisse finally slowed down. She drove to the car rental place, where she dropped off the vehicle and left the keys in the overnight box.

She had recognized the man. Clarisse had just pepper-sprayed Wilson Sullivan!

It was three in the morning and she wasn't quite sure what to do.

Then something occurred to her. Something that, for her, was truly outlandish.

Clarisse made the call, desperate to hear the other woman's voice for some reason. She was breathing so fast her body temperature had cooled, making her teeth chatter.

"Hello?" the voice said sleepily.

"Mickey, it's me."

"I know it's you since it's the phone you left me. Do you have any idea what time it is?"

"Can…can I come to see you? Right now? Something's happened."

Gibson said nothing for several long and, to Clarisse, disquieting moments.

"Mickey?"

"I'm…I'm here. You…want to come and see *me*?"

"Yes."

"What happened?"

"I...I was at Stormfield tonight."

"Why?"

"I was looking for the treasure."

"Did you find anything?"

"I...can't we do this in person?"

"What else happened?"

"Someone else showed up while I was there. He grabbed me."

"Who grabbed you!"

"Wilson Sullivan."

Gibson did not say anything for several seconds. Then: "Did you speak to him?"

"No."

"Did he identify himself to you?"

"No. But I knew it was him."

"How do you even know what he looks like?"

"It's in my best interests to know as much as possible about things that could affect me. It was him. He grabbed me and got a face full of pepper spray for his troubles."

"You pepper-sprayed a cop?"

"He didn't announce himself as a cop. And I pepper-sprayed him before I realized who it was. And what was he doing at Stormfield in the middle of the night?"

"It's a crime scene."

"He was by himself. And haven't they long since released the property as a crime scene? And what was so important that he showed up at this time of night?"

"I...he...where are you?"

"I can be there in twenty minutes. And Mickey?"

"Yes?"

"I can't tell you everything, maybe not much at all."

"Can you at least tell me your real name?"

"I've developed the habit of not trusting anyone."

"Then why are you coming to see me?"

"Because of all the people I know you're by far the closest to the person I believe I can trust."

"Your sudden change of heart is perplexing."

"I would say the same if the positions were reversed."

"I'm not doing anything illegal to help you."

"I wouldn't ask it."

"Do you prefer tea or coffee? Or something stronger?"

"Coffee will be fine."

"See you in twenty."

62

GIBSON STARED AT HER FRONT door and then her gaze shifted to the upstairs where her kids were sleeping. Part of her couldn't believe she was inviting a stranger—no, not exactly a stranger, but perhaps a *psychopath*—into her home in the middle of the night. The only thing standing between this visitor and her kids?

Me. Should I call the police and have them waiting to arrest her? But for what, exactly?

And Gibson figured the woman would be savvy enough to thoroughly check out the neighborhood for signs of police before exposing herself.

She fingered her pistol in her waistband. Whatever happened tonight, she was not going down without a fight. Hell, she was not going down at all.

Gibson went to the window and peered out. She had turned no light on in the house, so her presence at the window would not be visible to anyone on the street watching her place. She flinched when the figure came into sight. She was walking. Gibson looked up and down the street and saw no strange car parked at the curb. And she had not heard a car, either.

She watched her all the way up the drive. Tall, thin, her gaze pointed down, hands stuffed in pockets.

Gibson was waiting at the door when the person tapped lightly. She opened it and, finally, the two women came face-to-face after knowing each other only as voices.

Gibson looked her up and down, while Clarisse did the same right back.

The latter's hair was blond and cut short. Her cheeks were flushed, perhaps from the walk in the rainy, chilly air. Gibson looked her over for weapons. She would prefer doing a strip search after going through the women's bag, but opted to keep her hand on the butt of her gun instead as she stepped back and motioned her visitor in.

Clarisse noted the gun but said nothing.

Gibson closed the door behind them and locked it. Keeping her gaze on the woman, she pointed toward the kitchen. "Let's keep it down. My kids are asleep."

"Of course," Clarisse said.

They sat in the kitchen after Gibson had poured out the fresh coffees. Both women took it black.

Clarisse took a few sips and then stared down into the depths of her drink while Gibson studied her.

"You look familiar to me for some reason," she said. "Did we meet somewhere, sometime?"

"Do you want to talk about the past, or the present and then our futures?"

Gibson sat back and stared at her. "*You* called this meeting."

"What do you know about Wilson Sullivan?"

"I know he's a detective with the Virginia State Police."

"Is that all?" said Clarisse.

"Do I need to know more?"

"Knowing less is never a good thing. Is he aware of the treasure?"

"I did talk to him about that, yes. He didn't seem all that interested."

"I think he's very interested. I believe that's why he was at Stormfield tonight, looking for it. Why else would he have been there?"

"When I was a detective, I worked crazy hours. I would get a theory and want to test it."

"What theory needed testing at Stormfield? Daniel Pottinger was Harry Langhorne. Shortly before his death he was visited by a man while a woman waited outside in the car. Sullivan knew this but didn't tell you. Langhorne was poisoned and found in a secret room with a strange phrase on the wall written, you think, by two people."

"Would that be the man and the woman who had visited Stormfield? You know who they are, don't you?"

"I have my theories."

"And who are you really?" asked Gibson.

"Do you have a theory?"

"Two, actually. Either Francine Langhorne, or someone with the initials—"

"—RE. Yes, I know. You mentioned that before. What I really need for you to do is find out more about Sullivan."

"I can check into some things. But you could have asked me over the phone. Why come here and show yourself to me?"

"I don't *show* myself to anyone. Tomorrow I will look nothing like this."

"How about Doug Langhorne? Any idea where he might be?"

"He might be the man who visited Harry Langhorne right before he died."

"And the woman in the car might be Francine Langhorne? So are you saying that leaves you out of the running to be her?"

"Think what you want."

"I have little kids to take care of."

"I know that."

"Do you have someone to take care of, like maybe a parent?"

To her credit Clarisse showed no reaction to this question.

"What makes you say that?"

"Just something you mentioned in passing."

"I must be more careful in choosing my words with you, then."

"Is that a yes?"

"Everybody has problems."

"You had to take a call when we were talking one time. I think you believed you had disconnected our call but you hadn't. I noted the tone of your voice. It was like mine when I got a call that my dad had been taken to the hospital with chest pains. Trying not to panic, but barely keeping it together."

"You love your parents, right?"

"Of course."

"Well, that's where you and I differ."

Gibson said, "All right, so all you want out of this is the treasure? Is that it? Just money."

"Sometimes money is more than money," replied Clarisse.

"What then?"

"Debts must be paid, Mickey. Otherwise there are consequences."

"You were rattled tonight. By Sullivan. That's why you're here."

"I have found that in life strategic alliances are the only way to achieve certain goals. You are one of those alliances."

"An involuntary one."

"Break this case and you can name your own ticket. Unless you want to spend the rest of your life hiding behind a computer."

"Isn't that what you do?"

"Obviously not, or else I would not have been at Stormfield tonight where I indeed did find a clue."

Gibson looked intrigued. "Where and what was it?"

"In the old wine cellar. It was behind the label of an old bottle. Get it, message *outside* a bottle? It said that we're in the *twenty-first century* now, so act like it. And then it called the finder an idiot."

"Do you have any idea what that means?"

"It means the treasure is not buried somewhere for us to dig it up. Apparently we have to look at more *modern* devices."

"Any thoughts on that?"

"I will have them. Perhaps you, too?"

"Perhaps."

Clarisse glanced upward. "How are your children?"

Gibson's lips set firmly. "Sleeping. Peacefully. I want to keep it that way."

"Children are precious."

Gibson studied her. "I think you really mean that."

Clarisse sipped her coffee. "I lie. A lot. But not about that."

"I think that even if you do find this treasure, it will not be enough to pay off the debt that you're owed."

"How can you possibly know that?"

"I read a story in a newspaper about Harry Langhorne. How he liked to play with little girls in the most disgusting, repulsive ways." She paused and eyed the woman. "Were you one of his victims?"

Clarisse rose. "I think that I chose wisely, Mickey. You have been everything I could have hoped for. And more. But don't try to predict either my motives or my future. As good as you are, no one is that good. And you will check on Sullivan?"

"I will make discreet inquiries."

"Thank you."

"Do you want to stay here? Are you safe?"

These queries, earnestly given, seemed to stagger Clarisse for a moment. "Let your children sleep. Peacefully, tonight and every night. And me staying here would not be a good thing, for you or them. But thank you for the offer. And thank you for the coffee."

"Why did you bring me into all this? Really?"

"You had everything, Mickey. Everything. And you pissed it away. So maybe I just wanted to teach you a lesson. And maybe teach myself one at the same time."

Gibson's expression hardened. "What the hell are you talking about? Pissed what away? You don't even know me."

"I know you better than you think. Maybe better than I know myself."

She turned and walked out.

Gibson locked the door behind her and then put her back to it.

What the hell had that parting shot been about?

She had finally met the woman who had dominated her thoughts of late and not in a good way.

So did I just meet Francine Langhorne, or RE? Or a third party I haven't heard of yet?

And I had everything, but pissed it away?

Gibson went back to bed but didn't sleep a wink.

63

Tʜᴇ ɴᴇxᴛ ᴍᴏʀɴɪɴɢ, ᴀꜰᴛᴇʀ ꜰᴇᴇᴅɪɴɢ her kids and then handing them over to Silva, Gibson rushed to her office and fired up her computer.

Her search this time focused on Wilson Sullivan.

He had joined the El Paso police force at age twenty-one. He moved up there before heading to a comparable position in Arkansas, where he achieved his detective status. After that were short stints in South Carolina, then North Carolina, and, finally, Virginia.

That was a lot of hopping around, she thought. She didn't know if that was because he was just that type, or whether the police forces had asked him to leave. If so, she might be able to dig up something unless they had buried it, which, she knew, police departments often did.

And the thing was she could find nothing about him before he joined the police force in Texas. It was like a black hole. She went on sites that she used for ProEye to do more sophisticated searches and pulled a big fat zero on them.

Okay, put a pin in Sullivan and move on to something else.

She pulled up the photo she had of Francine Langhorne and compared it to her recollection of Clarisse from the previous night. Maybe a hint around the nose, the slightly off-kilter luminous eyes that gave them considerable depth, but she couldn't be sure that the decades-old grainy photo of a little girl with big, sad eyes was the adult woman who had been in her house.

She next pondered the clue that Langhorne had left behind.

It's the twenty-first century, act like it.

She knew better than most that there were many modern ways to hide money, assets, treasure. One didn't need a safe-deposit box, or a bus locker ticket, or a trunk and a shovel with which to dig a hole.

And if she had learned anything while at ProEye, it was that assets were liquid and nonliquid, but one could be made into the other with blinding speed and done so behind a wall of secrecy. And those assets could be transformed *and* transferred in ways that would make it nearly impossible to trace their origins.

The one twenty-first-century possibility that leapt to her mind was cryptocurrency. Ironically, this esoteric system of creating value—which was tied to reams of numbers spewed out by oceans of computers—could usually be traced fairly easily. This was because of the system's stringent registration requirements, which were the only things that made crypto valuable.

Even though it seemed that bitcoin had been around since the Roman Empire, it had only been created in 2008 by a still-unknown person using the alias Satoshi Nakamoto.

Once you registered an account online and took possession of your coins—which weren't really coins, but digital assets—your account was placed on a blockchain. The blockchain was the electronic ledger that kept everyone honest and the bitcoin worth anything. With that Gibson could find what you had, even perhaps if you later placed it in a secure wallet. This wallet wasn't made of leather; it was more likely in the form of a thumb drive–like device, but still tethered to the blockchain.

The FBI had long exploited the fact that persons using bitcoin for illicit purposes weren't as careful as they should have been. They got impatient, or tried shortcuts. That had cost the creator of the billion-dollar Silk Road drug operation his freedom, and it put in prison another ambitious criminal with a $150 million Ponzi scheme. And it had cratered a young Frenchman's multimillion-dollar embezzlement plan. All thieves using bitcoin. All caught and held accountable because they had messed up.

Gibson thought of the digital evidence left behind for the cops and people like her to find as Bitcoin Breadcrumbs.

But folks were getting more careful because if Gibson or the cops found you on the blockchain, it wasn't just one illicit transaction that would be exposed. It would be everything you ever did with crypto. Since crypto was a fairly recent phenomenon, Gibson knew that Langhorne had to have put his stolen mob money elsewhere for many years.

Gibson's fingers flew over the keys, and for the next hour she looked for the obvious places where Langhorne might have buried his ill-gotten fortune.

And she came up with exactly nothing.

Why would I think the asshole would make it easy?

She was about to try another search when her phone rang. Her real phone.

It was Zeb Brown.

"What's up?" asked Gibson.

When Brown didn't answer right away, she knew something was up. "Zeb?"

"Look, Mick, the company wanted me to email you, but I told them that you deserved better."

"What are you talking about?"

"I'm afraid ProEye is letting you go."

The blood drained from her face. "Letting me go? Why?"

"They didn't give me a reason, just a directive."

"I thought I was on leave. I thought that things had been explained. You told me so."

"I thought so, too, until the phone call I got."

"You're telling me you have no inkling why this happened?"

"Look, I'm not supposed to say anything."

"Say it anyway, Zeb, this is serious to me. I'm a single mom with two little kids."

"Someone here got a call from somebody. And that got it rolling."

"Who?" demanded Gibson.

"I don't know, but it was apparently someone important. But on the bright side, they're giving you two months' severance. And you already got the Larkin bonus, of course."

"There is no bright side to getting canned. And how about my family health insurance?" said a panicked Gibson.

"You can go on the marketplace."

"The open enrollment period has passed for this year."

"You can do COBRA."

"Do you know how expensive that is? ProEye was picking up the premium. And with no job what exactly am I supposed to use to pay for it?"

"I'm really sorry, Mick. But you'll get hired somewhere else. You're really good. I'll give you a reference. Again, I'm sorry."

"Can't you poke around and find out *who* got me canned?"

But he had already clicked off.

Gibson stared at her stunned reflection in the black of her dormant computer screen.

What in the hell had just happened?

64

CLARISSE SAT IN FRONT OF her computers, her notebooks neatly stacked beside her. Everything in her life seemed normal, at least according to her eccentric standards. But there was nothing normal about any of this anymore.

She glanced at one notebook that she had labeled HOW I DIE.

With Mickey Gibson she had voluntarily made contact with an actual person who might know who she was. She had pepper-sprayed a cop who was taking perhaps an unprofessional interest in the murder of Harry Langhorne and the treasure the man had left behind. She had a formidable person from her past hot on her trail. And this person also had her mother as captive. And lastly, an international criminal was counting on her to retrieve his money stolen by Harry Langhorne.

And if I disappoint him?

As soon as she had found the note in the wine cellar, she had thought about ways Langhorne could have concealed his fortune. Crypto had instantly occurred to her, as she was sure it had to Gibson as well. But she had one advantage over Gibson. She had known Langhorne, so she didn't think that was it. Crypto was fallible; one could lose enormous amounts of money in seconds. In that regard it was no more a currency than a highly volatile penny stock. Langhorne did not like to lose at anything. He would have opted for something with more certainty as to value. He would have most likely put the money into an *appreciating* asset.

She picked up her MICKEY GIBSON notebook and rifled through the pages. The truth was she could have looked for the treasure all on her own. But the reasons she had not, and why she had involved Gibson, were complicated, just like she had told Gibson they were.

She was the big girl on campus. She could have been anything. She didn't turn pro in basketball. She didn't even try her luck on Broadway. Then she became a cop. Okay, that was fine. But then she married that jerk and she let him ruin her life. How had the big girl on campus allowed that to happen? Now she's driving a mommy van and sitting behind a computer screen pissing her life away. I brought her into this to kick her ass, sure. But I also brought her into this to wake the woman the hell up.

She had filled six entire notebooks devoted to the life of Mickey Gibson.

Clarisse let her fingers drift over the computer keys.

But still, how pathetic is that? What right do I have to judge her decisions? And she was kind to me, when she didn't have to be. Of course I've changed my appearance so much that she didn't recognize me. But I remembered what she did for me. And it just kills me to see how… ordinary her life has turned out to be.

Mickey Gibson had been the odd combination of stud athlete and Bohemian artist. She was whipping balls to teammates one night and singing her guts out the next, while dressed as a French revolutionary in a college production of *Les Misérables*. And everyone adored her.

Clarisse could have easily hated her for that, but found she couldn't. The woman was nice to everyone, without a hint of an ego.

When I served her food in the cafeteria, or when I pulled wardrobe for her during the theater productions, she was unfailingly polite and always had a smile for me. Even though I was a poorly paid kitchen worker, an unpaid stagehand, whatever the university wanted me to be. Back then I just wanted a roof over my head and some food in my belly.

That was a simple life that part of her sometimes yearned for now. Her existence now was so complicated.

And Gibson had a loving family. Clarisse had none of that.

But she imagined that back at Temple she and Mickey Rogers had talked about roles they wanted to play. That Gibson had encouraged her, helped her with memorizing lines, given her the courage to audition.

Now that fantasy seemed laughable, and, even worse, pitiable.

You were such a loser you had to imagine you had friends.

But I could have been Mickey Gibson. I could have been the big girl on campus with adoring parents. And I wouldn't have thrown it all away like she did. I never got that chance, though.

And there had been that encounter on the campus, late at night when the creep had assaulted her. It had been terrifying and…Gibson had been there. Clarisse should have been immensely grateful but she hadn't been. It had made her mad, furious even, for reasons she couldn't really explain.

But maybe I can now. I didn't want to be saved by her, or anyone else. It just showed I had no control over any part of my life. Because, in the end, the only person who could save me was myself.

She had left the university the following day and started out on what had become her career: lying, cheating, stealing, manipulating, giving back to others what she had been force-fed most of her life. In her more rational moments, she knew none of it made sense. But for a long time now, it had become the only way she could make sense of the world. There were winners and losers. There were the strong and the weak. Those in control and those being controlled by others, and didn't she know the hell that came with that last one?

So when Clarisse had walked into Stormfield that day to find Harry Langhorne dead, her thoughts had pivoted instantly to the nearby Gibson. In her mind, the plan came together perfectly. She would show Gibson that she was actually the stronger one—the winner. And if Gibson did manage to help her find the treasure, all the better. Clarisse would have still won.

And what else really matters?

But she asked if I wanted to stay at her house. Whether I was safe.

No one had ever asked her those things before. But it didn't surprise her that Gibson had. She was a good person.

Unlike me.

Clarisse shook her head and wiped her eyes.

Get a grip, girl.

She refocused on a picture on her computer screen.

Wilson Sullivan. There was something about the man that was making her warning antennae scream.

While Gibson was looking for treasure, she decided to start looking at the Virginia police detective.

If that was all he really was.

CHAPTER

65

The next morning Clarisse watched from across the street as Sullivan left the police building in Virginia Beach and got into his state-issued sedan. It was drizzling and the skies were darkening, promising still more precipitation after the previous night's steady rainfall.

She put her rental car in gear and moved into traffic two vehicles behind him.

They drove a familiar route, and ended up back at Stormfield. She had turned off before they arrived there because traffic had thinned and she didn't want to be spotted. But she was certain that could be the only place out here that he would be going to.

She parked and approached the house on foot, drawing her hoodie closer around her as the air chilled and the rain picked up.

Clarisse moved past the mailbox and flitted through the trees until she reached the edge of the lawn opposite the front entrance. His sedan was parked there.

She ran across the grass and reached the east wing of the home, where she peered into one of the windows. It was dark inside, so she could really see nothing. The man must be using a flashlight. And then to confirm this theory she saw a stab of light cut through the interior. He was moving along the hall to the main staircase. And then he took it down.

Well, if he made it to the wine cellar he would find it bereft of messages. She licked her lips and remembered how the paper had tasted in her mouth.

"Hey, babycakes."

Clarisse turned at the sound of the voice, right as a cloth covered her face.

* * *

Clarisse awoke slowly at first, and then in a panicked rush of cortisol plowing into her bloodstream, she sat up, or would have if she hadn't been restrained.

She looked around at the decrepit room: paint peeling, floors wooden and filthy, one window, the single light bulb overhead feeble and pulsing. She was on a bed with her arms and legs tied to the bedposts. The smell here was not pleasant.

She could hear the rain tapping on the roof, in the distance a growl of thunder.

"Welcome back, babycakes. It was only a short ride down slumber lane for you. I know just how much to use. Helps me sleep at night."

Clarisse looked directly in front of her to see the woman sitting there in a hardbacked chair, one leg draped over the other. She could see her far better in this light than in her own apartment, when the woman had previously gotten the drop on her. She was heavier in the face and butt and hips, Clarisse noted. The hair had changed color, going from soft brown to stark red. It was not a wig, she could tell. It was the work of a colorist. A good job, but the shade did not flatter her complexion.

Clarisse managed to settle her head at a better angle on the pillow.

"And you thought this was a good idea, why? I was watching someone who is looking for the treasure, too."

"I know that," she said casually. "I know lots of things. Some more than you, some less. Which is why it *was* a good idea to bring you in for a chat. A *debriefing*, the law guys call it."

"What did you use on me?"

"Can't spell the name or pronounce it, but it works real good." She rose and drew closer. She was dressed in jeans and boots and a long sweater that covered her butt.

"You've really lost weight," said the woman.

Clarisse said, "I lost my appetite about twenty years ago. You, on the other hand, went the other way."

"I survived, so I ate what I wanted. You should try it sometime. You're too skinny."

She pulled her chair next to the bed and sat down.

"And my mother?"

"She's around here. You probably smell her pee and other stuff. We moved her to another room so we could use this one for you."

" 'We'?"

"Don't get curious. It's not a good look, and I'm not in the mood. Wilson Sullivan is the cop you were watching. Tell me why."

"Like I said, he's looking for the treasure. He may be a cop but he's not acting like one."

"Why's that?"

"Well, one compelling theory is that he, like us, is not who he once was."

The woman looked thoughtful. "And who might that be? The person he might have been, I mean."

"One of the gang from the old days who changed his appearance? That's one possibility."

"I don't think so. I recognized Bruce. I recognized *you*, even with all the shit you've done to yourself. I'd recognize anybody from the old days. I have a gift for it. And I work at it. For obvious reasons, survival being the top one. You know what they did to us. They're not getting a second shot. And I saw Sullivan before and my meter did not buzz once."

"Okay, where is the other half of 'we'?"

"Off doing things as 'other halves' often do. Busy, busy, busy."

"So you lied about him not being around anymore?"

"Let's get back to the mystery man. If not the old days, what else?"

"First, I need to see my mother," said Clarisse.

"Why?"

"Chiefly to make sure she's not dead."

"Again, why? You never loved her. You always wanted to kill the bitch. Don't try to lie and say that wasn't true. Or that your feelings have changed. Feelings don't change after that shit. No, I'm wrong, they do. They get stronger. So you just want to kill her *more* now, right?"

Clarisse shook her head. "It's not that simple. Maybe it was back then, not now. And I'm her caretaker. But just so you know I haven't totally turned into a wimp, I spent good money keeping her alive and if anyone's going to kill her, it's going to be me. Not you. So bring her to me. Now."

"Feisty today, huh? All tied up as you are? Sure, you can see her. I'll just wheel her right in. It's about time for her bathroom run, anyway."

"Has she been getting her meds?"

"Stop worrying. You were always a worrier."

"That doesn't answer my question. She's on a ton of meds and she requires oxygen, and she has special dietary needs and she's diabetic. And I hope you have her in a cleaner place than this. She has no immune system left."

"You always had a tight ass for rules. Do this, do that. But see, you're tied up and I'm not. So relax your shrimpy ass while I wheel her in." She smiled and held up a warning finger. "But don't you go anywhere." From the rear of her waistband she slid out a pistol. "Or bang-bang and Mommy is dead. By my hand, not yours. Because I don't follow rules anymore, I make them."

As soon as she left, Clarisse struggled against her restraints, but to no avail. She didn't have long to wait, as the door opened and there was her mother in a wheelchair, with an oxygen line in her nose and a canister of the stuff riding on the back of the chair.

She looked clean, well-groomed, and actually clear-eyed, even with the cataract in the one. She smiled at her daughter and waved like a little girl encountering a friend.

"Lovey, Lovey," she said. "See my new friend?"

Clarisse looked at the other woman, who said, "We got her med list and other requirements before we snatched her. What, you think we're monsters?"

"They snatched me, they snatched me!" exclaimed her mother happily. "Broke me out of my prison, way I see it. And they let me smoke, too, a little. But only with the oxygen off. Nobody wants to go boom."

Behind her the woman placed the pistol against Mommy's head. "And if smoking doesn't kill her, guess what will, babycakes?"

"Oh, don't say that word," screamed Mommy, putting her hands over her ears. "It's god-awful."

"Yes, it is," said Clarisse. "Only you didn't seem to care back then, did you? If you can even remember."

Her mother slowly removed her hands and looked directly at her daughter. "I remember. And I had to pick my battles."

"Well, you don't have to worry anymore."

"Really?" said Mommy with widened, hopeful eyes.

"Really," answered Clarisse.

"Did you do it?"

"I wish."

Mommy looked at the other woman. "Was it you?"

She shook her head. "Somebody beat me to it."

Clarisse said, "Bullshit. If not you, who then?"

"Don't know, do I?"

"They wrote on the wall. Same thing you wrote on Bruce's wall."

"Bruce I'll 'fess to. But that's all."

Clarisse focused on her mother and snapped, "And exactly what battles did you pick to fight? Because I don't remember a single one."

Her mother took a moment to eye both women. "You have

no idea what all they wanted to do. Not even *your* mother," she added, turning to look directly at the other woman. She saw the gun but didn't react to it. "I put my foot down there. I would have told."

"Like those assholes gave a shit," said the woman. "Fox guarding the henhouse. Well, not my issue anymore. And I don't live in the past." She shivered comically. "It's too s-s-scary."

"You *were* scared," said Clarisse. "We all were."

The woman stopped her fake shivers. "Well, you should be scared. Now. There are lots of bad people around and you're looking at one of them. So take it all in. For the memory books."

"You didn't use to be this way," said Clarisse while her mother worried at the cannula in her nose and eyed her lap.

"We didn't use to be lots of things. Now we are. All of them. Least I am."

"How is he?" asked Clarisse. "I mean really?"

"Who?" asked her mother, now looking a bit dazed, as though she had just expended all of her clarity in the last couple of minutes. "Who is she talking about?"

"Just sit there and suck on air, okay? This doesn't concern you." Clarisse looked at her captor. "Tell me how he is. Please."

The other woman's expression became less sure. "We've had a good ride. Bonded for life because of those years together and what happened."

"But you didn't have to kill Bruce. That was unnecessary."

"I didn't have to do lots of things. That's why we make choices. And there were things about Bruce you never knew."

"And Harry? Come on, you can tell me the truth. It's not like I'm going to the cops."

The other woman shook her head, a sad smile playing over her lips. "We just wanted the money. He was no good to us dead. So there you go. No motive. You have to check that. The cops do."

"I know you two went to see him. How did you find him?"

"Not something you need to know. But he was alive and kicking when we left."

"Then who did it?" asked Clarisse. "Who killed him?"

"If you find out, tell me. And I'll kill them because they screwed us over real good. Cost us the easy path to the money."

"He would never have told you where it was. He never made anything easy."

The woman brandished her weapon. "Now, what have you found out?"

"We apparently have to move into the twenty-first century if we want to find the treasure. At least that's what the note I found said."

"And what does that mean exactly?"

"That the treasure is not in some wooden crate somewhere. Or buried at Stormfield. It might be digital."

"Digital? Have you figured that out?" asked the woman.

"Not yet. But I will."

She placed the gun against Mommy's temple, and this time the old woman did flinch. "Then pick up your pace. I'm not getting any younger. None of us are, especially this hag. Right, babycakes?"

When Mommy cried out at this term once more, the woman placed a wad of moist cloth over the woman's face and she immediately slumped sideways in her wheelchair, unconscious.

"She has COPD, that stuff could kill her," cried out Clarisse.

"I guess we'll find out. And now it's your turn to go lights out. *Babycakes.*"

66

THE NEXT MORNING GIBSON RECEIVED an email from Art Collin:

Re your query. I cannot ever talk about that. I said what I said and
I have nothing to add to it. And you should forget about it. Nothing
anyone can do now. And the scum is dead, so there's that. Hang
in there. AC.

Well, thanks for the help there, AC.

But he had pissed her off, so she sent him another email basically implying that Langhorne had let himself be caught because he could feel the cops breathing down his neck on the child abuse thing and WITSEC would give him a get-out-of-jail-free card. And, on top of that, he could walk away with all the mob's money.

So there you go, super cop.

She waited for him to reply. And he never did.

Sam Trask had given Gibson a secure email address to write to him. She did so, telling him about her kidnapping by, presumably, his son, and the deal she had been forced to make with him.

Trask immediately wrote back. "I am so sorry. Call this number. It's untraceable, even by my bastard offspring."

He answered on the first ring.

"Are you all right?" was the first thing he asked. "Did he hurt you?"

"No, I'm fine. He just scared the crap out of me. And I'm just assuming it was him or his goons. I have no proof of anything."

"So he wants you to find the money that Langhorne, under the alias Daniel Pottinger, stole from him? And he'll pay you a five percent commission?"

"That's what he said. I didn't believe him, but I did believe the part where he threatened me and my family."

"Have you made progress?"

"I've found some clues, along with another person I'm working with."

"You mean Clarisse?"

Gibson almost swallowed her tongue. "You know about her?"

"She visited me before Pottinger was killed and then revealed to be Langhorne. She came in the form of a podiatrist that The Feathers has visit once a month. She played her part very well. Had all the official credentials and knew the lingo. Though I was the only patient she saw, I'm certain of that," he added with a chuckle. "She fooled me completely until she told me why she was really there. She actually did an excellent job with my toenails. But while she did so we talked about other things."

"Well, I'm glad she was so open with you. She never mentioned any of that to me."

"She was looking for Pottinger. She knew he had purchased Stormfield, and I assume she knew, or at least suspected, that Pottinger and Langhorne were one and the same. She told me that she discovered Pottinger had done business with my son—sex trafficking, on a corridor from Mexico and Thailand into the States. Incredibly lucrative because those being trafficked were also bringing in stolen artifacts, as well as drugs. So Langhorne and my son had three profit centers off one human being."

Damn, so Clarisse had been telling the truth about that. "Why didn't you tell me all this when we met the first time?"

"I didn't really know you. I have since had you checked out. You're one of the good ones. And you were kidnapped and threatened by my son. That alone is enough to make me confide in you and want to help you."

"And did you learn anything about Clarisse?"

"I had nothing to go on. She used latex gloves while she was here. No prints left behind. I could have tried and taken a DNA sample, but I thought that might be impolite. And while I'm a man, I'm old and on oxygen. I don't think I could have taken her."

Gibson had to stifle a laugh at these self-deprecating comments.

"That's not her real name, obviously," said Trask. "But she struck me as highly intelligent, focused, organized, and…"

"And what?"

Trask didn't answer right away. "Well, *sad* beyond all comprehension, despite the confident air she tried to display."

"I think she might be Francine Langhorne."

"That thought crossed my mind as well. She's the right age. And it would explain her motivation to find him."

"Did you know about the disgusting stories swirling around about Langhorne?"

"His affinity for young girls? Yes, I learned about them *after* he had gone into WITSEC. The man already repulsed me. That of course put my revulsion on a whole new plane."

"Couldn't he have been charged?"

"Unfortunately, no, it would have destroyed WITSEC. No one with a questionable history would ever come forward. And the majority of informers who go into WITSEC are criminals themselves. I wish, like you, that he could have been held accountable. But that matter was out of my hands. But if Clarisse *is* Francine Langhorne, then that would also explain the sadness. If she knew about it, or, even more heinous, if her own father…"

"Yes, yes, it would," said Gibson hastily. She teared up as the image of her daughter came into her mind. "Earl Beckett is a US marshal who was one of the Langhornes' handlers at their last stop in Albuquerque. He's been giving me info about the case. He never mentioned any sort of abuse."

"I doubt he would, particularly if it happened right under their noses. No federal agency wants to admit a mistake."

"I guess," said Gibson.

"So what are you going to do with regard to my son? I told you that I was still wired into certain players and agencies who see me as a possible way to bring him down. Your working for him now might provide you an opportunity to collaborate with us to accomplish that."

"There's nothing I would want more," said Gibson. "To answer your question, my best bet is to keep working away to find the treasure. With that I have a bargaining chip with him. The FBI will have to be ready to roll when I call you in. *If* I get a chance to call you in."

"From what I've seen, my money's on you. And one more thing."

"What?"

"My money's also on Clarisse. You know, *together* you two might be able to do what neither can do independently."

"I have been working with her. She's the reason I'm involved in all this. But I'm not sure our interests are totally aligned."

"Nothing in life is ever perfectly aligned. I worked with criminals to bring worse criminals down. I'm sure you did, too. Sometimes you just have to go for it and hope for the best. Trust people not based on anything neatly reasoned, but on your gut. Just food for thought from an old man who's seen far too much of that kind of life than was good for him. It might simply be me mellowing in my old age, or the fact that I wanted a daughter and never had one, but having spent some time with Clarisse and gotten a chance to think about her, I have arrived at one conclusion."

"What's that?"

"I would love to see her really smile at least once."

Gibson said goodbye and clicked off and stared at the wall as Sam Trask's words went round and round in her head.

Wanting to see Clarisse smile? After all the shit she's put me through? No, I'm not there. Yet.

CHAPTER

67

LATER, AS GIBSON SAT THERE she thought about something.

Parents.

Clarisse had talked about childcare for kids *and* parents.

Okay, play this out. What if she is Francine and has been taking care of her mother, Geraldine? What if the woman is in a nursing home or an assisted living facility somewhere?

Gibson next thought about the phone call Clarisse had gotten while she had been on the line with her. Clarisse, normally unflappable and in control, seemed close to losing control. This was a long shot, Gibson knew. But everything right now was a long shot, and it wasn't like she had lots of other leads to run down. She had asked Clarisse point-blank about what Gibson had overheard on the phone call, but the woman had evaded answering directly. However, Gibson could read people. Clarisse was definitely worried about something, about someone.

She went online and put in a fairly broad search request having to do with assisted living facilities and nursing homes, and any problems that had arisen in any of them over the last week or so — like people going missing, as she had heard the other woman say over the phone line, or maybe a death or an accident. She got a flood of stories and posts back on this.

Jesus, are these places dangerous or what?

She narrowed the search as much as she dared and hit the send key.

Ten items came back. That was better. She read through them all. Four pertained to some accident where someone had died. Two were shootings by relatives of their geriatric "loved ones."

Wonderful.

And the rest were about residents who had walked away or otherwise vanished from their facilities. She checked each one of these thoroughly, but couldn't draw any conclusions. She recognized none of the names, not that Clarisse would have placed her mother in the facility under the names Geraldine Langhorne or Geraldine Parker.

She put this search aside and was about to go get a cup of tea when an email plunked into her inbox.

It was from Jan Roberts, her contact at the *Star-Ledger* in Newark. She had finally replied to Gibson's earlier email.

You have time to talk?

She had left a number, which Gibson immediately called.

"Well this is a blast from the past," said Roberts in her booming voice that Gibson remembered so clearly. She had met Roberts through her father when she was working a case in Jersey City. Roberts had assisted Gibson in one aspect of the case and had been given an exclusive interview by her as payback, all done anonymously, of course, because of Gibson's being undercover for the investigation.

"How's your father?" Roberts asked.

"Ornery as ever," replied Gibson.

Roberts laughed. "Good, then we know nothing's wrong with him."

"How do you like Newark?"

"It's Jersey and I'm a Jersey girl. Hey, is it true that Harry Langhorne was found dead down your way? You are in Virginia now, right?"

"Yes. He was using the name Dan Pottinger. Someone murdered him."

"Well, I won't be crying. I didn't know the man, but from everything I've read about him he was a real creep, working with the mob and all."

"I also read Samantha Kember's story on him."

"She died too young. Rest in peace, Sam. Yeah, I had just started at my first paper when she wrote that story. I actually went back and read it when I heard about Langhorne's being dead."

"So was he a pedophile?"

"Nothing was ever proven in court because the guy vanished, but it sure as hell sounded like he was, unless all those girls were lying, which I don't believe."

Something had occurred to Gibson earlier and she wanted to run it by Roberts. "I learned from a third party that Langhorne was fingerprinted and a background check run so he could volunteer at, I suppose, a school. I wondered why a mob accountant would do that. But I guess now it makes sense."

Roberts said, "Seems he wanted to get very close to the source of his sick fantasies."

Gibson shivered at this thought. "Can you tell me more than was in the story?"

"Like what?"

"Langhorne had kids, a daughter and a son."

"Wait, and you think, what, he was abusing them, too?"

"I don't know. That's why I'm asking."

"You think his wife would have allowed that?"

"From what I heard she never stood up to Langhorne. And she apparently didn't stop him from molesting the other kids."

"Right, if she knew about it. What was her name again?"

"Geraldine."

"Hmmm, you sure that's right?"

"Yeah, that was her name."

"Oh, right. That's the name she *went by*."

"Hold on, did she have another name? And how would you know?"

"In addition to reading her story again, I dug into Sam's files for the story. The *Star-Ledger* never throws anything away."

"Why did you do that?"

"I thought with Langhorne's being found murdered there might be a follow-up story in there somewhere. I'm right now pitching it to my editor, in fact."

"Okay, makes sense."

"Sam was meticulous in her work and really taught me a lot."

"I'm sure, but what did you find?" said Gibson impatiently.

"Geraldine was the woman's *middle* name. She went by that because she apparently hated her given name. I would have, too, I suppose. It's not the prettiest."

"What was her given name?"

"Agnes."

Gibson glanced at her computer screen. *Holy shit.*

Among the articles she had found about things going awry recently at assisted living facilities was the story of an *Agnes* Leland, who apparently disappeared from one in Greenville, South Carolina, right around the time of the call to Clarisse.

Or was it now almost certainly Francine?

68

AFTER FINISHING HER CALL WITH Jan Roberts, Gibson just stared at the screen for a long time wondering what to do.

She believed she had just received confirmation that Clarisse was none other than Francine Langhorne. And her mother, Agnes Geraldine Langhorne (Leland), had gone missing from an assisted living facility in South Carolina, a facility in which perhaps the daughter had placed her mother. Had someone kidnapped her? Someone who wanted to gain leverage over the daughter? Maybe to ensure that they would get all or part of the treasure? Because it seemed like everyone was motivated by that goal.

Maybe me included, since I don't have a job right now and I've got two kids to feed, clothe, and take care of.

Sam Trask's words came rushing back to her, so she finally picked up *that* phone and called the woman.

"Yes?" said Clarisse, not sounding like herself.

"Did something else happen?" asked Gibson. "After you left my place?"

"I don't know what you mean."

"Can we just cut the shit, please? We both have a lot to lose here." Gibson paused and steeled herself for what she was about to say because, if she was right, it was going to be a tsunami for the woman, and she had no idea how Clarisse would react. "For God's sake, they kidnapped your mother, *Francine*."

Gibson had not turned on her stress analyzer app. She didn't have to. She was a daughter. She had a mother. And if what had happened to Francine's mother had happened to hers? She would be out of her mind with worry.

The woman said nothing. All Gibson could hear was elevated breathing.

"I put two and two together, Francine. I'm good at that, which I guess is why you brought me into this. I just found out your mother's name was Agnes, coupled with what you let slip about—"

"Okay, okay, you're fucking Sherlock Holmes!"

The call cut off.

Ten minutes went by and Gibson did nothing except stare at the phone. *Come on, come on, I can help you. I really can. I want to help you.*

When it rang she nearly fell out of her chair.

"I'm sorry about that," said a now-composed Clarisse.

"I'm sorry I dumped all over you like that," replied Gibson. "I just didn't know if we had time to waste. Do you have any idea where your mother is? Have they made contact? Do you know who it is?"

"Can you get away?"

"Yes."

"Meet me at this address in an hour."

Gibson wrote down the address of a restaurant in Newport News, clicked off, quickly changed her clothes, and headed out after checking in with Silva and the kids.

She took great pains to make sure she was not followed. When Gibson pulled up in her van there was a woman standing out front. She had on a hat and sunglasses. She walked over to the van and held up her hand.

Gibson unlocked the door and Francine Langhorne climbed in.

Francine took off her glasses and said, "You're right, we *don't* have time to waste."

"Okay."

"You want to drive while we talk? I don't like sitting here exposed."

Gibson put the van in gear and headed off.

"Have they made contact?" asked Gibson.

"She's made contact twice."

" 'She'?"

"Rochelle Enders."

Gibson looked puzzled for a moment. "Wait, is that RE?"

Francine nodded. "We were in Albuquerque together. Her family was in WITSEC, too. They lived right across the street."

"And BD? Bruce Dixon?"

"He and Rochelle dated some back then. Rochelle broke it off, I never knew why. Then Bruce's father died, and he and his mom left WITSEC." She looked over at Gibson. "Rochelle killed Bruce. I don't know the reason. She stole his identity as Daryl Oxblood to rent the van she used to take my mother from the facility in Greenville. She didn't have to kill him. She really didn't."

"And she killed your father, too?"

"She denied it. And she never denied anything if she had done it. Love her or hate her, she took responsibility for what she did."

"But who could have killed him then?"

"*I* was going to kill him when I got to Stormfield that night. Then I found him dead, and saw the phrase on the wall."

" 'Do as I say, not as I do'? What was that about?"

"It's what my father always said. But he meant it in a different way than normal."

"You're going to have to explain that."

"We always had to do *exactly* what he said. They were commands, not parental advice."

"So if she didn't kill him, whoever did would have known that?"

"Yes."

"Could it be your brother?" Gibson said, watching her carefully.

"Doug's with Rochelle."

"But I thought you and your brother left together. That he waited for you to turn eighteen."

"He was actually waiting for *Rochelle* to turn eighteen, not me. He loved her. I did go with them initially. Rochelle and I just never saw eye to eye. I'm not like her and she's not like me. But...we all endured shit that maybe allowed us to form a bond, at least for a while. Then she...made it clear I was not wanted."

"What sort of shit?" Gibson said slowly. "And just so you know, I read the story about your father molesting little girls from your old neighborhood in New Jersey."

Francine dropped her gaze. "Mr. Enders and my dad became really good friends. They each told the other about their backgrounds and why they were in WITSEC. They formed a bond around that. Mr. Enders had been a hit man for some Mexican cartel and then got nailed. So he flipped to keep himself out of prison and went into WITSEC with his family. Rochelle was an only child. Her father was scum; the guy had even killed little kids when working for the cartel. So of course he and my father got along great. We weren't supposed to tell anyone about who we really were, but they didn't give a crap about that. They just...rolled with whatever they wanted to do."

"When you were little, did your father...?"

"I think he wanted to. I mean, he acted really...weird around me, and Dougie. But...my mother..."

"She protected you both?"

"Yes. For the only time in her life."

"When you were older and living in New Mexico, did your father and Ender abuse you and Rochelle?"

Now Francine looked up. "In some ways it was worse."

"I don't understand."

"You ever read *Oliver Twist*?"

"I've heard of it of course, but I never read it."

"It's about a gang of street criminals, mostly kids. Oliver Twist becomes one. The leader of the pack is Jack Dawkins, nicknamed the Artful Dodger. He was trained by an old guy named Fagin."

"I'm not following."

"My father and Enders went into business selling product — and *Rochelle and I were the product*. They pimped us out to anybody with money. And for the rich assholes, they secretly filmed the stuff. And then they blackmailed the shit out of them. And the rich assholes all paid. Because we were way, way underage. And we were expected to steal whatever we could from the men while we were with them. If we came home empty-handed, we got beaten."

"Holy shit!"

"I slept with my first man at age thirteen. They even tried to pimp Dougie out, but he was too big and strong by then. He wouldn't do it."

"Then why didn't he stop them?"

"You never knew my father. It wasn't a matter of muscle. It was a matter of mind games. Of intimidation. Of putting you in mortal fear of your life. And no one was better at that than our old man. He ripped off the mob. Teenagers were not a challenge. My brother knew if he tried to stand up to him, Dad would've killed me and Rochelle without a second thought."

"And where was your mother in all of this?"

"Drunk and stoned. I think she had given up by then."

"I heard about what he did to knock you out of being in the school play."

She slid back her shirtsleeve to reveal a long scar. "That was in addition to him screwing me out of starring in *Twelfth Night*. And the cat I brought home that pissed him off? He burned it alive, right in front of me."

"Oh my God."

"God never came around to my house while all that was happening."

Gibson watched as two large tears fell onto Francine's cheeks.

She pulled the van over and gripped Francine's hand. "I'm so sorry you had to deal with all that…horror."

"It made me stronger in some ways. And totally blew me up in others. And you see the result."

"And Rochelle's mother?"

"She finally just bugged out, leaving Rochelle to fend for herself. FYI, I hate my mother. And I pity my mother. And I guess as the years went by the pity became stronger than the hate."

"So you took care of her?"

"There were no happy times with my father. There *were* happy times with my mother. If he hadn't been in the picture, things would have been far different. For all of us. Yes, she had her issues, the booze, and the drugs, but they were almost all because of him. So when I was old enough and had enough money, I found her and put her in assisted living."

"Couldn't you have gone to the US Marshals Service? They could have made all this stop, surely."

Francine glared at her. "Are you joking? The local marshals were *in* on it."

"What!"

"My dad offered me up to them. That way he got special privileges. They let him and Enders do whatever they wanted."

"What were their names?"

"One's dead. The other guy's in Norfolk now."

"Not Earl Beckett?"

"That's him. I got into his office when I was working on the cleaning detail for the federal building." She slid out a thumb drive from her bag. "And got this."

"There was no way he put any of that on a government computer," said Gibson.

"No, but they had a file on my father that I thought might be helpful. And, more importantly, I wanted to find out who *else* Beckett had guarded since."

"Did you get a list?"

"Yeah, but I haven't started checking it yet."

"You could have gone to the police, the school principal, somebody, Francine. Isn't there anyone that could have helped you back then?"

"My father was all about the details, so he had already thought of that. I have my mountains of notebooks, so I guess I take after him in that way. Anyway, no one knew he was Harry Langhorne who had been accused of pedophilia back in Jersey. He and Enders spread rumors, through the cops, the schools, our pediatricians even, that we made shit up. That Rochelle and I couldn't be trusted. My father and Rochelle's dad even made us write up confessions saying it was all a lie just in case somebody suspected. They threatened to kill us if we didn't."

Francine focused on a photograph taped to the dash of Gibson's kids. Next to it was a note that had a round face beside a large heart with the word "Mom" in childish scrawl.

"I can never have kids because of how forced sex at that age hurt me physically." She sighed and sat back. "Rochelle had it even worse. I don't know everything they did to her."

"Why was she treated differently?"

"Because she wouldn't cry. All the stuff they did to her, she refused to cry. And she wouldn't beg them to stop. That pissed them off beyond belief. I guess I was the weak one. I cried, and I begged. Not that it did much good."

Gibson sat back and looked at her with a conflicted expression. Francine noted this and said, "You don't believe me?"

"I want to, but—"

"—but I'm a liar. A good one. Yeah, I know. Well, it doesn't really matter if you believe me or not, does it?"

"But why involve me?" said Gibson. "You said you knew about me when I was a cop."

"It was before then. At Temple."

"Were you a student?"

"No. I worked in the cafeteria, and at odd jobs on campus.

I also helped with the theater productions. I did that for free because…well, I liked it."

"Why did you say I had everything and then I just pissed it away? I had to work my ass off for everything. I didn't come from money, Francine."

"I wasn't talking about money." She glanced at her. "Basketball star, the lead in all of those plays, a loving family. I would watch all of you walk around campus when they came to visit. There goes Mickey Rogers, the baddest badass on campus. You were a rock star. Everybody just…loved you. I…never knew how that felt. So, in my mind, you had it all. I thought you were going to be a pro basketball star, or rock the boards on Broadway."

"But I never did because I wasn't good enough, Francine. Playing ball in college and being in college theater is way different from doing it at the next level. The funnel gets really, really narrow."

"I wanted you to try. I wanted—"

"—to live vicariously through me?"

"Pathetic, I know. But I didn't have a whole lot else going on."

"And baiting me into all this?"

"I'll tell you the truth, though you probably won't believe it." She paused and looked directly at Gibson. "I wanted to kick your ass. I wanted to find the treasure before you did, even with all your resources at ProEye. You had failed at life, at least I saw it that way. But if I could beat you. If I could show the world that—"

"—that *you* were the real rock star, and, what, everybody would love you?" Gibson stared grimly at her. She pointed at the car seats in the back. "*I* made the choices in my life. I got married and had kids because that's what I wanted. I don't owe you or anybody else an explanation because it's nobody's fucking business but mine. So you waited all these years and decided to blow my life up and put my kids in danger all so you could feel, what, good about yourself? That *is* pathetic."

Francine didn't shrink under these harsh words. She simply nodded. "You're right. Everything you just said is true. I'm a pathetic loser. You hate me and you should hate me." She opened the van door. "I will take care of this. I'll get Trask off your case. I'll find the treasure and that will be that. So you'll be good to go."

"You can't guarantee any of that."

"Nothing in life is guaranteed. But I'll do my best."

Gibson's tone softened. "Look, I know you've had a shitty life. And I'm sorry for that. If that had happened to me, I'd probably be in an institution."

"I *have* been in an institution, and I wouldn't recommend it," said Francine bluntly.

Gibson stiffened at this. "What about your mother?"

"Once I have the treasure, I can buy her freedom."

"And Earl Beckett?"

"What about him?"

"Does he just get away with this?"

"I can't do anything about the people he's already hurt, but I'm going to do my best to stop him from hurting anybody else."

"So if you didn't kill your father, and Rochelle didn't kill him? Doug?"

"No, Doug wouldn't do that, not without Rochelle knowing."

"Did Beckett know about the phrase, 'Do as I say...'?"

"Sure. He used to lord that over us, too."

"Beckett said your father got away cleanly, as though he had help."

"I suppose so, yes."

"Could his help have been *Beckett*?"

Francine shot her a glance. "Why would he do that?"

"For a piece of the treasure?"

Francine closed the van door, fully reengaged. "You think?"

"And then your father did what he always did. He screwed the guy. But Beckett strikes me as one tenacious bastard. He kept looking. And he found the man. And he killed the man."

"If we could only prove that."

Gibson sat back and looked thoughtful. "The only thing I can't figure is that phrase was written by two different people. Which means if Beckett killed him, he might not be working alone."

"What about Wilson Sullivan?"

Gibson nodded. "It could be. I could find nothing on the guy past twenty years ago."

"That's interesting," said Francine.

"And it was Sullivan who brought Beckett into this thing. Maybe that was by design if they both killed him. And now they want the treasure. And you found Sullivan looking for it at Stormfield. We also have Nathan Trask out there. He expects the two of us to find it. Or else."

"Like I said, I'll take care of Trask."

"But you can just walk away from that. Claim you never found it."

Surprisingly, Francine shook her head. "I wasn't lying when I told you the sorts of crimes that Trask and my father were involved in. Sex trafficking of minors was a big one. They killed a bunch of them in San Antonio to keep them from testifying. That's why I went to Trask in the first place. I wanted to nail him. I didn't care about the money or the commission he might pay. I just don't want them to hurt any more kids."

Gibson sat back, looking conflicted.

Francine noted this and said, "I'm a bad person, Mickey. I've committed crimes. I've hurt people. But...I don't like men who do shit to kids and get away with it."

"It took iron balls to voluntarily go in and meet with that psycho," said Gibson. "When his goons snatched me I've never been more afraid in my life."

"I guess my only advantage is, I've had to deal with psychos my whole life, with my father being the predominate one. After a while, the fear is still there, but it's no longer paralyzing."

"Sam Trask told me you had been by to see him, as a podiatrist."

"He's a very nice man. I have no idea how his son ended up the way he did."

"He also suggested that we work together to get this done."

"Nathan Trask is very dangerous. And you have two little kids. I never should have let you go near the man. Look, *you're* going to walk away. You *have* to walk away. Now. I'll get the guy or die trying. And rest assured, no one will miss me if I get killed."

"I will."

Gibson let that statement hang out there for a few moments as the women locked gazes.

"You can't mean that. After all I've done to you."

"My father taught me to not judge someone unless I've walked in their shoes. I don't know anyone who's walked in *your* shoes. Yeah, I'm pissed at what you've done to me. But…you risked your life to take some really bad people down. As a former cop that counts with me."

Francine said, "But you've already got a job. And you should go back to doing it, starting right now. But you have my word that I will die before I let them hurt you or your kids." She glanced at the photo of Tommy and Darby again. "You have no reason to believe me, I know, but that is the truth."

"FYI, I got fired from ProEye. Now that I know about Beckett, I think he was the asshole who made it happen. And you know me, Francine, from way back. I don't give up. From what I know about you, you're the same as me."

"What exactly are you saying, Mickey?"

"Sam Trask thought we might be a stronger force working together than separately. Why don't we find out if he's right?"

69

THE MEDICAL TRANSPORT VAN PULLED away from The Feathers senior living community with four passengers in it.

Sam Trask had on a suit jacket and pleated slacks, and he absently read a newspaper as the van rolled along. His rollator was parked in the back, along with a wheelchair for another passenger. He carried a portable oxygen supply with him. The passengers would be picked back up at designated spots and at prearranged times.

Trask, for his part, was looking forward to seeing a movie for the first time in a while, inside a real movie theater while munching on popcorn. He glanced out the window. If he noted the black SUV following behind, he made no sign.

He was the third one to be dropped off. Using his rollator he walked inside the theater, bought his ticket and his small bag of popcorn, and made his way to his show. The black SUV parked across the street and a man got out, hustled over to the theater, bought a ticket, searched each of the interior theaters until he saw Trask sitting by himself and munching popcorn. There were a few other patrons scattered around as the lights went down. The man checked this all out and left.

As soon as Gibson saw the man leave, she scooted over next to Trask, while Francine did the same on the other side. Trask offered them popcorn, which they both accepted.

"The big bad wolf is gone, I take it," said Trask.

"I guess your son's muscle aren't into movies," said Gibson.

"I'm glad you took my advice and teamed up, ladies," he said.

"We're still feeling our way," said Gibson, glancing at Francine, who stared straight ahead. "And we might fall right on our faces."

Francine said, "Or we might not. Okay, the plan is, I'm going to deliver the goods to your son."

"Then you'll need the goods to deliver."

"That's where you and your people come in," she said. "He wants his money back. Fifty million dollars is what he told me when we met. A drop in the bucket to a guy like him, but it's not the money."

Trask said, "If he can get ripped off, he's vulnerable to the other hyenas in the jungle."

"Which is why Mickey surreptitiously planted certain information on the dark web that alludes to this having happened to him, and I, using multiple untraceable IP addresses, spread that muck around. That will make him desperate to resolve this. And desperation makes people less careful than they otherwise would be."

"Go on. I like how this is shaping up."

"And Mickey came up with an absolutely brilliant plan to tackle your son."

Gibson took up the story. "It comes from tracking down rich deadbeats online for the last two years. You learn some sources, methods...and tricks."

"Sounds intriguing."

Francine said, "Then you're going to love the next part."

However, as he listened Trask's smile faded. "I can't let you do that. It's too dangerous."

"It's the only way," said Francine. "And how many times did you risk your life for the greater good?"

"We know what we're doing, Sam," added Gibson. "And he already knows about us. If we don't pull this off that will be hanging over our heads forever."

Trask sat there for a few moments, munched his popcorn, and finally nodded. "All right, and I think I can provide the very help you'll need."

"Good," said Francine.

"Because it's going to take all of us," added Gibson.

70

Nathan Trask was not in a good mood when Francine walked into the same room they had met in before. He looked agitated and distracted. And when he glanced up at Francine his displeasure deepened.

"Did I come at a bad time?" she asked as she sat down opposite him.

"I don't know. You said you were successful?"

"It took a lot of work, but I finally located an account owned by Pottinger with about seventy million dollars in it, twenty mill over what you said he took you for. But who said a little bonus isn't in order?"

"How did you find it?"

"Proprietary information," she said, smiling disarmingly. "That's how I make my living. I'm sure you can understand."

"So how do we get the money?" asked Trask.

"I'm confident I have a way. And it's not in a traditional bank account. It's in bitcoin."

"Bitcoin! I didn't think Pottinger even knew what that was."

"Either he did, or he had someone advising him who did."

"So, again, how do we get it?"

"To do it, I need your help."

He looked at her in surprise. "You're getting paid to do this. Why do *I* need to be involved?"

"Trust me, if it were money in another type of account, I could handle it solo. But bitcoin is a different beast."

"Okay, tell me your plan and I'll tell you what's wrong with it."

She smiled again. "I like my clients to be proactive."

He sat forward, so they were almost knee to knee. "I'm not your client. I'm a man who let you into his world on a very temporary basis to see if you could solve a problem I have that nobody else seems able to handle. You do that, and you'll be fine. You start trying to elevate yourself in this situation to something you're not and never will be, then we have a problem. And that is never good for someone like you. Understand?"

"I understand."

"And another thing—my people who I pay to watch those things tell me that there are stories out there about this. About me getting taken advantage of."

"I wasn't aware of that."

"Wrong answer. You're getting paid to anticipate stuff like that and then do something about it."

He snapped his fingers and the door instantly opened. A large man came in, walked up to Francine, ripped her from the chair, slammed her up against the wall, and wrenched her arm up her back until she cried out in pain.

Trask nodded and the man let her go. She staggered over and fell back into her chair.

"I thought I was getting paid to find your money for you," she said quietly, rubbing her injured arm.

Trask nodded at the man, who slugged Francine in the jaw. She screamed and held her hands up in a defensive posture, as blood trickled from her mouth.

Trask said, "Again, wrong answer. You're not doing too well. See, when you work *for* me, you do everything above and beyond. You think of this shit. You deal with it so that it never touches me. I hire people who are smarter than me. If they turn out not to be, what good are they?" He sat back. "Now tell me the plan and maybe he'll have to hit you again. Only harder. Or my people might have to do something more than that to you. It all depends on what you say next. No pressure, just relax and start talking."

Francine composed herself, sat up straight, and wiped the tears from her eyes, then her expression hardened to stone. "Do you have a computer handy?"

"Why?"

"It's *bitcoin*. That's where it lives."

He studied her for a moment. "Why can't you use *your* computer?"

"I could, but then I'd just have to transfer it over to yours."

"Then that's what you're going to have to do."

"The thing is, Mr. Trask, if we do it that way, your account, passwords, and other information will be on my cloud. I'm not sure you want that."

"You can erase it."

"How will you know I did? Even if you have someone to check it? And I don't want you coming after me if anything goes sideways with respect to that, especially if someone hacks me before I can erase it. And how will I know you'll even let me walk out of here if there's a chance of that? I came here to finish the job and collect my commission, that's all."

Trask said nothing for about thirty seconds. "Okay, I'll play along, for now."

He made a call and a minute later a man walked in with a laptop and handed it to her.

"It's password protected," she said. "Can you open it up for me?"

He did so and she started typing, her fingers flying over the screen.

"Mind explaining what you're doing?" said Trask.

"I'm persuading a secure wallet, or hot storage, to believe that I'm Dan Pottinger with the private key."

"That's all you need, a private key? I thought this stuff was all secure with that blockchain crap."

"Which is why I'm *not* attacking the blockchain. That's thousands of computers tied together. I'm not beating that in my lifetime. But if you want to *do* anything with your bitcoin, you have to go on other platforms and digital exchanges."

"And how are you able to do that?"

"Before he died I hacked Pottinger's home Wi-Fi. I did so to see if I could capture his PII."

"What's that?" asked Trask.

"Personal identifiable information. With that I can hopefully capture his crypto private key."

"But he's dead. He's not doing things online anymore."

"Doesn't matter if he's dead, if he set up remote instructions to execute a transaction with his bitcoin on a certain date and time, that transaction will still be fulfilled."

"And did he?"

"Yes. And now I'm going to divert that transaction to *your* account."

"What, you mean now?"

"That's why I came here when I did. I've got the transaction set to run. I need your people to plug in your account info as the destination. Seventy million will be coming in, in five minutes, but we need the end account."

"Five minutes! I don't like to be rushed," snapped Trask.

"Okay, but this is the only shot we have because he has no other remote instructions pending. The bitcoin will be lost forever unless he willed the private key to someone. And if so, *they'll* get the money."

"But you said you got the key. Why can't you go in anytime you want and empty the account?"

"Because Pottinger was smart. He used a onetime private key system. I got the one. It's good for this transaction and only this transaction. After that, it becomes useless."

"Shit!" Trask sat up and looked at his assistant. "Get George to plug the Zurich account in. Hurry up." He looked at Francine. "A little more notice would have been good."

"I just found all this out. Digital works on its own schedules with not a lot of warning. That's why I asked to meet with you immediately."

The man got on his phone, and two minutes later another man hurried in. He was around thirty, skinny, and wearing an ill-fitting suit.

He sat down at the laptop and hunched over so no one could see what he was typing in.

"Okay, it's done," said George.

"Now George here is going to watch every keystroke you hit," said Trask. "He sees anything out of the ordinary, and I mean any little thing that shows you're trying to screw me, you get a bullet in your head." He nodded at the man who had hit Francine. The man took out a gun and placed it against the back of Francine's head.

Francine noted George's fearful look. She smiled reassuringly, her big eyes growing ever larger, threatening to swallow the man whole. "No pressure, George. We'll get through this, okay?"

She squeezed his hand reassuringly even as her other hand started hitting the keys. He smiled back at her, his gaze drifting over her for a few moments.

"Okay," he said.

Francine's fingers were flying so fast that even the tech-savvy George looked impressed.

She filled him in on what she was doing as she typed, keeping up a running commentary as he nodded in understanding, continually looking at her, just as Francine intended. He glanced at Trask and said, "She's really good, sir."

Two minutes later she said, "Okay, you are seventy million in bitcoins richer, Mr. Trask." She looked at George. "Feel free to confirm."

George took the laptop and clicked some keys. He smiled and looked up. "She's right, sir. Seventy mill in bitcoin just came in."

"And it's like cash," she said. "No ownership trail because I had the private key. A dead man just paid you off, Mr. Trask. But with companies in crypto going bankrupt left and right, my advice would be to cash out as soon as you can."

Trask waved his gunman away and chuckled. "I don't understand any of that crap, but I do understand seventy million dollars."

"Less my commission of three point five million. I'll be happy to take it in bitcoin. And then I'll cash out."

Trask considered this. "Why not?" He waved at George. "You able to do the transfer?"

George did not look confident. Francine said, "You confirm the bitcoin figure and I'll do the transferring. That way we all know where we stand and the numbers are what they are. And you don't have to access any of your own funds, only the stuff I just got for you. So you're golden."

George looked at Trask, who nodded. "Do it."

He confirmed the amount and then Francine got back on the laptop and started hitting keys. A minute later, the transaction complete, Francine said, "Nice doing business with you, Mr. Trask."

"Can you do anything about this shit floating around on the internet?"

"Yes I can. And I will, right away."

"And there was another woman. She went to see my father. She was looking for this stuff, too."

"Well, you snooze you lose. And since you have your money back plus a nice little bonus, if I were you, I'd forget about her."

"I think you're right."

Francine shook George's hand. "Nice working with you, George."

"You too."

"Let's grab a coffee some time."

He smiled and nodded, and Francine felt her heart quiver, because she knew George was probably now a dead man.

I'm sorry. But it was either you or me.

The golf cart took her to the gate, where she walked quickly off.

She went into a store, did a costume switch in the bathroom using clothes and a wig she had previously hidden there, and walked out through another exit.

Four blocks later she climbed into a white van.

Three stern-looking representatives of the FBI stared back at her as they sat in front of a bank of computers, along with Gibson, who was smiling.

Francine said, "I take it you were you able to follow the entire transaction after I put the keystroke tracking software on?" she said.

"Oh yeah," said Gibson. Then her smile faded when she saw the bruises on Francine's face, and how her right arm was hanging funny. "Shit, those assholes beat you up."

"I've been hit a lot harder, trust me."

"We got every line of code's worth," said one of the men. "And access to all his accounts. That was good work. You took a big risk going in there naked like that."

"Well, it makes life interesting."

Another agent looked at Gibson. "We could use people like you two."

"Quite frankly, I don't think you can afford us," said Francine, causing Gibson to hold back a snort.

Francine climbed out of the van and kept walking.

A few moments later Gibson joined her. "Are you sure you're okay?" she asked.

"I'm fine."

"That was really brave what you did."

"It was necessary to get to the end result."

"You always this transactional?"

Francine stared directly at her as she wiped more blood off her lips. "Welcome to my world."

"I'm starting to figure you out, you know."

"Don't waste the time. After this is all over, if I'm still alive, you'll never see me again."

"Off to pull more 'transactions'?"

"If I find the treasure, there's a place in France I've been looking at."

"But if *I* find the treasure?"

"Then you and your kids can go live in France. I'll forward you the Zillow listing."

Gibson looked at her pensively. "Maybe I haven't figured you out."

"There's no maybe about it."

71

Two days later the news of the arrest of Nathan Trask and numerous of his associates made global news.

It seems the man had made the mistake of stealing seventy million dollars from a federal bitcoin depository. And in doing so, had made the glaring technological error of opening up his own digital files to the government. So not only were they going after him for the bitcoin theft, but everything else that was revealed. And by the broad smile on the US attorney who announced the arrest, it was a lot.

No one could explain why a man like Trask had made such a bold and ultimately costly move in trying to steal from the government. Some news pundits were saying it was clear the man thought he was untouchable, because he had escaped responsibility for his alleged crimes for so long. His lawyers had made the predicted responses—that this was a witch hunt, that Trask had been set up—and they vowed to have any and all evidence gathered by the government ruled inadmissible. But the legal commentators had already noted that that would be an uphill battle considering that the man, or his lackeys, had inadvertently offered up this treasure trove of facts about his criminal doings to the very government he had waved a middle finger at for so long.

One commentator noted: "If that isn't irony piled on top of irony, I don't know what is. They couldn't catch Capone on his really awful crimes, but they got him on tax evasion. The history books may write that Nathan Trask was brought down by his own arrogance. But this clearly shows that no person is above the law."

Sam Trask was interviewed by all the major networks, since a global criminal having an FBI father was, to say the least, not typical.

His responses were articulate and professional, but all of them were accompanied by a satisfied smile.

Trask and his inner circle were being held without bail since the man was definitely a flight risk. As formal charges were readied, it was clear that Trask would be in prison for a long time before his trial even started.

When told this during one of the interviews, Sam Trask said, "Oh, what a beautiful day it turned out to be."

* * *

Rick Rogers phoned his daughter that morning.

"Do I want to know?" he asked anxiously.

"Not really," she replied.

"Are you sure you're safe from this guy?"

"Yes, Dad, I am."

"I'm not telling your mother any of this."

"I wouldn't, either."

* * *

Several days after Trask's arrest, at the same movie theater, Francine and Gibson sat on either side of Sam Trask, who had maneuvered his rollator that day with an extra spring in his step.

As they munched on popcorn Trask said, "I've spoken with some former colleagues at the Bureau. The DOJ is positively giddy about prosecuting my son and all his fellow scum. The evidence they have is mountainous, they tell me. And despite his lawyers' arguments to the contrary, completely admissible even without a warrant because Trask freely opened his records to the government in the course of his cybertheft. And they can't argue entrapment because they're missing a critical piece of evidence."

"Me," said Francine. "And I don't work for the Bureau. They must have been tracking me somehow and that led them to Trask," she added with a smile.

"Exactly. And what is his alternative explanation going to be? He was just getting back money his partner stole from him, and which came from sex and drug trafficking? Ha!"

Gibson said, "But we have more work to do."

"Can I help?" asked Trask.

Gibson gave his arm a squeeze. "You've already done all the helping you needed to do, Sam. I suggest you sit here, finish the movie and popcorn, and revel in your victory."

The two women left.

Francine said, "Nathan Trask might have been the easy part."

"I was thinking the very same thing," said Gibson.

72

WILSON SULLIVAN CAME OUT INTO the waiting room at the police station to see Gibson sitting there.

"I wasn't expecting you," he said, looking annoyed.

She rose and smiled disarmingly. "I like to keep people on their toes."

"What's up?"

"Can we go back to your office?"

He took a long moment to make a decision. "All right, but you have to make it brief. I've got a full plate."

"Let's go."

In his office, she sat down across from him.

"Oh, did you hear about Nathan Trask?" he said. "It's the talk of the police world. No one thought that son of a bitch could be touched."

"Just shows what happens if you keep trying," noted Gibson.

"The Bureau must be jumping for joy. Quite the catch for them. Wonder how they did it."

"Yeah, me too. Speaking of the FBI, Cary Pinker came by to see me."

"I know."

"I don't think he likes me poking around this case. I assumed I didn't hear from you because he told you to put the kibosh on what we were doing?"

"I don't work for the FBI," replied Sullivan.

"So we're good on that score?"

"I told you from the first there are things you can do to help and there are things I can't let you get involved in."

"So how is Pinker? Making progress?"

"He's working the case."

"With you?" asked Gibson.

"He's working *his* case, and I'm working mine."

"Fair enough. So look, I wanted to fill you in on what's happened since we talked last."

"Okay."

"First thing, I got canned by ProEye." She had mentioned this to see his reaction.

"What the hell? I talked to your boss."

"I know. Apparently somebody else contacted them and they decided to cut all ties with me."

He fiddled with the pen he was holding. "And what, you think that was Pinker?"

"If you were me, would he not be on your list?"

Sullivan said, "Well, he never mentioned that to me. I would have told him it was a bad idea."

"Okay, I appreciate that." She glanced at the old wound on his neck from being injured in the line of duty. "Does that still hurt?"

"Only when people ask about it," he snapped. "What else? Any progress on the money Langhorne left behind?"

Gibson was about to answer when she started coughing, which became more and more pronounced.

"Allergies," she gasped. "Water? So I can take a pill?"

He hurried out, and came back in with the water. She drank it while tossing down a vitamin C pill.

"Whew, thanks. That hasn't happened in a while."

"Sure. So any progress on the money?" he asked again.

"I think so. He left some clues behind."

"More than what you already told me?"

"No, but I've been giving it some thought and I might have some leads. I did a bunch of legwork on the computer. The guy had a ton of companies and accounts, all of which were cleaned out fairly recently."

"Meaning he might have been accumulating cash?"

"Yes, either to hold or to use to buy something. I'm going to try to track that down. By the way, when was the last time you were back at Stormfield?"

"Why?"

"I was just wondering if you had found out anything else."

"The last time I was there was with you."

She showed her poker face at this lie, and nodded. "Any luck finding Francine or Doug Langhorne?"

"None. When they disappeared, they really vanished."

Yes they did, thought Gibson. "And no leads on whoever killed Langhorne?"

He shook his head and already looked detached from this conversation.

She stood. "Well, I'll let you get back to things."

"Right."

She left without a single positive thought of Wilson Sullivan in her head.

And here I thought we might have been friends. Or maybe more.

Gibson reached into her pocket and pulled out the plastic baggie in which she'd placed the pen he'd been handling while he was out getting her water.

Let's find out who you really are, shall we?

73

Through her new friends at the FBI, Gibson got them to run the print she'd taken from Wilson Sullivan.

"His real name is Mark Gosling," Gibson told Francine as they sat at an outdoor café having coffee in Williamsburg.

"Why would he change it to Wilson Sullivan?"

"I don't know. He wasn't in WITSEC; they confirmed that. And it's not illegal to change your name. And he has no criminal record under that name. That would have made it problematic to become a cop."

"Wait a minute. Gosling?"

"Yeah, why?"

Francine pulled her laptop out of her bag and opened it. Then she slid a thumb drive into the dongle port and brought up the information on it.

"This is the stuff I got from Beckett's computer." Her fingers flew over the keyboard. "Okay, here it is. I thought I recognized that last name, and not because of Ryan Gosling."

Gibson shifted her chair next to Francine so she could read off the screen. "Helen Gosling was in WITSEC years ago. She'd fallen in with a guy who was a member of a militia group that did some really bad stuff. People got killed and a federal building was bombed. She turned state's evidence and was put in WITSEC."

"And she was moved to Alabama where she was under the protection of Earl Beckett, among others," added Francine.

"And she killed herself. They found her hanging in her bedroom."

Francine hit some more keys. "Here's a photo of her."

"Wow, she was gorgeous," noted Gibson.

"Yes, she was," said Francine, eyeing Gibson steadily. "Maybe *too* gorgeous."

Gibson shot her a glance. "Wait, you think—"

"—that Beckett tried it on with her? Oh hell yes, I do. This was right after we left New Mexico. He must have gotten transferred."

"Do you think he had something to do with her death?"

"Well, let's say she was brave enough to threaten to out the man for his shit. Is that a motive for murder?"

"You bet it is. And Sullivan—or Mark Gosling, rather—is her...?"

Francine pulled a notebook out of her purse. Gibson saw that it was labeled TAKING DOWN EARL FUCKING BECKETT.

"Do you have a notebook for everything?" Gibson asked.

Francine gave her a knowing smile. "Oh, you have no idea." She skimmed through some pages and then pointed at some written notes. "This is what I found out. Mark was her younger brother. I didn't know at the time that he was also Wilson Sullivan."

"You think she might have confided in him? So he might have known what was happening to his sister?"

"And he became a cop to bring justice to his sister?" said Francine. "It's certainly plausible."

Gibson had a sudden idea. "I thought Gosling might have been following Langhorne and then killed him. But can you see where Beckett was assigned over the years?"

She turned some more pages in the notebook. "After Alabama he was in El Paso. Then Arkansas, South Carolina, North Carolina, and now Virginia."

"That's it."

"What?" said Francine.

"Starting with El Paso those are the same places that Mark Gosling has been a cop as Wilson Sullivan."

"So he's been following *Beckett*?"

"Sure as hell seems that way," noted Gibson.

"But you said you thought they were working together."

"And I was clearly wrong about that. It's probably the only way Gosling could see of taking this guy down. He might have jumped at the chance when he found out Pottinger was Langhorne. With his cop connections he could easily have found out that Beckett knew Langhorne back then. He could use that as a plausible basis to ask for his help on this case. And that way get closer to the guy and hope something dropped and he could nail him."

"So he's not a bad guy, then. But why was he at Stormfield that night?" asked Francine.

"He lied and said the last time he was there was when he and I were at the place together. And he asked me about the treasure when I met with him."

"So maybe he really does want a piece of it?"

"Hell, who doesn't?"

Francine stared at her. "Does that include you, Mickey?"

Gibson looked uncomfortable. "I need money as much as the next person, especially now with no job. But it's all dirty money, Francine. It would be like stealing."

The other woman nodded and slowly closed her notebook. "I used to think that."

"Used to?"

"There are haves and have-nots. I was in the latter group for most of my life. I'm not saying the world owes me anything, but it does owe me the right to make my own way. And if we recover the treasure, shouldn't we be due a finder's fee? I mean, isn't that how those things work? Even Trask offered you and me one."

"Well, yeah, that makes sense. But I hope it's a better percentage than ProEye pays. I found them two hundred mill and they gave me a lousy five grand."

"Oh, honey, we can do so much better than that."

"How do you know? We'd have to negotiate."

"Oh, we will. *After* we find the treasure so our leverage is at its maximum." Francine rose. "So let's get working. You on the treasure, and me on finding my mother. We're clearly going to need one for the other because Rochelle is not leaving empty-handed. And despite all the shit she let happen to me, I would actually like my mother back."

74

FRANCINE SAT IN HER ROOM with the lights out and noise-cancelling headphones on. She had been drugged by Rochelle at Stormfield at one forty-five p.m. or close to it. She remembered looking at her watch right before she fell unconscious. When she had awoken in the bed all trussed up she could still see her watch. It was one minute past two. She had to be carried to a car. Two to four minutes to accomplish that. Then an eight-minute drive to where she had been taken and several more minutes to carry her in and tie her up and then she had to regain consciousness.

She closed her eyes and trained her mind to focus exactly on what she wanted it to focus on. She had done this back in Albuquerque when she was with the men who had paid her father, or else with Darren Ender, who loved to hear her scream. She had read about the technique in a book. It was a way of transporting your mind to another place while your body was engaged elsewhere. Prisoners of all sorts often did it, to get by. She could understand why.

It had allowed her to survive without losing her mind.

The roads around Stormfield were winding and the area was not heavily populated. The reality was you couldn't get anywhere fast. The place she had been taken to had to be isolated so pesky neighbors wouldn't be around to see her lifted out of the car and carried in. She calculated the time and distance and settled on a two-square-mile area with Stormfield as its epicenter.

She made her mind go blank for a moment and then proceeded

to fill it up with as much as she could remember about the room she had been in.

There would have been an easier way to do this, but Rochelle had been smart enough to turn off Francine's phone so she couldn't go back and track where she had been taken.

She recited out loud, "Plank floor, small bed, tattered drapes, one window, peeling paint, cold, though the day had not been especially chilly."

She didn't remember much sun coming in the window. So perhaps lots of shade trees?

"Wooden two-panel door, looked old. Smell was musty, place was dusty."

Abandoned house? That would make sense.

Now she focused on sounds, or lack thereof. No nearby traffic. No train rumble or whistle. No aircraft, so not on a flight path, presumably.

But there had been a sound. Consistent, loud. Mechanized.

A farm tractor?

She turned on the light, took off the headphones, opened an app on her phone, and plugged in her mileage parameters with Stormfield as the center.

She grabbed her car keys. And a Glock pistol she had purchased. She might need it against Rochelle's knife or gun. It would certainly take the treasure to get her mother back. And it might take something more. Whichever it was, she was willing to pay the price. She wasn't exactly sure why.

But I am willing to pay the price. Because I know Rochelle is.

* * *

Gibson had arranged for her parents to come over and watch the kids. Her dad had hugged her especially tight, something her mother noted but did not comment on.

"You look okay," muttered her father into her ear.

"That's because I am."

"So it's really over then?"

"That part is."

"That part! Oh my God, I feel another ulcer coming on."

"Just pop some Rolaids. Works for me."

She left her parents with Tommy and Darby, and headed to her home office.

She fired up her computer. While Francine was looking for her mother, Gibson was going to make one more all-out assault on Langhorne's treasure.

While they had used the cryptocurrency subterfuge to ensnare Nathan Trask, Gibson hadn't thought that Langhorne was involved in that type of digital currency at all. But as she went over some records of Pottinger's financial accounts again, she saw an intriguing bit of code that had been left there, like a dangling participle.

She copied the line of code and pasted it into an online search. She sat back and waited for the search to run.

"Damn!"

Harry Langhorne had just thrown her a curve.

The search had taken her to a site that sold NFTs, or Non Fungible Tokens, basically digital assets separate and apart from bitcoins. Each NFT was unique and equated to a specific asset. They ran the gamut from a one-of-a-kind meme autographed tweet, to a fractional ownership of a Banksy work, to a digital sports trading card signed by a superstar in very limited quantities. The very first tweet, from Twitter founder Jack Dorsey, had sold for nearly $3 million as an NFT.

Now that is some crazy shit, but, hey, it's only money. Or bitcoin.

One could buy an NFT with cryptocurrency, or, with some platforms like PayPal and Robinhood, a simple credit card would suffice. If crypto was used, the buyer would need a digital wallet to hold both the NFT and the crypto.

She'd chased down debtors who had stashed some of their wealth in NFTs. Thus, she knew that most NFTs were Ethereum based.

Ethereum was a blockchain-based economic trading platform. In fact, many NFT marketplaces would take only Eth tokens as payment. You had to have a user account to create a transaction on Ethereum.

So had Langhorne bought an NFT? And if so, why? Was that the treasure?

She might be able to find out because, while NFTs were not bitcoin, they were pieces of digital information housed on blockchains. While one bitcoin could replace another, NFT tokens represented a unique digital asset. She wasn't sure why someone would spend a ton of money on a tweet or sports card that anyone could take a screenshot of and claim it was original. But then collectors were strange beasts, and the blockchain would prove the authenticity of the NFT and its concomitant value, at least in theory. So there was that.

But the thing was NFTs could not really be traded for other NFTs or traditional currency. So once you bought one you really could sell it only for crypto. And recently, NFTs had been taking a beating in the news and financial markets because of fraud and hidden fees and the cost of or impossibility of maintaining the article on the Ethereum blockchain, as well as a host of other issues. Gibson wasn't sure whether the whole market wouldn't implode at some point, but she didn't care about that. She just wanted to find the treasure, if it existed.

Okay, here we go.

On blockchains she started searching for ERC-721 tokens, upon which NFTs on Ethereum were based. She had to find some that had been owned by Langhorne and then used to buy one or more NFTs. There were many places to buy NFTs, platforms like OpenSea, Rarible, AtomicMarket, and SuperRare, among others. Hell, apparently even Amazon was thinking about selling them. She worked away, following one trail, which took her to another one. Some ended in dead ends. In fact, all of them did.

Until one did not.

75

It took about two hours, but Francine finally found what she thought was the place to which she'd been taken.

A farm was within earshot and she could hear the tractor, approximately the same sound she had heard while being held prisoner.

The dilapidated house was down a curvy, dirt road. It was clearly abandoned, which made sense. Rochelle had always been stingy, even with the proceeds from a diamond haul in the bank. She wouldn't be shelling out money to rent a safe house to keep Mommy hostage when she could do that for free.

Francine knelt next to a bank of trees and surveyed the place.

She didn't see a car, but it probably was parked in back, just in case anyone came down this far.

She wondered if there was electricity even turned on in the place. If not, there was no way they had an oxygenator in there. They were probably providing her mother's oxygen needs purely from tanks. She wondered how they had managed that. That cost money, and the place you got it from delivered the tanks. She doubted they would haul oxygen canisters to a place like this.

Had they ripped off the supply from the assisted living center they had taken her from? Rochelle had intimated something like that when she had spoken to a trussed-up Clarisse. That was more in Rochelle's line. Why pay if you could steal?

But that's sort of my mantra, too.

She stiffened when he came out of the house.

And she felt her heart grow both soft and sad.

Her tall, handsome brother had not aged well. He looked too thin and bowed, and…just worn out.

Shit. What the hell have you two been doing? But then look at me. I know what I've been doing. Leading a life I had to manufacture to forget the other one.

Her brother had always been sensitive and aloof. Her father had called him stupid, inept, useless. And those were the kinder terms the monster had used. That just ground you down, year after year. And now all these years later, here, perhaps, was the result.

He smoked a cigarette, idly flicking the ash away. His hair was thinning and he'd grown a mustache that looked wispy and far too small for his broad face. His clothes were cheap and hung baggy on him. She remembered them together as kids, before their father had revealed his abominable ways. They had loved each other, had fun together, supported each other, eventually forming a little two-person army to keep all the shit at bay.

Too bad the shit won.

She had hoped that he would have found happiness and good health and something altogether better than had been available to him as a member of the Langhorne family.

He didn't seem to have achieved any of that.

Part of her instinctively wanted to call out to him.

But her brother clearly was not the same person he had been all those years ago.

His life could have turned out so differently, but for Harry Langhorne.

I wouldn't blame you, Dougie, if you'd killed him.

Now if I could only get you away from Rochelle.

There was a noise from inside the house. Then the door opened and Rochelle joined him. She took a puff off his offered smoke and gazed around. She had on jeans and a hoodie, and was barefoot. Her substantial hip butted up next to Doug's slim one. She smiled and kissed him.

And he smiled back, and in that smile Francine had to admit that her brother looked like a little boy again. The one she remembered. He looked...happy.

She put a hand in her pocket and felt for the gun there. This could turn out fabulously. Or this could be the worst day of her life, and that would be saying something. She drew a deep breath and transformed herself into what she knew she could be when the need arose: commanding, confident, and courageous. Like she had been with Nathan Trask, conning him and his people just enough to allow her to survive. To allow her to win.

She stepped out into the open. "Lovely spring day, isn't it? And how is Mommy doing? Spry and spirited?"

Rochelle took a step forward, putting herself between brother and sister.

"Oh, like I would ever hurt my *brother*? But you shouldn't give me such a tempting target, Rochelle."

Francine looked past Rochelle, and her tough facade faded for a moment. "I would never hurt you, Dougie. Never. For so long we were all each other had."

Francine wasn't sure if he reacted to this, though he did drop and grind out his smoke.

He nodded at her, she supposed, in hello. Her brother had never been loquacious.

"How did you find us?" asked Rochelle. "I turned off your phone."

Francine walked closer. "Never reveal sources and methods. And is my swagger still there?"

Rochelle pointed to the gun. "What's that for?"

"You brought a gun last time. Only fair that I have one. So, how is Mommy?"

"The same as when you were here before," said Rochelle. "And you better hurry up and find the money because I can't deal with the woman much longer."

"Is there electricity in there? Otherwise, how are you managing the oxygen?"

"We rigged it off a feeder line. At least Dougie did. He's real good with stuff like that. And we got an oxygenator."

"Where?"

Rochelle's mouth curved to a grin. "Sources and methods."

Francine glanced at her brother. "Did Mom recognize you?"

He shook his head and looked off.

"I'm sorry."

He glanced back at her. "Why?" His voice was husky and dull and unfamiliar.

She drew closer, pointing the gun to the dirt. "Because she's our mother. In spite of all the shit."

"Forgive and forget?" said Rochelle in a sneering way.

"Neither. But we can move forward."

"Maybe you can. That shit messed us up but good," said Rochelle. "Just treading water now. Probably forever."

"And you think I'm the picture of perfect mental health?" said Francine.

"I don't know. Are you trying to be?"

"All I try and do is get out of bed every day."

"Us too," said Doug. He added quietly, again looking off, "Us too, really."

"And Bruce?" asked Francine.

Her brother glanced nervously at Rochelle. "I did it," he said.

"Why?"

Doug once more glanced at Rochelle and shrugged. His gaze fixed on his shoes.

"You didn't know Bruce like I did," said Rochelle.

"But you two were dating," retorted Francine.

"No we weren't. He had some crazy-ass fantasy about me. Told me I was Wonder Woman to his Superman. He creeped me out. I told him to leave me alone. But unlike Doug, Bruce had no problem playing in the reindeer games."

"What are you talking about?"

"He paid my father to have sex with me. And it was not voluntary. My old man had to hold me down."

"He never tried that with me."

"He wanted to, trust me," said Rochelle, who was now looking off like Doug had been.

"Then why didn't he?"

"Because he had me instead. I figured if he did the shit to me, he'd leave you alone. In fact, I made him promise to leave you alone."

"Why would you do that?"

"*Twelfth Night?*"

"What?"

"You were a much better actress than I was. I could never get Viola's cadence right. Or really get into the spirit of her character. I just memorized the lines and regurgitated them when I was supposed to."

"I heard the performance was well received."

"It should have been you onstage, not me." Rochelle paused. "That was one reason why I let Bruce do what he did to me."

"And the other reason?"

Rochelle looked at Doug. "You're his sister. That means you're precious to me. And just in case you're wondering, as soon as Bruce saw us when he opened the door at his house he went after Dougie with a machete. Dougie didn't have a choice. It was him or Bruce."

"Why did you even try to find him?" asked Francine.

"He had something of mine that I wanted back."

"What?"

In answer Rochelle lifted a small gold necklace off her chest. "Your brother gave it to me. Worked his ass off doing construction when we were in New Mexico. Bruce took it one time when I was forced to have sex with him. Next thing I knew his father croaked, and he and his mom vanished."

"How did you find him?"

"Remember, I worked at the marshal's office cleaning shit, too. I found what I needed to find. Unlike us, Bruce and his mom kept in touch with the WITSEC folks. But old Bruce thought we were there for another reason, I guess. Like revenge for raping me. Anyway, he tried to cut Dougie's head off before Dougie showed him who was the better man."

"I saw the aftermath. Didn't look to be much of a struggle."

"We cleaned it up. And put Bruce in the bed. We knew the cops would probably figure shit out, and they'd never believe it was self-defense, even though it was. Dougie was a lot bigger than Bruce, but I guess Bruce still thought he was Superman."

Francine looked at her brother, who was now rummaging in his pocket. He pulled out another smoke and lit up.

She turned back to Rochelle. "You cut my neck."

"I never said I was completely good," noted Rochelle. "Or entirely sane."

"You went to visit Harry. How and why?"

"We were looking for him all that time. Finally found him. Dougie went in to negotiate with him. Basically, he gives us a share of the money if we don't expose him. Then Harry tells Dougie that he's dying and basically to fuck off."

Francine said, "I talked to the housekeeper. She said Dougie told her to get another job and it was because he knew Harry was dying?"

Doug nodded. "Yes."

Francine slid the gun into her jacket pocket. "I'll get the money. Tell Mommy I said hello, and that I'll be back for her. And that we'll all live happily ever after." She started to walk away and then turned back. "It was good to see you, Dougie."

Her brother nodded, and didn't glance away this time. He watched her leave, even as his fingers curled around Rochelle's in a firm, unyielding grip.

76

"Can we meet?" said Gibson.

She was on the phone with Francine, who had just gotten back from her encounter with Rochelle, and her brother.

"Yes, same place?"

"I'll be there in an hour."

Gibson drove over in her van and found Francine waiting for her in front of the café. She had on a floppy hat, glasses, and a dark blue suit.

They sat outside with iced teas, and Gibson opened her laptop.

Before she could show what was on it, Francine said, "I found my mother. And I saw Rochelle and Dougie."

"What! How?"

Francine explained her method for tracking them down.

"Pretty ingenious," noted Gibson. "But you left her there?"

"She's actually far happier with them than she was at the facility in Greenville. And they won't let anything happen to her. They want the money."

"Okay. So...how was your brother?"

"In some ways the same, and in some ways different. I was going to try to figure out how to get him away from Rochelle."

"And?"

"And then I realized he was happy with her. In fact, I think they were made for each other. Sort of threw a wrench in my plans."

"Of what, reuniting your family?" Gibson said dubiously.

She gazed off. "I've spent so much time alone that…well, I thought I might try another slice of life."

"But?"

"But I can see now that that won't work. Too much time has passed. We're all too different." She looked at the laptop. "So, show me what you found."

"You know about NFTs?"

"I do, but don't tell me my father did, too?"

"It looks like it." Gibson clicked on some keys and then held the laptop at an angle so Francine could see. "I found a bit of dangling code on one of the accounts that your father had closed out. I think he did that on purpose, sort of another breadcrumb to the treasure. So I followed it up."

"Well, NFTs are definitely twenty-first century," remarked Francine.

"Yes, they are. So that fits in with the note he left."

"But what sort of NFT could he have dumped a half billion dollars on?"

Gibson gaped. "Is *that* how much money we're talking about?"

"That's what I calculated, yes."

"Holy shit."

"'Holy shit' probably doesn't cut it."

"I found this." She hit one more key, and an image came up on the screen.

"That's a room," noted Francine. "Where is it?"

"Heard of the metaverse?"

"The nonreality reality where we all have avatars doing shit we could either do for real, like going to a party or attending a concert, or insane stuff we would never do for real, like BASE jumping in a wingsuit."

"Right," said Gibson. "And you can also buy stuff that *doesn't* actually exist. Well, it does in the metaverse. Including real estate. Anything from a house to ad space at a football stadium, at least virtually." Gibson pointed at the computer screen. "That room is in a piece of real estate Harry bought on the meta-verse."

"Where is it located?" asked Francine.

"That I'm not sure about. The digital trail was obscured for some reason. Usually, it's pretty well laid out."

"What's that on the walls?"

Gibson hit a key to zoom in. "Artwork."

Francine leaned in for a better look. "What sort of artwork?"

"Digital images of famous pieces of artwork. I've already iden-tified them." She used her cursor to hover over each. "This is a Degas, that one's a Monet, the one on the left is a Vermeer. The three along this wall, the first one is a Winslow Homer, the next a Mary Cassatt, and the last one is a John Singer Sargent. There are others, in other rooms. But you get the gist."

"Okay, but these are digital copies, not the real things. How much could they be worth?"

"I checked on that, too. These are authorized one-of-a-kind copies with blockchain provenance. I guess museums and people who own these works saw a way to make some money without actually selling the original. Everyone's getting in on it. I calculated that all told, these NFTs add up to about five million bucks total. I think that was pretty much a vanity purchase. I mean, who would want to shell out that much money for a digital copy, even with authentic provenance? I doubt he could resell it or make money."

"But that's nowhere near the fortune that I calculated he left behind. And he ripped off Trask, too, so there has to be more." She glanced at the screen. "And is there any way to at least get ahold of these NFTs?"

"Not without the private key."

"Is that contained in some other clue we haven't found yet?"

"It might be. I did learn that your father used things like sub-stitution ciphers when he was doing the books for the mobsters. So he might have employed that here, too."

"Really good work, Mickey, but we seem a long way from getting any money out of this."

"I know."

"And let's not forget the very real possibility that my father has screwed us over."

Gibson glanced nervously at Francine. "So, tell me more about seeing Rochelle and your brother. Did you learn anything new?"

"I learned that back in New Mexico Rochelle rode shotgun for me in a way I didn't realize."

"Meaning?"

"Meaning she took shit from some others so they would leave me alone."

"Why would she do that?"

Francine slid her sunglasses down and eyed Gibson. "Principally, because she loves my brother. My brother loved me. So, as she said, I was *precious*. She sacrificed her body for mine."

"Damn."

"And all this time I had seen her as the enemy."

"And Bruce Dixon?"

"Dougie admitted to killing him, but Rochelle said that Bruce came after him with a machete when they showed up at his place. Dougie had no choice. It was him or Bruce."

"Why would Bruce do that?"

"According to Rochelle, Bruce was not nearly as nice a guy as I thought."

She went on to tell Gibson about Dixon raping Rochelle and then stealing her necklace.

After a long moment of silence Gibson said, "What happened to Rochelle's father?"

"Don't know. He disappeared pretty soon after my dad did. I told you her mother had done a runner already, like mine. So when Rochelle and I turned eighteen, we got the hell out. There was no reason to stay. And, as I told you before, Dougie and Rochelle later went off together. They've been together ever since."

"How did your brother look?"

"Physically, not great. But..." She paused and glanced at Gibson. "He seems really happy with Rochelle. And she with him." She cleared her throat. "That's more than I have." She frowned. "Sorry, that's self-pity bullshit, I know."

"I think it's just being human."

Francine's next words were said in a businesslike tone. "And if we can't get the money right now, there is something we can get."

"What?"

She pulled a notebook from her bag and held it up. "Earl Fucking Beckett."

77

I'M PRETTY BUSY," SAID WILSON Sullivan as he stood in front of Gibson in the waiting area at police headquarters.

"Just wanted to catch up again and see how things are going. I thought we were working this together."

"Well, things change. I got a dressing-down from the top. They don't want collaborations with civilians."

"Damn, that's too bad. And just when I thought our working relationship was really hitting its stride."

"Yeah, well, I'm sorry about that. Now, if there's nothing else?"

"No, that's about it."

Sullivan turned to leave.

"Hey, *Mark*!"

He whirled around to see Francine Langhorne standing there.

"I think it's time we talked," she said.

* * *

Sullivan sipped his coffee and looked down at the table. They were in the police cafeteria, which was empty at this time of the morning.

"How'd you do it?" he asked.

"Just connected the dots," noted Gibson. "Principally, your career trail matched Beckett's."

"That doesn't tell me how you got my real identity."

"I took your prints off the pen you were using when I visited you last time. We suspected you weren't who you said you were. Past twenty years ago, Wilson Sullivan didn't really exist."

He eyed Francine. "And you're really Harry Langhorne's daughter?"

"In the flesh. Sorry to use an old WITSEC tactic to out you by using your real given name, but we had to make a move on the chessboard."

"And where do we go from here?"

Francine tapped the table. "Earl Beckett. I know what he did to me and others. And we suspect what he did to your sister."

"He raped her and when she threatened to tell, he murdered her."

"But it was never proven?" said Gibson.

"Obviously not, since he's a free man."

Gibson glanced at his neck. "I checked your record. You were never wounded as a cop like you told me. So where'd you get that scar?"

Sullivan pulled his shirt collar up to cover the mark. "Let's just say in my despondency over the death of my sister I attempted something very foolish. Luckily, I didn't succeed."

Francine and Gibson exchanged a glance.

"Okay," said Francine. "We need to make sure we nail him now."

"On what charge?" asked Sullivan.

"Murdering Harry Langhorne," answered Gibson.

Sullivan looked at them both. "Can you prove it?"

"Maybe. With your help."

He leaned forward. "How?"

"You're working with him on this case. We think he's taking advantage of that relationship to find the treasure that Langhorne left behind." Gibson paused. "A treasure that you seem interested in, too."

"My sister had a little girl, my niece. My parents raised her after Helen died. She's now a grown woman and she has some intellectual disabilities. I was hoping if there was any money..."

"Well, we think there *is* money. And we believe we can use that as bait to reel Beckett in."

"Okay, I'll help you however I can."

"Exactly what we wanted to hear," said Francine.

78

"WHAT'S UP?" ASKED EARL BECKETT as Sullivan popped his head inside the man's office at the federal building in Norfolk. It was a couple of days after Sullivan's meeting with Francine and Gibson.

Sullivan took a seat across the desk from the marshal. "Look, can I talk confidentially?"

"Why, you think somebody's eavesdropping on us in here?" Beckett said with a wry grin.

"No, but what I'm about to tell you I don't want to go any further."

"Okay." Beckett sat up straighter and put his elbows on his desk as he took in the serious expression on the Virginia police detective's face. "Shoot."

"The Langhornes?"

"What about 'em?"

"I think I've found Francine and Doug Langhorne. And the mother."

Beckett exclaimed, "What? Where are they?"

"The last place was an abandoned cottage about two miles from Stormfield."

"What the hell are they doing there? And how did you find them?"

"It was actually Gibson who did the heavy lifting. She had some specialized software program on her computer that ProEye provided her. It's a tracking device that takes in like ten thousand different factors."

"How do you know they were there? Did you see them?"

"Gibson said she did."

"*Said* she did? And you believed her?"

"She sent me these. Took them with a long-range camera."

Sullivan pulled his phone out and held it up. "Just swipe across."

Beckett did so and glanced up at Sullivan.

"Well?" said Sullivan. "You knew them, I didn't. Could it be them?"

"It could be," said Beckett slowly. "Can you text me those pictures?"

"Sure." Sullivan took a few moments to do so. "So, do we head over there and arrest them?"

"For what?" said Beckett.

"For murdering their father. They might be intending to do the same to their mother, for all I know. And they're after the treasure. Gibson is sure of that. She's tracked some stuff down online and she says she can trace their digital signatures back to Francine."

"Francine always was the smart one," Beckett said absently.

"Yeah, so if we arrest them and make them talk, they can tell us where the money their father stole is, and that will all go to the government. It was mob money, after all. We'll both probably get medals for that," he added with a grin.

"Yeah, medals," said Beckett absently again, his mind clearly elsewhere. "Did Gibson have any idea where the treasure is?"

"She's convinced it's somewhere at Stormfield."

"Where? It's a big place."

"Gibson might be able to find it. Or we can get that from Francine."

Beckett leaned forward and began speaking slowly and intently. "See, what I'm thinking is Francine is never going to tell us squat. You didn't know the girl, but I did. She doesn't give up anything without a fight. But if we can find the treasure on our own? That's a whole different story."

"But what about arresting them?"

"They can keep. Just put them under surveillance for now so they can't slip away."

"Okay, yeah. And then if we find the money we turn it in. Hold a press conference. Maybe the governor will come. And somebody from Washington. It'll be a big deal. I've been waiting a long time to bust a big case like this."

Beckett rubbed his chin and gave Sullivan a sideways glance. "Yeah, I bet you have. You really think Gibson can find it?"

"Well, she found the Langhornes. So my money would be on her. And she sounded really confident when I talked to her. Said she had it all figured out. This is what she does for a living, after all. And what could it hurt to see?"

"Couldn't hurt at all. Sure save us a lot of trouble. You want to arrange things with her? Maybe the three of us can go there?"

"The three of us? I thought we would take a *team* over there tomorrow and just go through everything."

"Tomorrow. Yeah, I guess that would make sense. Is Gibson at home now?"

"Yeah, she's got the kids and all. I can contact her and set it up for tomorrow. You want to meet out there, say around ten?" Sullivan rose. "This could be really big for both of us, Earl." He held out his hand. "Here's to good luck tomorrow."

Beckett stood and shook his hand. "Yep, to good luck *tomorrow*. I'll see you there."

Sullivan left, and Beckett immediately made a call.

79

THE DOORBELL RANG AROUND NINE THIRTY that night at Gibson's home.

When she answered the door, there stood Earl Beckett.

"Marshal, what can I do for you?" she said, looking surprised.

"Got your address from Sullivan. Mind if I come in?"

She stepped back and he walked past her, taking off his hat as he did so.

They sat in the small living room.

"Guess your kids are asleep?"

"Oh, yeah. They go down around eight thirty and explode again at around six."

"Never had any kids," said Beckett. "Guess my career was my family."

"It is for a lot of people."

"Look, Sullivan came by to see me today."

"Right, he said he was going to do that."

"I saw the pictures. Sure looked like the Langhornes to me. He said you used a software program to find them?"

"That's right, proprietary software that ProEye uses."

"Damn, I wish we'd known about it. We could have found them a long time ago."

"Well, the software has only been available for a couple of years."

"Thing is, I'd like to see them if I could. I wanted to let the kids, well, they're not kids anymore, know that I was thinking about them. And—"

"—and you're wondering if they killed their father?"

He looked uneasy with the query. "Look, I don't want to think they did that. And it's not my case to go after them. It's Sullivan's."

"But still?"

"Of course they would have a motive to do it. He treated them bad, real bad. I told you about the play and how he wouldn't let Doug do any sports."

"Yeah, sounded really awful."

"I told Sullivan to keep eyes on them."

"Unfortunately, they disappeared before he could do that. But we'll get on their trail again," she said when Beckett looked stunned.

"Sullivan also mentioned that you know where the treasure is?"

"It's what I do for a living. In fact, I was thinking that if I found it, I might get a finder's fee. I'm a single mom with kids and, as you can see, I'm not rich. So the money would be very welcome."

"But with Francine and Doug in the area, what if they're after it, too? What if they get there first now that you lost them?"

Gibson looked alarmed. "Shit, I didn't think of that. You believe they might?"

Beckett started talking fast. "If they killed him, they were probably after the treasure, too. You said they left the place where you saw them. Well, they might be at Stormfield right now. Sullivan said we would go there tomorrow, but what if that's too late?"

"Damn, if they get there before we do?"

"So you really think you know where it is?"

"I do."

"Look, I'm going to call Sullivan and tell him to meet us out there as soon as he can. Let's go right now." He snapped his fingers. "Oh, but you can't leave your kids."

"That's not a problem. My mom's here. She can look after them. You call Sullivan and I'll let her know that I'm leaving and that I'll be back later."

"Sounds good," said Beckett.

* * *

While they were traveling to Stormfield in Beckett's truck a storm system blew in and it started to lightning and thunder, the wind picked up, and the rain started to fall. It was nearly eleven when they arrived. With the cloud cover the place was totally dark.

Beckett and Gibson pulled out their flashlights.

"I don't see Sullivan's car," noted Gibson.

"The weather might have slowed him down."

"Okay, let's go. He can catch up when he gets here."

They ran through the storm to the entrance.

The front door was unlocked.

They went in and shook the water off their clothes; Gibson pulled her wet hair out of her face.

"So where is the hiding place?" said Beckett as their twin beams cut through the gloom.

Gibson shone the light on her face, looking triumphant. "The room where Langhorne was found is *not* the only secret room in this place."

"What!"

"Yeah, I did a rundown on Stormfield's history, and it seems that the man who originally built it was of Scottish ancestry. Well, the Scots are famous for putting hidden rooms in their castles. I spoke with John Turner, who sold the place to Langhorne. He said there's a second secret room down in the wine cellar, and he told me how to access it."

"Damn. Good work, Gibson."

"Thanks. I actually patted myself on the back with that one."

They headed down the stairs.

On reaching the wine cellar, Gibson hurried over to a far corner where a wooden wall with wine bottle shelving attached was situated.

"Shine your light right there," she instructed Beckett as she pointed at the lower right-hand corner of the wall.

He did so and she set her light down, and gripped at a corner of the wood. First she pushed inward and there was an audible click. Then she pulled and the entire section of wall rotated out on hinges.

"Voilà." She picked up her light and shone it inside the small, dank room.

At the rear, under some old blankets, was a box. She opened it while Beckett kept his light pointed at it. Inside was a key.

Gibson held it in her hand and looked around. "Okay. What do you open?" Then Gibson started probing and prying in the middle of the rear wall of the room. "Shine your light," she said urgently.

He did so and she pulled away a bulge of bubbled paint, revealing a keyhole.

"Damn, how'd you see that?" asked Beckett.

"Easy, the rest of the wall is a slightly different shade of blue, and they couldn't completely cover the bulge of the lock underneath."

She inserted the key and turned it. The wall that had now become a door swung open. Revealed was an inner room that contained five large trunks. She tried the same key in each trunk's lock, until, with the fourth one, the lock turned.

She slowly opened the trunk, and Beckett illuminated the contents with his light.

"Holy shit!" he said.

It was full of cash.

She knelt down and examined the money. "These are all hundred-dollar bills," she said.

She did a quick calculation. "If all of these trunks have this same amount of cash in them, we're looking at probably a couple hundred million bucks."

She dusted off her hands and pulled out her phone. "I'll take pictures, and then I'm going to try Sullivan again and tell him what we found. This is going to hit the national press for sure."

"No, it won't," said Beckett.

When Gibson glanced up, his gun was pointed at her.

CHAPTER

80

"WHAT THE HELL ARE YOU doing, Earl?"

"Getting what's rightfully mine."

"This is Langhorne's mob money."

"Nothing personal, but this is *my* money and I've waited a long time for it."

"What are you talking about?"

"I helped Harry clear out of WITSEC. We were supposed to meet up and he was going to give me my share, but that asshole never showed. Been looking for him for over twenty years. And I finally found him right here in this house."

"Wait a minute—*you* killed Langhorne?"

"Ran into him when he was coming out of that little hidey-hole of his in the library. I was fair. I gave him a choice. Tell me and he dies with no pain. Don't tell me and he dies awful. He chose the poison."

"And when Sullivan approached you?"

"I figured it wouldn't hurt to piggyback on your efforts. Found out you were really good at finding hidden money." He motioned at the trunks with his light. "And I have to say you lived up to your rep."

"You can't get away with this. Sullivan is on his way."

"Jesus, get with the program. I never called him."

"My mother knows you and I left together."

"Which means I have a little unfinished business back at your house. Don't worry, it'll be quick. And I won't touch the kiddies. And now, we have to take care of you."

"Drop it, Beckett," the voice called out.

Beckett whirled to see Wilson Sullivan and two uniformed officers, guns drawn, emerge from the darkness.

Beckett cursed under his breath and put his gun down. He eyed Gibson. "You set me up, you bitch."

Francine appeared next to Sullivan. "Hey, Earl, remember me? Francine?"

Beckett's eyes took her in. "Long time no see."

He smiled. And Gibson did not like that smile.

Francine stepped up to Beckett and kneed him in the crotch.

"Hope the reunion was memorable," she said as the man dropped to his knees, moaning.

The next moment a series of gunshots were fired from the open doorway. Two slugs hit one of the uniformed officers, and he collapsed to the floor. Another round hit Sullivan in the shoulder and he went down, too. The other officer fired back at the doorway.

Gibson pulled her pistol from her ankle holster, but Beckett had already recovered. He grabbed Francine and his gun, and pulled her out of the wine cellar. Gibson heard a click.

She raced to the door and found that it was locked.

"Francine!"

Gibson looked around, and saw that the cop who'd been shot was dead. His colleague was bending over Sullivan, who was panting heavily and holding his arm.

She ran over to him. "How bad?"

"In and out, but it's bleeding like a bitch. Who fired those shots?"

"Beckett obviously didn't come alone."

Gibson said to the officer, "Tourniquet his arm, and call an ambulance and more backup."

She ran over to the door, and fired two shots into the lock, then kicked at the door and it popped free.

She did a turkey peek to see if they were waiting to gun down anyone who came out of the cellar. With the coast clear, Gibson ran after them.

She was now back in Jersey City cop mode, running down another suspect.

Only this one had a hostage.

CHAPTER

81

GIBSON COULD HEAR THE SOUNDS of footsteps pounding away in front of her, though she didn't know how close; they had a decent head start.

She silently berated herself for allowing this to happen. She knew it was likely that *two* people had written the phrase on the wall in the secret room. At first, she thought it might have been Francine and her brother. Next, it might have been Rochelle and Doug. But when that was disproved and she had figured Beckett as the killer of Harry Langhorne, she should have remembered the second hand that had contributed to the message. That oversight had cost one cop his life and Sullivan a gunshot wound.

And maybe Francine her life.

But who was the other person?

She reached the main floor and peered around a corner. She no longer heard the sounds of footsteps.

"Look out, Mickey!" screamed Francine.

Gibson ducked down. Two shots slammed into the wall where Gibson's head had been moments before.

She heard a thud and Francine screamed in pain.

Gibson couldn't fire back because she might hit the woman.

When she heard them run off again, Gibson followed. She broke into a sprint when she heard one of the huge front doors slam against the wall.

The storm was still raging outside. She had no idea how long it would take for the police or an ambulance to get here. But if Beckett got away with Francine? Gibson knew they would find only her body, if they even managed that.

She stepped off the front steps when she saw the headlights of Beckett's truck pop on as the engine fired up. Next to it was another vehicle. That must be the ride for whoever was working with Beckett.

Gibson ran forward, knelt down, took careful aim, and shot out the two front tires, and then popped two rounds into the radiator.

The side doors flew open. Beckett appeared on the driver's side of the truck and another man on the passenger's side. In front of the other man was Francine, with a pistol against her head.

Beckett screamed, "You're gonna get her and you killed."

"You're not leaving here with her. Then she's dead for sure."

"She's dead now," called out the other man.

"The cops will be here any second," said Gibson.

"And we got two guns and you got one," said Beckett. "So this is not ending well for you."

"Just like it won't for you," Gibson snapped, the rain streaming down her face.

A massive bolt of lightning hit nearby, and struck a tree. That explosion, combined with an unholy crack of thunder, made them all look at the now-flaming tree about a hundred yards away.

The man holding Francine grunted as someone hit him, knocking him down.

Gibson saw this and called out, "Run, Francine."

Francine sprinted away as the man rose and fired several shots in her direction before he was pounced on again by his assailant. This person pounded the man's face until he fell limp.

Beckett, seeing what was happening, tried to run over to help his partner, but Gibson shot the man in the leg and dropped him in the dirt, where he lay screaming and holding his wounded limb.

Gibson ran forward and scooped up his gun where it had fallen. She held up a finger. "You move one inch, I finish the job."

Right as Gibson turned to run over to the other man, Beckett slipped a second gun from a side holster. He was about to fire when a muzzle was placed against his head.

FBI Special Agent Cary Pinker took the gun and said simply, "You're under arrest."

Gibson turned, saw what had just happened, and said, "Thanks for having my back."

"No, thank *you*. I've been after this SOB for a long time."

Gibson hustled over to the other side of the truck to find Doug Langhorne hovering over the unconscious man. Gibson shone her light on the man's battered face.

"Who is he?" she asked.

His chest heaving and his clothes soaked through by the rain, Doug said, "Rochelle's father, Darren Enders."

When they heard the scream, they both turned and ran toward it.

They stopped near the tree line, where they saw Francine standing over something on the ground.

"Rochelle!" cried out Doug. He pushed past his sister and knelt next to Rochelle, who had a bloody bullet wound dead center of her chest. Right as Doug gripped her hand, she opened her eyes, saw him, mumbled something, and died.

Gibson looked in disbelief at Francine and then back where Darren Enders lay unconscious. "When he fired at you—"

"—he hit Rochelle," said Francine, swaying on her feet.

Gibson managed to catch the woman right as she fainted.

82

THE DEAD HAD BEEN COLLECTED. The crime scene was still being processed. Witness statements had been gathered. The wounded Sullivan was at the hospital undergoing emergency surgery, as was Earl Beckett. The battered Darren Enders was also in the hospital and under arrest.

Gibson, Francine, and Doug were sitting in the federal building in Norfolk in a small conference room, with warm blankets around them, sipping hot, strong coffee.

Agent Pinker walked in and closed the door. He carried a file with him. He drew out a chair and sat down. "How are you all doing?"

Doug just stared at the table. Francine's gaze was on her coffee cup.

Gibson answered, "As well as can be expected. Is Sullivan going to be okay?"

"I talked to the doctors. He's going to be fine."

"Do you know his real name?" said Gibson.

"Mark Gosling, yes."

"When you arrived on the scene, I thought you were there to investigate Langhorne's murder."

"In a way, I was. But I was really after Beckett."

"So you knew what he had done?"

"We strongly suspected. We had heard stories. A few people had come forward over the years. There were enough irregularities to get our suspicions up. I don't like dirty cops. And what Beckett did was far worse than just getting paid off to look the other way."

He glanced over at Francine and Doug. "I know some of what happened to you. I know it probably means very little, but I'm sorry. It should never have happened."

Francine acknowledged this with a nod. Doug didn't show that he'd even heard.

"How did you come to be out at Stormfield?" asked Gibson.

"We were tailing Beckett. We followed him to your house and then to Stormfield. We saw the other man drive up and enter the house after the two of you did. We were outside when all hell broke loose and people started running out of the place and shots were fired. I'm glad I was there in time to prevent him from shooting you."

"Me too. Did you know that he had teamed up with Darren Enders?"

"We knew he was working with someone, but we didn't know it was Enders. Apparently, Langhorne had promised both of them some of the mob money."

"That's what Beckett said, too. He's been hunting Langhorne all this time. And he confessed to killing him. Sullivan and the other officer heard him, too."

"Oh, we have him dead to rights. He will never breathe another day of freedom. He or Enders." He tapped his file. "So, you set him up with the treasure?"

"What he thought was the treasure. Sullivan found out from the former owners that there was another secret room in the wine cellar. So Francine and I had the idea of conning Beckett. We knew he wanted the money. So we got the trunks and Sullivan and his people filled them with cut-out paper, but hundred-dollar bills topping each stack. The former owners told us where the old key was to open the other door inside the secret room. We blobbed some paint on the keyhole to make it look like it was hidden. You didn't even need a key to open the trunks. I just used it so Beckett wouldn't get suspicious." She paused. "I also just found out that he was the one who called ProEye and got me fired."

"Why would he do that?" asked Pinker.

"Probably because he wanted me to be desperate to find the treasure, so he could take the whole thing."

"And you had to know that he would try to kill you when you found it."

"That's why I had Sullivan and two of his men hidden in the wine cellar. I didn't figure that Beckett had brought his partner along for backup. It cost a cop his life." She shook her head and looked miserable.

Pinker glanced over at Doug. "And I'm very sorry about your friend, Mr. Langhorne." This time Doug nodded but didn't look up. "It was very fortunate that you were there to help subdue these men."

Doug looked at his sister, not Pinker. "We took turns watching the place. Rochelle was there last night. When she saw the cars coming in, she called me and I came right over. I saw Enders and Beckett. I knew who they were right away. When I saw you run and he was going to shoot you..."

Francine put a hand on her brother's arm. "You saved my life, Dougie. You were always there for me. And Rochelle."

His eyes filled with tears. "'Cept last night." He bent low and started to sob.

Francine wrapped her arms around him and held him, whispering soothing words into his ear, while Gibson and Pinker looked away.

83

WELL, WE GOT EVERYTHING ON our bucket list except the treasure," noted Francine.

She and Gibson were seated in the latter's home office. Tommy and Darby were with Gibson's parents.

"Yeah, but that's a big one. How is your mom, by the way?"

"I got her into a facility near here, at least temporarily. Dougie is with her right now. He's decided to cremate Rochelle's remains and sprinkle them at a lake where they lived for a while and were happy."

"So they came here looking for Beckett and your father, too?"

"They wanted revenge, but they also wanted the money, like I did." She looked at Gibson's twin computer screens. "NFTs. It just doesn't strike me as something that Harry would dump money into. And it was only five million bucks."

"I've looked at everything a dozen times."

"So the dig deeper clue. The 'twenty-first century' clue. That's it, right? No other clues left behind?"

"Yeah, that's..." Gibson looked at her screens. "That's actually *not* right."

"What do you mean?" asked Francine.

"I forgot to tell you. I tracked down a bunch of companies that Langhorne had. If you incorporate you have to have a registered agent in the state of incorporation, so if you get sued, there's someone in the state to accept service."

"And the point?" asked Francine impatiently.

"There was one agent I reached out to who got back to me immediately." She started clicking keys on her computer and pointed at the screen. "Dexter Tremayne from South Dakota. He's the registered agent for DPE. That's Daniel Pottinger Enterprises, obviously."

"What did he say when he got back to you?"

"That Pottinger aka Harry had called him and left a message for Tremayne to give to anyone who contacted him after he was dead. DPE was pretty well buried behind some other shells. It took me some time to dig through."

"What was the message?"

" 'Now you see it, but then you don't.' "

"That's it?"

"No. He also said to take away the eight. And then to use the leftovers for Sesame Street."

"That makes no sense at all."

"Agreed. Now, the usual phrase is slightly different. 'Now you see it, *now* you don't.' "

"So Harry had changed 'now' to 'but then'?"

"That's right. I was going to dig down deeper, but then I got sidetracked with everything else and forgot all about it."

Francine took a notebook from her purse and flitted through the pages.

"What's that?" asked Gibson.

"My TREASURE notebook."

Gibson gave her a funny look.

"I actually have a half dozen devoted just to you. A record for me."

"Well, I guess I should feel honored somehow. Do you think he just got the phrase wrong?"

"No. He was the most detailed person I've ever met."

Gibson glanced at the notebook and the precise writing on the page she was reading. "You mean sort of like you?"

"I do it so I can have some control over my life. He did it to screw people over."

"So if he added the 'but then,' there was a reason?"

"Most definitely." She turned another page and tensed. "Wait a minute. You said you found out that my father used secret codes and substitution ciphers to keep his mob account books secret?"

"That's right."

"Then maybe this phrase is a substitution code. Do you know how they work?"

"Pretty much. You substitute one alphabet letter for another. The parties trying to communicate have the key, so you know what letter to substitute for another. Dates all the way back to at least Julius Caesar."

Gibson started clicking keys and increased the font size so the phrase loomed large across the screen.

NOW YOU SEE IT, BUT THEN YOU DON'T.

"So you think each letter represents another letter?" said Francine.

"Possibly. I actually have software that drills down on that, because the debtors I chase use all sorts of stuff, including secret codes." Gibson opened a program and then plugged the phrase into it. "It works fast, but it's not always conclusive."

Five minutes later the program disgorged several possibilities that, to both their minds, seemed nonsensical.

"Harry's housekeeper told me that he was almost never there," said Francine. "And Nathan Trask confirmed that."

"Okay, so where was he the rest of the time?" asked Gibson.

"At another hidey-hole of his, probably. Wait, what if the treasure is at one of those hidey-holes and this code is giving us the location?" suggested Francine.

Gibson glanced at the words with renewed interest. "If it *is* an address, it would probably be both numbers *and* letters."

"Which complicates the unraveling even more, I know," Francine mused. "Okay, let's try the simplest first. Let's take the first letter of each word and give it its alphabetical numerical equivalent. So breaking the phrase down, each first letter is N-Y-S-I-B-T-Y-D. Now give each letter the alphabetical equivalent."

Gibson executed on this and looked at the line of numbers corresponding to their place in the alphabet: "Fourteen, twenty-five, nineteen, nine, two, twenty, twenty-five, and four. Anything strike you?" she asked.

"Yes, confusion," said Francine.

"Could it be a hybrid?"

"Meaning?"

Gibson said, "Some substitution of numbers for letters, but then maybe some of the letters actually represent words."

"Okay, which ones?"

"I don't have a clue."

"Let's take Harry literally. The letters *b* and *t* from the words 'but then' are represented by the two and the twenty. Is that significant? Since it's clear he added 'but' before 'then' to make it 'but then.' "

Gibson looked at her notes. "Wait a minute, we forgot about the 'take away the eight' part."

"Okay, but how do we do that?"

"Well, if we follow the same substitution cipher, eight represents the letter *h*."

"So we take away the *h* in the word 'then'?"

"So it becomes 'ten,' " said Gibson.

"Which means it now reads, 'Now you see it, but ten you don't.' " She looked at Gibson. "What the hell does that mean?"

The blood slowly drained from Gibson's face. "Oh my God."

"What, what is it?" Francine said quickly.

"It's all a convoluted mess, really, which I'm sure was intentional. 'But then' was really the key. I'm pretty sure that was a shortcut that Harry offered up because the word was so unusual in this context."

"What word?"

She typed out something and then sat back for Francine to see.

"One ninety-nine *Button* Road, Yarden, New York. 'Button' equals 'but ten.'" She glanced at Francine to see if she was following her logic. "You don't know?" Gibson said. "It's not in one of your notebooks?"

"What?"

"This is the address of the house where your father first lived."

84

Gibson steered the rental car down the street in Yarden, New York.

She and Francine had flown in and were now pulling up in front of the small house that Harry Langhorne had lived in as a child.

It looked exactly like the picture that Gibson had earlier pulled up on Google Maps.

A car was parked in front. Flowers were in the flower beds. Everything looked neat and trim. There were four other homes on the street. They all looked the same. Cars in front, flowers in the beds.

But what Gibson had subsequently found out was that each of these homes was owned by one corporation that she had finally tracked to one of Daniel Pottinger's companies. And she had also found out that a management service had been hired to keep the outside of the homes in good order and to look after the vehicles. And that there was a housekeeping service to look after the interiors of the other homes. But they had not been given access to 199. No one apparently went in there.

They got out of the car and approached the house.

There was an alarm pad next to the front door.

"Little unusual being on the *outside*," noted Francine.

"There's no key lock on the front door, only a handle. My guess is this is where Harry lived for the most part. Now we need the code to get in."

Francine opened her notebook and looked at the numbers she had written down there: 14, 25, 19, 9, 25, and 4. These represented the numerical equivalent of each first letter in the phrase Harry had left with his registered agent after leaving out the words "but then."

"The *leftovers* for Sesame Street?" said Gibson.

"As in 'open sesame,' we hope."

"Here goes nothing," Gibson said, as she punched all these numbers into the alarm panel.

The red light on the pad turned green and they heard a click.

Francine gripped the handle and pulled the door open. "After you," she said to Gibson.

The women walked in and Francine closed the door behind them.

The house was small, the rooms plain but spotless. The kitchen was functional, if rudimentary. They noticed that the windows were simply facades. There was no light coming in from them. The air was cool, and they could hear the hum of the HVAC system.

"The lights and HVAC must be on a program," noted Gibson.

They turned the corner and walked into what looked like the living room, which was the largest space thus far. There was track lighting on the ceilings and the lights were pointed at the walls.

And on the walls—

"Holy shit," both women exclaimed at the same time.

Arrayed on all four walls were paintings. And not simply any paintings.

They drew closer to one of them. It was a simple depiction of a room: a tile floor, and part of a blue door. But the focus of the work was clearly a wooden chair with a straw seat that held what looked to be a pipe and cloth on it, and—

Francine pointed to the name that appeared on a wooden box sitting behind the chair that contained some vegetables.

"'Vincent'?"

"As in…Van Gogh?" mumbled Gibson. "The NFTs were just misdirection, or maybe a digital sampling of the real thing?"

Francine took out her phone, did a search, and showed the screen to Gibson.

"Van Gogh signed his first name in odd places on the pieces he thought had some merit apparently. This one is entitled *Vincent's Chair*. He painted it in December 1888." She kept reading. "It was housed in the National Gallery in London." She paused and then jerked her head up. "Until it was stolen eleven years ago." She looked around. "It wouldn't surprise me if all of these paintings had been stolen."

"So Harry bought them from whoever stole them, and housed them here where he's the only one who gets to enjoy them. And he bought NFTs of all of them and housed them in a metaverse room that is probably a duplicate of this one." She looked around at what was clearly world-class artwork from a series of masters. "What a dick."

"Who cares?" Francine leaned against the wall, closed her eyes, and let out a long, calming breath. She opened her eyes, looked at Gibson, and allowed herself an ear-to-ear smile. "We just found the treasure."

85

THE VARIOUS MUSEUMS AND PRIVATE collectors whose works had been stolen were thrilled to have them back in their possession. So happy, in fact, that the finder's fees paid to Gibson and Francine were quite generous.

On the flight back from meeting with one of the museums, which had had two of the paintings stolen from it, Francine turned to Gibson.

"That night at Stormfield?"

"Yeah?"

"You saved my life."

"Well, you did the same for me. If you hadn't warned me, I'd be dead."

Francine slowly reached over and gripped Gibson's hand. "Can I ask you a favor?"

Gibson looked at her curiously. "What?"

"Can I...? Oh never mind."

"What!"

Francine seemed nervous and unsure of herself. "I was just wondering, if I could meet...your kids."

By Gibson's expression, this was not what she was expecting. However, she said, "Sure, my parents have been watching them. You can meet them, too."

* * *

"This is my friend, Francine," said Gibson, introducing Francine to her parents. "She was at Temple when I was there."

The Rogerses shook hands with Francine. Gibson's father shot his daughter a glance and mouthed, *Francine Langhorne?*

She smiled but didn't answer.

"So how did you know Mickey?" asked her mother.

Francine said, "Well, she was pretty famous on campus. But we were both involved in the theater program. Do you remember her in *My Fair Lady*? She was fantastic as Eliza Doolittle."

Rick Rogers looked guiltily at his daughter. "I must'a missed that one. But I saw all her home basketball games."

"Did you act in plays as well?" asked Dorothy Rogers.

Francine said, "Sometimes it seems like I've been acting my whole life."

"Are you here on business?" asked Rick, with a sly look at Gibson.

"Actually, I am. In fact, I'm sort of in the same line of work Mickey is. Asset recovery."

"And the kids?" asked Gibson. "Francine wanted to say hello."

"Naptime is just about over," said her mother.

Gibson led Francine upstairs and into her kids' room.

Tommy's eyes were open and he was looking sleepily around.

Darby's eyes were still closed. Her thumb was in her mouth, and her other hand was clenched around her favorite stuffed animal, a Winnie the Pooh that had been so "loved" its button nose had worn off.

Francine knelt down next to Tommy and held out her hand. "Hi, Tommy, I'm Francine."

Tommy glanced up at his mom, who nodded. Tommy put out his hand and the two shook.

"Hi," he said in a small, uncertain voice.

"Did you have a good nap?"

He nodded.

"You look very strong. I bet you can throw a ball pretty far."

He smiled and nodded.

"What's that, I wonder?" said Francine. She reached behind his head and pulled out a Nerf ball and held it up.

Tommy's eyes popped out as she handed it to him. "Okay, give it a whirl." She backed up and squatted down like a catcher.

Tommy sat up, rubbed the sleep from his eyes, looked at his mom, who nodded encouragingly, and got to his feet.

He wound up and threw the ball to Francine, who caught it and then shook her hand, pretended it was stinging. "Wow, you really can throw."

She tossed it back to a beaming Tommy, who neatly caught it.

"Who you?"

They all looked up to see Darby awake and staring at Francine.

She rose, went over to Darby, and knelt down. "I'm Francine. And you're Darby, right?"

She nodded, her thumb back in her mouth.

"I had a Winnie the Pooh just like that one, and you know what?"

"What?" mumbled Darby.

"He lost his nose, too." Francine laughed and Darby looked at her Pooh and giggled.

Darby took her thumb out and said, "Pooh can't schmell."

"That's okay. He can still see and hear, right?"

Darby nodded energetically.

"And he won't have to smell stinky things."

"Tommy stinky," said Darby.

"Am not," protested her brother.

"Well," said Gibson. "I think she has you there, buckaroo."

"Can I shake Pooh's hand?" asked Francine.

Darby held him out.

Francine reached out and shook the bear's hand and said, "Well, look at that. Did you know Pooh had this?"

Darby quickly sat up. "What?"

Francine held up a locket shaped like a heart.

"What dat?" asked Darby.

"It's a locket. Do you know what you can do with it?"

Darby shook her head so vigorously that her pigtails flew around.

Francine opened the locket to reveal the compartment. "You can put a picture in here." She glanced at Gibson. "Maybe of your mommy? And when you get older you can put the locket on a necklace, here like mine." She showed Darby the one she had on. "And anytime you want to see your mommy, you just open the locket and there she is."

Darby slowly took the locket and looked at her mom with excited eyes.

"We can pick out a picture to put in there," said Gibson. "Maybe the one of both of us at your birthday party?"

Darby nodded, then she lay down, closed her eyes, and went right back to sleep.

As they walked out of the house later, Francine said, "Your kids are beautiful. You must be really proud."

"I am most days, except when they're fighting, won't eat, or puke on me."

"Motherhood in all its glory."

Gibson said, "And you didn't have to do that, Francine. The gifts, I mean."

"A Nerf ball and a locket. Not all that much, really."

"You looked like you've played catcher before."

Francine looked both wistful and sad. "My brother. Harry never let him do any sports. He never let him do anything. So I found some balls and gloves when we were kids, and he would pitch to me in the backyard."

"That's really nice."

"Sometimes it's the little things." She paused and added, "The little things, actually, were all we had."

"The locket was a sweet idea."

Francine fingered hers.

"Whose picture is in it?" asked Gibson.

When Francine looked at her, Gibson had wished she hadn't asked the question.

"I never had a picture in it." She paused and then added, "But maybe one day I will."

86

A MONTH LATER FRANCINE WAS back in Williamsburg, in Gibson's backyard, where the two women were watching Darby and Tommy playing. Agnes Langhorne sat in a wheelchair with her oxygen tank and seemed delighted with the kids' antics. Doug sat next to his mother and seemed in better spirits than he had been. He had scattered Rochelle's ashes over the lake; Francine had gone with him to lend her support.

Gibson and Francine were sitting on swings on a brand-new play set that Gibson had purchased with some of her finder's fee. Part of the money had gone to fund the kids' college accounts, and the rest had gone into the bank, until she decided what to do with it.

Francine had given half her finder's fee to her brother. They had decided that Agnes would live with her son and that she would have round-the-clock care until the end. Francine had also provided funds to the other victims of Earl Beckett. And she and Gibson had both given monies to Sullivan's niece to help her with her challenges.

As they slowly swung back and forth Gibson said, "Beckett and Enders did plea deals. But they'll both die of old age in prison."

"Hopefully, sooner rather than later," remarked Francine.

"Sullivan is doing well and his sister has been avenged. He can just go on being a cop now, without having to move all the time to keep up with Beckett."

"Nothing wrong with not staying in one place too long."

"So does that mean you'll be heading on soon?"

Francine glanced at her. "Why?"

"Just wondering. I was…sort of getting used to having you around."

"You can go do anything you want, Mickey. Buy a big house. Travel the world."

"All a little heady for a Jersey girl."

"You can pull it off. You really can."

"Not if the desire isn't there."

"So what *is* your desire, then?"

"You go first."

Francine looked embarrassed. "I…I got through an entire day without writing something down in a notebook."

"Hey, that's progress."

"The notebooks were important to me. The shrinks have a lot of fancy names for it. But it just came down to being afraid of losing the little I had."

"They were also a wall for you, Francine."

"What?"

"Your notebooks were a way for you to build a wall around yourself. And the different personas you used? That way no one could ever get to know the real you. And if they never knew the real you?"

"They could never hurt the real me," Francine finished.

"Trust me, you're not the only one who built walls or played roles because they were scared, or to keep from being hurt. You just took it to another level. But you had good cause to do so."

"That does make sense."

"I've been meaning to ask—how did you end up at Temple?"

"I wanted to get as far away from New Mexico as I could. And I'd been to Philly before, when I was a kid, before we went into WITSEC. I liked it. So I went there, and I got a job at the university. In the cafeteria."

"Did you really serve me food?"

"I really did. But I looked a lot different back then." She paused. "I guess I really became obsessed with you at that point, basketball star and all, and a *girl* on top of it. And when I found out you were in the drama program, it was like it was an omen. I mean, I had always dreamed of being a famous actress. And here was my idol doing that very thing. I also went to all the home basketball games." She shot Gibson a glance. "You were one vicious point guard."

"Had to be. I was a lot shorter than most of the other gals. Did we interact at all in the theater?"

"I helped get you into costume, helped with the sets, that sort of thing. You were a great mentor to the other drama students. You just always seemed so put together. Never anxious about anything."

"That was my best acting job because I was dying inside from nerves. Same on the basketball court."

Francine shook her head. "Well, it never showed." She paused. "And...you saved me once on campus."

"What?"

"Some asshole attacked me late one night. Stupidly, I was there late by myself. The guy jumped me. He had my blouse halfway off when—"

"Oh my God. I drilled him in the face with a basketball. I was coming back from practicing three-pointers by myself in the gym. That was you? You ran off. And so did he."

"I was scared and embarrassed and, I don't know, just messed up. I left Temple right after that and reinvented myself, put those walls up, like you said. The intervening years sort of raced by."

"Until you came back into my life."

"Hardly in a way you wanted. I'm sorry for all that I did. I'm sorry for all that I said and thought about you. It was...I was...so wrong about everything."

Gibson gripped her hand. "Francine, after all that you went through, the fact that you're even functioning is a damn miracle."

Francine glanced away, watching the children again. Tommy was running in circles, and Darby was doing awkward forward rolls and coming up laughing after each one.

Perhaps reading her mind, Gibson said, "You know, you can adopt. You'll be a rich single mom, the world at your feet."

Francine shook her head. "You're clearly mother material. I don't think I am."

"I never thought I would be. You sort of grow into it." She glanced at Tommy, who was now seeing how loudly he could burp while Darby egged him on by laughing uproariously. "And here I am raising two Einsteins of my very own."

Francine gave Gibson a mischievous look. "They're going to end up ruling the world and you know it."

"With an aunt like you teaching them, they probably will."

Francine gaped. "Aunt?"

"I have two brothers who can't even dress themselves. You think I'm letting them be role models? It's all yours if you want it."

"Mickey, I don't know what kind of a role model I would be to anyone, much less your kids."

"First of all, it's high time you called me Mick, which is what the people I care about call me. And second, you don't have to decide right now. And last but not least, I think you'd be a great example to them. I don't really care about the stuff you did back then." She looked over at Francine's mother and brother. "What I care about is that you have a heart, a big one. And in the end, you did the right thing."

"We did make a pretty good team," noted Francine.

"I think the term you're looking for is *world class*. And there is a lot to be said for doing something interesting and worthwhile with your life."

Francine said, "I have always done *interesting* things, but I don't know how worthwhile they've been."

"Life is but a series of second chances."

"Do you really think so?"

"It's just a matter of whether the will is there." She paused. "So do we perform our next act together?"

In answer, Francine held out her hand, which Gibson shook.

"I think that we do, *Mick*."

ACKNOWLEDGMENTS

To Michael Pietsch, Ben Sevier, Elizabeth Kulhanek, Jonathan Valuckas, Matthew Ballast, Beth de Guzman, Ana Maria Allessi, Rena Kornbluh, Karen Kosztolnyik, Brian McLendon, Albert Tang, Andy Dodds, Ivy Cheng, Joseph Benincase, Alexis Gilbert, Andrew Duncan, Janine Perez, Lauren Sum, Morgan Martinez, Bob Castillo, Kristen Lemire, Briana Kuchta, Mark Steven Long, Marie Mundaca, Rachael Kelly, Kirsiah McNamara, Lisa Cahn, John Colucci, Megan Fitzpatrick, Nita Basu, Alison Lazarus, Barry Broadhead, Martha Bucci, Ali Cutrone, Raylan Davis, Tracy Dowd, Melanie Freedman, Elizabeth Blue Guess, Linda Jamison, John Leary, John Lefler, Rachel Hairston, Tishana Knight, Jennifer Kosek, Suzanne Marx, Derek Meehan, Christopher Murphy, Donna Nopper, Rob Philpott, Barbara Slavin, Karen Torres, Rich Tullis, Mary Urban, Tracy Williams, Julie Hernandez, Laura Shepherd, Maritza Lumpris, Jeff Shay, Carla Stockalper, Ky'ron Fitzgerald, and everyone at Grand Central Publishing. Thanks for being terrific partners for over twenty-five years. You make my life a lot easier with your support and enthusiasm.

To Aaron and Arleen Priest, Lucy Childs, Lisa Erbach Vance, Frances Jalet-Miller, Kristen Pini, and Natalie Rosselli, for being great friends and counselors.

To Mitch Hoffman, for a great editing job and being a wonderful listener.

To Joanna Prior, Jeremy Trevathan, Lucy Hale, Trisha Jackson,

Stuart Dwyer, Leanne Williams, Alex Saunders, Sara Lloyd, Claire Evans, Jamie Forrest, Laura Sherlock, Jonathan Atkins, Christine Jones, Andy Joannou, Charlotte Williams, Rebecca Kellaway, Charlotte Cross, Lucy Grainger, Lucy Jones, and Neil Lang at Pan Macmillan, for being a stellar publisher and always innovating.

To Praveen Naidoo and the wonderful team at Pan Macmillan in Australia, for outstanding work.

To Caspian Dennis and Sandy Violette, who have been by my side from day one.

To the charity auction winners, Arlene Robinson (Gloucester-Mathews Humane Society) and Wilson Sullivan ('Sconset Trust), I hope you enjoyed your characters.

And to Kristen White and Michelle Butler, for being the A Team!

DAVID BALDACCI is a global #1 bestselling author and one of the world's favorite storytellers. His books are published in over 45 languages and in more than 80 countries, with 150 million copies sold worldwide. His works have been adapted for both feature film and television. David Baldacci is also the cofounder, along with his wife, of the Wish You Well Foundation, a nonprofit organization dedicated to supporting literacy efforts across America. Still a resident of his native Virginia, he invites you to visit him at DavidBaldacci.com and his foundation at WishYouWellFoundation.org.

Facebook.com/writer.david.baldacci
Twitter@davidbaldacci
Instagram@davidbaldacciauthor

Set in the tumultuous year of 1968 in southern Virginia, a racially charged murder case sets a duo of white and Black lawyers against a deeply unfair system as they work to defend wrongfully accused Black defendants.

A CALAMITY OF SOULS

AVAILABLE APRIL 2024

PLEASE TURN THE PAGE FOR A PREVIEW

CHAPTER 1

ON ANY OTHER DAY THE dead quiet coming from this room would have concerned no one, because the elderly couple usually napped peacefully, sat stationary as cats, or read their twin King James Bibles in silence, aged fingers turning pages replete with wisdom, tranquility, and violence.

The latter was on embellished display, for the man was sprawled on the floor on his back, while the woman was draped across a finely upholstered chair. Life had been rent from them with a grim certainty of purpose.

They were not remarkable in any way that mattered to most. What *was* memorable was the grand upheaval that would define and qualify the full measure of their deaths. It would fuel a calamitous surge of energy, like that of a sawed-off shotgun randomly discharged into an unsuspecting crowd.

Their violent end would be gossiped about in Freeman County, Virginia, for decades.

"You got the right to remain silent. You hear me, *boy*?" the first lawman said to the only suspect in the room.

That suspect was on his knees, his hands shackled behind him, the cuffs cutting deeply into flesh. The only signs of his granular fear were the trembling of fingers, and the quick exhalations of breath.

"This coon don't look like he can talk even if he wanted to," countered the second deputy. He was six feet, cattail-lean, with a soft jaw and eyes that resembled creased bullet holes. A policeman's hat was tipped far back on his head.

The debilitating humidity, wicked off the nearby McHenry River, spread everywhere, like mustard gas weaving through the war trenches. The sweat dripped off the deputies' faces, darkened their starched shirts, and, like gnats flitting around nostrils and eyes, added annoyance to their rage.

The first deputy continued to read off the little white card he'd drawn from his pocket. He was short, and squat as a tree stump. He had just arrived at the part about an attorney being provided if the accused couldn't afford one, when his partner, clearly troubled by these new legal rights, interrupted once more.

"You tell me what lawyer in his right mind would represent this here colored boy, LeRoy. 'Cause I sure as hell would like to know the answer."

Raymond LeRoy ignored this and continued to read off the card, because he hadn't yet memorized the words. He actually doubted he ever would; the will was just not in him. He had no idea who this Miranda fellow was, but LeRoy knew that the legalese upon the paper was designed to help *those* people, who had committed crimes, usually against white folks. And that transformed every word, which he was compelled to read by the decision of nine robed men hundreds of miles away, into bleach on his tongue.

"You understand what I just read to you?" said LeRoy. "I apparently got to hear your answer accordin' to those sonsabitches in Washington, DC."

His partner gripped the butt of his holstered .38 Smith & Wesson. "Why don't you just take off them iron cufflinks and tell him to run for it? Save the good folks of this fine county payin' for his trip down to Richmond and the chair."

"They ain't doin' executions no more, Gene. Say it's cruel and unusual."

Gene Taliaferro bristled. "And what the hell has he just done to *them*, LeRoy?"

In one corner an overturned table had upset the items that had long rested upon it, chiefly, a photograph taken over fifty years ago of the couple in their courting days. He with his slouch hat in hand, along with a pair of brooding eyes, she with a bonnet resting on her small, delicate head, the hair parted in the middle, making her resemble a child. They were framed by an arch of fragrant honeysuckle and jasmine that was hosting both bees and butterflies, tiny, whirring apparitions trapped by the flash pop and shutterbug.

Now the photo lay on the floor, its front glass shattered, a cut across the picture bisecting the woman's face and reaching to the man's left eye.

LeRoy said, "We ain't gonna shoot him, Gene. Boy's in custody."

"He's only a g-d n——!" exclaimed Gene.

"I *know*," bellowed an out-of-his-depth LeRoy. "Do I got me two eyes or what?"

"Well then?" demanded Gene. "Ain't be the first time we done it."

"Well, it's not like that no more, is it?" countered a disappointed LeRoy.

"A hundred years ago where was the capital of the Confederacy?" Gene pointed to the floor. "It was right chere in Virginia. And nuthin' can change that. Granddaddy four times removed owned boys just like this one." He stabbed his finger in the direction of the kneeling man. "Owned 'em! I got me a picture! They ought 'a fry his ass."

"Then let 'em," muttered LeRoy. "But I ain't havin' a bunch 'a Negro lawyers comin' after me. And now that that Dr. King got hisself killed down in Tennessee, coloreds are riotin' all over the damn country."

Gene snorted. "He weren't no real doctor!"

"Gonna let my son take up the cause. We got to keep fightin'. Hundred years, thousand years, it don't matter."

Gene sucked in a long breath and let it go. The gesture seemed to sap the core of his fury like cold mist on a candle's flame. But then the lawman's expression grew cagey. He squatted down on his haunches next to the only suspect in the room and slipped a wooden billy club from his belt. Along the wood were cut a dozen horizontal notches.

"I don't remember tellin' you to get on your knees, boy. Now stand up." Before the prisoner could move, Gene struck him full in the gut with the head of the billy club, propelling the man to the floor.

Gene rose. "I told you to get up, not fall on your damn face. Now get your ass up boy, right now. *Now*, or you get some more of the wood."

Slowly, the prisoner managed to come once more to rest on his haunches.

Gene knelt next to him and said in a near whisper, "Now who told you to get your ass off that floor?"

He battered the prisoner on the back of the head with the club, sending him down once more, now bleeding from his scalp.

Gene stood up and said, "Jesus, you ain't too smart, and here you wanna be equal to the white man. Now get up. Get up." He jabbed the prisoner fiercely in the ribs with the club. "I ain't tellin' you again, boy. Up!"

The prisoner, inch by tremulous inch, levered himself back onto his knees.

Gene knelt down again. "Good, good, boy." He grinned at his partner. "Who says you can't teach critters new tricks, LeRoy, huh?" He turned back to the bleeding, woozy prisoner and eyed the band on the man's finger. "Hey, now, you got yourself a woman?"

Gene walloped the suspect with the club on the side of his head. "I asked you a question. You ain't got no choice 'cept to answer me."

"Y-yes."

"Yes, what?"

"Yes...sir."

He leaned in closer. "Good, good. Bet she's pretty. She pretty, boy?"

The prisoner nodded, which got him another clubbing to the head.

"You speak, boy. You don't never nod at no white man. It's disrespectful."

His eyes closed, the man said, "She real pretty, *sir*."

"Good, good. Now, you got you kids?"

"Y-yes sir."

"Fine, that's fine. How many babies you got?"

"Three, sir."

"Three!" Gene looked at his partner. "Boy say he got him three colored babies." He turned back to the prisoner. "Okay, now after they fry your ass over in Richmond I'm gonna go see your pretty wife and your babies with some friends of mine. Now let me tell you what we gonna do to all them after we finish havin' some fun with her."

He leaned close and whispered in the prisoner's ear.

The man roared in rage, knocking Gene down with his maddened, gyrating bulk.

The deputy slid across the floor, grinning. He took off his hat, swiped back his hair, and gripped his billy club extra firm. He rose and headed back to the only suspect in the room, who was now sprawled helplessly on the floor.

Gene said triumphantly, "Resistin' arrest plain as day. You seen it, LeRoy."

And he raised the club.

CHAPTER 2

JOHN ROBERT LEE, WHO WENT by Jack to all but his mother, finished pumping Esso gas into his ancient, four-door Fiat pillarless saloon car. The front doors opened regularly, back to front, but the rear doors opened front to back. It had a long hood terminating in a fancy grille with silver cased headlights that sprouted from the front slim fenders like incandescent daisies. Its four-cylinder engine could hit fifty-three miles an hour with a decent tailwind. He paid over a crisp single and two dull quarters to the attendant, who was studying the funny-looking car with interest.

"What the hell is that thang?" he asked.

"It's a Fiat," answered Jack.

"A fee-ought?"

"It's Italian made."

"I-talian? Ain't that where the pope's from?"

Jack nodded. "That's right."

"You Catholic?"

"No, I'm agnostic," said Jack.

The man screwed up his face. "What's that? Like Presbyterian or Methodist?"

"It's actually a skeptical man's faith," replied Jack.

He climbed into the Fiat that his father had gotten from a car cemetery and resurrected back to the road. It was a gift from his parents when he'd graduated from law school. It was not a prestigious law school, like the mighty University of Virginia, or Richmond's or William and Mary's illustrious legal institutions. However, he had passed the Virginia State Bar exam on his first attempt, while he knew some from the glorified universities who had failed to do so. They still got the jobs in the big firms because that was where their daddies labored, too, selling their professional lives in hour incre-ments for handsome compensation, prestigious homes, and golf memberships at the country club. They also married lovely, elegant women with fine pedigrees and firm skin, who ended up drinking too much, or bedding the gardener or the pool boy because of all the extra time on their hands.

Jack was a white man, thirty-two years old, at least for a bit lon-ger, and eight years out of law school he was just getting by, and still unmarried, much to his mother's chagrin. As the 1970s approached, men were wearing their hair far longer, but his was as short as when he'd been in the Boy Scouts, though he was starting to grow out his sideburns. He was two inches over six feet, broad shouldered and slim hipped and a bit too lean; he had never earned enough from his law practice to eat all that well. A six-pack of peanut butter crackers and an RC Cola was often his end-of-day repast.

The Second World War had made everyone underfed and over-worked. Then the fifties had ushered in a roaring economy with a chicken in every pot and a Ford or GM loitering in every driveway. Then the sixties had come along and proceeded to upend all that dollars-and-cents progress. It had also foisted stark changes upon society at large that were far too swift for many.

He drove over to his parents' modest house in a working-class neighborhood where the husbands primarily used their muscle to earn their daily bread and their wives handled everything else. He had been born there in the main-floor bedroom, and he was fairly certain both his parents would die there, barring something unfore-seen. No fuss and no muss, that was the Lee way.

He pulled into the gravel drive. All the homes here had been carved out of a plantation that more than a century ago had grown tobacco as a cash crop. Nearly all the residences looked the same: brittle asbestos siding, high-pitched roofs with black asphalt shingles, one front door and one in the rear, three bedrooms total along with one bath, set on a quarter acre of solid red clay with a grass veneer.

At his parents' house there was an aging weeping willow tree out front, and an apple tree in the back that had never been honestly pruned, and consequently sagged with the weight of the coming harvest. There was also a detached garage sitting where the gravel drive ceased. At the very rear of the property was the grave of the dog that had been Jack's faithful companion as a child: a black-and-white Belgian shepherd as loyal and good as God ever made canines. He'd toppled over one morning in his ninth year of life and hadn't lived the day. Jack and his younger brother had cried like they'd just lost their best friend, and, in some important ways of little boys, they had.

The Lees also had a second bathroom upstairs, thanks to their father, who was quite talented at creating useful things from castoffs. Then there was a galley-sized kitchen, an eight-by-ten dining space bleeding off that, a small living room, and a TV den containing a faux-wood Motorola with two dials big as saucers on its face.

Jack climbed out of the Fiat and put on his suit jacket.

He could smell through the front screen door chicken breasts and legs popping in a frying pan of sizzling Crisco. And he imagined the potato salad resting in the small almond-white Frigidaire, and the heated pots on the electric stove top, the coils red-hot and holding pans of simmering green beans and stewed tomatoes his mother had harvested and then preserved from the kitchen garden. The meal would be concluded with chocolate sheet cake and Maxwell House coffee purchased from the A&P.

The dinner tonight was to commemorate Jack's thirty-third year on earth. At 7:10 p.m. on this day in 1935 he had emerged headfirst into a world still devastated by an economic collapse. His birth had occurred in the downstairs bedroom, while his nervous father had prowled the hall outside smoking his American-blend Camels. After a spank on the ass Jack had given his first cry and hadn't stopped for four years, according to his mother.

He'd grown up to play myriad sports, loved to debate folks, and was an avid reader from a young age. And every morning from the age of twelve until his junior year of high school, he'd risen long before the crack of dawn to deliver the *Virginia Times Dispatch*.

Many of the parents from his childhood still lived in the neighborhood. Their children, like him, had moved on. Most, unlike him, had married and now had their own swelling broods. He'd see them occasionally disgorging a passel of kids from battered station wagons to go visit grandparents who were getting more fragile and forgetful by the day. Yet sometimes the natural cycle of life was broken and children remained closer than Mom and Dad might desire.

And didn't Jack's parents know that.

He opened the screen door.

"Hello?" he called out. "Birthday boy's here." He'd seen his father's tan GMC pickup by the garage. It was their only vehicle because his mother didn't drive.

"Hello?" he said again.

His sister edged around the corner from the dining room, where he could see the dinner plates laid out on the small table purchased years ago on layaway. There was a balloon tethered to a closet door handle, the words "Happy Birthday" stenciled upon it.

"Hey, Lucy girl," said Jack.

His elder sister rushed over and gave him a hug that nearly cracked his back. She'd always been strong, and he'd always believed it was nature's way of balancing out what was missing upstairs.

It had begun with his mother's trip to the dentist to remove a painfully impacted wisdom tooth. She'd been given laughing gas as a sedative, a term Jack had later learned was for the compound nitrous oxide. Only she hadn't known she was with child at the time. Eight months later his sister had been born. And a year after that, when Lucy was not developing as she should, some specialists had diagnosed her with "severe and irreversible mental retardation," or so his daddy had told him years later when Jack had questions about his sister.

She was now thirty-seven, a grown if physically stunted woman, with the innocent mind of a child. Her blond bangs hung right above eyes so extraordinarily blue it was the first thing folks noted about her. Jack had the same eyes that she did, only with something of a different sort behind them.

He kissed the top of Lucy's head and said her dress was very pretty. It was light brown with vivid blue dots that nearly matched her eye color and had puffy sleeves that hung down to the crooks of her delicate elbows. His birthday was probably the only thing that she had talked about all day.

"Momma, Daddy, it be Jack," Lucy bellowed over her shoulder.

She pulled him over to the balloon, poked it, and laughed as it oscillated on the end of its tether. Jack laughed, too, but there was a definite hollowness to it. He'd often wondered what his sister would have grown up to be if the dental visit had never occurred. Perhaps Lucy Lee would have been the lawyer in the family.

His mother had never forgiven herself for her daughter's fate, though there was no fault in her ignorance. She had had two more children, Jack and his one-year-younger brother, Jefferson, who went by Jeff to all but his mother, who always referred to him by his full name. His mother had employed a midwife and taken no drugs for her sons' deliveries, preferring to endure the unique pain of childbirth as perhaps penance for the daughter who had never been allowed to truly grow up because of the mother's bad tooth. And ever since, she had refused any and all medication, including aspirin, though she was susceptible to migraines that sometimes forced her to lie in agony for hours in the dark.

"Momma?" he called out expectantly.

And he heard the woman coming.

CHAPTER 3

Hilda Lee, known to all as Hilly, appeared, dressed in a crisp white T-shirt, faded Wrangler jeans, and flat canvas shoes, with an olive green apron tied around her middle. It was a tomboy foundation comfortably twined with a domestic facade.

She was quite tall and sinewy lean, and her short hair was light brown with a reddish tint attributable to her Scottish ancestry; it was also now liberally laced with gray. Her nose was straight as a razor blade. Her calm, pale green eyes gave the impression that no matter the challenge not only would she persevere, Hilly Lee would also conquer all comers, with grit to spare.

The woman's veined, wiry, tanned forearms were festooned with sunspots because she liked the outdoors. However, when she was outside, Hilly moved with force and had some purpose, tending the kitchen garden, mowing the grass, helping her husband to reshingle the roof, felling a dead tree, or repainting the backyard wire fence. She had been raised on a mountain ridge on the far western edge of the state that to this day had no electricity or running water. His mother rarely spoke of her hardscrabble time there, and that in itself articulated volumes.

Hilly wiped her hands on the apron and gave her oldest boy a hug. "Ten minutes to go, Robert." She had never called him anything other than Robert. *John was your father's idea, Robert was mine, so Robert it will be, at least for me.* And they had left it at that. With his mother he had left many things at *that.*

If she'd had her way he would have officially been Robert E. Lee, after the gallant Confederate general who had sacrificed all to carry the mantle of the Army of Northern Virginia against his birth country in defense of states' rights, or so the old story went.

But they were not *those* Lees. No First Families of Virginia lived on this street or even in this blue collar parcel of Freeman County. The homes weren't big enough, and neither were the opportunities.

"Yes, ma'am," he said back.

Her expression turned somber. "I still can't believe they killed JFK's brother."

"I know," he replied. A little over a week before, America had had another Kennedy running for president. Now they simply had another Kennedy to mourn.

"And Dr. King just two months ago. What is this durn country coming to where we have to settle things with guns?"

"World is a troubled place. Look at Vietnam."

He shouldn't have brought that up because of his brother, but perhaps it had slipped out intentionally, Jack thought. He'd had that sort of verbal sparring relationship with his mother from an early age. She usually seemed to relish the jousting.

And he had always found it bewildering that she venerated a long-dead Confederate general at the same time she shed tears for the recent deaths of two men who held views diametrically opposed to all the Confederacy had stood for. But then he had found much about his mother to be irreconcilable.

"Walter Cronkite said it was a man with the same two names who did it."

"Sirhan Sirhan," Jack told her.

She said, "What kinda name is that?"

"He's from Palestine."

"How did his kind get close to Bobby Kennedy of all people?"

"They say Kennedy was walking through the kitchen at a hotel in Los Angeles, and the man was waiting and shot him."

"This Sir-han will probably hire himself a fancy lawyer like you and get off."

He smiled at her. He would never be a fancy lawyer. "Doubtful."

"Well, you're the attorney in the family, Robert," she said. Hilly's gaze flitted to her daughter, who was still poking the balloon and giggling each time it moved in response to her jab. In his mother's eyes Jack could read the unspoken thought: *The family I have left.*

"You seeing any girls I don't know about?" she asked, turning back to him.

"You'd know. The gossip chain in Freeman is top-notch. Where's Daddy?"

"He'll be in shortly." She gripped his arm. "Miss Jessup came by today."

"Miss Jessup? What'd she want?"

"What she wanted was *you*, but didn't say why. She didn't look good at all, Robert." She added hastily, "Not that I ever had much contact with her, obviously."

"You think she's sick?"

"You're not a doctor."

"She have family around?" Jack asked.

"Yes. Her husband's long dead. But she has children and now grandchildren. Maybe great-grandchildren," she added ruefully, making Jack sense his mother was thinking that she had none of those future generations lined up.

Jack went over to the door and stared up the street to the only house in the neighborhood that didn't look like all the others. A retired lawyer by the name of Ashby owned it. And he'd added to it over the years, usually when he'd gotten a big client, or made a few bucks in the stock market. Thus, it was rambling and had oddly mitered wings and loose joints.

Jack had read that there had been nearly one hundred slaves on the sprawling plantation once situated here. They and their progeny had labored all their lives for not one penny in return to make their wealthy owners richer still. Almost nothing had been recorded about them other than their actual numbers. And that reportage was apparently solely done for the benefit of their master's ego.

Ashby had six children, all long grown now and with their own families to run. His wife had died many years ago, but not of illness. Well, Jack supposed it was a sickness to go to your garage, stuff a towel in the tailpipe of your Plymouth, lie across the front seat dressed in your finest cocktail dress, and, sipping on a Mason jar of Old Fashioned, start the engine, and stay there until you were dead. Ashby had reputedly focused his final years on imbibing as many bottles of Rebel Yell bourbon whiskey as he possibly could.

Miss Jessup was Ashby's maid, cook, and nurse; Jack had never known her first name. Years before Jack had been born, she had gone to work for the lawyer and his family. Now she was probably single-handedly keeping the old man alive.

Growing up, Jack and all the other children in the neighborhood always called the woman Miss Jessup, the only sign of respect she probably ever received on the western side of Freeman County, and the only attention, too, unless items went missing and someone was needed to blame or indict. She was the only Black person who ever came around here, which lent her a certain novelty, at least in the eyes of the white youngsters.

He flicked his gaze back to his mother. "What did she say other than she wanted to talk to me?"

Hilly deftly pulled a heavy glass vase from Lucy's clutching fingers before saying, "Nothing. She walked right in the front door without a by-your-leave and just asked for you. But she was upset, so I made allowances."

"It's not like Miss Jessup's a stranger. We've known her a long time."

"We don't really *know* her kind."

"Times are changing," he said, not really wanting to go there on his birthday.

She pursed her lips. "I'm sure she'd feel the same way if I barged into *her* house. Tell all her friends about that crazy white woman and how she came barging into her house."

"So what did you tell her then?"

"That you'd be here for dinner and that I didn't appreciate her intruding. Scared poor Lucy half to death. Took me forever to calm her down."

She reached out and hugged placid Lucy to her bosom.

"Okay, but how did you leave it with her?" Jack asked patiently.

"I didn't leave it any which way with her. I just asked her to *leave*."

"Just like that?" he said, clearly annoyed.

His mother checked her slim Timex. "You were born one minute ago, Robert. Happy birthday, son."

CHAPTER 4

COMING HOME FROM DELIVERING THE morning paper Jack would sometimes see Miss Jessup get off the bus that stopped at the corner. She always exited from the rear. He wondered why that was so until, as a teenager, he rode the bus one day into the city with his brother, and found that all the Blacks congregated in the back, while all the whites gathered in the front. Each group seemed to willingly accept this arrangement as fine, and thus so did he and his brother.

Jack would wave to her as he sailed past on his Schwinn bike, and she would wave back. Some mornings she looked tired and spent as though the mere act of living had done her in, while other times she looked full of fire, her eyes searching for a fight. He would think about this as he rode home and then his mind would turn to other things, and Miss Jessup's meager place there was always crowded out until next he saw her.

Occasionally she would call out to him. "How you doin', honey?" Or, as he got older, "You lookin' more like your daddy every day. Move like he do, too. With a *swagger*," she added, smiling, which made him smile in return.

Sometimes she would ask if he had a spare newspaper. She would tuck it away in her bag, and always thank him profusely.

"You're certainly welcome, Miss Jessup," he would say back because his parents had taught him to be unfailingly polite to all.

"Rich, poor, colored, white," his father would say. "We're all God's children. We all deserve kindness and respect. We may not break bread with colored folks, but we don't break bread with rich folks, either. Did little colored children have a say where they were born? No, they did not. You don't have to marry one or have a meal with them to respect the fact that they're people, too. You remember that, boys, and pass it on."

"Yes, sir, Daddy, I sure will," Jack and Jeff Lee had each dutifully said back, but now also starkly aware of differences between Blacks and whites, and rich and poor.

Miss Jessup would wear her maid's uniform, starched and crisp, on even the hottest summer days. Her wide feet were squeezed into uncomfortable black lace-ups. Her hips were broad and grew wider still over the years. He could remember going over to play with the youngest Ashby boy, and some other children from the neighborhood, and having Miss Jessup bring out glasses of lemonade with little chips of ice. She would also have some cookies and paper napkins with designs on them. This was how Jack knew the Ashbys were rich. They had napkins and lemonade and cookies on a platter in the afternoon, and a colored maid to carry it all right to them.

He would watch as Miss Jessup trudged back inside, her hand slipping to the cookies left on the platter and several of them would disappear into her apron pocket. He never begrudged the woman any of that. They weren't his cookies after all and the Ashbys had plenty more. The rich always had plenty more.

He hadn't really thought of the woman that much since he'd become an adult. That is until he had seen her about three months ago when he'd come to his parents' house early one morning to pick up some papers he needed for court and had mistakenly left there the previous night. She was just getting off the bus, her hair still wavy and abundant but also all gray now. The driver had closed the door so fast it clipped her in the rear end. And he sped off with such velocity that she got a lungful of exhaust fumes to start her workday.

Jack could imagine the driver thinking what a good deed he had done putting a Black woman in her place. Although ever since Rosa Parks and others had come along, Miss Jessup could ride anywhere on the bus she wanted. Yet Jack knew legal rulings were one thing, making folks live in accordance with them was quite another.

This made him remember something. When he was a little boy he had once heard Miss Jessup talking to Ashby's wife. There seemed to have been a disagreement between the two women, for Mrs. Ashby looked upset and Miss Jessup was saying, "I got me my place and you got you your place and they's oil and they's water and they just don't mix. Fo' sho' they do *not* mix, *ma'am*."

A flustered and teary-eyed Mrs. Ashby had quickly gone on her way, while Miss Jessup had just stood there, hands on hips, shaking her head and looking—at least to Jack—like she'd just finished dressing down a youngster for doing something foolish.

"Hello, son," said a familiar voice.